D1481376

KAREN HAWKINS

A Belated Bride

AVON BOOKS

An Imprint of HarperCollins*Publishers*

This is a work of fiction. Names, characters, places, and incidents are products of the author's imagination or are used fictitiously and are not to be construed as real. Any resemblance to actual events, locales, organizations, or persons, living or dead, is entirely coincidental.

AVON BOOKS
An Imprint of HarperCollins*Publishers*
10 East 53rd Street
New York, New York 10022-5299

Copyright © 2001 by Karen Hawkins
ISBN: 0-7394-1455-0

All rights reserved. No part of this book may be used or reproduced in any manner whatsoever without written permission, except in the case of brief quotations embodied in critical articles and reviews. For information address Avon Books, an Imprint of HarperCollins Publishers.

Avon Trademark Reg. U.S. Pat. Off. and in Other Countries, Marca Registrada, Hecho en U.S.A.
HarperCollins® is a trademark of HarperCollins Publishers Inc.

Printed in the U.S.A.

For my mother Damaris Evelyn Berry Smith—
who blessed me with a lust for life,
a love of laughter,
and a very strange imagination.

Mom, thanks for just being.

And to all the readers who sent tons of
cards, letters, and emails after reading
The Abduction of Julia—don't worry!
Nick's story will be next.
Thank you for all of your support.

Chapter 1

Yorkshire, England
November 1814

"**L**awks, Wilson! Why'd ye go an' do that?"
The carriage jolted to a sudden halt, sending a basket of raspberry jam crashing to the floor. In alarm, Arabella Hadley threw open the carriage door and peered through the night gloom. "Ned? What's happened?"

"Come quick, Miss Hadley!" the stable hand called. A stout, simple lad of seventeen, he also served as footman, errand boy, cook's assistant, and did every other odd job Arabella could not afford to hire out. "Wilson's done it agin."

The old groom's voice lifted in protest. "Hush your blatherin', boy! There's no need to call the missus."

Arabella stepped across the spilled jam and clambered out of the carriage. She only hoped Wilson hadn't run over another hapless pig. Lord Harlbrook still hadn't recovered from the loss of his prize livestock from last month. She halted when she came to the front of the carriage. "Why have we stopped?"

Ned pointed to Wilson, who stood muttering to one side of the coach. "He was drivin' the coach like a madman agin, and—"

"I was not," Wilson protested.

"Were, too. As we came 'round the corner, it musta frightened the man's horse cause it jus' bolted up and—"

"*What* man?" Arabella interrupted.

Wilson pointed with a grubby hand to the side of the road.

Arabella turned with apprehension. In the dim light, she could just make out the form of a large man lying prone in the dirt. Her heart sank when she noted his multi-caped coat and the unmistakable gleam of a costly pair of Hessians, shined to mirrored perfection.

"Heavens!" she managed in a faint voice. "Is he . . . dead?"

"Lawks, no." Wilson jerked his thumb toward a fat, craggy tree. "He jus' smacked his head on that branch when his horse reared."

The low-slung limb quivered as if still recoiling from the blow. Thank God Wilson hadn't run over the poor man; the last thing she needed was the attention of the local constabulary.

The old groom poked at the man with the tip of his worn boot. "Must not have much of a seat, to lose control of his mount."

"A green 'un," agreed Ned. "Pity his horse ran off. Master Robert would have liked such a prime goer."

"The last thing my brother needs is a horse that rears at the slightest provocation," Arabella said in a dry tone.

"Give me the lantern. I must see how badly this poor man is injured."

"Don't get too close," warned Wilson from a safe distance. "He might come awake and be none too happy to find hisself a-lyin' on the ground."

"If he lunges at me, I give you full permission to shoot him." Arabella bent to examine the man by the lantern's light. "Judging by the quality of his clothing, he must be a gentleman of some means."

Wilson snorted. "He may look a gent, but ye ne'er know. Don't get any closer, Miss Arabella. Lady Durham and Lady Melwin would never forgive us if anything happened to you."

Arabella thought her aunts would be more upset that they had not been present for such an exciting episode. Aunt Emma and Aunt Jane were both addicted to flights of romantic fancy. Fortunately, life had cured Arabella of that fault long, long ago.

She bent closer to the fallen man. He lay on his side, his broad shoulders rising and falling in a reassuringly steady rhythm. Black as midnight, his hair fell across a large purple lump on his brow, while the rest of his face remained obscured by the folds of a woolen muffler.

The wind rose, carrying with it the faintest taste of snow. Arabella shivered and tugged her cloak closer. She had little choice but to take their guest back to Rosemont. Her aunts would look after him until the doctor could be sent for.

As Arabella was turning away from the fallen man, something caught the light. A gold signet ring set with a huge square-cut emerald glittered on the stranger's shapely hand. Hardly aware of what she was doing, she set the lantern on the frozen road and sank to her knees.

Sweet heaven, it can't be— Every thought in her mind froze.

"Look at that gewgaw!" Wilson said, awed. "Must be a nabob, to have a ring like that." His brow creased. "Ye don't think he'll be angry at me fer scarin' his horse, do ye?"

Her heart pounding in her ears, Arabella barely heard the groom's words. She reached for the muffler, numbed as if she were in a dream. Just as her fingers closed over the wool, a powerful hand enclosed her wrist like a band of warmed steel. The man's eyes opened and met hers.

Slumberous and seductive, his gaze held her prisoner. Framed by thick curling lashes, his green eyes were as beautiful as an angel's.

She knew those eyes. Knew them better, perhaps, than her own. She knew, too, what she would see beneath the muffler: golden skin and a bold, patrician nose over a sensuous mouth designed for forbidden pleasures.

"Lucien." The forgotten feel of his name whispered across her stiff lips. Though his hand still gripped her wrist, she pulled the muffler free, her knuckles brushing against his stubbled jaw. A bolt of raw heat lanced through her fingers and settled in her breasts, then slid lower.

Arabella hunched her shoulders at the strength of her reactions, panic rising. God help her, but she was still under his spell. With a strength she didn't know she possessed, she yanked her hand free, cradling it to her chest as if burned.

His gaze flickered and his mouth curved in a lazy smile.

But Arabella refused to respond. Whatever she may be, she was no longer an inexperienced miss of sixteen. "Damn you, Lucien. Why did you come back?"

His mouth parted as if he would answer, but then his eyes slid shut and his head fell to one side as unconsciousness once again claimed him.

"Ye know him, missus?" Wilson's voice quavered between hope and fear.

Arabella stumbled to her feet, her hands clenched in the folds of her skirt. "He is Lucien Devereaux, the Duke of Wexford."

"*A duke!* They'll hang me fer certain."

Ned gawked. "Jus' fer scarin' his horse?"

"It don't take much with the gentry."

Arabella glared down at Lucien, hating him anew for disrupting her life yet again. For an instant she contemplated leaving him where he lay, alone and helpless.

But the brisk wind cooled more than her burning cheeks. Neither her conscience nor her aunts would allow her such a luxury. With a heavy sigh, she picked up the lantern. "Help me get him into the coach. My aunts can tend him until we locate his mount."

Grumbling at the inconvenience, Wilson and Ned carried Lucien to the coach and pushed and pulled him onto the leather seat. Arabella had just gathered her skirts to climb in herself when Ned stopped.

"Gor', mistress," he whispered hoarsely. Eyes wide, he held out his hand.

Blood glistened on his fingertips.

Wilson blanched as Arabella pushed Ned aside and climbed onto the seat. She fumbled with Lucien's greatcoat, tugging at the heavy material. Ned hurried to assist her, and between them, they removed it and the tight-fitting coat beneath.

From the snug fit of his breeches to the intricate folds of his cravat, Lucien Devereaux looked every inch the

Duke of Wexford. Only the rip in his shirt and the blood-stain around it marred the perfection.

Ned shook his head, disgust wrinkling his nose. "Ne'er knew a duke to bleed so. Must not eat much bread pud-din'.' "

From the door, Wilson watched as Arabella struggled to undo the mother-of-pearl buttons on the waistcoat, his face pale with anxiety. "If'n he dies, they'll hang me."

"He will not die," Arabella said sharply. "I've waited ten years to tell this pestilent cad what I think of him and I'll not wait longer."

Wilson managed a weak chuckle. "Aye, that's the way to talk him into livin', missus. Ye jus'—" He stopped and looked over his shoulder. "What's that?"

Above the sound of the wind came the baying of dogs on the hunt. The howling echoed across the mist-shrouded moor and dissipated into the black night.

Wilson turned a white face to Arabella. "Constable Robbins's dogs."

Not now. Please, God, not now. She had been so care-ful, so cautious that no one learn the reason for her late-night jaunts. Heaven help them all if she was discovered.

Unaware of the tension, Ned rubbed his chin where a small layer of red fuzz had lately begun to grow. "He's probably out lookin' fer smugglers. I heard tell he's made a vow to catch 'em all afore winter."

Wilson swallowed noisily. "Perhaps we should be get-tin' under way, missus."

The dogs bayed again, the sound bone-chilling and ominous. Arabella turned back to Lucien. "To Rosemont, Wilson. And quickly."

She heard him barking orders to the hapless Ned. The stable hand scurried off, Wilson hard on his heels, and within seconds the coach was careening down the road at breakneck speed.

The lantern swayed, the light flickering across Lucien's pale face. Arabella set to work loosening his cravat, but the stubborn knot held. Frustrated, she shoved it to one side and pulled his shirt free, ripping it open when it resisted her efforts. She faltered at the expanse of naked skin.

He was more muscular than she remembered. Not that he'd ever been anything other than fit and beautiful. But the Lucien Devereaux she had known had been a self-indulgent viscount kicking his heels in the country while waiting for the season to begin.

Wildly handsome, he had been a shameless hedonist and a Corinthian of the highest sort, excelling in every sport from fencing to riding. Still, he hadn't possessed the raw strength and power evinced by the man bared before her.

She used the edge of his torn shirt to wipe the blood from his shoulder so she could see the wound. The tree branch had inflicted more damage than a bump on the head. A long, jagged gash followed the curve of his shoulder across sinew and muscle. Though it bled steadily, it didn't appear to be very deep. Relieved he was not mortally wounded, she looked about for something to serve as a bandage, but found nothing.

"Wonderful," she muttered. "I suppose I shall have to use my new petticoat. I should have left you in the road, Lucien Devereaux, and let the mice have you."

Scowling fiercely, she lifted the edge of her skirt and ripped a long strip free. Then she folded it into a neat square and strapped it into place with the thick muffler, tying the ends as tightly as she dared.

"There. That should hold you until we get to Rosemont." Arabella pulled the heavy carriage blanket from beneath the seat and tucked it around him, more for her peace of mind than for his comfort. It was disconcerting to sit in the same carriage with all those rippling muscles and smooth, golden skin only an arm's length away.

Holding her cloak closer, she sank into the corner of the carriage and fervently prayed that a rabbit would cross the path of Constable Robbins's well-trained hounds.

A faint smile tugged her mouth at the thought, though it did little to untie the knots in her stomach. She was so close to success. If things continued to progress, everything would be taken care of within the next year—her father's debts, Robert's doctor bills. She might even have enough left to complete the improvements on Rosemont. All she needed was time. Time and a little luck.

Of course, luck did not seem to be favoring her just now. She stole a glance at Lucien from beneath her lashes. He lay sprawled in the corner, muttering restlessly at each bump and dip. Though she knew it was childish, Arabella only wished he were fully conscious so she could enjoy his discomfort.

The lumbering coach struck a particularly deep rut and Lucien let out a low groan, his hand reaching for his wounded shoulder. Arabella dived across the coach just as his fingers settled about her hastily tied dressing. His brows lowered and he struggled to free himself from the bandage.

Refusing to give way, she held tight, wrapping both of her hands about his. After a moment, he subsided and slipped sideways until his head rested in her lap, his breathing shallow but steady.

Arabella waited until his brow had smoothed before she carefully pulled the blanket back into place. He looked peaceful, his thick lashes resting on his cheeks, as innocent and guileless as a boy.

But she was not fooled. She knew him too well. Leaning forward, Arabella whispered into his ear, "If you live through this, Lucien Devereaux, I just may kill you myself."

Chapter 2

Lucien awoke slowly, adrift in muted sensations. His head lay nestled in a warm, soft cushion while the delectable scent of raspberries sparked visions of lazy summer days.

Except for the occasional sway and creak of a poorly sprung coach, he could almost believe himself to be ensconced in a wondrously soft bed, suffering from no more than an enthusiastic night of brandy.

He shifted and an icy cold stab dispelled his pleasant fantasy. No night of overindulgence had ever hurt this much. He raised a hand, his fingers instinctively reaching for his shoulder.

"Be careful how you move," commanded a feminine voice. Husky and low, the faint Yorkshire accent sparked a distant memory. For an instant, Lucien had a clear vision of warm brown eyes and petal-soft lips.

Distracted from his pain, he forced his eyes open. A

sweet, heart-shaped face stared down at him, the delicate sable brows lowered.

His heart thudded an extra beat. He knew those eyes, had felt those rosebud lips beneath his, long, long ago. His gaze dropped to the soft, rounded breasts that loomed above him. "Bella."

Her hand, once lying so trustfully beside his cheek, balled into a fist. "Perhaps Your Grace would find it more expedient to address my face and not my bosom."

Frost crackled along the prim voice and Lucien winced. Steeling himself, he dragged his gaze to hers and offered an apologetic grin. But he knew there would be no forgiveness; he had sinned against her in ways much worse than a thoughtless comment.

She pointed to the opposite seat. *"Move."*

There was nothing for it but to comply. Lying with his head in her lap was not an advantageous position from which to argue; not to mention the effect her nearness was having on his unsteady senses.

He levered himself upright, faltering against the sea of black spots that swam before his eyes and the pain that laced through his shoulder. "Good God," he muttered through clenched teeth. "What in hell happened?"

She leaned as far away as possible, unmoved by his agony. "You don't remember?"

"No." At least, not anything that made sense. The images of a cliff in the chill night air, the tang of the ocean so strong he could taste it, slipped through his muddled brain. He'd been on his way . . . somewhere.

Lucien rubbed a hand to his temple, wincing when his fingers brushed a knot the size of a walnut. "Did I fall?"

"Your horse reared, and you hit your head on a tree branch." She stopped as if uncertain how to proceed, then retreated behind a severe frown. "My groom may have been traveling a bit fast for such a narrow road."

Her glare implied that he was somehow guilty of the deed himself. Lucien touched his forehead, where the dull ache seemed to grow by the moment. "It hurts like hell."

"You'll live. It would take more than an oak to dent that hard head."

His lips quirked. Somewhere along the way, his Arabella had developed a sarcastic wit. He regarded her with a narrowed gaze. She sat as rigid as a board, her hands clasped in her lap, color staining her cheeks, a hint of tiredness making her eyes appear even darker. With her tousled honey and brown curls and large dark eyes, she appeared younger than he'd remembered. Younger and even more beautiful.

His chest tightened, his amusement fading. Damn the Home Office for sending him to Yorkshire. He'd refused to go when they'd first told him of the assignment. He was needed in London while his sister prepared for her first season, but they'd brushed aside his objections.

Left with no recourse, he had planned to arrive under cover of night, discover what he could, and leave without anyone the wiser. Of course, that was before Arabella's coachman had seen fit to run him down.

He moved his shoulder and winced at the sparks of pain that shot through it. "Bloody hell. It feels like I've been shot." He caught her gaze and lifted a brow. "You didn't by chance put a ball in me?"

"If I had shot you, Lucien, you would not be here now."

No, had Arabella shot him, he would be stretched out on the ground, a hole through his forehead while she danced around his lifeless body in wild celebration. He had taught her the rudiments of gunplay when she was fifteen, and she'd had an uncanny ability even then.

Lucien placed a hand on the makeshift bandage. Neatly tied, it bound him so tightly he could scarcely breathe. He forced a smile. "I suppose I have you to thank for—"

The coach hit a rut. Thrown back, Lucien's shoulder slammed against the cracked leather squabs. Spots of color exploded as coal-hot agony lanced down his arm. Gasping for breath, he fell forward, almost tumbling to the floor before Arabella caught him. Her arms encircled him and held him close.

The coach continued to sway while his breathing slowed to a more normal pace. As the pain subsided, Lucien realized his cheek rested against Arabella's breast, the soft swell made all the more beguiling by its proximity to his mouth. The heady scent of raspberries once again drifted to him and he savored the contact, soaking in her warmth and remembering all that should have been.

"If you cannot sit on your own, I will have the footman come and hold you upright." As brisk as a mountain spring, her voice yanked him rudely into the present.

Unable to resist the challenge, Lucien lifted his head to look into her eyes. A scant inch of charged air separated their lips. Her eyes darkened; the chocolate depths swirled with mysterious gold flecks. He leaned closer, his gaze drifting to her plump lower lip.

He should have forced himself to walk out of her life yet again. But his body burned with a demanding heat that left him dizzy, as punch-drunk as a youth sampling his first mug of ale. Every sensation seemed amplified—the cadence of her voice, the beckoning curve of her breasts, even the outraged whisper of her starched skirts. A light sheen of moisture glistened on her lips and he would have traded every shilling he possessed to taste her then and there.

God help him, he'd spent his entire life running from this woman. What was he doing, subjecting himself to such unbearable pleasure, such exquisite torture?

Yet he could no more stop reaching for her than he could cease breathing. Without releasing her from his gaze, he brushed a stray chestnut curl from her cheek, his fingers entangling the silken hair. Her eyes widened in alarm, her mouth parting in murmured protest.

Then he kissed her, slanting his mouth hard across hers. Pleasure swirled and built until he was drowning in sensation. It was all he could do to keep from crushing her to him, demanding more and more until she cried out with the need for her own release.

With a muffled protest, Arabella broke free and slapped him, her hand cracking sharply against his cheek, jerking his head sideways.

Agony screamed down his neck and pooled in his shoulder. "Bloody hell!" he ground out, clutching his arm.

"Your base passions do not interest me, Your Grace. I am no longer a green girl of sixteen." Distaste laced each word with prim poison.

Unwilling to let her see his disappointment, Lucien sneered. "More's the pity."

She gasped in outrage, but he ignored her, moving his jaw gingerly. Thank God she hadn't thought to double up her fist. He caught her wary gaze and forced a cold smile. "I understand you quite well, madam. I shall stay on my side of the carriage." *And after this evening, out of your life.*

A dangerous light sparkled in her eyes. "I am sure your *wife* will appreciate your noble efforts."

The words penetrated his brain like shards of glass. He rubbed a hand across his eyes. If Arabella thought Sabrina would have disapproved of his actions, she was wrong. His wife would have laughed long and hard to see him so overset with passion that he forgot everything but the woman he was with.

But Sabrina was not here. Guilt simmered in his belly, hot and bitter. "My wife died three years ago."

Arabella's gaze widened, then she retreated into her corner, unconsciously pulling her skirts back so that they no longer brushed his knee.

He watched her without comment. It was what he expected, what he deserved. Thankfully, he no longer possessed any illusions about who or what he was. Sabrina's death had taken care of that. He leaned his aching head against the seat and closed his eyes.

"I'm sorry." Arabella's voice drifted to him, as soft as an angel's breath.

Lucien refused to look at her, to see the pity he didn't deserve. "Don't be. It was mercifully quick. For both of us."

The coach swayed around a corner and slowed. Lucien glanced at the covered windows. "Where are we?" His voice sounded cool even to his own ears.

"On the cliff road to Rosemont."

"And my horse?"

"He bolted across the moors. I will send Ned to look for him as soon as we are home."

Then he would be free to complete his mission. Lucien placed a hand over his greatcoat and rested his fingers across the heavy leather packet that weighed down the pocket. Thank God it had not come dislodged during his fall.

He slid his hand away and almost laughed at his furtiveness. Who would have imagined that he, Lucien Devereaux, the sixth Duke of Wexford, was one of the Home Office's most prized infiltrators? He fixed his gaze on his companion, wondering if she suspected anything. "Arabella, why are—"

"We will arrive at Rosemont shortly." She kept her gaze fixed on the swaying curtain, her tumbled curls at odds with the prim line of her mouth. "It would be best if you sat quietly and rested your head."

Disappointment soured his curiosity. So that was the game she wished to play. Very well. He owed her that much, if not more. "Of course. As soon as my horse is found, I will be on my way."

The thick crescents of her lashes shadowed her eyes to black. "If it is the lack of a mount that keeps you here, I would be more than happy to loan you one. It may not be of the quality to which Your Grace is accustomed, but it will serve the purpose."

Lucien scowled and slumped against the seat. He hated the way she called him "Your Grace" as if he were some kind of toplofty lord. Yet despite his dissatisfaction, he found himself noting the way her hair curled about her face and framed her determined chin and the smooth, untouched line of her cheek and throat.

God, how he had loved her—loved her with the undisciplined passion of a willful twenty-year-old, spoiled by his family and his circumstances. He had loved her, but then been forced to turn and walk away.

He rubbed his aching shoulder absently and wondered about her life in the years that had passed. Had she wed a local gentleman? Or a farmer, perhaps? A big, bumbling Yorkshireman with rough, callused hands and a broad, simple face?

The idea of such an unappreciative clod touching Arabella made his stomach roil. Lucien shook his head at the sudden rise of nausea. He must be more severely wounded than he thought. Indeed, his whole side burned, while his mouth felt as dry as a coal bin.

The carriage suddenly jolted to a halt. Arabella

frowned and pulled back the edge of the leather curtain. "Wonderful," she muttered under her breath, her face pale as she dropped the curtain back into place. "It is Constable Robbins and his men."

"What do they want?"

She hesitated a second before answering. "My coachman believes they are out searching for smugglers."

Lucien leaned past her to lift the edge of the curtain. He could barely make out a large group of horsemen in the pale moonlight. "A dark night like this is perfect for moving shipments inland."

Clear brown eyes met his. "You sound as if you know a great deal about the smuggling trade."

Damn it, what was wrong with him? He rubbed a hand across his eyes and wondered why he felt so light-headed. "I know a good deal about a lot of things."

"I'm sure you do," she replied in an indifferent tone, peering out the window once again.

He should have been glad for her disregard, but it stung nevertheless. A voice arose from outside and Lucien realized there could be serious consequences for Arabella if she were discovered alone with him. He had dishonored her once; he would not do it again.

The unmistakable sound of an argument lifted over the wind, then the altercation ended abruptly, followed by a tense silence. Lucien struggled to stay upright, but his head pounded mercilessly. He pulled a flask from his coat pocket and tried to undo the stopper, but his hand seemed leaden, his arm weighted and numb.

Swearing under his breath, he handed the flask to Arabella. "Open it."

Arabella regarded the flagon with disapproval. How could he even think of imbibing at a moment like this? Of course, he could not realize how much was at stake. She forced a frozen smile to her lips. "It would be better if you—"

"Arabella." His eyes narrowed unpleasantly, his mouth white. "Open it."

A shiver lanced up her spine at the implied threat in his voice. There it was, that indefinable difference from the Lucien of her childhood. This Lucien was older, harder, and more dangerous than ever. Even the air about him hummed razor-sharp and deadly.

From outside, a gruff voice called for assistance. Footsteps came toward the door, halting at Wilson's loud protest. Arabella hurriedly undid the flask, wrinkling her nose at the cloying odor of brandy.

Lucien swallowed the burning liquid with a murmur of approval. Arabella sniffed and he cast her an amused glance, the green of his eyes shimmering unnaturally in the lantern light.

She tried not to watch as he tugged at his cravat, revealing his muscular bronze throat. The sight triggered a flood of hot memories. Arabella clasped her hands together and said, "Pray lace up your shirt. It wouldn't do for the constable to see you thus attired."

"Of course," he murmured in reply, then downed the rest of the brandy, his gaze never leaving hers. The corded muscles of his throat rippled as he swallowed and Arabella warmed as if she were the one imbibing the potent drink. Handsome and dissolute, Lucien Devereaux was lethal.

Only this time, she would not weaken. She determinedly held each painful memory to her, a shield against his seductive power. "I will tell Constable Robbins you are a friend of Robert's and have sustained a fall from your horse. That will explain why I am here, without a chaperone."

"It won't be enough."

"It will be if you close your eyes. You can hardly seduce me if you are asleep."

His gaze locked with hers for an agonizing moment before he glanced away, the lines about his mouth deepening. "I will do this only to save you from embarrassment." Though it must have pained him, he tugged his coat back into place and pulled the carriage blanket over his shoulder. He closed his eyes just as the door swung open.

Reeking of garlic, Constable Robbins thrust his lantern into the doorway. "Good evening, Miss Hadley."

"Good evening, Constable. Is anything wrong?"

His suspicious gaze raked the interior. "Who is this?"

"A friend of my brother's. He arrived this afternoon."

"Did he, indeed?"

"Yes. My aunts and I hope he will be leaving soon."

The constable brightened at the mention of her aunts. "Lady Melwin promised me a tonic fer my sheep. Said it'll make them produce twice the lambs."

"I'll be sure to ask her when it will be ready."

"There's no need. I can ride over and ask myself." Before Arabella had time to properly digest this unwelcome bit of news, he sniffed the brandy-soaked air and eyed Lucien with a lifted brow. "Ape-drunk, is he?"

She cast a repulsed glance at Lucien. "Fortunately, he will be leaving tomorrow."

Constable Robbins shook his head like a big bear. "Like that, is it? Your brother should mind which of his friends he invites to Rosemont."

Arabella mustered a brave smile that seemed to meet the constable's approval, for he stopped his perusal of Lucien and smiled back at her with evident admiration.

"Your concern is such a comfort," Arabella said. "Things have been so difficult since my father died, and then Robert returned to us, and . . ." She fumbled in her reticule for a handkerchief, but found none.

The constable dug in his pocket and triumphantly produced a wrinkled scrap of linen.

She held the dubiously clean kerchief between two fingers. "Oh, thank you. You are too kind." Arabella bit the inside of her lip until a tear welled in her eye.

"Now, now! No need to get in a bother," he said hastily, looking wildly about for help. "I wouldn't have stopped you at all except there's been a report that a shipment of brandy . . ." His voice trailed off, his attention fixed on Lucien's still form.

She followed the constable's gaze. The blanket had slipped from Lucien's shoulder, where a large patch of red showed clearly against the snowy white linen. Arabella's hands clenched about her skirts, her fingers sinking into the sticky fabric. She looked down at the red smear with relief. "Jam."

The constable's thick brows lowered.

"Raspberry jam." Arabella gestured to the floor, where a large red stain gleamed wetly in the lantern light. Part of the smear was indeed caused by the raspberry jam, but more of it came from Lucien's wounded shoulder.

She wiped her jam-smeared fingers on the constable's handkerchief and hoped he did not notice how her hands trembled. "A rabbit leapt in front of the carriage and startled poor Wilson. It caused the horses to rear and the basket slipped from the seat."

"Did it, now?"

"Oh, yes." She handed the handkerchief back to the constable. "We were splattered head to foot."

He took the sticky handkerchief and sniffed, his brow clearing as he gave a little chuckle.

"Have you found something?" came a strident voice from outside the carriage.

The constable gave Arabella an apologetic shrug. "Lord Harlbrook," he said with a noticeable lack of enthusiasm. "He demanded to come. He's sure some smugglers are usin' the Red Rooster to hand off their goods." The constable leaned forward to whisper loudly, "I'm thinkin' he's jus' angry to miss his share of the profits."

Harlbrook's voice raised again. "Robbins! What is it?"

The constable grimaced, but replied dutifully, "No one but Miss Hadley and a friend of her brother's who is covered in raspberry jam."

A fleshy figure pushed Robbins from the doorway. "Young Hadley has no friends."

Arabella had to grit her teeth against the urge to plant her foot squarely between Lord Harlbrook's narrow eyes. "I don't believe you've met all of Robert's acquaintances. Perhaps—"

"I've told you to call me John, my dear," he said with pompous civility. His thick mouth pursed in disapproval as he caught sight of Lucien's prone form. "Who is this ruffian?"

A wave of ire strengthened her resolve. In as haughty a tone as she could muster, she announced, "This is Lucien Devereaux, the Duke of Wexford."

"Duke?"

"The sixth duke, to be exact. Of course, you are but lately arrived to the neighborhood and wouldn't know that he and his family often came during the hunting season years ago. Robert and Lucien have corresponded regularly ever since."

Lord Harlbrook's disbelief was palpable. Arabella gave a silent prayer of thanks that they had not stumbled upon her two hours ago, when the carriage had been loaded with casks of prime French cognac.

As if aware of her relief, Harlbrook asked, "If this man is a friend of Robert's, then why are you escorting him?"

"We were visiting our tenants, the March family, when Robert took ill. He returned home earlier."

"And left you alone? I shall have a word with him about this."

The proprietary tone stiffened Arabella's back to ramrod straightness. "I assure you, that will not be necessary."

Deep in feigned sleep, Lucien stirred and began to snore in a most annoying fashion. Arabella took the opportunity to pull the door as far closed as she could with Lord Harlbrook standing in the way. "Thank you for your concern, my lord, but we must be returning home to—"

His hand closed over her wrist, his breath hot on her cheek. "Pray don't be so belligerent my dear. I have the right to ask anything I wish, and you know it."

Arabella yanked her hand away. "You have no rights where I am concerned. The debt will be paid and our association will be at an end."

"Forget the money." He wet his lips with a swift swipe of his tongue, his hungry gaze roving across her face. "Arabella, you must know that I—"

"Lud, what's this?" Lucien's voice rumbled across the coach, husky like aged whiskey. He slid forward until his arm rested along the back of the leather seat. "The coach has stopped. Have we lost a wheel?"

All Arabella had to do was lean back and she would be comfortably ensconced in his embrace. The idea made her tingle in the most astounding places. She cleared her throat. "This is Lord Harlbrook, Your Grace. He is my neighbor."

"How exciting," Lucien murmured in a wearied voice. "May we continue to Rosemont? I am tired."

Harlbrook puffed out his chest. "Your Grace, I was unaware of your presence in our neighborhood or I would have immediately ridden over to—"

"I came for a private visit," Lucien said softly.

There was no mistaking the intention of that carefully uttered phrase. Harlbrook bristled. "You will forgive my curiosity, Your Grace, but I myself have an interest at Rosemont."

Lucien stared at the pudgy lord for an inordinate length of time, his gaze narrowing. Arabella could feel the anger building in the tense figure at her side. He proffered a polite, humorless smile and slid his hand another inch down the seat until his fingertips rested against her shoulder. "Rosemont is a lovely house. I, however, find its occupants more to my liking." Heated green eyes turned to Arabella. "Don't I, love?"

The soft words settled in the silence and Lucien placed his hand on the side of her neck, his thumb moving in slow, easy circles.

She tried to swallow, but failed. Her entire body focused on his warm hand and the sensuous movement of his thumb.

Harlbrook choked, his face bright red. "This is insufferable!"

Lucien looked surprised. "For whom?"

Although Lucien's actions were highly improper, Arabella had to fight the urge to giggle. She'd put up with Lord Harlbrook's unwanted advances for so many months that it was a pleasure to see him glaring, his jowls quivering like an outraged hog.

She forced herself to say politely, "If you'll excuse us, my lord. His Grace and I really must return to Rosemont. My aunts will worry if we are late."

"So true!" Lucien exclaimed. "We must not tarry." Leaning past her, he grabbed the door and slammed it shut, barely missing Harlbrook's nose. Without waiting another moment, Lucien thumped on the ceiling.

Wilson immediately hawed the horses into action. The lantern flickered against the walls as the carriage swayed along the road.

Lucien's breathing filled the tense silence, ragged and shallow. "How long has that bastard been forcing himself on you like that?"

"He is usually not so persistent. I must say, you certainly set him in his place."

"I'd like to have set him in a much wetter, much muddier place."

She bubbled with laughter. "It was a wonder to see him so confounded he could not even speak." She glanced at him shyly. "Thank you."

"Don't thank me," he snapped, his voice harsh, his eyes as hard as agates. "My damnable temper—" He broke off, controlling himself with an obvious effort. Then, in carefully restrained tones, he said, "Once that fool tells every person in town what he saw here, you will be ruined."

Arabella chuckled. "Pish-posh. No one will believe a word he says. Besides, I don't care what anyone thinks."

"But I do," Lucien ground out, his jaw set and hard.

Arabella had to fight an overwhelming desire to kiss away the bitter turn of his lips. Shocked at her thoughts, she turned to fasten down the curtain that flapped against the window and said breezily, "Oh, I've been ruined before. As painful as it was, I lived through it."

"You should not suffer because of me." Lucien's warm voice sounded at her ear. "Never again, *Bella mia*. Never again."

She turned and found herself drowning in his sea-green eyes. She knew she should speak, say something cutting. After all, this man had taken her heart and discarded her as if she were of no more importance than a wrinkled cravat. His heartless actions had hurt her with a pain that had been as soul-deep as it had been long in duration. She could still feel the sting of his rejection.

At the time, she had believed she would never forgive him. She had dreamed of the day when she would have the chance to face him. But the words she had imagined herself saying for so long fled, and all she could do was stare at him: at his incredible eyes, the smooth, golden line of his face, the sensual shape of his mouth.

"So beautiful," Lucien murmured. As if sensing her longing, he lifted a hand to her cheek. His eyes glistened with hunger as he lowered his mouth to hers.

Arabella was lost at the first touch of his lips. Once again she was sixteen, pledging her love to the only man who had lifted her senses to such heights. Waves of desire raced through her, stealing her breath and tangling her in feelings she had no strength to deny.

A slow heat began to build inside her. She gripped him closer, and felt his groan rumble deep in his chest.

Abruptly, Lucien's mouth slipped away and he fell back against the seat.

Arabella stared down at him.

Lucien Devereaux, the dashing and dangerous Duke of Wexford, had fainted.

Chapter 3

Lady Melwin sat knitting, her needles clacking through the red yarn like a barnyard full of hens. "*Something* must be done."

"Indeed." From the other chair pulled close to the fire, her sister, Lady Durham, looked up from her embroidery. "More than one thing, if you ask me."

Jane silently agreed and forced herself to knit at a slower pace. The last time she'd knit so furiously, she had inadvertently lost count and poor Wilson's sweater had come out with one arm a good five inches longer than the other. She always felt a twinge of regret every time she saw the sleeve drooping over his hand. She sighed. It was just one of many things that needed correcting at Rosemont. "It's a disgrace, the way poor Arabella runs from dawn till nightfall, staying out far too late."

Emma stabbed her needle into the material. "She works much too hard."

"As if she were a servant. Though it is improper to

26

speak ill of the dead, our brother was derelict in his duty to his daughter. The ninny, losing everything on faro."

Emma lifted her brows, her blue eyes owlish behind her spectacles.

"Don't look at me like that," Jane said defensively. "Whist is an entirely different matter. Besides, James had an addiction. I, meanwhile, merely enjoy an occasional game of cards."

Emma snorted, but offered no more comment. Glad to see that her sister was disinclined to argue, Jane glanced at the painted wooden box in which she kept her winnings. At one time it had been satisfyingly full, and she'd thought to help Arabella with the debts left after James's death. Now, however, she'd be lucky to find a shilling for a single game.

Unaware of her sister's musings, Emma tied off a thread. "It is beyond me how our foolish dolt of a brother could be a descendent of a man like the Captain." She turned her gaze to the portrait that hung over the mantel and, as one, they both stared in silent admiration.

The picture was of a decidedly rakish man dressed in the height of fashion for 1551. A red silk doublet sat across his wide shoulders, the slashed sleeves revealing the rich blue velvet of his tunic. Cream-colored hose encased his muscular legs, outlining their fine shape. One hand rested casually on a sword set with jewels.

But it was his expression that arrested one's attention. There, the artist had outdone himself. The Captain's blue eyes blazed with genuine humor, a quizzical half smile lighting his handsome face.

This portrait did not show him in his dashing captain's uniform, as did the one in the main salon. No, this portrait was of a later time, after a certain damsel had settled the lusty pirate's need to wander. Emma and Jane sighed. No man had ever been so handsome as Captain Richard Hadley, the Pirate of Rosemont.

Jane pulled a handkerchief from her pocket and delicately wiped the corner of her mouth. "The Captain would have known how to handle our Arabella."

"Oh, yes." Emma adjusted her glasses, a beatific expression on her face. "He'd ride into the courtyard, brandishing his sword, and take her." She tilted her head, her white curls gleaming in the firelight. "Would that be incest? He *is* her great-great-great—"

"*Emma!* To suggest such a thing!" Jane tucked her handkerchief away and rose to check on the tonic she had brewing in a small kettle over the fire. She lifted the heavy ladle and sniffed. "It needs something. . . ." She took a tiny bottle from the table and dropped a few dried leaves into the bubbling mix.

Emma came to stand beside her. "You had better add more; Constable Robbins's sheep are quite large."

Jane added a smidge more to the pot, dropped the lid back into place, and replaced the ladle. "I wish we could do something for Arabella. If only there were more eligible men about."

"Mr. Francot showed some promise. He visited every day last summer."

"But he is only a solicitor and much too old for her."

"True." Emma sneezed as she resumed her seat, her plump bosom straining against her laces. "I believe I am catching a complaint."

"You are *always* catching a complaint."

Emma ignored her and removed a small brown bottle from her pocket. The sweet smell of cognac wafted through the air as she sipped delicately. She had long since forgone using a spoon for her "medicine."

Jane shook out the last of a knot and began a new row.

"Arabella needs someone as strong-willed as she. Someone capable of understanding her high spirits."

"Someone with wealth and position. And a title. Nothing less than a viscount." Emma recapped her bottle and returned it to her pocket.

The fire crackled and Jane held her toes out to the warmth. As difficult as things were, at least they maintained some of the basic comforts. Since they could not afford to keep the morning room heated during the winter, she and Emma had turned the old nursery into a private parlor. The room was small enough to warm with just one fire, and decorated with enough rose chintz to give it a cozy, welcoming air. The only remnant of the old nursery was a wrought-iron bed that stood in the corner.

The clicking of her needles increased in tempo as Jane considered the fate of her niece. Arabella was much too attractive to stay alone. Though the current rage seemed to be for tall, fair women, Arabella had garnered more than her fair share of masculine attention. She was small and well-rounded, her skin flawless. She practically glowed with good health.

Perhaps that was one of the problems. Jane scowled at the tangle of yarn that suddenly appeared at the tip of her needles. Besides her vigorous health, Arabella refused to use any of the thousand or so feminine wiles designed to attract a man. It was a pity her niece had inherited the famed Hadley pride. Jane's knitting needles clacked faster. Well, with or without her niece's help, she was going to find a husband for Arabella.

A heavy thud sounded down the corridor before the door opened, and Wilson and Ned staggered in carrying the limp form of a large man.

Jane leapt to her feet and scurried to open the door wider. Her gaze locked on the red stain that stretched across the man's torn shirt. "Good heavens! Put him on the bed."

Emma dropped her embroidery and clambered to her feet as Wilson and Ned struggled to lay their burden on the cotton counterpane, breathing heavily from the exertion.

"Who is he?" asked Jane, peering over their shoulders.

Panting, Ned placed his hands on his knees. "Fell . . . we thought . . . he . . ."

Doubled at the waist and breathing even harder, Wilson nodded. "On the . . . road . . . tried to . . . had to . . . and then . . ."

Emma plopped her fists on her generous hips. "Sweet Sampson! Spit it out!"

Jane sniffed suspiciously. "Have you two been drinking?"

"No . . . it were him," managed Ned, his color returning to a more normal shade. He jerked a thumb at their unconscious guest. "He's a dook."

Emma, on her way to the washstand, stopped in midstep. "A what?"

"A dook, m'lady," Wilson said. "A real 'un."

Jane pulled open the torn shirt and regarded the neat bandage, recognizing Arabella's handiwork. "How was he wounded?"

"I'm afeared I frightened him into fallin' off his horse," Wilson said, adding hastily, "though it weren't my fault. He was ridin' in the middle of the night, gallopin' acrost the road like a devil. Nigh frightened me to death."

Ned nodded. "If ye hadn't run 'im down, someone else would 'ave."

Jane's face must have registered her confusion because Wilson added, "The missus bandaged him up right quick. He's hardly bleedin' now."

"Fortunately for you." She would just have to wait to speak with Arabella to discover the true story. Jane went to the cupboard to remove the roll of cloths she kept for such emergencies. "Was he injured anywhere else?"

"He bumped his head." The old groom pushed the sleeve of his sweater up where it fell over his hand. "Miss Arabella seemed quite taken with the gent."

Oh? This was getting more interesting by the moment. Jane set the roll of bandages on the bed and returned to the cupboard for clean cloths. "Remove his clothing and cover him with the sheet. We must be certain he is not injured elsewhere."

Moving quickly, Ned helped Wilson. After a few awkward tugs and muffled oaths, they succeeded. Ned stood back with an air of satisfaction. "Wait till I tell 'em down at the Wild Stag 'bout this. I've never undressed a dook afore."

"Where is Miss Arabella?" Emma asked.

"Out in the barn," Ned said. "Waitin' to see if Constable Robbins is followin'."

Emma blinked. "The constable? What is he doing out at this time of the night?"

"Lookin' fer smugglers." Ned frowned. "Miss Hadley seemed a bit put out to see 'im. Mayhap she didn't want 'im knowin' she had a real dook in the carriage."

Jane exchanged a glance with Emma before shooing the men from the room. She firmly closed the door behind them and returned to the bed. There she stared down at their new visitor, her mind alive with possibilities. "He is certainly handsome."

Emma poured some water into a basin and came to stand beside her. "Very handsome. But then, I think most dukes are."

"I have often thought it a tragedy that there weren't

more of them about." Jane retrieved her sewing shears from her pocket and began to cut the cloth into strips while Emma removed Arabella's crude bandage. The wound was shallow, but the severity of the jagged tear required stitches.

Emma gathered her sewing silk, and they went to work. *Tsk*ing over the angry edges of the torn skin, they bathed the wound, sewed it with tiny, perfect stitches, and then packed it with a cold poultice. As they worked, they marveled over each inch of the golden skin. Muscular and well defined, he reminded Jane of a statue she'd once seen in Italy. The only difference was, of course, that this statue was incredibly warm to the touch.

Emma tied off the fresh bandage, then lifted the duke's hand and examined his ring. "This must have cost him a few pence."

"At least he is a *successful* duke." Jane stood back to admire him in his entirety. "He is certainly tall."

"Hmm. I wonder why Arabella did not wish to speak with Constable Robbins."

They exchanged a look, and Jane heaved a mournful sigh. "Something is amiss and I suspect it has to do with our guest here."

"I was thinking the same thing." Emma looked at the duke with a regretful shake of her head. "A pity, too, for a duke would have been just the thing."

Jane could see it all now—the wedding would have been lovely. The gentleman, so tall and well proportioned, and Arabella, beautiful in the pink frock Jane and Emma had prepared almost six years ago. Every year, they added something to the bodice of the dress—a lace collar, a flounce, handcrafted beadwork, a silk bow. This year they had outdone themselves, adding ten rows of hand-sewn rosettes.

Emma cleared her throat. "It is a bad habit for a duke, to wander around at night and startle servants. Still . . . there are so few qualified men available."

"True," Jane said slowly, looking down at the glittering emerald on the duke's hand.

"And no man is perfect," her sister continued. "In fact, you could almost hold that no man is perfect *until* he meets the right woman."

Jane beamed. "All our duke needs is a good woman who will break him of galloping around at night and scaring people's servants to death."

Emma turned to the portrait over the fireplace. "Like the Lady Meaghan broke the Captain of his insatiable bloodlust."

"Exactly!" They both stared at the smiling portrait. Somehow, the blue eyes seemed to twinkle merrily, as if the Captain could discern their bold thoughts and heartily approved. A gust of wind arose outside the manor and rattled the shutters with satisfying vigor.

Emma gave a delicious shiver. "Oh, my! It seems the Captain agrees with us."

Jane strongly believed in signs. "Of course he does. A duke is not so very different from a pirate, after all." She tapped a finger on her chin. "His wounds will keep him abed a week, but no more. We must induce him to stay longer."

"Fortunately, it won't take long for him to fall in love with Arabella, and—" Emma stared down at Arabella's future husband, her brows lowered over the bridge of her upturned nose. "He is very handsome, but I wonder . . ."

Jane didn't like the frown on Emma's face. "What?"

"What if . . ." Emma had to swallow twice before she could continue. "What if he's not . . ." She blushed, then whispered loudly, *"Adequate."*

Jane looked down at the duke's face and noted the thick lashes and the strong line of his jaw. He seemed too handsome to be anything *other* than adequate. But one could never tell. "Perhaps we should look, just to make certain."

Emma's mouth rounded into a perfect O. "Look? *Us?*"

Jane smoothed her hands over her neatly starched skirt and nodded sternly. "Think, Emma. What if he is deformed? Or worse?"

Seeing Emma's mouth firm into a stubborn line, Jane added, "You wouldn't buy a melon without thumping it, would you?"

No one was more devoted to selecting quality fare for the table than Emma. She blinked down at the duke. "No, I wouldn't."

"Would you choose Arabella's husband with less care than you choose a melon?"

Emma looked positively dazed. "I hadn't thought of it quite that way. I . . . I suppose you are right, sister."

"Furthermore, who is better to judge if the man is fit to be wed? After all, we were both married for over thirty years. Here, I'll even go first," Jane said bravely. She took a calming breath, and then folded the sheet back until the edge of one muscular leg showed. Bronze against the white linen sheet, it would ripple as he walked.

"Oh, my," breathed Emma. She pressed a plump hand to the lace at her even plumper bosom. "Oh, my, oh, my!"

Jane gestured toward the bed. "Your turn."

Face furrowed with determination, Emma stepped forward and folded the sheet back farther, revealing the trim line of his hip and the lean edge of his stomach. The two women studied the exposed area in silence. Finally, Emma turned to Jane. "Are you ready?"

Unable to do more than nod, Jane grabbed the sheet and lifted.

There was a moment of reverent silence.

Then Emma closed her mouth, reached out and took the sheet from Jane's still fingers, and carefully lowered it back into place.

Without looking at one another, she and Jane tucked the sheet in, replaced the blanket, and returned to their respective seats by the fire.

A strained silence filled the once-peaceful room. Emma pretended to embroider, though it was painfully clear her mind was elsewhere, since her needle had no thread.

Jane didn't even attempt to knit. She just sat, staring ahead.

After a prolonged stillness, she let out her breath. "He is definitely a *real* duke."

Emma sank against her chair in relief and fanned herself with a weak hand. "Arabella *must* marry him."

Jane looked up at the picture over the fireplace. The Captain's blue eyes met hers, and suddenly she knew what was destined to happen as clearly as if she were a seeress. "Oh, yes, Emma. Our Arabella must marry her duke. And the sooner, the better."

Chapter 4

Lucien awoke slowly, pulled from deep sleep by a pounding headache that surged against his eyelids and forced them open. Squinting against the sunlight, he surveyed his surroundings.

The room had the unmistakable look of a feminine retreat. Lace frills hung from the curtains and covers, and embroidered roses adorned every conceivable surface. The cacophony of color made his head spin. Lucien raked a hand through his hair and winced as his fingertips brushed a lump that felt the size of a cricket ball.

From across the room, bright blue eyes surveyed him with interest. Gray, plump and bespectacled, his observer tugged her companion's cuff. "Jane, look! He's awake."

Jane turned and regarded him with blue eyes that were an exact replica of her companion's. "So he is, Emma. I thought he'd sleep the rest of the day away."

Emma scurried to his side and beamed at him like a

cordial fairy. "My, you have the most beautiful eyes!" She called over her shoulder, "Jane, come and see!"

Small and neat as a wren, Jane advanced and peered down her arched nose. She stared intently, assessing him as thoroughly as if he'd been a stallion on the block at Tattersall's. It was damned irritating, but before he could protest, she straightened. "I once had a cat with green eyes. Best cat I ever had."

It was too much for his clouded mind to decipher. Lucien turned away. As he did so, the soft rub of crisp cotton brushed across his knee and caused him to start. Bloody hell, he was completely naked. *Where the devil are my clothes?*

Emma retucked the edges of his blanket as if he were no more than ten years of age, the distinctive scent of cognac swelling as she leaned near. "We sent them to be cleaned."

Lucien crumpled the edge of the sheet between his fists. The papers from the Home Office were still concealed in his greatcoat. If they were discovered—

He caught sight of his coat slung casually over a small chair in the corner, the telltale outline of the packet clearly visible. He relaxed against the pillows.

Unaware of his turmoil, Jane returned to the table by the fire, saying over her shoulder, "Your shirt was ruined, you know."

"As was your cravat," Emma said. "You lost lots of blood." She beamed pleasantly and added in a singsong voice, "Lots and lots and lots of blood."

Somehow Arabella had forgotten to mention that her aunts were completely, unequivocally mad.

"Fortunately for you," Emma continued, unabashed by his lack of response, "Jane had some of her tonic already

in the making. It is wine-based, you know. Very tasty."
Emma's cupid's bow mouth pursed into a pout. "My niece
is not fond of having spirits in the house. The supply has
dwindled sadly since she took over the estate."

"Arabella runs the estate?"

"Oh, yes. Since her father died two years ago."

"Surely her brother assists her."

"Oh. You don't know about . . . Robert is not well,"
Emma said, a tremor to her voice.

"Humph," Jane said, returning to the bed with a metal
cup. "Robert would be fine if you and Arabella would
cease coddling him."

Flags of color flew in Emma's cheeks. "We do not cod-
dle him; we just want to help him. If you weren't so
unfeeling, you would want to help him, too."

"The doctor says we should force him to use his legs."

"Ha!" Emma scoffed. "And what does the doctor know
about paralysis? Has *he* ever been paralyzed?"

"Of all the silly—"

"How did Robert come to be injured?" Lucien interrupted hastily. His shoulder was stiff and painful, his head
throbbed a relentless beat, and his bandages were so tight
he could barely breathe. The last thing he needed was to
have two elderly women arguing across his bed as if it
were a chessboard and he a hapless pawn.

Emma sent a darkling glare at Jane. "Robert was paralyzed *in the war.*"

"No," returned Jane evenly. "Robert was not paralyzed
until two weeks *after* he returned. He rode his horse all the
way up the coast to Rosemont the day his ship landed and
even bragged he'd made record time."

"But he was pale," Emma said quickly. "And he had
horrible nightmares those first weeks. We thought he'd get
better once he'd had time to adjust. But . . ." Her voice

faded to a thread. "One day, he didn't come down to breakfast."

Jane fished in her pocket for a handkerchief. "We found him by the bed, trying to reach the door to call for help." She met Lucien's gaze with a pained smile and pushed her kerchief into Emma's waiting hand. "That was two months ago."

If Arabella was indeed overseeing the estate, as well as the care of an invalid brother and her two crazed aunts, it was no wonder she'd appeared so tense the evening before. Lucien moved restlessly under the sheet, feeling as if a weight were pressing him into the soft mattress. "Is there no one to help administer the estate?"

Jane sighed. "Emma and I try, but I fear we are more often a burden than not."

Maybe he could do something. God knew, he certainly had the funds. He would talk with Arabella, offer to underwrite her expenses until—

Bloody hell, what was he thinking? Arabella Hadley would no more accept help from him than she would a gift from the devil. Even at sixteen, she had possessed far more than her fair share of pride; it had been one of the things that had drawn him to her. The women Lucien had met in London had either been bored society misses or shameless paphians. Arabella had been different. An engaging mixture of innocence and excitement, she had experienced life second by second, throwing herself wholeheartedly into whatever she did. She'd been an amazingly sensual lover, her emotions completely engaged. And he had been utterly besotted.

Not that it mattered now. Whatever sentiment she'd once felt for him was long gone. The sooner he removed himself from Rosemont, the better she would like it. But once he left, he would find a way to be of service to her, perhaps through a third party, so she would not suspect his influence.

He would send for Hastings, complete his assignment for the Home Office, and return to London. Then he would set his solicitor to investigating the state of affairs at Rosemont. The idea gave him a surge of strength. "Has my horse been found?"

"Arabella sent Ned to search for him, but it will be hours before he returns," Emma said placidly.

Jane held out the metal cup. "Drink some of this and you'll feel much better."

The scent of cinnamon and cloves wafted through the air. Lucien's stomach rumbled and he was suddenly aware of how high the sun stood in the sky outside the window. It must be late afternoon. No wonder he was famished.

Still . . . he looked at the brown liquid in the cup. The two women reminded him far too much of the witches in *Macbeth* to drink any brew of their making. He gently pushed the cup away. "If you could just send for my valet, I could find Satan myself—"

"Oh, no. You will not be rising for many days to come," Jane said. "You are too ill."

"Nonsense. A few days' rest and I will be as good as new."

"Oh, but we cannot allow that to happen!" Emma said.

His astonishment must have shown, for Jane immediately added, "What Emma *meant* to say was that we cannot allow you to risk your health. Besides your shoulder, you also have a grievous wound to your head." She thrust the steaming cup under his nose. "Now drink this."

"But I—"

Jane neatly tipped the cup into his mouth. He was instantly assailed with sweet warm wine mixed with cinnamon, cloves, and just the faintest hint of nutmeg. He took a second drink. Swirls of delight trailed down his throat and into his empty stomach.

She pressed the cup into his hand and straightened his covers. "There. We'll have you feeling the thing in no time at all."

He took another sip, savoring the ambrosia before swallowing. "What is this?"

"Mulled wine and tonic," Emma said. "The sheep love it."

He blinked into the cup. "You waste *this* on sheep?"

Jane sent a quelling glance at her sister. "Emma, get the poor duke another blanket. He looks chilled."

Lucien sipped his wine. Not only were his aches receding with each passing moment, but his mind was acutely clear, as if he'd spent his entire life looking through a clouded fog that had suddenly been blown free. By God, he would have Hastings learn how to make this magnificent tonic and serve it every night before bed. Lucien tilted the cup over his open mouth and let the last few drops fall onto his tongue. Hell, he just might drink it with every meal.

Emma helped Jane spread a blanket over his legs. "We get so few dukes in Yorkshire."

"True," agreed Jane. She removed the tumbler from Lucien's nerveless hand and set it on a side table, then slipped his arm under the blanket and tucked it in so tightly that he couldn't move. "Barons, viscounts, and an occasional earl, but very few dukes."

"And *such* a duke." Emma cast an admiring stare his way, her eyes hideously magnified by her spectacles. "I vow, I shall not know how to go on."

Lucien smiled and would have waved a hand, had one been free. "Pray do not bother yourself, Lady . . ." He trailed off, wondering foggily if he knew their names.

"Where have our manners gone?" Jane exclaimed. "Allow us to introduce ourselves. I am Lady Melwin." She issued a short, jerky curtsy and then waved a hand at her plump counterpart. "And this is my sister, Lady Durham."

Wreathed in smiles, the rotund lady dipped a curtsy that caused an unholy crack to sound. Her cheeks reddened. "Pardon, Your Grace. Age, you know." She brightened. "Fortunately, I have my medicine right here." She withdrew a small bottle from her pocket and took a swig. A whiff of prime cognac wafted toward Lucien.

Jane stared down her aquiline nose at her sister. "Pray forgive Emma. She has a consumptive complaint."

"I've never been consumptive a day in my life." She turned to Lucien and said in a voice dripping with mystery, "I have Female Problems."

Even in his now-hazy state of mind, Lucien found this bit of information alarming. But he was spared an answer when the door opened and small booted feet walked briskly across the floor.

Lucien knew it was Arabella before she came into sight. The air charged with heat and his body responded as if he'd been stroked by a velvet hand. He should have been dismayed by his instant reaction, since it was clearly outlined by the tightly tucked blanket. But somehow his sense of propriety had completely vanished, and along with it, his ability to feel his own feet. Instead, he was innately proud of his attributes and wondered if Arabella would notice.

Unfortunately, she was too preoccupied with the tray she carried. The silver salver was so heavily loaded, Lucien wondered that she didn't stagger from the weight. With quick, competent steps, she crossed to the small table by the fire and set the tray on the polished surface with only a slight clink of silver.

He watched as she adjusted the dishes and removed covers, the light from the window highlighting her hair to warm mahogany. Dressed in a faded frock that would have been in fashion five years ago, she appeared neat and proper. Even the unruly curl of her hair had been tamed, tucked into a tidy bun. Yet the pink of the dress echoed the warm color of her cheeks and lips and made him yearn to touch her.

He became aware that Aunt Jane was closely watching him. She smiled, clasped her hands together, and announced, "Arabella, allow me to present you to the gentleman you rescued last night. His Grace, the Duke of Wexford."

Emma nodded vigorously, her iron-gray curls bobbing. "And *this,* Your Grace, is Arabella Hadley, our lovely, *lovely* niece."

Even swimming in a tonic-induced sea of euphoria, Lucien recognized such a blatant attempt at matchmaking. Normally he would have depressed such presumption, but he was too full of good cheer and all too aware of his nakedness beneath the thin blanket to be prudent. "She is indeed the loveliest of women. Her skin flawless, her eyes exceptionally bright and fine, and her form—"

"Oh, yes," Jane interrupted hastily, tucking a stray white curl behind her ear. She gave a nervous laugh when she caught Arabella's amazed expression. "My! His Grace is certainly pleased to meet you."

Arabella's gaze narrowed on him for a moment. "I think he's drunk."

"Nonsense," he protested with good humor. "But even if I were, just seeing your beauty would sober me in an instant." Somehow, that didn't sound quite as good when said aloud.

Emma tittered. "Isn't this lovely? All of us here,

together." No one vouched an answer and Aunt Emma's excitement dimmed as she floundered, "Ah, did Your Grace know that Arabella—"

"His Grace and I are well acquainted," Arabella said abruptly.

"Oh?" Jane fixed him with a stare. "You didn't mention that."

"You didn't ask," Lucien pointed out, then smiled sweetly.

Jane's eyes narrowed, but she did not reply. Instead, she turned to the tray and began peering beneath the covers of the dishes. "My, what a nice hot luncheon."

"I thought you would be hungry, having spent all day playing nursemaid." Arabella encompassed her aunts with a smile that left Lucien feeling slighted.

Emma blinked behind her spectacles. "But there are only two plates here. What about the duke? What did you bring him?"

"Cook is making some gruel. Once His Grace has had his fill, I am sure he will wish to be on his way."

Somewhere in the back of Lucien's mind, an elusive thought skittered into sight before it drowned in the tonic's fumes. Arabella was right: There *was* a reason he should wish to be gone—but for the life of him, he couldn't remember what it was. "I hate gruel," Lucien announced.

"Then leave," Arabella said. "I hear the Golden Lion has an excellent board. Shall I lend you a horse?"

To Lucien's intense pleasure, Aunt Jane immediately protested, "Arabella Hadley! The duke is our guest!"

"And you cannot send a duke to a common inn!" Emma added, *tsk*ing loudly.

Lucien could have kissed them both. Sad as it was, Arabella's aunts appeared to be his only friends. He wanted to publicly declare his gratitude for their championing, but to his intense dismay, he discovered that his tongue was getting more numb by the second. He scraped it across the edge of his teeth and found that he couldn't feel his teeth, either.

Meanwhile, Arabella leveled a cool glance at him that faltered when she caught him with his tongue half out. The situation struck Lucien as quite comical and as soon as he could get his tongue back into his mouth, he grinned, delighted to find that his lips still worked.

Her brows lowered. "What is wrong with you?"

Though his tongue seemed unable to work, he managed to say, "I am ravenoush, and gruel ish not enough food for a man like me." He grinned, glad that he had only slurred one or two words.

While his tongue was numb, every other sense was amplified. The smooth linen of the sheet abraded his skin, the low flames from the fireplace heated one side of his leg with a gentle insistence, and the faint prick of a feather through the pillow beneath his cheek all served to push his senses to a new height.

But more discomfiting was the undisciplined nature of his mind, which was imagining Arabella walking toward him, her arms wide, her clothes . . . missing.

As if she could read his thoughts, she crossed her arms over her ample charms and glared. "If His Grace is well enough to imbibe spirits, then he is well enough to stay at an inn."

Jane took a seat by the tray and removed the remaining covers from the dishes. "He will be leaving soon enough."

Emma took the seat opposite her sister. "Oh, yes. With a little rest and some good food, he will gone within a week."

Arabella choked. "A week?"

"Oh, yes. We looked him over from head to toe and he is very, very healthy. Why, a horse isn't as well hun—"

"*Emma!*" Jane's red cheeks matched the rose embroidered on the pillow beside her. "I am sure Arabella does not wish to hear any more about the duke. She has made her feelings on the subject quite plain. We can only assure her that, as soon as he is well, he will be up and on his way."

Lucien couldn't think of a single reason to leave his wondrous haven. It seemed the perfect place to be, comfortably tucked into bed and protected by the loving ministrations of his two champions. The smell of cinnamon lingered, as did the sweet taste of mulled wine. The sun shone brightly through the window while delectable, winsome, beautiful Arabella stood only a few arms' lengths away.

The only way his life could get better would be if Arabella were *in* his bed and not beside it.

He worked free a hand so he could wave it in the air. "Bella, my love, I must salute your aunts for their kindness. They are the loveliest of ladies." For emphasis, he blew a kiss into the air and imagined he could see it floating off to land on each pale, wrinkled cheek.

They tittered like schoolgirls and Lucien grinned in response.

Arabella's brows rose. "If he's not drunk, then what's wrong with him?"

"Nothing is wrong with him; Jane and I just gave the poor man a little something to ease his pain."

Arabella covered her eyes with her hands. "Not your tonic!"

"We only gave him a teaspoon or so," Jane said stiffly. "Not enough to cause any harm."

"What's wrong with the tonic?" Lucien asked, suddenly alert.

Jane plucked uneasily at the lace on her sleeve. "Nothing, Your Grace."

Arabella snorted. "Tell him about the tonic."

"Really, I don't think he needs to know—"

"Tell him."

"Oh, very well," Jane said in a testy voice. "The tonic is actually made for . . ." She stopped and cast a longing glance at the door.

"For what, damn it?" Lucien asked, his alarm rising by the minute. Good God, what were they afraid to tell him?

"It is used for mating," she blurted out, then bit her lip. "If we feed it to the sheep before they mate, they tend to . . . ah, relax."

Emma nodded, wiping crumbs from her chin. "We have the most fertile sheep in all of Yorkshire. Why, just last year alone we had three times the lambs as Sir Loughton, with only half the number of ewes."

"It is a very healthy mixture," Jane added. "A little chamomile, some St. John's wort, a goodly dash of rose hips."

"And some laudanum," Emma said.

"There is no laudanum in the tonic."

"Not usually, but I added a drop," Emma managed to say around a mouthful of plum pudding. "Thought it might help the duke to sleep."

Lucien closed his eyes. "Bloody hell, I've been poisoned."

"Nonsense," Jane said briskly. "You will be up and about in no time at all."

Emma pushed her spectacles back up her nose. "Sooner than most men, I would imagine."

"For the love of—" Arabella's hands fisted at her sides. "Lucien Devereaux is no different from any other man."

That hurt. Lucien opened his mouth to protest, but Jane

leaned close to her niece and whispered loudly, "Trust me, dearest. This one is a bit *better* than average, even for a duke."

"Sweet Sampson, yes," agreed Emma, fanning herself. Her gaze wandered toward Lucien and he could have sworn she stared at his leg.

Arabella placed a hand on her forehead, where the slightest ache was beginning to pinch. It had been a long and arduous day, filled with a visit from her steward regarding the shambling state of the barn in the west field, and Wilson's dire predictions about having a wounded duke in the house. She wanted nothing more than to seek out the quiet of the library and lose herself in a good book.

Instead, she was arguing with her aunts, while a drugged Lucien watched with an amiable, witless grin. It was more than she could bear.

Well, if Aunt Jane and Aunt Emma wanted to keep their precious duke, they were welcome to him. They could tend him until they were sick and tired of his autocratic ways and ready to kick him head over heels all the way back to London.

His complete victory over her aunts caused a pang. It was rare that they championed anyone's causes over hers. Of course, they did not know about Lucien and his desertion all those years ago. At that time, both Jane and Emma had had households of their own in faraway Devonshire, and rarely visited Rosemont.

Arabella sighed. Come what may, he would be gone in a week. Surely one simple week wouldn't hurt her. "If you are so determined to keep him here, then so be it. But let me warn you—I am far too busy to care for him. You will have to do it yourselves."

"Of course, dear," soothed Aunt Jane, coming to lead

Arabella to a chair by Lucien's bed. "In the meantime, you sit right here and eat something."

Arabella locked her knees in place and refused to sit, despite the pressure her aunt placed on her shoulders. "No, thank you. I've already—"

Aunt Emma stepped past Aunt Jane and shoved the tray into Arabella's lap, forcing her into the seat. "Here, dearest. You must be famished and I— Oh, my! No bread!"

Jane was already standing by the door. "We'll be right back with hot bread and the duke's gruel. Don't leave the poor duke alone, Arabella. He is drugged, you know, and may move and tear his stitches."

Before Arabella could protest, two sets of feet scurried down the stairwell. She looked down at the heavy tray and her disgusted gaze fell on a plate of hot bread, steam gently wafting from the top piece. "Damn," she muttered.

"Such language," a low, sleepy voice mocked.

Arabella jerked her gaze to Lucien. He regarded her through half-closed eyes, his mouth curved in a lazy grin. She had an instant impression of his warmth surrounding her, the firm line of his jaw scraping against her chin just before he claimed her mouth with his, the possessive feel of his hands as he molded her body against his. . . . Damn the man. She thought she had quelled her unruly memories years ago. But ever since Lucien had kissed her in the carriage, it was as if a door had been thrown open. To her horror, she discovered she could remember every nuance of his touch—from the texture of his skin to the satisfying pressure of his mouth on hers. It was unbearable. Worse yet was having to endure such blatant matchmaking from her aunts. Heat flooded her face. "I cannot think what my aunts are doing, forcing us together in such a manner."

Laughter rumbled in his chest. "Don't look so crest-fallen. Napoleon wouldn't have stood a chance against such steely determination."

Arabella managed to say in a quite normal voice, "They can be quite determined once they take a notion."

"I noticed," he said dryly.

Despite her irritation, a smile tickled the corner of her mouth. "They are as gentle as lambs, really. Just stubborn."

"A family trait, I would say."

Her smile disappeared. "If you are saying I am stubborn, then I—"

"I was speaking of the portrait." Lucien's gaze slipped past her to the picture of the Captain hanging over the fireplace. A far-off look entered his green eyes. "Now, *there* is a man who knew what he wanted. You can see it in his eyes."

She favored the portrait with a brief glance. "He was a wastrel and a philanderer. Legend has it that his ghost appears to warn of impending danger and when one of the family marries their . . ." *True love.* She hesitated, then closed her mouth. Lucien did not need to know more.

"Have *you* ever seen the Captain?" His eyes were strangely bright, evidence of Aunt Jane's tonic.

"Aunt Emma sees him quite frequently. Or so she claims." She really should get up and go to her room, but the sight of the bandage on his chest stayed her. If he tore his stitches, he would be here that much longer. She shifted impatiently in her chair. "What can be taking them so long?"

Lucien captured her wrist and, before her astonished gaze, carefully uncurled her fingers one by one until her hand lay open before him. "You have dimples on your knuckles," he murmured.

She wrinkled her nose and he laughed. The rich sound sent a tremor through her, warming her all over as if *she* had imbibed too much tonic.

Arabella glanced at him from under her lashes. She had not allowed herself to remember this part of Lucien—his quick laughter, his tenderness, the ease with which he could make her smile. She had even forgotten the heady sensuality that he wore about him like a cloak. It made her yearn to brush her fingertips over his cheek, his jaw, his chest.

Lucien lifted his gaze to hers. Moving ever so slowly, he lifted her hand and placed a kiss on her wrist, his mouth lingering on her bare skin.

Her every sense filled with him—the heady scent of cinnamon, the exquisite scrape of his stubbled jaw along her wrist. . . . Arabella caught herself just before she was swept over a waterfall of desire. She yanked her hand free and tucked it securely by her side. For added measure, she wrapped the memories of his betrayal tightly about her heart. "You should rest, Your Grace. My aunts will return soon."

Something flickered in his green gaze and then was gone, replaced by a careless shrug that hurt worse than any words could. He yawned and snuggled farther into the bed, favoring her with a drowsy smile. "You may not remember as I do, but it doesn't matter. We shall just have to find new memories, you and I." His eyes slid closed and he murmured, "What fun that shall be."

With that last, cryptic phrase, the infuriating Duke of Wexford fell into a deep sleep.

Chapter 5

Arabella grasped the handle of the damper and pulled. The rusted metal groaned as if mortally wounded, but didn't budge. She gritted her teeth against her irritation.

While she loved Rosemont, it was a Herculean task to maintain. Built in Tudor times, the rambling stone house possessed large, inefficient fireplaces, leaky windows, and rusty door hinges, just to name a few inconveniences. She tried not to think of the major repairs the house so desperately needed.

She planted one foot on the side of the fireplace, wrapped her hands more firmly about the handle, and yanked with all her might.

Cook stopped on the threshold, a bowl of dried apples in her hands. "Missus! Whatever do ye think ye are doin'? Let Ned deal with the likes of that."

With a frustrated sigh, Arabella straightened, pushing her skirts back down more modestly. She hated to ask for help. Surely if she just put a little more effort into it, the damper would come unstuck and she could— She gave one last pull.

Whoosh! A chunk of soot dropped into the fireplace and poofed a huge black cloud into the room. Arabella stumbled backward as Cook screeched, both of them gasping for breath and waving their hands in the murky air.

"Lawks, missus!" choked Cook. She grabbed a clean cloth and tossed it over her apples, then scurried to open a window. "Ye'll have soot in the tarts if ye keep that up! Whatever will the dook think then?"

Arabella tried to answer, but her nose and throat were too full of soot for her to do more than sneeze repeatedly.

Cook used her apron to wave as much of the gray cloud out of the window as she could. "Thank ye fer tryin' to help, missus, but I'm goin' fer Ned. There's less than three hours left to dinner and I need the fire."

Arabella rubbed her nose. "But I can—"

"Not when I've a dook to feed, ye can't." Cook gave one last wave of her apron, grabbed up her cloak from the hook beside the door, and marched outside.

Coughing, Arabella went to stand in the doorway and gulp the fresh air as she watched Cook pass through the gate to the stables. For two days, now, all she'd heard from Ned and Cook was "the dook" this and "the dook" that. Even Mrs. Guinver, the persnickety housekeeper who took pride in disliking every male she met, had grudgingly admitted that "as far as dooks go," Lucien was by far the best-behaved.

It was infuriating. Since his arrival, Lucien had gone out of his way to charm her servants, but Arabella was not fooled. She knew exactly who Lucien Devereaux was, and being a duke did not lessen his imperfections one bit.

It was just like him to ride carelessly into her life and

disrupt her carefully laid plans. And despite her best efforts, she couldn't stop wondering about his cryptic comment about making "new memories." He must know he was not welcome back into her life, no matter how "improved" he wanted everyone to think him.

Though it irked her to admit it, she could understand her servants' awe. Lucien did possess more than his fair share of handsomeness. And one would be hard-pressed to find a man who managed to carry himself so very . . . dukelike. But that, too, was a product of his birth, and not a result of any goodness on his part.

Lucien Devereaux was an ordinary man who deserved no special treatment whatsoever. She glanced at the elaborate dinner preparations already under way: An uncooked rack of lamb sat on a platter liberally sprinkled with crushed mint, and a thick tub of cream had already been whipped with sugar into a frothy sauce for the apple tarts, while various other succulent dishes sat in varying stages of completion. Each one represented a week's worth of food for the inhabitants of Rosemont.

Arabella scowled to think of their winter supplies dwindling just to feed a worthless, unappreciative duke, but nothing she said swayed her servants from acting as if they had been blessed by his majestic presence. Cook had even opened the last sack of fine sugar for the tarts.

Drat the man. If he didn't leave soon, they'd be forced to eat dried beans and bland pottage the rest of the winter.

She stared at the table and toyed with the idea of over-peppering the rack of lamb. The image of Lucien choking and turning a bright red held immeasurable appeal. But Robert was more likely to suffer than Lucien, for her brother adored roasted lamb. She hunched a shoulder toward the table and turned away. The idea was beneath her dignity anyway.

It seemed as if she was doomed to suffer until Lucien was healthy enough to leave. She felt more hopeful since the arrival yesterday morning of Lucien's imposingly correct valet.

Without saying a word, Hastings had managed to convey the impression that he found Rosemont less than adequate housing for his exalted master, with the guest room's smoky chimney and the upper floor's drafty hallway. To see Hastings's pinched expression, one would think Lucien was above residing in a fine house like Rosemont.

"Ha! I could tell them a few stories," Arabella muttered. Of course, her stories concerned a young and reckless viscount given to seducing young country innocents, not a handsome duke who, with his lineage and fortune firmly behind him, was clearly above reproach. It was maddening.

She resolutely pushed away all thoughts of her unwanted guest. She already knew what would happen if she weakened for any reason—he would take his pleasure, steal her heart again, and then leave under the dark of night like a coward while she drowned in her own feelings.

The old wounds ached, and Arabella sighed and returned to the stuck damper. Lucien would be gone soon enough and her life would return to normal. But there was something very odd about the way he had reappeared in her life. What on earth would possess a duke to ride unattended through the wilds of a Yorkshire moor on a moonless night?

She frowned. There was something almost sinister about his presence. Despite being confined to his bed, he carried on an amazing correspondence, sending several letters a day. But when Aunt Emma had offered to have

Wilson carry the missives to Whitby, Lucien had refused, saying he didn't wish to bother the household. Instead, Hastings made daily trips to town in his fancy curricle.

Wilson had taken offense at that. He'd muttered darkly about "secret dooks" and taken to staring glumly at Hastings whenever he saw him.

Cold air stirred through the kitchen and swept the last bit of soot from the air. Arabella closed the window, then returned to the fireplace to wrestle one more time with the stubborn damper. She would succeed at *something* today or go to bed sore and tired from trying. But it was becoming obvious that yanking on the handle would not open the damper.

Arabella dropped to her knees before the chimney, peering up into the dark maw. Perhaps a brick had fallen and wedged itself in the opening. Leaning away from the flue, she rattled the damper handle.

"What is all the racket?" Robert's voice came from the doorway leading to the front hall.

Arabella wiped her hands on her apron and stood. "I am trying to get the damper open." She watched him wheel his chair into the room. The sun glinted off his chestnut hair and highlighted the faint shadows under his eyes.

"You didn't sleep well," she said, worry sinking her stomach. He was still so very frail. He looked as if the faintest puff of wind would blow him away.

A sudden frown drew his brows low, signaling his impatience with even that small display of sisterly concern. He pushed the wheelchair to the table and reached beneath the cloth to steal an apple slice, his gaze moving restlessly around the room. "The way you've been banging about, I thought you'd found the Captain's treasure and were removing it from the chimney one sack of gold at a time."

"No one but Aunt Emma believes that old tale."

"I believe it," he said so promptly that she almost laughed.

She settled for a grin. "I suppose you also believe in the Captain's ghost lurking about, watching after the family."

He took a bite of apple, his gaze thoughtful. "There are times I wonder. You must admit things often happen at Rosemont that cannot be explained."

"Like what?"

"Like the time you fell asleep in the dinghy and it drifted out to sea. Father swears the Captain led him to the shoreline and showed him where you were."

"Pish-posh. That was just one of Father's stories."

"There are other examples. Think about the duke's strange arrival. And not just any duke, either, but Wexford himself. Don't you think that is odd?"

Arabella had wondered if Robert remembered anything about Lucien's visit over ten years ago, for her brother had been a mere child then. She should have known Robert remembered everything. He'd always had an uncanny knack for ferreting out the truth and discovering falsities. And it was obvious he mistrusted Lucien.

Well, she wouldn't argue with that. She brushed a finger across her mouth. Though it had happened almost two days ago, the pressure of his lips seemed to linger still. She'd thought youthful imagination had romanticized the relationship, but the sensations he'd roused in her told her otherwise. She trailed her fingers up the curve of her cheek, feeling once again his heated breath on her skin. A tremor rose as she remembered how quickly her ardor had risen to match his.

"Well?" asked Robert impatiently. "Don't you think it is odd the way the duke was tossed into your path?"

"Are you suggesting it was because of a matchmaking ghost?"

"It is possible."

She managed a grin. "The next time the doctor comes, I am requesting a mustard plaster and a good dose of cod liver oil. That should rid you of these fanciful notions."

He grinned in return and took another apple slice. "It would solve all of our problems if we could find that treasure, wouldn't it?"

"If it existed." Something about the sudden gleam in his eyes made her add hastily, "But you know as well as I that Father would have found it if it had been here. He nearly tore the house apart looking for it."

Robert absently rubbed one of his knees. "Perhaps he missed something."

"How could he? He knew every crook and crevice of Rosemont. Now, stop eating all of Cook's apples. She'll blame me for it and I'm in no mood to be scolded."

A reluctant smile flitted across his face and he pushed his chair beside her. Though they were brother and sister, their similarity began and ended with their chestnut hair. Where her eyes were dark brown, his were silver-gray. Where she was small, fair-skinned, and round-cheeked, he turned bronze at the slightest show of sun and possessed Father's broad, athletic figure.

At least he had before the war. Now it made her throat catch to see him so pale, deep circles beneath his eyes, his long legs beginning to thin from disuse.

She rattled the iron damper handle one last time. "I suppose I shall have to ask Wilson to take a look at this. If we find the Captain's treasure embedded in the stones, I will fetch you immediately."

"Will you?" He rolled back to the table and took

another apple. "You have always been good at keeping secrets, Bella. Even better than Father."

"Secrets? What secrets could I have?" She grabbed the broom and began sweeping the hearth. "Unless you call my growing dislike of this smoking chimney a secret. I could happily yank the damper out and toss it into the sea."

"Not you; you would be much more likely to rebuild the entire chimney to make it work properly, whether it wanted to be rebuilt or not."

"What do you mean by that?"

His pale gaze flickered toward her before he looked away. "I only meant that if anyone could find a way to fix something, it would be you. And you would do it all by yourself, too. One stone at a time." He wheeled the chair toward the door, stopping to say in a mild tone, "Wash your hands and face before you go anywhere, Bella. You might scare someone."

She set the broom aside and looked down at her hands. If she had even a quarter of the amount of soot on her face as was on her palms, she must look a fright. "Is it bad?"

"I'd hate to meet you in a thunder-wrought mansion."

Arabella picked up a shiny pot and peered at her reflection. Streaks of black ran across her cheek and nose. It was a good thing Lucien was still confined to his sickbed; she was in no state to face a "dook."

Of course, it wouldn't matter if Lucien did see her looking like a scullery maid. He had no real interest in her, even if he had attempted to kiss her every time he regained consciousness. That was the way of a rake—to flirt shamelessly and then waltz away. Still, it wouldn't do for him to see her looking like a positive ragamuffin. Perhaps she should run up to her room and—

"Are you through gazing at yourself?"

Arabella hastily replaced the pan and pulled a handkerchief from her pocket. "At least *I* don't have a mangled cravat knotted about my throat! If you decide to leave the house, pray tie a napkin over that hideous thing. It has two lumps on one side while the middle stares out like a hideous eye."

He laughed, the tired lines on his face easing. "I may well have to do that: Aunt Jane has a burning desire to visit town. I suppose I shall have to accompany her."

"I daresay she also asked that I sit with our injured guest while she was gone."

Robert's lips twitched. "I believe she did."

Arabella wiped her cheek one last time, then balled up the handkerchief and threw it at him. "Oh, yes, make light of my suffering! Just don't come crying to me when you find yourself the victim of her odious matchmaking."

His wan smile faded. "That will never happen."

"Don't be too sure. Once I marry the village smithy just to escape her hideous schemes, she will turn her evil eye on you."

His eyes flashed and he said vehemently, "What woman would ever want *me*?"

The despair in his voice stabbed through her like a knife. She refused to believe he would not awaken one day and be back to his old self, healed as quickly as he'd become ill. But she could see from the darkness in his eyes that he did not have such high hopes: Robert believed he would never walk again.

Arabella bit her lip. She tried to take care of her family, to overcome all of the hardships that faced them. Yet she could not do this one thing—the most important thing of all. She was no better of a provider than Father.

Desperately seeking to comfort them both, she swallowed her tears. "The doctor believes your paralysis is due to nervous tension. In time, when the memories—"

"No." His voice dropped into a cracked whisper. "Every night I see it all—again and again and again." He closed his eyes and pressed his fists to the closed lids. "I see it until I would rather die than fall asleep."

Arabella reached out a hand. "Robert, don't—"

"*I cannot help it!*" The cry was torn from him. He dropped his fists to his lap and lifted haunted eyes to her. "The memories are with me all the time; I will never forget."

She pulled back her hand and clutched the folds of her skirts to keep herself still. He would reject her sympathy and withdraw from her as he did from so many people. The wound was too new, too raw to be so directly addressed. She pasted a tremulous smile on her face and said with a confidence she did not feel, "Give it time, Robert. It has only been two months."

His mouth twisted. "I am going to find Wilson."

Arabella watched as he pushed the chair out the door, his dark head bowed. Her heart ached, as if it had swollen too large and pressed into her breastbone.

The back door opened and Ned stomped in, Cook jabbering as she followed. "The damper has gone and rusted closed, if ye ask me. Ye'll have to shake it loose."

Ned nodded wisely. "Can't let the dook go without his dinner." Without another word, he went straight to work on the damper as if it were of vast importance.

Cook watched Ned intently, saying over her shoulder, "Oh, Missus. I almost fergot to tell ye. Mr. Francot stopped by earlier and said he had some papers for ye. He said he would come back this afternoon." Cook scrunched her nose. "I don't like that man."

"Mr. Francot? Why not?"

"He's dishonest. I can see it in his eyes. Lady Melwin don't like him, either."

"Aunt Jane dislikes everyone who is not a member of our household or who is not an eligible bachelor with an income of at least two thousand pounds a year. Mr. Francot has assisted us more times than I can count, and he refuses to take so much as a shilling in payment." In fact, now that Arabella thought about it, Mr. Francot was much more worthy of her servants' attention than a wastrel duke.

"Hmph," Cook said. "The only reason that sniveling whelp hasn't seen fit to give ye a bill is because he has his sights set on ye."

"Nonsense!" she said, astounded. "Why, he is almost fifteen years older than I!" Arabella untied the broad apron and carefully removed it from her dress. Despite her best efforts to protect her gown, soot dotted the right side of the skirt. She brushed at the spots and only succeeded in making them larger. "Lovely. Now I shall have to go upstairs and change."

"If ye're doin' that fer Mr. Francot, ye're wastin' yer time. He would think ye looked like a princess even if ye wore sackcloth and ashes."

"He is being kind and nothing more," Arabella said with great certainty, deciding suddenly not to change her dress after all.

Mr. Francot's continued attendance was due solely to the fact that he felt an obligation to Father, who had helped him establish his practice when he'd first arrived in Yorkshire. "If you don't need me in the kitchen, I am going up to my room to wash."

Cook shooed her on her way, her attention now focused on Ned's formidable efforts to loosen the damper.

Arabella mumbled under her breath as she went. She had half a mind to march into Lucien's room and demand to know what he was doing here in Yorkshire. But that would only put her at the disadvantage, for it would mean she had to see him—and she didn't think her shaken composure was quite up to such a thing.

She reached the top step and turned the corner, still lost in thought, when the door to her aunts' sitting room opened. Arabella came to an abrupt halt. There, standing in the doorway, his bare chest only partially covered by a bandage and a makeshift sling, stood Lucien. The sunlight from the room outlined his muscular body in vivid relief.

Arabella took in the expanse of broad chest that tapered to a firm, flat stomach. A tantalizing line of hair dusted his chest and then narrowed to a thin line that drew her gaze to the snug waistband of black breeches that clung lovingly to his hips and powerful thighs.

Her heart thudded an extra beat, and her mouth watered as if she were looking at a plate full of Cook's famous apple tarts.

His gaze flickered over her, resting on her face and traveling down the front of her dress. A sudden crease appeared between his eyes. "What in the hell have you been doing? You are covered in soot."

Lovely. Facing a half-naked Lucien had made her forget all about her fight with the damper. She clenched her hands into fists and resisted the urge to lift the hem of her skirt and scrub her face. "I was assisting Cook in the kitchen."

"How? By climbing into the fireplace to stir a pot?"

There was nothing more lowering than meeting the man of one's dreams while looking as raggedy as a chimney sweep. "Never mind how I look; you shouldn't be in the hallway without proper clothing."

He leaned one hand against the doorframe, a faint hint of amusement sparkling in his eyes. "You are fortunate I had on my breeches. Until Hastings arrived, I was completely nude." He lowered his voice to an intimate level. "A pity you didn't visit me then."

"I've been busy," she replied shortly, wondering if he could tell how wildly her heart was beating against her ribs. She remembered how he looked without his clothing all too well—every detail was etched in her mind in indelible ink, from the hard plane of his stomach to the bronze of his skin.

It was just one of many memories she fought every night. But those hot, scorching reminiscences were nothing compared to the relentless reality of the man who stood before her.

Arabella pressed her damp palms against her skirt. "I'm glad to see you are so well. Shall I have Wilson saddle your horse? I'm sure you are anxious to be on your way."

His gaze narrowed a moment before he took a step forward, his legs brushing against her. "Your Aunt Emma says Rosemont is renowned for its hospitality."

"You lost your rights to our hospitality ten years ago."

He flinched as if she'd slapped him, but Arabella knew him too well to believe she had hurt him. He was a consummate actor, able to breathe words of passion and deliver hot, ardent looks with an air of sincerity that many a player would kill to possess.

"Bella, we need to talk about what happened—"

"What happened ten years ago belongs where it is—in the past. Leave it there."

His face darkened. "But I want to explain. It wasn't—"

She turned on her heel and marched to her room, painfully aware that his dark gaze followed her every step of the way. She had no desire to revisit the mistakes of her past. At sixteen, she'd been a bit wild, the product of being left to her own devices after the death of her mother. Father had rarely been home, always off chasing a dream, and leaving her to care for Robert and watch after affairs at Rosemont. The responsibility had been onerous until Lucien had freed her. For one brief summer, she had left her inhibitions behind and been young and careless. And she had regretted it every day since.

Once she reached the safety of her own room, Arabella closed the door behind her, turned the key in the lock, and sank onto the edge of her bed. Her knees quivered, her heart pounded in her throat.

No matter how hard she tried, she could not stop the way her body reacted to his. It was a weakness, an illness she could not overcome.

Fortunately, whatever mischievous imp of fate had brought Lucien Devereaux back to Rosemont would soon spirit him away. And this time Arabella was determined to watch him leave with her chin held high, her pride intact.

Taking a deep breath, she crossed to the washstand and caught a glimpse of her ash-covered face. She grimaced at the sight. For one day, just one simple day, she wished her life would be easy. Sighing, she plunged her hands into the icy water and began to scrub her face clean.

Chapter 6

"**B**loody hell," Lucien choked. "What's this?"

Hastings paused in the middle of unpacking a valise to regard the glass Lucien held at arm's length. "I believe it is a restorative beverage of some sort. Lady Melwin brought it early this morning while you were still abed."

Lucien gingerly sniffed the contents, then snarled a curse. *"Cinnamon."*

"Ah," said Hastings, as if that explained everything. "Cinnamon *is* the devil's own spice, is it not, Your Grace?"

"You don't know what's in this potion." Lucien set the glass onto the nightstand so hard that liquid sloshed over the sides. "Take it away."

The valet picked up the glass and carried it to a tray by the door. "I suppose I should return the plate of tea biscuits to the kitchen as well. They seem to have been flavored with . . ." he took a cautious sniff, then shuddered. *"Nutmeg."*

"Very funny," Lucien said.

Hastings bowed. "I try my best, Your Grace."

"You wouldn't laugh if you had been under the care of those two harpies. Trust me, Hastings—have nothing to do with anything either Lady Melwin or Lady Durham prepares for you."

Hastings's mobile face folded into a frown, all traces of humor gone. "Are you suggesting they are attempting to poison you?"

"Those dainty old ladies kept me drugged for two days. I missed meeting my contact, and now I don't know a damn thing about the jewels." Not to mention the unpleasant side effects: Aunt Jane's tonic had left him so taut with desire that he could barely think.

And he'd let that unrelenting desire ruin his one chance to speak with Arabella. This morning, he'd been on his way to find Hastings to move his things to the guest room, when Arabella had suddenly appeared in the hallway. She'd been dressed in a worn frock, the thin material clinging to her curves in a familiar, loving way. Soot was streaked across her creamy skin and made her eyes appear that much darker. She looked flushed, hot, and utterly desirable.

But then, she always had.

Hastings held up a dressing jacket. "Your Grace, if you will lift your arm, I believe I can get this over your bandage."

Lucien allowed his valet to assist him, then simply knotted a cravat about his throat, unable to create a more fashionable arrangement without the use of his hurt arm. It didn't really matter if he had the chance to speak with Arabella; it wouldn't change things. And she was right: He had worn out his welcome at Rosemont ten years ago.

The best course was to finish what he had come to do

and leave as quickly as possible. He'd already sent one report to the Home Office telling them of his accident and his failure to meet the contact. Now all he had to do was reschedule the meeting, discover the extent of the operation, and report back to London. The Home Office would handle everything from there.

Lucien absently rubbed his shoulder. A pity he hadn't made it to his meeting before being run down by Arabella's carriage. "Hastings, have you seen to Satan?"

"Yes, Your Grace. I fear he has made himself quite at home. In fact, he challenged the horse in the next stall to a fight. Fortunately, that stalwart equine specimen was too well bred to accept."

Lucien chuckled. Like Hastings, Satan was full of bluster and had a deplorable tendency to puff off. However, when the chips were down, Lucien could not think of a better, more reliable mount—nor a more trustworthy, though irritating, valet.

Truthfully, Hastings possessed a large number of unusual skills. Lucien wasn't quite sure of the details of the man's past. Several years ago, Viscountess Hunterston, a reformer and the wife of Lucien's closest friend, had begun a servant referral service wherein she gathered slum dwellers and prostitutes of London's lowest streets and trained them for respectable positions. Once they had completed their training, Julia then foisted them onto hapless members of the ton.

Somewhere along the way, Hastings had become one of the viscountess's special projects. To Lucien's chagrin, Julia had decided that her newest project merited the household of a duke. By then, he was the only duke who did not run in the opposite direction whenever he saw her coming, mainly because she was married to Alec.

Lucien had had his doubts as to whether Hastings

would make a proper valet, but these misgivings were soon put to rest—the man had an amazing ability to blend in with any surroundings. It was one of a wide variety of unusual skills the valet possessed.

He glanced at Hastings now. "Did anyone stop by the inn after my accident?"

The valet paused in the middle of polishing a silver brush. "A Mr. Mumferd inquired after you, Your Grace. He was most upset to discover you were not present."

"Did he leave a message?"

"No, but I must say that he was uncommonly vulgar." Hastings wrinkled his nose as if he smelled something foreign. "I ventured to follow him. He traveled by decrepit nag to an inn called the Red Rooster."

"*You* followed him?"

Hastings bowed. "Of course, my lord. By then, it was apparent that something had gone amiss with your venture." The valet finished polishing the brush. He laid it down and picked up a mirror and began to work on it, careful not to meet Lucien's gaze. "I find it most distressing when you do not return as scheduled, Your Grace."

"I sent for you as soon as I was able."

The valet gave the mirror handle one last swipe and said, "I am aware of that, and I thank you."

Lucien smothered a sigh. There were times when Hastings's devotion became a damn irritation. Still, he couldn't imagine where he would be without the implacable valet; it had been due to Hastings's extraordinary knowledge of gemstones that Lucien had managed to turn the Devereaux fortune around in just a few short years.

In the three years Hastings had been with Lucien, the duke had never asked his valet where he'd come by his knowledge of gems, and Hastings had never offered to explain. All in all, it was a very satisfactory arrangement, one that allowed Lucien to keep the vow he'd made when he'd realized the mistake he'd made in marrying Sabrina: to never touch one pence of her money. It was the only way he knew to atone for his sins.

However, allying himself with an heiress had accomplished one thing—it had reassured his creditors that their debts would be met. They'd ceased clamoring for payment and were willing to extend their terms. Heavily aware of his responsibility toward his sister, he'd sold every horse in his father's stables, as well as a few he himself owned, and had taken the capital down to the docks. There, with the help of his solicitor, he'd invested the money in everything from tea to a diamond mine. The tea had paid handsomely, as had several other ventures, but because Lucien could not tell a quality diamond from a flawed one, he lost all of his profits in the mine.

Sick with the knowledge he'd have to start over again, Lucien had imbibed far too much brandy and confessed the whole to his new valet. Hastings had patiently explained to his inebriated employer the merits of various quality jewels and how to detect flaws. Even in his tipsy state, Lucien had recognized the man's wealth of knowledge. The next morning—once he'd rid himself of a massive headache—he offered to pay Hastings twice his salary if he would teach Lucien all he knew.

Hastings agreed and Lucien began to study gems as single-mindedly as he had once pursued pleasure. Within a year he knew more than most Bond Street jewelers. Within two years, by judicious buying and selling, Lucien had amassed a small fortune. It was then that he'd had his brilliant idea.

Most of the money to be made in jewels came after the transformation of a quality stone into a piece of jewelry. Hastings's connections came into play once more, for he knew the owners of a questionable business on the East End who welcomed the opportunity to turn over a new leaf. Lucien made sure he paid his new employees enough so they'd have no desire to pilfer his coffers. To his surprise, they were amazingly loyal.

Once everything was in place, Lucien anonymously purchased one of the largest jewelers on Bond Street, known to have the business of the Prince Regent himself. The transaction went almost unnoticed, since the past owner stayed on to run the shop.

Since Lucien had his sister's reputation to worry about, he never let it be known that he dabbled in anything as common as trade, though he freely admitted his interest in gems to any who asked. All of the ton soon knew the Duke of Wexford had a passion for jewels. What was not acceptable as a means to earn a fortune *was* acceptable as a leisure pursuit. Often he would receive word of someone who had fallen on difficult times and might be interested in selling some family heirlooms.

It was through his seeming hobby that the Home Office had recruited him. When the war began, Lucien had wanted to join in the effort, but the circumstances of his title had forced him to stay in England.

By a chance encounter with another collector, Lucien had learned of an illegal jewelry auction near London, the proceeds reputedly going to fund Napoleon's efforts. His reputation as a collector had held him in good stead, and when he had attended the sale, he was able to discover the names of the sponsors of the nefarious plan—information he had immediately turned over to the Home Office.

Lucien sighed and leaned back in his chair. In all the times he'd run these little errands for the Home Office, not once had he failed. It was irritating to think that this time might be different.

That was the real reason he was hesitant to leave Rosemont, he decided with a sense of relief. It wasn't because of Arabella; it was the desire to succeed. And to do so, he needed a better understanding of the Yorkshire smuggling mechanism. Lucien looked at the bottle of fine cognac Aunt Emma had thoughtfully placed in his room. The cut-crystal decanter sparkled with a thousand rainbow lights, sending splinters of color across the carpet.

Hmmm. Perhaps the answer was closer than he realized.

"You seem distracted, Your Grace," Hastings said. "Quite unlike your usually cheerful self."

Lucien quirked a brow. "I need to meet with Mumferd. It is the reason I came to Yorkshire."

The valet paused in the midst of replacing a coat in the wardrobe. "Shall I visit the Red Rooster and attempt to locate him?"

Lucien rubbed at his bandage, his gaze resting on the decanter. "No, I don't want you risking yourself. It won't hurt to wait another day. In the meantime, we will remain at Rosemont."

"Very well, Your Grace." Hastings closed the wardrobe door. "May I ask if you have yet had the opportunity to write Miss Devereaux?"

Though Lucien winced at the mention of his sister, he nodded. "I've written her every week." Liza would be furious with him for disappearing and leaving her in London at the not-so-tender mercies of their Aunt Lavinia.

"Very good, sir. I hope you will forgive my presumption, but your sister particularly tasked me to remind you of your obligations, should the opportunity arise."

That would be just like her. Strong-willed and deplorably independent, Liza would be a handful for whatever man took her to wife.

The valet opened a portmanteau and withdrew a writing case. "Miss Devereaux feared you would fail to remember her once you became engrossed with your travels. I ventured to assure her that that would never happen."

"Of course I won't forget her," Lucien muttered, pulling himself to his feet and adjusting the sling that held his arm. "She's far too busy trying to manage my affairs to allow that to happen."

"Very good, Your Grace. I shall see to it that paper and pen are waiting in the morning room." The valet gathered the writing case and slipped out the door.

Lucien stared after him thoughtfully. His instincts tugged at him. There was a connection between Rosemont and his quarry; he would bet his life on it. And that meant that somehow Arabella was involved, whether she knew it or not. Lucien rubbed a hand over his freshly shaved chin. Perhaps he should arrange another visit with his reclusive hostess—only this time, he would be sure he stayed within the bounds of propriety.

Lucien adjusted the knot in his cravat to a more comfortable position and wondered what secrets lay behind those deceptively innocent eyes. It would be a joy to discover them for himself. A joy and a battle, in light of their unfortunate history.

Still, he was not without allies. Humming softly, Lucien collected the glass of tonic from the tray and then crossed to the window. He leaned out, shivering at the chilled afternoon wind. To his relief, no one moved in the garden below. He poured the tonic across a particularly sturdy rosebush, set the glass on the window ledge, and then headed for the door.

Arabella turned the page of the ledger and stifled a sigh. She'd hoped to bury herself in a sea of numbers and banish the thought of her encounter with Lucien earlier this morning, but it was not to be. After a restless hour, she closed the ledger with an impatient thump. Across the room, Robert's fingers tapped an impatient tattoo on the edge of his chair as he stared absently up at the portrait of the Captain.

The noise was annoying, but Arabella was glad to see him without a scowl marring his brow. He looked lost in thought, a strange light in his eyes.

The door opened. "Mr. Francot," announced Mrs. Guinver, stiff with outrage.

A tall man, nattily attired in an olive-green coat and a drab kerseymere waistcoat, checked abruptly on the threshold when he saw Robert sitting by the fire. "Ah, Mr. Hadley!" He spoke loudly, as if Robert's impairments had affected his ears rather than his legs. "How are you this cold winter day?"

Arabella closed her eyes. No matter how many times she hinted, Mr. Francot did not understand that his patently mannered way of talking to Robert infuriated him.

Robert turned to Arabella and said in an equally loud, overenunciated manner that bore a striking resemblance to Mr. Francot's, "If you will excuse me, dear sister, I will go and see to our aunts." Robert wheeled himself from the room without even a glance in the solicitor's direction.

The door closed and Mr. Francot made a wry face. "I offended him, didn't I?"

"Don't mind Robert. He is just in a foul mood."

Mr. Francot shook his head, his expression subdued. "It is something deeper than that; he dislikes me."

"Then you are in good company, for he tells me daily that he cannot stand me." She smiled and indicated a chair by the desk. "I am surprised to see you out on such a cold day. Surely there is no urgent business at hand?"

He took the chair she offered and slid it closer, pulling out a sheaf of papers from a leather folder and setting them on the desk. "I need your signature, and . . ." He hesitated, his eyes darkening.

"Yes?"

"I hate to mention this, but . . . a payment is due at the end of the month."

"You will receive the money Tuesday morning."

He blinked. "You . . . Can you?"

Arabella raised her brows.

"I'm sorry! I only meant I . . ." Mr. Francot clasped his hands together on the desk, apparently struggling with some great decision.

Silence reined as Arabella wrote her name on first one, then another tenant contract. Really, she didn't have time for histrionics today. She still had the ledger to see to, and Wilson needed help fixing the wheel on the carriage.

Just as she lifted her pen from the last paper, the solicitor burst out, "Miss Hadley, I should not say this, but I feel I must mention . . . I know how you feel about things, but . . . there *is* a way you can pay off all of your father's debts and still have enough left for you, your brother, and your aunts to live quite comfortably."

"Is it legal?"

His mouth dropped open. "Of course it is legal. I would *never* suggest that a lady such as yourself, so gently reared and educated, would do anything that was not impeccable—"

"Yes, yes," she interrupted, stifling a sigh. She should have known better than to tease such a serious man. "What is your idea?"

He took a deep breath. "Sell Rosemont."

"Are you mad?"

"I realize it has been in your family for a long time—"

"For almost three *hundred* years!"

"Which is exactly why it must be sold. Just look at this place. It is falling down around your ears." He gestured to the room and, for an instant, Arabella saw it the way he saw it—the worn and faded carpet, the cracks in the plaster, the smoke-stained fireplace.

She put the quill back into the inkwell. "So long as one wall is standing, the Hadleys will *never* leave Rosemont."

"Miss Hadley, please." He splayed his fingers across the smooth surface of the desk, his throat working nervously as he tried to find the right words. "There is a buyer. A very *eager* buyer."

"Mr. Francot, I am not selling Rosemont. Not now, not ever."

He raked a hand through his hair. "Even with today's rental agreements, there is no way you can collect the money necessary to pay Lord Harlbrook."

"We had a record number of lambs this year. Even more than Sir Loughton."

"If your sheep produced a hundred lambs a day, it still would not be enough. And as for the tenants . . ." He waved a dismissive hand at the papers she'd just signed. "You will spend more in upkeep on the cottages than you will receive in rent. You do the same every year, though you refuse to listen to me."

"You would have these poor families living under leaky roofs and with horrid, smoking chimneys?"

He shook his head, smiling slightly, the light from the window glinting off the gray streaks in his hair. "You think with your heart and not your head, Miss Hadley. It does you credit as a woman, but not, I fancy, as a financier."

Arabella fought the inclination to yank out her heavy cash box and toss it into his witless face. Instead, she slid the papers across the desk. "Thank you for your concern, Mr. Francot, but there is no need for it. We will come about some way or another." She placed the contracts in his hand. "Please don't let me keep you longer."

He stood when she did, obviously bewildered by her dismissal. "Forgive me for suggesting . . . I hope I haven't offended you or . . ." He broke off, his face as red as the carpet. "You don't even know what the buyer has offered!"

"It doesn't mat—"

"Yes, it does." To her astonishment, he named a sum so outlandish she almost choked.

"That is absurd! Why would anyone pay more for a house than it is worth?"

His voice deepened with intensity, he answered, "Perhaps he fell in love."

"More likely he is completely mad," she retorted. "Has he recently sustained a fall of some sort? Did he injure his head?"

"When a man loves something, he will do whatever he must in order to possess it." Right before her eyes, calm, dependable, orderly Mr. Francot surprised her with a look so full of admiration that she almost fell back into her chair.

Heat fanned Arabella's cheeks. Cook had been right. "It is getting late and my aunts wish to go to town. Thank you for bringing these papers to my attention."

White lines appeared about his mouth as he hurriedly stuffed the contracts into the leather case and laid it on the desk. "Miss Hadley, I only want what is best for you." He grasped her hands and held them tightly. "Please listen. You must—"

"There you are, Mr. Francot!" Aunt Jane stood in the

doorway, her shrewd gaze taking in the situation at a glance. "How good of you to stop by, and in such weather!"

He reluctantly dropped Arabella's hands and turned. "Lady Melwin, how good to see you."

"Wilson has brought the carriage around. We are off to town before the road worsens. I wonder if you would be so kind as to escort us."

"I—"

"Thank you." She smiled graciously. "Such a gentleman!"

He cast an anguished glance at Arabella, who studiously ignored him. Shoulders sagging, he picked up his leather case and gave Aunt Jane a jerky nod. "Of course. I would be delighted to escort you and Lady Durham."

"I am sure you will be of immense use if we slide into a ditch." She looped her reticule over her wrist and fixed her bright blue gaze on Arabella. "Robert will be joining us as well. The fresh air will do him good."

"Don't keep him out too long. He didn't sleep well last night."

"What that boy needs is more exercise and less mothering." Aunt Jane adjusted the bow on her hat to a more sedate angle. "Mr. Francot, don't you need to collect your horse?"

Arabella watched with amusement as Aunt Jane herded the poor solicitor from the room, alternately admonishing him to hurry while thanking him for his "offer" to escort their party.

Jane watched him leave with obvious satisfaction, then returned her attention to Arabella. "Have you enough to keep you occupied while we are gone?"

"Indeed I do." She pulled the accounts closer.

"Don't pore over the books too long, dear. You will go blind."

"Hmm." Arabella pinned her aunt with a gaze. "What about the duke?"

After two days of trying every ploy known to try and trick Arabella into the sickroom, Aunt Jane's shrug was something of a surprise. "He should be fine. I left a bell on the table beside him in case he needs anything. But if you're anxious, pray feel free to visit him. I'm sure the company would be most welcome."

Aunt Emma rustled through the doorway, a vague look of worry on her plump face. "Arabella! Thank goodness I've found you!" She pressed a hand to her round cheek and announced in accents of doom, "I've lost my embroidery pattern."

Aunt Jane fixed an unforgiving eye on her sister. "You just had it in your hands a moment ago."

"I know. But then I couldn't find my blue half boots and I set the pattern down to look for them, and then I heard the carriage come around and I knew I should hurry, and now I can't remember where I left the silly thing."

Arabella looked down at Aunt Emma's tiny feet. "But you are wearing your red boots, not the blue."

"Oh, yes! The blue ones pinch my feet so I decided to wear the red, after all."

Jane snorted. "Shatterbrained old woman. Did you look in the sitting room?"

"I've looked everywhere. I even checked the attic."

Arabella refrained from asking why Emma thought her pattern would be in the attic. "Where is the last place you remember seeing it?"

"In the morning room. But I already looked there and it

is nowhere to be found. I am beginning to think . . ." She sent a meaningful glance at the portrait of the Captain.

Jane gave a brisk nod. "Yes, he does seem to be quite active lately." She leaned toward Arabella and said, "I lost two pair of stockings just last week."

Emma blinked. "What would the Captain want with your stockings?"

"He is a *pirate* ghost, you ninny. Pirate ghosts can't help but be attracted to naughty items like stockings. It is in their blood."

Emma appeared much struck by her sister's undeniable logic.

Arabella took Emma's arm and led her to the hallway. "You had better leave before the weather turns." Promising to find the missing pattern, Arabella walked her aunts to the door and handed them over to Ned, who helped the elderly ladies into the carriage.

With a sense of relief, Arabella watched the coach clatter down the drive, a forlorn Mr. Francot riding behind. Finally she would have some peace and quiet to finish the accounts.

She started to walk past the morning room, but stopped. Most likely Aunt Emma's lost pattern was right where she'd left it, on the table by her favorite chair. Arabella entered and walked briskly to Aunt Emma's chair, placed by the window to catch the morning light.

"There you are," said a voice from behind her.

Arabella slowly turned around.

Lucien sat in a wing-backed chair by the fireplace. His black hair still damp from a bath, his jaw scraped clean of whiskers, and his shirt hanging disgracefully open at his neck, he looked dark, handsome, and arrogant.

Arabella forced herself to remember what a treacherous dog he was. She was helped by the sight of Aunt

Emma's favorite shawl laying across his lap, clashing horribly with Aunt Jane's best scarf of India silk that was tied about his arm like a sling. Even confined to the sickroom, he had managed to work his magic over her aunts.

He gestured to the chair opposite him, separated only by a low table bearing a silver tea tray. "We have a conversation to finish, madam." His mouth curved in a lazy smile, his green eyes glinting with humor. "So . . . will you run? Or will you stay?"

Chapter 7

"What do you want, Lucien?"

"Conversation. Pray have a seat." Lucien regarded Arabella, from her worn boots to her mussed hair. Her drab gown served as a foil for the riot of color that brushed her cheeks and lips. Arabella made Sabrina's cold, perfect beauty fade into nothingness.

Her gaze flickered over him, lingering for an instant on his chest before she looked away, adorably embarrassed. "Did my aunt have anything to say to your traipsing about the house half dressed?"

She may have been embarrassed, but he was assailed with the desire to bare even more just to watch her delicious reactions. Heated by his own wayward thoughts, he cleared his throat. "Your aunt had plenty to say about my attire. The Hadley women are not known for their meek ways." Her eyes flashed and he chuckled.

His Bella had developed into a woman of extremes, with a temper as rich as her passion. He had an instant vision of Arabella, flushed from passion, her hair streaming across her white shoulders and—

Lucien stirred, his manhood taut and ready. He tugged Aunt Emma's shawl farther across his lap and silently cursed his too-vivid memory.

Arabella's eyes darkened with suspicion. "I hope you didn't upset Aunt Jane."

"Don't be absurd." In Lucien's opinion, Aunt Jane was a woman-shaped piece of cold, hard steel covered with a very thin veneer of lace and muslin. Before Arabella could harangue him further, he added, "I don't wish to discuss your aunt."

He half expected her to refuse to speak to him. But, pluck to the backbone, she showed her teeth in a chilly smile. "What *would* you like to discuss, Your Grace?"

He gestured to the chair. She eyed it warily as if she suspected he had placed a spider on it. He grinned. "What's wrong, Bella? Afraid?"

That lit the fires. "Of *you*? Ha!" She marched to the chair, but perched on the very edge it, ready to fly at a moment's notice. "What do you want?"

Lucien hooked her chair with one foot and pulled it closer, ignoring how the delicate wood scraped past the small table and jostled the creamer.

Arabella gasped, her hands clutching the thin armrests. As soon as he pulled her within touching distance, she favored him with a cold, flat stare. "You have two minutes, and then I'm leaving."

She could not have appeared more disinterested if she'd fallen asleep in the midst of the sentence.

His eyes narrowed. In his drug-induced dreams, she had not been disinterested. No, she had reacted much the same way she had in the carriage, with a throaty moan and a wild sensuality that had flamed his passion even higher.

He leaned forward and pushed one of the waiting cups toward her.

"I don't have time for tea."

"Why not?"

"It is Thursday. I always work on the accounts on Thursday."

Though he wasn't vain, it irked Lucien that an attractive woman would think a dry list of numbers of more interest than sitting with him. In London, he was considered quite a catch. The only way he'd found respite from the hordes of matchmaking mamas was to wear unrelenting black to every social function, obliquely announcing his widower standing to one and all.

A flicker of something unusual flared in his chest. Arabella was a challenge: a woman who knew her worth and questioned his. And the fact that it was she who challenged him made it all the sweeter.

He shamelessly used the one topic he knew would melt her icy facade. "Your brother visited me earlier."

"Did he?" She hesitated, then added, "He can be discourteous at times. He so hates it when people pity him."

"I'm hardly in a position to pity anyone other than myself, especially after being in the care of your aunts for two entire days."

A smile hovered on her mouth before she regained control, her lashes dropping to conceal her expression. "Robert chafes under such constant attention. I'm sure he is glad to have some male company. He is quite outnumbered in this household."

It was fascinating the way her face softened when she spoke of her brother. "I found him to be remarkably intelligent."

Her gaze darkened. "Yes, but much too quiet."

"Not when he wins at chess. I'm sure you heard him crowing throughout the entire house last night."

She chuckled, the sound rising from her throat and spilling over her lips until he wished he could capture it with a kiss. He focused on her plump lower lip and the shorter one above it. Together, they formed the perfect mouth, one that would part sweetly beneath his.

Lucien bent his leg slightly and rested his knee against the edge of the table to hide his too-obvious reaction to her presence. *Bloody hell, all this from just looking at her.* Heaven help him if she accidentally touched him.

Damn Aunt Jane's potions. How long did it take to recover from that vile mixture? He took his emotions firmly under control. "So many things have changed since I was here. How did Robert come to be confined to his chair? And your aunts, when did they arrive?"

A speculative gleam lit her gaze, then she settled her shawl about her shoulders and reached for the teapot. "I shall tell you all about my family," she replied coolly, "after you tell me what brings you to Yorkshire."

So that was the way of it? She still couldn't resist a direct challenge. Lucien hid a grin. "I was on my way north to meet someone regarding a purchase." Not for land, of course, but there was nothing wrong in letting her think otherwise.

"It was very improvident that your horse bolted across the road just as our carriage rounded the bend. You could have been killed."

"But I wasn't." He watched her elegant, capable hands as she poured the tea and wondered what it would take to get her past her anger and back to the passion she'd once felt. The idea tantalized him.

"Tell me something," she said abruptly. "Why were

you out riding the moors at that time of the night? Surely you were not meeting someone so late?"

He met her gaze with a direct one of his own. "What were *you* doing out on the moors at that time of night?"

"Visiting one of the tenants," she said, her answer clearly practiced. "Mrs. March was ill and I took her some soup." She lifted the cup and held it out to him. "You may ask Aunt Jane if you do not believe me."

He had little doubt that Aunt Jane would confirm every blasted word. Lucien took the cup, barely keeping himself from making a face. He hated tea. "Speaking of your lovely aunts, do they often conspire to keep wounded guests confined to their sitting room by dosing them with sheep tonic?"

"Oh, no. You are the first." She dropped not one, but three lumps of sugar into her cup. "You should be flattered that they believed you to be of such value. It isn't often that they leap to such heights of impropriety."

He watched, fascinated, as four dollops of fresh cream followed the sugar. "How did they come to stay with you?"

"They were widowed within a few months of each other. When Father got sick, I asked them to stay."

"And your brother?"

She took a sip of her tea, grimaced, and then added another lump of sugar. "My brother has seen more sadness than any person should. He was in the light cavalry at Waterloo. His unit was decimated."

Lucien whistled silently. The fate of the cavalry at Waterloo was almost legend. They had led the charge with a rousing roar, fighting with a frightening fierceness and skill that had allowed them to bring down ten times their number of the enemy. But they had paid dearly for their bravery and only a handful had survived the final battle.

Arabella set down her cup and placed a crème cake on

a plate. "Two of his childhood friends were there, fighting alongside him. Neither survived." Her eyes darkened and she placed the plate on his side of the table. "Robert will not speak of it, but I know it grieves him greatly."

Apparently Arabella wasn't the only member of the Hadley household whose every action could be traced to stubbornness and pride. Lucien thought of the thin, quiet boy who had so single-mindedly played chess with him the night before. "Perhaps he just needs time."

She nodded absently and sipped her tea. He watched her over the rim of his cup. She was fuller than he remembered, lush-bodied like a Boucher painting. Her hair curled in thick, luxurious waves over her brow, across her ears, and clung to the white column of her neck. The ribbon she wore to confine her hair had failed miserably and now hung in dejected splendor over one of her shoulders, threaded through the abundant curls.

Yet, for all her loveliness, there were faint purple shadows under her eyes and an aura of bone-deep weariness. It was as if she carried the burdens of the earth on her rounded shoulders.

Impulsively, he picked up the plate of cakes. "Here, take one."

Color touched her cheeks. "No, thank you."

"Nonsense. They are exceptionally good." He lifted one from the plate and held it out.

Her gaze seemed drawn to his hand, but she shook her head. "No."

"You must. Aunt Emma threatened to have my head if I didn't eat them all."

A reluctant smile curved her lips. "Oh, very well, though I shouldn't." She looked down at herself and sighed. "I fear I like them far too much as it is."

He scowled and placed not two, but three cakes on her

plate. "What a lot of nonsense. You look perfectly fine the way you are." Better than fine, in fact. Arabella was every bit as succulent as the rich cakes.

She was not the usual thin, wasted beauty that abounded in London society. Womanly and soft, she was breathtakingly beautiful. If circumstances were different—hell, if *he* were different—he'd have had no compunction in luring her to his bed and keeping her there for days as he discovered every inch of her sumptuous body.

He shifted in his chair. "You never married." *Bloody hell, what made me ask that?*

Her earlier humor evaporated. "No. Unlike you."

And he'd lived to regret it with every breath in his body. But he'd had no choice. Meanwhile, Arabella . . . He flicked a glance over her face, noting the thick curl of lashes and the lush line of her cheek. The men in Yorkshire were either scarce or blind. Perhaps there was someone who was waiting to sweep her away. Someone with whom she'd shared her incredible passion.

Someone other than him. He scowled.

There was the pig who had stopped their carriage with the constable. What was his name? Hartlebrook? Hartboot? Whoever he was, it was obvious that Arabella had not favored his suit. Lucien wondered if there were any other suitors about.

What of the staid-looking gentleman he'd seen ride out with Aunt Jane? Surely there was no romantic interest there—the man had to be forty years old, if a day. Lucien glanced at Arabella. Sitting in the chair opposite his, eating a cake, a dab of crème on her chin, she looked barely nineteen.

"I saw your aunts leaving for town. Who was the man who escorted them?"

Arabella frowned, a half-eaten cake held in midair. "Ned? He's the stable hand."

"No," he said, his tone perilously tense. "The older one—the dandy."

She put the cake back on the plate with obvious regret. "Oh, that was Mr. Francot, our solicitor."

It seemed to Lucien that her voice lowered intimately as she said the name. "Does he visit often?"

Eyes as rich as the peat floor of the forest on an autumn day challenged his. "I don't think that is any concern of yours."

"I just wondered," he answered, suddenly irritated that he was making such a fool of himself. But the man couldn't be totally unaware of Arabella's charms, regardless of the legitimacy of his claims on her time. "He looked familiar."

Her brow creased and she absently licked crème from one of her fingers. "Perhaps you met him in London. He was located there for some years prior to his arrival in Yorkshire."

Lucien forced himself to sip his tea, wishing it was brandy, something to banish the lingering cobwebs left by Aunt Jane's infamous tonic; cobwebs that were trapping him into such unfamiliar feelings and frustrations. He glanced around the room, looking for some of Aunt Emma's cognac.

The thought gave him pause. It had been exceptionally fine . . . a very rare quality indeed. He looked more closely at the room, noting the darned curtains and the worn appearance of the furniture. Where *had* Aunt Emma gotten such prime cognac in the wilds of Yorkshire?

He frowned. Free traders were a close-knit group, and it would be an easy thing to use already established smugglers to move in something new—especially something as small as a pouch of jewels.

But Lucien had to tread carefully. To many, smuggling was a way of life, seen as an honest occupation that had been unfairly singled out for prosecution by the crown. The attitudes of the nobility assisted the business, for they welcomed the better-quality goods, especially when they didn't have to pay the high duties placed on all imports due to the war.

Truthfully, he could care less about a little judicious free trading. His own father had supported the habit of several free traders, gaining quality port for half the usual price. But supporting Napoleon's armies was another matter. Lucien had seen the men who returned from the war, and he knew of the devastation, the pain many had paid. Just like Robert.

Arabella set her cup down. "It is my turn to ask a question. Tell me about your wife."

The abrupt question should have removed his attention from Arabella's mouth, where some of the crème clung to her lower lip, but it didn't. He couldn't stop staring, his whole body focused on the dab of sweetness. His gaze must have alerted her, for she touched her napkin to her mouth and then ran the tip of her tongue over the spot.

His throat contracted painfully.

"Lucien," she said, frowning. "I asked you about Sabrina."

He cleared his throat. Sabrina was the last thing he wanted to talk about. But he would much rather Arabella hear the story from him. Struggling to clear his mind, he took a sip of tea. "It was a needless death. She foolishly rode a horse that had never been ridden."

"Did she know the horse was dangerous?"

"Yes." He couldn't tell Arabella the whole truth: that to

Sabrina, riding a dangerous horse had been far preferable to staying in the same house with him. She had blamed him for every unfortunate event in her life and, by the time they had been wed a year, he'd begun to believe her.

Even though he knew her anger stemmed from her madness, some small part of him had wondered if she'd been right—if perhaps he was partially responsible for her illness. He, who lived with her and should have recognized her wild antics and frantic moods were the result of something more than an indulgent lifestyle, had merely avoided her cloying company. The wilder she became, the more he stayed away, until eventually they were more strangers than man and wife.

By the time Lucien realized that there was far more wrong with Sabrina than a mere excess of nerves, it was too late—she was too far gone in her madness to be saved. Had he been a steadfast husband, there was a chance that Sabrina might be alive today.

Lucien absently pressed a hand to his shoulder where it throbbed. Such speculation was useless, he knew. He had wasted a lifetime on exactly that type of empty thought and had almost lost himself to it.

He met Arabella's curious gaze with a carefully guarded expression. "Sabrina is gone. There isn't anything more to say."

Spots of color appeared in her cheeks. "I didn't mean to imply that you—"

"I know you didn't. I just didn't want you to think . . ." What? That he should never have left Arabella? That he should have been more attentive to his own wife? That he seemed destined to cause pain to those he loved and those who loved him? He'd told himself those things hundreds of times.

He forced a smile. "I would rather talk about you. Arabella, I know this is ten years too late, but we need to clear the air."

She set her cup down with a snap. "I have no wish to speak about what happened ten years ago."

"But I do," he said. She turned her face away, but he continued, "I have never forgotten you."

"And I have never forgotten you, either," she said coldly.

How could she *not* hate him? He'd left without a word and had never returned to explain. But at the time, he couldn't bring himself to face her, knowing that if he did, he wouldn't be able to leave. "I'm sorry to have caused you distress. Circumstances prevented me from returning, though that is no excuse."

A flicker of something crossed her face and was gone. She cleared her throat, her hands unconsciously smoothing her skirt. "I must help Cook with dinner. Do you need anything else before I leave? More tea? Another pillow?"

It was as if a wall had been erected between them, fifteen feet high and ten years thick. Perhaps it was better this way. He would stay focused on his mission and leave before things became even more complicated. "If you don't mind, I would like some cognac before you leave. It will ease my shoulder."

"Of course." She crossed the room to a large ornate cabinet and withdrew a decanter. She poured some golden liquid into a glass and then returned to place it on the table in front on him. "If you need anything else, ring the bell. Mrs. Guinver will be delighted to assist you."

He picked up the glass and watched her through narrowed eyes, waiting until she had almost reached the door before he said, "Arabella, where did you get this cognac?"

She stopped so suddenly that her skirts swung forward. "I beg your pardon?"

"The cognac. It is an excellent quality and I want to

purchase some for my estate in Derbyshire. I could get you a nice price for it."

Her color fluctuated wildly. "No," she said in a strangled voice. "It came from our cellars and I have no wish to sell any."

His stomach tightened, his instincts on the alert. "Bella, are you—"

"There is no reason for you to stay at Rosemont, Lucien. I want you gone, and the sooner, the better. Tonight."

"Your aunts will not like to hear that."

"They will if I tell them what once happened between us."

She had a point. Lucien set his glass down and sighed. "By the time Hastings packs, it would be dark."

"In the morning, then."

Her tone brooked no refusal. Lucien pursed his lips thoughtfully. So he had indeed struck a nerve, had he? "Very well. In the morning."

"Good." With a stilted curtsy, she swept from the room.

Lucien stared at the closed door. He couldn't doubt it now—she knew something. He stroked his chin thoughtfully. But perhaps it wasn't just some*thing*. Perhaps it was some*one*—whoever was smuggling the prime cognac. And perhaps he wasn't just smuggling spirits to the local gentry; perhaps he was smuggling in something much more sinister.

Lucien sighed and leaned his head against the cushion. The suspicion that Arabella knew the smuggler and was protecting the villain made him that much more determined to stay at Rosemont. Lucien smiled grimly. His stay was about to become prolonged.

But who was Arabella protecting? One of the servants? Lucien picked up his glass and absently swirled the golden liquid. No, her reaction had been too strong. Perhaps sweet little Aunt Emma, or determined Aunt Jane? But no, the idea was laughable. Neither had the wits to organize such a grand scheme. And Robert was bound to a wheelchair. . . .

Or was he? The doctors seemed to question the truthfulness of his paralysis. Perhaps Robert could indeed walk and it was all a ruse to avoid suspicion.

Sighing, Lucien stood, walked to the window, and pulled the heavy curtain aside. Outside, snow blew lightly over the pane, frosting it with swirls of white. It looked as if Rosemont were surrounded in a pristine sea, an island of enchantment locked in the icy grip of a sorcerer's spell. He dropped the curtain back into place.

Whether she knew it or not, Arabella was in danger. The free trader who supplied her family with cognac could also be one of Napoleon's agents. And if she knew his identity, she could become a dangerous liability.

Lucien was unable to shake off a sense of gloom. Frowning at his thoughts, he went to the small desk tucked into a corner and opened his writing case. With bold, decisive strokes, he addressed a letter to Mr. Mumferd of the Red Rooster Inn.

It was time he quit dallying and got back to work.

Chapter 8

Hours later, Arabella entered her aunts' room with an impatient step. "I need to speak with you."

Jane looked up from her knitting, noting the tense expression on Arabella's face. Emma must have noticed, too, for she gave a nervous start. "Whatever is wrong?"

Arabella pulled up a stool and sat on it. The pose struck Jane as being both mature and youthfully forlorn. She noted, too, the faint circles under her niece's eyes and wondered for the tiniest instant if perhaps she'd been wrong to throw the duke and Arabella together.

Arabella clasped her arms around her knees. "This is rather awkward. I need to talk to you about Lu—" She flushed. "About the duke."

"The duke?" Emma beamed. "He mended my pen for me this afternoon! Such a gentleman."

"He can be amiable when he wishes, but—"

"He is *perfectly* delightful! Why, I knew the moment Jane and I laid eyes on him that he was—"

"He is not the man you think," Arabella said sharply. With an abrupt move, she stood and began to pace.

Jane stopped knitting. "How so?"

Arabella paced faster, her face strained. "There was a time, long ago before either of you came to stay, that I met . . . someone. I was young and foolish. Father tried to warn me." She stopped and gripped her hands together, the knuckles showing white. "You know how stubborn I can be. I—I didn't heed him."

The corner of her mouth curved down and, to Jane's horror, a tear quivered on her niece's eyelash. Arabella *never* cried. Worse yet was the realization glimmering in Jane's brain. "Do you mean to say the duke is the same man who—"

Arabella nodded miserably and sank back onto her stool. "His father came hunting every year. I so looked forward to his arrival; it was the one thing that made life here bearable after Mother died. Then, one year . . . he arrived and we just *knew*." She gave a bitter laugh. "Or, at least, *I* knew. I thought he felt the same."

"Where was James when all this was happening?"

"Father was involved in a horse venture at the time, and he wasn't at Rosemont for weeks on end."

"James was a fool." Jane looked down at the tangled yarn in her lap. "I suppose you were indiscreet."

Another tear slipped down Arabella's cheek. "I thought he loved me."

Emma reached out to grasp her niece's hand. "Dear! *Don't* say another word. We know all about it. Your father wrote us some time after . . . after your friend returned to London."

Jane nodded, her own throat tight. "He didn't name the man, of course, or we'd never have placed the duke in your path."

The dark head drooped, a dusky curl following the line of her cheek. "I should have known you'd heard something; Father told everyone."

Emma patted Arabella's hand. "How uncomfortable for you, dear. Though I have to wonder . . . are you *sure* it was the same duke? I mean, there are other dukes, and—"

"Of course I'm sure it was him! He was twenty at the time, but except for being more . . ." She flushed, then continued doggedly, "Except for being older, he is exactly the same."

Jane sighed. It certainly sounded damning. And if it was true, it ruined everything.

Or did it? All of the signs had pointed to the fact that Arabella and the duke belonged together. Why, Jane's bad luck was already beginning to turn for the better. And then there was the way the duke looked at Arabella, his green gaze intent, as if fascinated beyond his control. Jane pursed her lips. "Perhaps he is sorry."

Emma nodded, her face brightening. "I daresay he is *very* sorry! It is wretched knowing one did something as a youth that one should not have. Why, I remember once when I stole a kiss from old Mr. Frothington and I—"

Jane started. "Our tutor?"

Emma nodded, a beatific expression on her plump face.

"But he was married!"

"Yes, well, as I said, one does things that one might not be proud of."

Some women, perhaps, but not Arabella. Not unless . . . Jane raised her brows. The child must have been incredibly in love to have so heedlessly thrown propriety to the winds. In fact, now that she thought about it, there was reason to believe that Arabella's feelings were still engaged. It would explain why she hadn't shown the slightest interest in any of the eligible young men Jane had planted in her way over the past four years.

Arabella gently untangled her hand from Emma's and stood. "I just felt I should tell you so you would cease your efforts to throw Lucien and me together. It is untenable."

Jane saw the hurt in the dark eyes and it made her own heart ache.

As if realizing she was revealing too much, Arabella straightened her shoulders and turned toward the door. "I need to see Cook about dinner." She stopped by the door and smiled weakly. "Thank you both."

The door closed behind her.

"I suppose this changes things," Emma said dolefully. "I feel sorry for the poor duke; he seems so smitten."

"And how could he not be? Arabella is the most beautiful, the sweetest—"

"The most capable," added Emma helpfully. She reached down to untangle her embroidery where it had fallen to the floor and twisted about her boot heel. "Do you think he did it on purpose? Just rode in, took advantage of her, and left?"

"I daresay. I understand he was quite a rake at one time."

"But what rakehell would stay so quietly in the country? He seems content here."

"Exactly," Jane said. "I think the duke has changed and Arabella has not yet realized it."

"I don't think she *wants* to realize it." Emma's round shoulders slumped. "Oh, sister, I wonder if she can ever forgive him."

Jane and Emma sat silently, one plucking absently at a loose thread, the other chewing on her lip. Finally Emma sighed, reached into her pocket, and withdrew her bottle.

She took a thoughtful swig. "Perhaps she still cares for him."

Jane nodded. "My thoughts exactly."

"Despite his past, I cannot see how a wealthy, titled suitor could make her anything *but* happy. Especially one who is so well hu—"

"Developed," finished Jane hastily. Before Emma could offer more insight, Jane reached across to take the bottle. Pinching her nose, she took a quick swallow. Cognac burned its way down her chest. She coughed, handed the bottle back to Emma, then took out a lace handkerchief and delicately wiped the corners of her mouth. The fiery liquid infused her with energy. "This calls for action."

"What can we do? She won't have him. Perhaps Mr. Francot could be convinced to renew his suit."

"I'd rather have a rakehell for a nephew-in-law than that mawkish worm."

"Heavens, Jane! Mr. Francot has always been very kind."

"He isn't right for Arabella. But the duke . . . that is another matter altogether." Mr. Francot didn't have the ability to shake Arabella's confidence. Nor could he make her flush with a mere indolent smile, yet Jane had witnessed the duke doing all of these things. There was a bond between her niece and their visitor, and she was not about to ignore such a promising opportunity. Of course, it would take a good deal of address to smooth over this little bump. But Jane had faith in the duke's ability to win her stubborn niece. A man with a face like that, and such a fine figure—all he needed to do was make an effort. But he would have to use all the weapons at his disposal— every last one.

Perhaps she should have word with their duke. Yes, that

was what she would do. And once she explained what his responsibilities were, she was sure he would know exactly how to go about winning his way through Arabella's defenses. After all, there were two hearts at stake in this game, and Jane was determined that neither would go to waste.

Satisfied, she picked up her abandoned knitting and began untangling the knots.

Chapter 9

Buoyed by the duke's brooding glances at her niece during dinner, and further encouraged by Arabella's frigid refusal to acknowledge those glances, Jane waited for Arabella to retire and then marched into the library. Lucien stood by the fireplace, staring into the flames, a cheroot in his hand.

He turned when she came into the room and hastily tossed his cheroot into the fire.

"I wish you hadn't done that," she said, sending him an encouraging smile. "My husband enjoyed his cigars. I miss the scent of fresh tobacco." She took a chair and patted the arm of the one beside her. "Come and sit, Your Grace. I wish to speak with you."

It was amazing how quickly his face shuttered, but he did as she invited and took his seat.

Once there, he leaned back and regarded her, his handsome face inscrutable. "Yes?"

The man certainly had a gift for being direct. Jane liked

that almost as much as his title. "I have come to warn you."

"Oh? Am I in danger of some sort?"

"Arabella told me about your . . . past relationship."

He went very still, lines of white bracketing his mouth. "What did she say?"

His voice held an edge that made her sit a little straighter. "Not much, really. Only that you knew her, took advantage of her, and left." Jane met his gaze straight on. "Is it true?"

"Yes," he answered harshly. "It is all true."

She sighed. "I was afraid you'd say that."

Lucien stood abruptly and turned away to stir the fire with the toe of his boot. "I will not lie to you. I was young, a thoughtless cad, and—there are not enough names for what I was." He made a gesture as if to push the memory away, his mouth thinned. "I went heedlessly through life, ignoring my responsibilities. I was unprepared to step into my father's shoes and I suffered for it, as did Arabella." His green gaze rested on Jane for a moment, burning with intensity. "But I never forgot her."

Jane's disappointment softened. There was such sincerity in his gaze, such a depth of emotion that she felt her own eyes grow damp. For Arabella's sake, Jane pressed on. "Did you love her?"

His hand fisted at his side. "Yes."

Do you love her still? The words burned on Jane's tongue, but she held them back. She doubted whether he knew what he felt. *Yet.* Instead, she said in a mild tone, "You hurt Arabella quite badly."

He gave a short, bitter laugh. "I have a history of hurting all of the women in my life."

"But Arabella did not deserve it. She loved you dearly."

He turned away, but not before Jane saw the agony in his gaze. "I know she did."

She waited for him to say more, but he stood, silent, head bowed. Finally she said, "Surely there were extenuating circumstances. Perhaps you fell ill and could not return?"

"If you are searching for an excuse for my behavior, you will not find it here. What I did was inexcusable. At the time, I thought—" He stopped, desolate lines carving his face. "It doesn't matter what I thought. Suffice it to say that I did irreparable harm to an innocent girl and I have regretted it every day since."

His pain was almost palpable. Jane regarded him silently for a long moment, thoughts tumbling through her mind like water over a fall. "I won't say you are wrong, but fortunately it won't be a matter for either of us to worry about. I expect Arabella will wed shortly."

"To whom?" The question snapped across the room like the crack of a gun.

Jane hid a smile. "Lord Harlbrook has been most insistent lately—"

"*No.*" The duke's jaw tensed. "Good God, Harlbrook is a pig! Even I saw that, and I was in his company but a moment. You cannot let that happen."

"I may have no choice. Things are not well at Rosemont and Arabella feels responsible for us all."

He turned to pace before the fire. "Perhaps I can make some arrangements . . . send my man of business with a draft—" He stopped and turned a bleak gaze on her. "She would refuse."

"Most likely. She has the Hadley pride, you know."

He gave a wry grimace. "I had noticed. It is one of the things that annoy me the most about her, yet at the same time, I cannot imagine her otherwise." A smile softened his mouth. "She is the most damnable woman."

Jane had to bite her lip hard to keep from jumping from her chair and rewarding him with a fierce hug. Whatever had happened to the boy who'd once been Lucien Devereaux, it had made him into an exceptional man.

The perfect man for Arabella.

Jane kept her face blank. There was still much to do. "The past is the past. What I want to know, Your Grace, is what you intend for the future."

He was quiet for a long time, staring into the fire. The light flickered across his face, softening the planes with a golden touch. Jane sighed. He was indeed a most beautiful man. Her gaze traveled across his broad shoulders and down to his snug breeches. One day, Arabella would thank her for her help. And if she didn't, then her niece was a bigger fool than Emma.

Lucien sighed. "You are right, Lady Melwin. I will do what I should have done when I first arrived."

Jane leaned forward in her chair, her throat tight with hope. "Yes?"

He shoved himself from the mantel with a fluid movement. "I will leave immediately. I had planned—" He shook his head abruptly. "But you are right. I will tell Hastings to pack and we will leave this evening, if possible."

"Bacon-brained fool!"

Lucien stopped, unsure he'd heard her right. "I beg your pardon?"

Bright spots of color touched Jane's thin cheeks. "You cannot leave."

Resentment flared, followed by hollow amusement. "As much as you might wish it, you cannot order me about. I will leave tonight."

"No, you will not. It is time you stopped running from

your responsibilities. You, sir, will fix what you broke all those years ago."

"And what is that?"

"Arabella's heart." Jane regarded him with a martial light in her eyes, her back ramrod straight, her feet planted firmly on the floor.

Lucien shook his head. "She won't allow it. You are greatly mistaken if you think otherwise."

"Do you mean to tell me that you would leave Arabella here, to rot in this rambling house with her crippled brother, whilst you go gallivanting back to your amusements? Your gambling, and your drinking, and your bits of muslin?" Jane sniffed. "Hardly the gentlemanly thing to do."

It was hardly the ladylike thing for her to mention "bits of muslin," but he prudently didn't point that out. "There is nothing I can do to help her if she won't let me."

"I disagree. It is time you set things right."

"Set things right? You don't understand. She cannot stand the sight of me. I would gladly give her a draft to cover the complete renovation of this place, but she'd throw it in my face."

"My niece has yet to recover from what happened ten years ago, and if you don't do something, she never will. Look around you. Her situation is desperate."

Lucien glanced about the shabby room. Jane was right: he owed Arabella too much to just walk away. Perhaps he could begin here, with the house she loved so much. For a short time, he could relieve her of some of the weighty responsibilities she'd assumed. Determination settled between his shoulders and he straightened. "You are right, Lady Melwin. I owe her too much to leave. If she'll let me stay, I will." He saw the quick flare of excitement in Jane's eyes and held up a hand. "I am not talking about marriage. I am the last man she would ever want to wed."

Jane frowned. "Then what are you talking about?"

"I will convince Arabella to let me assist her in renovating Rosemont. The least I can do is make sure she has a decent house over her head."

"She will try to force you to leave."

"I will refuse. Until she agrees to accept my help, I am fixed at Rosemont."

A pleased flush rose in Jane's cheeks. She stood and measured him with a narrow gaze. "Excellent. I'm sure a man of your considerable . . ."—her gaze dropped to his legs—"address will find a way to win her over."

Lucien looked down to see if perhaps he'd spilled gravy in his lap at dinner, but saw nothing. He frowned. Had the gaze been from anyone other than Arabella's prim, elderly aunt, he'd have thought she meant . . . He yanked his gaze back to Aunt Jane, but she was already gone, the door closing behind her.

He stared at the door for a full minute. What had she meant by that? That he should use seduction? *Surely not.* Still . . . the idea of seducing Arabella was vastly appealing. He warmed just thinking of it, remembering the piquant flavor of her skin, the tempting weight of her breasts in his hands.

He turned restlessly and paced to the window to stare blindly into the night. Such pleasant fantasies were just that. If he wanted to stay long enough to help repair Rosemont, he would have to find a way to overcome Arabella's pride. Leaning his good shoulder against the window frame, he let the chill ease his spirits.

Arabella had changed in the ensuing years; gone was the impulsive, warm sprite who had so enchanted him.

Instead, she had subdued her inner fire and sealed it away in an icy shroud of duty. She had changed, just as he had.

He fisted his hand against the window and rested his forehead on it. Ice melted where his breath clouded the glass and a slow trickle of water wove its way to the sill, followed by another, then another.

Lucien traced the fall of water, watching as it made its way over ice and ridge and then joined its sisters in a small puddle. He could see the reflection of the room in the glass: the peeling plaster, the worn carpet, a damp spot in one corner of the ceiling.

Rosemont had suffered right along with her mistress. He would face his past actions and make amends. The thought sank roots and wrapped around his bruised heart. There was danger in such a plan; his emotions were still finely wrought where Arabella was concerned. So he would stay only until Rosemont was on the way to being repaired, long enough to show Arabella that he was genuinely sorry for his past actions. *Long enough to force her to move forward with her life—to find her happiness elsewhere.*

He clenched his jaw against the idea of Arabella with another man, but it had to be. He'd brought nothing but ruin to the lives of the two women who had depended on him most. He would not let it happen again.

But how could he get Arabella to allow him to stay at Rosemont? She would never believe he wished to help merely to make up for his past sins. How could he convince her otherwise? He rubbed his hand along the wet window and cleared a small circle. Outside, the night gleamed beneath a blanket of cold.

An idea slowly formed and Lucien smiled. What if she thought he stayed for something *other* than mere kindness of the heart? She already thought the worst of him; perhaps he could use that to his advantage.

The last drop of water wended its way down the windowpane and came to rest in the small puddle. There was more than one way to thaw an icy heart. All he had to do was melt her resistance—one heated drop at a time. By the time he finished, she would accept his assistance just to be rid of him.

The terrace door burst open and Lucien turned as Robert wheeled in. His hair and cloak glistened with water. Eyes fixed straight ahead, he pushed his chair past Lucien without even seeing him.

Lucien watched as Robert pushed himself to the desk and removed a huge leather tome. He flipped through the pages with obvious excitement. "Looking for something, whelp?"

Robert's head snapped up, his eyes wide. "The devil, Wexford! You scared me to death."

Lucien made his way to the fireplace. "A bit damp for a stroll, isn't it?"

"I don't have much else to do."

"Oh? Run out of hapless visitors to brutally slay over the chess board?"

A reluctant grin lifted the corners of Robert's mouth. "That was a crack move, wasn't it? I learned it from Vicar Haighton. He comes every Saturday."

Lucien wondered if the elderly vicar was the only company Robert had, other than his aunts and sister. "I'm surprised your sister allows you to wander about in the cold."

"I like it," Robert said defensively, brushing at the drops that glittered on his cloak. "The wind clears my head."

"It is more likely to freeze you to death."

"Death isn't the worst thing that can happen to a man."

His low voice gave Lucien pause. The boy's eyes burned, his face set. He scowled when he caught Lucien's gaze. "Don't think you have to tell my sister every move I make. She would go into a fidget and worry me to death."

"Odious whelp. Do I look as if I would carry tales?"

Robert's face softened into a reluctant grin. "No. But you can never be too careful."

Lucien had to laugh at that. "True." He crossed to the side table to pour a splash of cognac into a glass. He gave the boy's pale face a long look, and then added another measure.

Robert took the glass with a faint smile. "Arabella doesn't like me to drink." He took a small sip and grimaced.

Lucien poured himself an equally generous amount and took a chair opposite Robert, stretching his legs toward the fire. "Your sister cares about you."

"Thus she wraps me in wool."

"It could be worse. She could leave you to yourself." Lucien flicked a glance over Robert's thin frame. "I've an idea you wouldn't bother to eat unless forced."

Robert's gaze darkened. "It is Arabella that I worry about. Aunt Jane and Aunt Emma do not realize the half of what she does. But I do." He looked down at his legs, his hand white about the glass, a bitter set to his mouth. "And I am in no position to help."

"Don't punish yourself for what you cannot change."

"I don't answer to you, Wexford. You are nothing but a chance guest. You don't belong here any more than I."

Lucien raised his brows. "Rosemont is your home."

"I am as necessary to this place as a lame horse." His shoulders drooped. "Perhaps less." Robert set his glass on the table beside him and slanted a glance at Lucien. "Since this appears to be a night for sharing, what keeps *you* at Rosemont?"

"The cognac. It is exceptional."

"Nonsense. There must to be something more."

"London palls. I find myself tolerably amused for the first time in months."

"What about my sister?" Robert gave Lucien a direct glance. "I was quite young when you and she knew one another, but I remember it quite well."

Lucien took a drink of the cognac. This was not a conversation he wished to have. But if he was to win his way back into Arabella's life, perhaps it would make sense to begin here, with the one person she loved enough to let under her guard. "I should have realized you'd remember something of that time."

"Do you know what I remember most?" There was a wistful tone to Robert's voice. "The way you looked at her. Someday I want to look at a woman like that and—" He broke off and shot an embarrassed glance at Lucien.

"I never should have left. I still regret it."

Robert regarded him for a long minute before looking down at the leather book that rested in his lap. He ran a hand lightly over the cover. "We all make mistakes."

Lucien wondered if Robert was talking about his own youth, the one he'd lost in the heat of a bloody battle. Abruptly, he said, "I usually prefer my tomes to weigh less than I do."

Robert shot him a shy smile. "Actually, I prefer to read the *Post,* but I found this the other day. It is our family history." He shrugged. "If it was good enough for the Captain, then it is good enough for me."

"The Captain?"

Robert gestured toward the portrait that hung over the mantel. "See? He is holding this book."

The picture was extraordinarily well done, the Captain's expression lifelike, his blue gaze seeming to follow one across the room. Lucien studied it thoughtfully. "It appears to be the same book."

"It is. I'm sure of it." Robert gazed down at the book, a strange gleam in his eyes. Carefully, so as not to disturb the ancient pages, he opened it.

Lucien could not shake the idea that there was more to the boy's interest than mere family pride. He rose and strolled to look over Robert's shoulder.

Robert shut the book with a snap, his thin hands clutching it to him.

Lucien clasped his hands behind his back. "You are certainly enthusiastic about your family history."

Robert nodded, a mulish set to his jaw.

"Perhaps I should get you pen and paper so you can begin making charts. I understand that is an important part of the process."

"That will not be necessary."

"And mayhap," Lucien said, warming to his subject, "you can convince your aunts to set aside a wall to display your research."

"You are too kind," Robert said with telling sarcasm.

Lucien turned to the large expanse of wall beside the door. "And here," he said, tilting his head as if deep in thought, "we can put your more significant findings. If you run out of room, perhaps you can plaster the hallway, as well."

Robert's lips twisted into a reluctant grin. "Stop being a gudgeon."

"Then tell me what you are really about. Something is afoot and I know it."

The boy hesitated, his gray gaze assessing Lucien. After a moment, he shrugged. "Oh, very well. But you will just laugh and think it is silly."

"Try me," Lucien said, recognizing Robert's strained

pride. He was determined not to laugh, even if the boy admitted to attempting to bring one of his illustrious ancestors back to life with incantations and a smoking candle.

Robert traced the edge of the leather book with a thin hand. "Since I cannot be of any help to Arabella in working the land or seeing to the repairs on the house, I thought I might as well see if I could find . . ." He took a deep breath. "The Captain's lost treasure."

Lucien raised his brows, but offered no reply.

A light flush touched Robert's cheeks. "You think I am crazed."

"Nonsense. Everyone dreams of finding a treasure. And if you believe it is possible to locate it, then by all means, search away."

"You are mocking me."

"No, I'm not," Lucien said quietly.

Robert stared at him for a long moment before he flashed a relieved smile. "I thought you'd . . . Well, I'm glad you understand." He rolled his chair forward and opened the book. "There is so much evidence that it exists. See? This a record of the family history and it contains some direct quotes from the Captain's journal. The Captain writes about putting away a fortune in jewels for the care of his wife in case he did not return from one of his ventures. I think it is here, perhaps as close as the garden."

"What would you do if you found this fortune?"

A slow smile curved Robert's mouth. "Arabella has always wished to visit London. That would be the first thing. And then I would fix Rosemont for Aunt Emma and Aunt Jane."

"And for yourself?" Lucien refilled his empty glass. "Surely there is something you've been dreaming of?"

Robert's gaze slid to his useless legs before he turned

his head away. "At one time I dreamed of having my own sailing yacht. Perhaps even a fleet of them."

"You had better hope that the Captain was a thrifty man."

"Oh, I hope for more than that. I hope he was enormously wealthy."

Lucien chuckled. "For your sake, I will hope so, too. Now go to bed, jackanapes. It is late and your sister will worry."

"Very well," Robert said in a grudging voice, though he had to stifle a yawn to say the words. "And I promise not to wake with the ague. If Arabella discovered you had plied me with spirits, she would cheerfully boot you out of the house."

"She has already tried," Lucien replied in a cool voice.

Robert looked surprised. "Surely not. Arabella would never be so rude."

"She had extreme provocation. But don't worry, whelp; I am refusing to go."

It was Robert's turn to chuckle. He shook his head and smiled shyly. "I'm glad. It is nice to have another man about the house." From down the hallway came a brisk step and Robert grimaced. "Speak of the devil."

Arabella walked into the library. "There you are, Robert! I came to see if you were already abed." Her gaze anxiously scanned him and she frowned. "Why do you have your cloak on?"

A dark cloud descended on Robert's brow and Lucien hurried to intercede. "That is my fault."

Arabella stiffened. "Is it indeed? I suppose you were encouraging him to go out in this foul weather?"

Robert sighed. "Leave it, Bella. Lucien didn't tell me to do anything of the sort. I came in through the terrace doors and he was already here."

"What were you doing outsi—"

"Lucien," interrupted Robert, hunching a shoulder in his sister's direction. "Perhaps tomorrow we can play another game of chess?"

"That will not be possible," Arabella said in a frosty accent. "His Grace is leaving." She shot a hard glance at Lucien. *"Early."*

"No, he's not," Robert said, surprising Lucien. "I have invited him to stay as *my* guest."

Arabella's full mouth drew into a straight line. "You invited *him*?"

Robert met her gaze solidly. "Rosemont is my house, isn't it?"

She swallowed, her eyes darkening. "Of course."

"So I thought," he said in a deceptively mild voice. He turned and caught Lucien's eye. A moment of fraternal camaraderie passed between them before the younger man wheeled his chair to the door. "I'm very tired. G'night, Bella. Lucien, I will see you tomorrow."

Arabella barely waited until the door had closed before she spun to face Lucien, her eyes sparkling in anger. "What have you done to my brother?"

Lucien downed the remainder of his cognac and returned the glass to the table. "I played chess with him. Nothing more."

Her hands clenched into fists at her sides. "You have cajoled him into believing you like him."

"I do like him. He is starving for male companionship."

"Vicar Haighton comes once a week."

"The vicar is four times Robert's age. It isn't the same thing."

"He was fine before you came," she said in a voice that hovered on the brink of tears.

"Was he? I get the impression he hasn't been well in a

long time. He is a remarkable young man, Bella. But he is in a lot of pain."

"Which is exactly why you should leave," she snapped.

"You do your brother a disservice, treating him as if he were a lad of fifteen."

"He is not much older than that; he is only twenty."

"He has seen a war, Bella. He will never be young again."

Her eyes filled with tears, before she regained control and glared at him. "I know you, Lucien. You will be a charming companion until you tire of his presence. And then you will disappear."

The words stung. That was how he had failed Sabrina—by not being there when she needed him most. And he'd committed the same crime against Arabella. He hadn't freed her from a life of financial ruin by walking away all those years ago. He had, instead, left her to deal with the harshness of life, alone and unprotected.

His heart ached anew. "Perhaps I have changed."

Her mouth thinned, showing her disbelief more plainly than words. "Robert has been hurt enough. Leave, Lucien. Before it is too late."

She had so much reason to question his motives, but he was sworn to stay. Sworn to help her, whether she wished it or not.

Lucien reached out and ran a finger down the curve of her cheek. "I am staying, Bella *mia.*" *At least until I can find a way to help you through this mess.* Afterward . . . he didn't know about afterward. Somehow, his thoughts would not go that far.

Arabella turned her face away, her eyes dark. "Then there is nothing more to say."

He shoved his hand into his pocket and curled it into a

fist. "Very well." He bowed and went to the door. "Good evening, my dear. I will see you at breakfast."

She stood, arms crossed, staring at the fire. His heart heavy, Lucien left.

Chapter 10

Lucien stepped onto the terrace and lifted his face to the pale winter rays. For December, the air was tinged with a surprising hint of warmth. And that was a good thing, considering his chilly reception in Rosemont since Robert had invited him to become an official guest of the house. Between Aunt Emma's open hostility and Arabella's frigid demeanor, it was a wonder he hadn't frozen to death. Thank God for Robert and Aunt Jane.

The scent of warm bread drifted from the kitchen as Lucien headed for the stables. He would take a quick ride to the Red Rooster, just to get a feel for the place, and then return and get to work. He lifted his arm and moved it in slow circles. Aunt Jane had meticulously plucked the stitches from his shoulder just this morning and he felt as if he were back to full strength, ready to attack the most difficult repair project Rosemont had to offer. Just today, he'd straightened the hinges on several doors, fixed the stuck damper in the kitchen, and replaced three loose steps on the main stairway.

Lucien rounded the corner of the house, whistling silently to himself. Out of the corner of his eye, he caught sight of the ungainly shed that sat beside the stable. Last night, after Arabella had retired, pleading a headache, Lucien had slipped outside and found enough of Aunt Emma's prime cognac resting in the back of the shed to furnish eighteen houses the size of Rosemont. The barrels, missing the requisite excise stamp and still damp from being hauled indoors, had been stacked neatly, a tarp hiding them from sight. Someone at Rosemont was purchasing goods from a free trader. But who?

The only one with enough business sense was Arabella. Without her expert guidance and commonsense management, Rosemont would be in a far greater state of ruin. Yet he could not see Miss Outraged Virtue involved with such an under-the-table effort. Perhaps one of the servants was responsible.

Lost in thought, he opened the gate—and froze. Across the small yard, Arabella strode toward the stables. Reaching the wide wooden door, she glanced over her shoulder as if to make sure no one followed, then slipped inside.

Lucien blinked once, twice. It wasn't just that she was slinking about like a sneak thief intent on mischief. It was more than that: Arabella Hadley was wearing breeches.

Soft, woolen breeches and black leather boots that clung to her rounded legs and calves in the most damnably alluring fashion. Lucien tugged at his cravat and wondered how defined her derriere would be, encased in what must be her brother's cast-off clothing. A pity she'd worn such a long coat. Fortunately, he could easily verify his fevered imagination.

With a careful glance around, Lucien continued toward

the stables. He'd never met such an infuriatingly independent woman. Someone should take Rosemont's mistress in hand—from what he could see, Arabella was long overdue.

But what was she doing dressed in men's clothing? Lucien scowled and increased his pace. *Bloody hell.* Perhaps she was indeed a link to the smugglers.

The thought clenched his jaw. It was implausible. Still, as soon as the barn door was opened enough to let him slip through, he dropped low and crept into the shadowed interior until he could just see over the stall door. Arabella stood before a pile of hay, sunlight trickling through the slats in the walls and dappling her hair with red-gold beams.

Behind her, an old worn farm horse stretched his neck over his stall door as far as he possibly could, his yellow teeth bared as he tried to reach her pocket. Arabella laughed, her voice rich with delight as she turned to pat the horse's nose.

Lucien closed his eyes at the sound of her laughter. He remembered another time when she'd laughed like that, her mouth still swollen from his kisses, her luxurious hair tangled beneath them both. She had been an amazingly sensual lover, giving herself in every aspect of their passion with an unbridled eagerness that had amazed and delighted him.

He had been the experienced one, having sampled the bountiful avenues of pleasure available to a young London blade. But Arabella, although an innocent, had drowned his senses with her unrestrained reactions.

He opened his eyes and banished the flood of memories. He was not used to chasing insufferably independent women into the stables, regardless of how appealing they looked dressed in their brother's cast-off clothing.

Lucien slumped against the stall door, suddenly realizing the ridiculousness of his situation. What was he doing, spying on her like a lovesick twelve-year-old? Arabella murmured to the horse and Lucien lifted his head again. She patted the animal for a moment, crooning to him in a low, soft voice. Then, with a heavy sigh, she turned and picked up a shovel.

A shovel? Lucien frowned as she set to work. She wasn't just shoveling—she was mucking out the stables, lifting steaming piles of soiled straw into a small handcart. He straightened, forgetting to conceal himself. How had things gotten to such a pass that a gently bred woman had to muck out her own stables? A twinge of guilt struck him. Without his thoughtless interference in her life all those years ago, she might have wed someone in her own station—someone who would have taken care of her and kept her from such labors.

The thought pained him. He clenched his hands into fists and took a hasty step forward, instantly regretting it when the old farm horse swung his large, bony head in his direction. The horse snorted loudly and pawed the floor, whinnying a distinct challenge that caused Hastings's gentle bay to retreat to the back of his stall in alarm.

Cursing silently, Lucien stooped back behind the door, but not before Satan's large black head appeared over the stall door beside him, roused from a doze by his companion's complaints. His ears flicked forward when he saw Lucien, and he whinnied a loud welcome.

"What you complaining about?" Arabella said over her shoulder to the horse. "*You* have the easy part."

Where was Wilson? Or Ned? Patting Satan's nose to keep him quiet, Lucien peered back over the stall door.

Arabella leaned on the shovel, shoving a wisp of hair from her forehead with a gloved hand. Her face was flushed from her exertion, her brow damp, a tendril of hair curled about her cheek.

Dissatisfied at being so summarily ignored, Satan tossed his head and knocked Lucien's hat to the floor. The horse snorted with laughter when Lucien scrambled to catch it.

"What are you doing here?"

Lucien froze. It would be a long time before he brought Satan another lump of sugar. He flicked a hot glare at the horse before straightening and meeting Arabella's accusing gaze. "Ah! There you are! I saw you slip in here, and for an instant I thought . . ." He stopped. Somehow he didn't think she would be amused that for one horrible minute he'd assumed she was involved in smuggling cognac for her hazy Aunt Emma.

Arabella's gaze narrowed. *"Well?"*

It was infuriating, the way she could look at him as if she could hear what he wasn't saying just as plainly as what he was. He barely managed to keep his smile intact. "I was looking for . . ." His desperate gaze found the hat clutched in his hand and he held it aloft. *"This."*

She arched a brow, her dark eyes shadowed. "And how did *that* get into the stables?"

"I lost it when I came to visit the horses last night." He patted Satan's velvet nose, then reached a hand toward the farm horse. The horse jerked his head away, then bared his teeth and lunged.

Lucien snatched his hand back just in time. "Vicious, conniving bag of bones," he growled. "I ought to—"

"Sebastian doesn't recognize you," Arabella said bluntly. "And I did not notice your hat when I came in."

"No? Perhaps it was hidden in all this hay." He made a great show of cleaning the beaver brim. "Damnable thing. Can't keep my hands on it."

Her lips quivered for an instant before she severely repressed them into a straight line. "Now that you have found your errant hat, you may leave." Then she glowered. "I don't know how you tricked Robert into giving you an invitation, but it doesn't give you leave to sneak up on me when I am alone."

"I will leave when I finish."

"When you finish what?"

"Helping you." He shrugged out of his coat, untied his neckcloth, and tossed them both over the railing, then closed the distance between them. He boldly placed his hands over hers on the shovel. Her chin jutted out and her eyes sparkled, the color deepened by her long lashes.

She tried to pull the shovel free. "I do not need your help."

"Yes, you do." And she was going to get it, whether she wanted it or not.

Arabella stopped yanking on the shovel to glare up at him. "Why are you here, Lucien? What do you hope to gain?"

She was the most ungracious, most stubborn woman he'd ever known. And she knew him far too well. "Perhaps I am being chivalrous."

She raised her brows in disbelief. He couldn't even plead common decency without facing her incredulity. It was galling. Galling and just the tiniest bit reassuring.

He sighed. "Very well, then; maybe I am bored. Your aunts won't even let me step outside without making Hastings wrap me from head to foot in wool."

Arabella stared at him an interminable length of time.

Finally some of the tension left her body. Her gaze flickered to his shoulder where his shirt opened at the neck, revealing the edge of his bandage. "Perhaps if you had acted less like an invalid, my aunts would not have coddled you so."

"We'll never know, will we?" He enjoyed the spark of irritation that shone in her eyes. "Fortunately for us both, this little chore will afford me some much-needed amusement." His gaze drifted over her, dwelling longer than necessary on the gentle flare of her hips. "Unless you have a better idea of how we could amuse ourselves. Here. Alone. In the stables."

Her jaw firmed. "No. Now let go."

She was not going to give an inch. Though he had managed to assuage some of her suspicion, it would take something stronger to get her to relax her hold on the shovel. He glanced at her hand, her slender fingers so tightly wrapped around the thick handle that he couldn't help but wish she had her hands wrapped around him, her strong fingers stroking, tightening. The idea lifted his manhood to painful readiness.

Damn it, if he didn't get away from her soon, he would lose what little control he had over his traitorous body. Fortunately, he knew exactly how to make Miss Arabella Hadley release the shovel. Without giving her time to say another word, Lucien leaned over and brushed his cheek across hers, igniting a jolt of raw passion. Heat spiraled to his stomach and he had to grit his teeth to keep from tossing the shovel aside and yanking her to him.

But his abrupt move accomplished its purpose—with a muffled curse, Arabella spun away and stumbled backward. In her haste to get away from him, she left the shovel in his hands.

She stood, a hand on her cheek as if he'd struck her. "That was uncalled for."

"So is your resistance to a polite offer of help." He hefted the shovel in his hand to begin, but Arabella stepped between him and the pile of soiled hay.

"I cannot let you do this," she said.

"Why not?"

"Because you will mar your clothing."

He should not have allowed her words to goad him further, but they did; she seemed to think him the most frivolous, empty-headed, selfish man to walk the earth. Perversely, he decided to prove her right. Smiling faintly, he leaned the shovel in the crook of his arm and began to undo the remaining buttons of his shirt.

Her eyes widened.

"What are you doing?"

"As you said, I can hardly clean out the stables while wearing white linen. Hastings would have an apoplexy."

"You don't have to remove your shirt." Her voice had an edge of desperation that urged him on.

"Oh, but I do." He pulled his shirt over his head, the cold air sending a welcome chill across his skin, cooling his ardor and allowing him to think clearly for the first time since he'd seen her in those damnable breeches. "There." He gestured with the shovel. "Now move."

Arabella stared at his chest as if fascinated and horrified at the same time. With apparent difficulty, she raised her gaze to his. "But you've never mucked out the stables in your life!"

"Then I am due, wouldn't you say?"

She glanced from him to the muck, a reluctant smile tugging the corner of her mouth. Lucien would have given his entire fortune to taste that smile, to plunder those soft lips and join the heat inside her mouth. The thought swirled straight to his loins and engulfed him in a wave of hot lust. To keep his thoughts away from his errant manhood, he stepped around her and went to work.

Arabella watched him, clearly struggling with herself before bursting out, "I am quite capable of doing this myself."

No one took their responsibilities as seriously as Arabella Hadley. Lucien supposed some sober and virtuous men would find that an attractive trait in a woman, but he found it damnably irritating. She possessed more pride than any ten women he knew.

Lucien rested the shovel on the floor and leaned over it until his mouth was inches from hers. "Arabella, I am going to muck out the stables. I am here, I am willing, and I can get it done in half the time it would take you."

"I doubt it," she snapped, not backing off an inch. "Dukes are notoriously poor at mucking out stables."

He grinned. Apparently she had regained her wits along with her temper. "Watch me," he said, and went back to work.

She raised her brows and looked away, her nails curled into her palms.

He shoveled steadily, flicking a glance her way now and again. Her back was rigid, her face a sea of conflicting emotions. In her brother's clothing, her hair a mass of wild curls across her shoulders, she looked all of eighteen and furious enough to slit his throat. It was not a propitious beginning. If she fought him every step of the way, he'd never get anything done. Hell, he'd almost had to undress to keep her from wrangling the shovel from him.

The thought unexpectedly amused him. Here he was, bare-chested and almost blue with cold, all from fighting for the right to muck out the stables. He chuckled.

"Put your shirt back on; it is freezing."

"Nonsense. It is warmer in here than it is in most of Rosemont."

Arabella forced herself to look away from that broad, muscular expanse of chest. Though it galled her to admit it, the old house did have the tendency to soak in the first chill of the season and hold it long into summer.

Arabella deliberately kept her gaze from Lucien. Had it been anyone else, she would have gladly accepted the offer of assistance. But she didn't trust him. Lucien Devereaux was a pleasure-seeking rake whose promises meant less than the soiled straw under her feet.

But try as she might, she could not dismiss the memory of Robert's face when he asked her if she did not believe him to be the master of Rosemont. Had Robert demanded that she leave off running the estate, she would have done so with a light heart. But since his return from the war, he had shown no interest in anything. Arabella could not refuse him the one and only request he'd made since his return—to allow Lucien to stay as his guest.

Unaware of her regard, Lucien bent to thrust the shovel deeper into the soiled hay. She scowled. Damn it. How was she supposed to argue with him when he stood before her half naked, the sunlight dappling his broad shoulders with gold, his muscles rippling beneath smooth skin she knew would be deliciously warm to the touch? Despite her vow otherwise, she found herself watching him.

He worked surely and smoothly. There was an innate grace to him that was as masculine as it was primal. It made her want to watch him whether he was on horseback, dancing in a crowded ballroom, or working like a common laborer.

He slanted a green gaze her way. "Do you always muck out the stables yourself?"

Arabella could only hope her voice sounded normal.

"Ned usually does it, but he's helping one of his sisters today. He has three of them and they all seem to believe he is theirs to command."

"And Wilson?"

Sebastian stole this opportune moment to nudge her. Arabella patted the horse, glad for the distraction. "He should be back this afternoon. He is helping one of the tenants patch a hole in their roof."

Lucien shoveled a mass of matted straw into the wagon. "How many tenants do you have?"

"Five families; they raise the sheep for us. We get twenty percent of their lambs and fleece."

"Only twenty?"

"I don't want them to starve," she replied defensively. It was an argument she and Mr. Francot had had many times.

Lucien quirked a brow. "You don't raise any sheep yourself?"

"Wilson, Ned, and I are much too busy. We supply the land and the cottages, and the tenants do the work."

"And Aunt Jane supplies the sheep tonic."

She nodded, then, unable to help herself, she blurted, "Lucien . . . just why *are* you here?"

"I am too wounded to travel."

"You couldn't shovel if your shoulder was still mending."

He regarded her a moment, his lashes casting shadows until his eyes appeared black. "Perhaps I found that I like the moors. They are quite beautiful."

"You cannot expect me to believe that."

His gaze narrowed and he set the tip of the shovel on the ground and rested his arm across the handle. "What *would* you believe? That I am staying for my own amusement? That the only reason I am here is to see if I can win my way back into your bed?" He reached out and brushed her lips with the rough edge of his thumb, his expression intense. "Would you believe that, Bella *mia?*"

Arabella was unable to move, unable to speak. All she could do was stare at him, fighting the longing his touch evoked. His hand lowered, skimming her throat and hovering where her coat parted to reveal her shirt. Her heart skipped a beat, and she waited . . . waited to see if it was leaping with joy or thudding to a tragic halt.

Pulling herself together, she took an unsteady step backward. "You shouldn't be here. You belong in London."

His hand dropped to his side as his face shuttered. Without a word, he returned to his work.

Arabella swallowed, feeling as if she'd hurt him in some way. Strangely, the idea left her feeling bereft. "If I were you, I would return to London as soon as possible. There is nothing for you here."

"No?" His gaze raked across her, making her prickle in places she'd rather not think about. "Are you certain?" His voice, soft and low, sent a trill of excitement through her.

Arabella had to fight the impulse to stamp her foot. It was frustrating, the way he could imply without words that she was the reason he was staying. To look at her so intently that she could feel the touch of his gaze like the brush of a feather on bared skin.

Suddenly the stable felt remarkably close and intimate, and she wanted to look anywhere other than at him, at his muscled chest and finely wrought thighs, outlined so well in his snug breeches. Arabella spun on her heel and clomped across the ground, glad for the solid thump of her worn boots. Muttering about the work she had to do, she set about harnessing Sebastian to the cart.

From the corner of her eye, she watched as Lucien

dropped the last shovelful into the handcart and then tugged his shirt over his head. The linen stretched smoothly over his shoulders and fell in soft creases to his waist. With his hair raked back from his forehead, his shirt undone and hanging free, he looked wild and untamed and as delectable as warm sugar cookies.

Trying to steady her breathing, Arabella gathered an armful of the short fence rails Wilson had prepared that morning. What was she doing, staring at Lucien like a moonstruck calf? She began to load the rails into the wagon, keeping her back to him so he wouldn't notice her hot cheeks. "I'll be back soon," she announced. "These need to go out to the south field. The fence must be mended before it rains."

"Then we'd best hurry." His voice sounded just behind her, husky with implied meaning, his breath caressing her ear.

Arabella squenched her eyes closed, a tremor of aware-ness making it difficult to think. If she didn't get some space between them soon, her traitorous longings would become obvious to the one man who should have no effect on her. Keeping her face averted, she said, "Thank you very much, but I don't need your assistance. I will see you when I return."

He didn't take the hint. Instead, he reached over and took the remaining rails from her arms and carried them to the wagon. He stacked them on top of the others, oblivi-ous to the damage done to his fine shirt.

It was, she decided with a dismal sigh, yet another example of the differences between them. The Duke of Wexford would never consider the cost of one simple shirt, even one that cost more than any two dresses she owned. "Hastings will not be pleased if you ruin your shirt."

Lucien ignored her and continued to load the wood

alongside her, stepping out of her way whenever she neared the wagon. After the last piece was placed inside, he slanted a hot glance her way. "Is that all of it?"

"Yes." She gathered her coat closer. "If you don't mind, please inform Mrs. Guinver that I will return in time for dinner." Without waiting for him to answer, she climbed into the wagon, sitting squarely in the center of the seat so that there was no room for anyone else.

She gathered the reins, aware of Lucien's warm gaze. Her breasts tingled as if he had stroked her through her heavy wool coat. Castigating herself for a fool, she had just reached over to release the brake when Lucien climbed onto the seat beside her, his coat slung over one shoulder. He unceremoniously nudged her aside with one hip, his large body pressed intimately against hers, his broad shoulder enticingly near.

"What are you doing?" she demanded, scooting away until the seat edge pressed into her thigh. Her entire right side burned from his touch.

"I'm helping you," he said.

"Please get down."

He shrugged into his coat and settled back, his feet planted firmly on the floor, his face set in immovable lines.

"Lucien, I will not have you—"

He bent and kissed her, his mouth claiming hers with a suddenness that gave her no time to prepare. His lips sent every last vestige of her control toppling, burning through her defenses until she moaned and clung to him as if she feared she'd fall.

Seconds later, Lucien broke the kiss with a muffled curse, his breathing loud in the stillness of the barn.

Arabella pressed her fingers over her lips. "What was that for?"

A smile softened the harsh lines of his face. "I just wondered if you tasted as good as I remembered." He picked up the reins from where she had let them drop and hawed Sebastian into motion. "And you do—just the way I remember. Like honey, all sweet and spicy. As if the bees had gotten into an herb garden."

It was nonsense, pure and simple. Practiced gibberish he used to trap innocent women into hopeless passion so he could abandon them when he desired. But she could not still the rapid pounding of her heart. "I did not wish to be kissed."

"Didn't you? I rather thought you did. Why else would you make such a fuss about my simple offer of assistance unless . . ." He slanted a long, slow glance her way.

She gathered her coat at her throat. "Unless *what?*"

"Unless you are worried my presence will awaken feelings you wish to deny."

"*Oh!* Of all the vain, useless, ridiculous things I have ever heard—"

"The lady doth protest too much."

Arabella balled her hands into fists and rammed them into her coat pockets. The braggart! The arrogant, conceited fool! She would love to box his ears until he begged for mercy. She shot a hot glare up at him and met his amused gaze. "I am *not* attracted to you, Lucien. Not anymore."

"Then you won't mind if I idle away my spare time by assisting you in your chores. I find them far more amusing than playing whist with your Aunt Jane."

Arabella set her jaw. Damn the man. What sins had she committed to deserve such a fate? She ground her teeth and stared at the passing fields. If she were fair, she would admit that it wasn't Lucien's fault that she became a mass of quivering jelly at the feel of his muscled thigh resting beside hers. After all, she had no illusions about him and he was being very honest about his reasons for staying— he saw her as a challenge, a passing game of fancy.

It was a good thing she had tight control over her passions, or she'd be lost for certain. At least she knew that whatever his dark purpose was in staying at Rosemont, it would soon come to an end. So long as she kept that firmly in mind, she was safe.

To make sure he didn't get the idea that she welcomed his presence, she leaned as far away from him as possible and said in an ungracious tone as they neared the far gates, "Turn right."

Soon the cart was bouncing down a narrow dirt road at a smart pace. They slammed into one particularly deep rut and Lucien swayed, his broad shoulder pressing against her breast.

Arabella tried to swallow, but found she couldn't. Frowning, she said, "The south field borders Lord Harlbrook's land and he is most insistent we keep our sheep away from his prize swine." She sniffled, her nose numb in the cold. "He is an experimental farmer, you know. He had three hogs brought over from Germany. Unfortunately, Wilson ran over one on the way to town a few weeks ago."

"Ah. That explains why His Lordship is so distraught to see the Hadley crest."

"He never knew it was us, though he suspects it. We buried the creature out in the moor."

"I suppose you volunteered this information when Lord Harlbrook came searching for his prize pig?"

"Of course not."

"How unneighborly of you."

"Wilson and I joined the search party," she said defensively. "We even invited Lord Harlbrook to dinner afterwards."

"And served ham, no doubt," he said, grinning as he pulled the cart up to the broken fence. He immediately hopped down and reached up to help her alight.

She hesitated, aware that her blood was already pounding from sitting by him.

His eyes lit with amusement. "Afraid, Bella?"

She stepped into his arms without another thought. As soon as his hands closed about her waist, she knew her mistake. The bounder didn't even have the decency to hold her through her coat. Instead, he had slipped his hands inside the heavy wool so that nothing but the thin linen of Robert's cast-off shirt and her own chemise separated Lucien's warm hands from her naked skin.

To make matters worse, he didn't release her as soon as her feet rested securely on the ground, as a true gentleman would. He stood holding her, his hands splayed across her sides, his fingers following the curve of her ribs, his thumbs nestled beneath her breasts.

The cold air disappeared, replaced by a thick, warm mist that seemed to draw her toward the wide plane of his chest. She remembered it well, knew the feel of those crisp hairs between her fingers, knew the curve of his hard muscles. At one time, she had reveled in the broad planes of his shoulders and the strength of his arms, nipping and tasting every bit of him.

Her cheeks hot, Arabella yanked away. "We have work to do," she said in what she hoped was a brisk, businesslike tone. She turned and began pulling the planks from the bed of the wagon.

After a moment, Lucien joined her and silently began to unload the remaining boards. For several minutes, they worked side by side. Despite the unnatural tension, Arabella grudgingly admitted that the extra assistance was a welcome relief, and for a few brief moments it was as if they were equals.

But no, she reminded herself bitterly, a pang flickering in her heart. Lucien would never consider himself her equal. He was a duke and well aware of his position. She tried to think of all the reasons he might be avoiding London. Gaming debts. Family obligations. An angry mistress, perhaps. *Probably all three*, she thought glumly. Regardless the reasons, once he'd completed whatever idle task had sent him to the wilds of Yorkshire, he would leave in the middle of the night and never return. It was his way.

Only this time, her brother would be hurt, as well. Having another man about had buoyed Robert's spirits. He was more vigorous, more alive than he had been since he'd returned from the war. What would happen after Lucien left?

But even her fears for her brother's welfare didn't help Arabella fight the flood of emotions that were being stirred to life by Lucien's presence, by the hot touch of his gaze, the lingering caress of his hands.

Pushing aside her untoward thoughts, she watched him slide the last slat into place. Hurrying, she climbed into the wagon before he could offer to help her up. The wind had risen during their labors, and heavy black clouds now loomed on the horizon. Lucien climbed into the wagon and took his place beside her, picked up the reins and then set Sebastian to a brisk trot.

He glanced down at her, his gaze hooded. "Well?"

"Well, what?"

"Aren't you going to thank me? I deserve that much, at least."

"Pish-posh. I'm sure it was all very healthy for you." She made a vague gesture. "The exercise. The fresh air. I daresay it is the most *useful* labor you have ever done."

She'd thought to insult him, but he merely grinned and said affably, "Most likely. But you are wrong on one account; the air was not fresh when I was shoveling out the stables."

She had to bite her lip to keep a chuckle from escaping. Somehow, her memories of him had not included his sense of humor. She wondered what else she had chosen to forget.

Lucien turned the wagon into the drive at Rosemont and pulled Sebastian to a halt in front of the house. "Here we are. Off with you, now."

"But I need to unhitch Sebastian and—"

"You don't need to do anything but get into the house. It will rain at any moment and at this temperature, you would be frozen solid in about two minutes."

It *was* cold and her shoulders ached from all of the shoveling and lifting. "Well. If you are sure you know how to—"

"Don't even say it." He glowered, a crease between his brow. "Just get down and let me take care of the horse."

"But you've never—"

"Damn it! Must you argue with everything I say?"

"Yes," she bit out, her pent-up emotions pouring forth. "I am a capable woman, Lucien, able to take care of myself and my family without your interference."

He stared at her a moment before saying in a quiet voice that nearly undid her, "I didn't mean to insinuate that you were anything else. I just wished to help, that is all."

She swallowed. "I'm sorry. I'm just not used to . . ." What? Handsome dukes who stripped to the waist and made her feel hot and restless?

Lucien's mouth quirked into a smile. "You are a stubborn woman, Arabella Hadley. Fortunately for you, I like stubborn women." He moved until his mouth was a scant inch from hers. "I like them best of all when they're within kissing distance."

She stared at his mouth, so sensuous and inviting. Pride, she decided, was a costly thing. Too costly when faced with temptation of such magnitude.

Gathering her wavering virtue, she scrambled down from the wagon and stiffly marched into the house. She barely stepped into the foyer when a huge rustle of wind signaled the beginning of a heavy rain. *Perhaps that will cool his ardor on the way to the barn.*

Muttering to herself about the difficulties of dealing with self-satisfied, conceited dukes, she tromped upstairs to change for dinner.

Chapter 11

"*By yonder blessed moon I swear . . .* " said a deep, mocking voice.

Arabella closed her eyes. *Please, God, not again.* She looked down from where she perched on a small stepladder trying desperately to juggle a hammer, three nails, and a broken shutter outside one of the library windows. Lucien stood below her, dressed for riding, his cravat immaculate, his Hessians gleaming. His arms were crossed over his powerful chest, his head tilted back as he watched her.

But his gaze was not fastened on her face. Instead he was openly admiring her posterior, which was embarrassingly at eye level. Thank goodness she was wearing a thick wool dress and a sturdy coat that had once belonged to Cook. She only wished the coat hung a bit lower.

"Perhaps it isn't a moon, after all," he murmured, "but the round warm sun, rising in the east."

She fought the temptation to toss her hammer onto his

rock-hard head. Every day for the last week, Lucien would find her engaged in some effort at setting Rosemont to rights, and he would pester her until she gave up her tools and allowed him to finish the task.

Actually, *pester* wasn't quite the word for his lingering glances and warm touches. But she had to admit that he'd managed to accomplish an amazing amount of work in the past week.

Until he was free to return to London, she would derive what benefits she could from his presence. She only hoped he would stay long enough to help her replace the broken door on the shed.

Not that Lucien showed any inclination to leave. In the ten days he'd been at Rosemont, he had entrenched himself so firmly that she was beginning to believe she would have to burn down the house to get rid of him. The worst part of the situation was the fact that Aunt Jane seemed to have ignored Arabella's confidences and sided with Lucien, doting on him constantly. That hurt more than it should.

And then there was Robert; he became positively surly if anyone so much as suggested something might be less than perfect with his new hero. Even when Lucien had disappeared two nights in a row and had not returned until dawn, offering no explanation to anyone, Robert had refused to admit there was anything untoward in such behavior.

Fortunately, she was made of sterner stuff. Arabella glanced down at Lucien and then pointed to the stables with her hammer. "Satan desires your presence in the barn. He is restive today and has twice tried to bite poor Sebastian."

"I daresay that broken-down nag deserved it."

Arabella couldn't argue with that; Sebastian was furiously jealous of the young gelding. "You should see to him. And while you are in the barn, you can feed and water the horses."

Lucien raised his brows, a flicker of amusement lighting his eyes. "I will gladly feed and water the horses, madam, once I finish here." He tilted his head to better examine her backside. "This landscape is far more to my liking."

Arabella didn't deign to answer, just tried to get the nail into the loose shutter so that she could hammer it in. For some reason, though, her hands seemed to have lost their ability to hold anything correctly and she dropped yet another nail into the bushes.

She stared at the thick shrubbery where the nail had disappeared. For the first time in her life, Arabella was at a loss. She had never felt so pursued, so hunted, and so out of control. Lucien Devereaux may have fooled her aunts, but he had not fooled her. She knew he was not visiting the taverns in Whitby to sample the ale.

Why was he still here? It was the first thought she awoke to and the last she had before falling to sleep, and she was determined to discover his underhanded reasons for herself.

Arabella glanced over her shoulder to find his gaze hooded and intent. He leaned against the railing, his arms crossed as if he planned to stay till doomsday.

He quirked his brows. "Shall I hold the ladder for you? I wouldn't wish you to fall."

The idea of him standing so close made her stomach tighten into a knot. "I am fine, but Satan won't be if you keep him waiting."

"What? And miss this lovely horizen? This breathtaking display of—"

"The barn has just as impressive a landscape. You can tell me about it when you return."

"You are much too modest. I've never seen a more impressive—"

"*Don't say it.*" Another nail slipped from her grasp and fell to the ground, joining a half a dozen of his slippery fellows. Arabella felt an urge to just toss everything—the hammer, nails, her whole wretched life—onto the ground and leave it all there to rot. She focused her ire on the nearest object. "Lucien, I wish you would quit standing there with that idiotic grin on your face."

"I cannot leave; the scenery holds me captive." His gaze ran over her, lingering on her face and hair, then returned lower. "Well rounded, full and complete . . ."

Arabella could just imagine his strong, lean hands on her, touching, seeking, causing her to burn as they once had. His fingers were long and elegant, his skin always warm as if an inner fire simmered just beneath the skin. Strange that she should remember that about him—the constant warmth of him even in the cold. Stranger still that he could heat her from three feet away.

A tremor shook the stepladder, and Arabella grabbed the edge and glanced down. Lucien's foot rested on the bottom rung, his knee grazing the back of her calf. He flashed a grin, his face just below hers. "It is certainly taking you a long time to fix that. Shall I help?"

She had a sudden image of his body pressed intimately against hers, of their legs entwined—"*No,*" she said, so firmly his lips quirked into a grin. "Move, Lucien. I need more nails." Indeed, she only had two left, hardly enough to complete the job.

Lucien shrugged and removed his foot from the ladder, though he did not step away. Arabella almost cursed aloud; there was no way to climb down without ending up quite literally in his arms. It was maddening.

Determined to ignore such impertinence, Arabella

climbed down and immediately rounded on him. "Isn't there something else you should be doing? Something *inside* the house, perhaps?"

Humor lit his gaze and he grasped the edge of the ladder with his other hand until he held her within a cage made of his strong arms. She leaned away, the rungs pressing into her back.

Lucien gave her a slow, lazy smile, his eyes gleaming the green of a moss-filled stream. "Poor Aunt Jane has sent me away for tangling her yarn. I am completely at your disposal."

"Lovely. A worthless duke. Just what I need."

"I am not worthless." He lowered his chin and whispered, "Just untried."

She choked. "In house repairs, perhaps."

"True," he replied. "In other areas, I am more capable."

"Yes—in philandering, worthless prattle, and being an alarming nuisance, I would say you are indeed a master."

His mouth hovered at her temple, his breath warm against her skin. "Don't forget kissing, holding, touching. . . . Would you like a demonstration of the areas I truly excel in?"

"Just fix the blasted shutter. I am not interested in anything except the work I have to do today."

His hand closed over hers, around the wooden handle of the hammer. "No?" His voice deepened a notch. "I remember a time when you were interested in many other things. When you begged me to show you more."

Embarrassment closed her throat. She yanked her hand away and he caught the hammer just as it fell. "I cannot believe you would mention that to me."

"Why not? Not all of our memories were bad." His gaze rested on her mouth. "Some of them have become my fondest dreams."

He was more stubborn than she remembered. And definitely more skilled in seduction. But *not* more trustworthy. She hunched a shoulder, refusing to look at him as he gave her one last smile, then turned and climbed the ladder.

"What am I to do up here, sweet? Just bang about until I hit something?"

Reluctantly, she told him what to do. It was already well past noon and she had a list of other repairs to see to before dinner. As he worked, she gathered her scattered tools and placed them back in the workbox. Perhaps Lucien's continued presence had something to do with his late-night journeys into town. If she could discover his true reason for lingering in Yorkshire, she might find the key to convince Robert to send him packing.

Lucien glanced down, his hair falling across his brow. "Are there any more nails?"

Arabella gathered the last of the fallen nails from the shrubbery and handed them up to him. A distinct jolt ran down her arm when his fingers closed over hers.

"Thank you," he said, glinting a smile that shook her to her toes.

She managed a brief nod, then moved away to watch him, mulling over his late-night trips. Most nights, he returned early enough to play chess with Robert. But each time, he reeked of smoke and stale ale. Almost as if he'd been visiting a lowly tavern.

Could that be it? Had he begun a flirtation with a tavern maid to while away the times he was not at Rosemont? She crossed her arms, an inexplicable wave of anger rising. It would serve her right for letting her imagination get the best of her, for occasionally daring to think that perhaps he was different, that perhaps she'd never before seen such a look of intensity in his eyes. Damn the man.

But she had to admit that Lucien was right about one thing: The view from the ground was exceptional. His strong thighs were braced against the rungs of the ladder, his backside outlined against the blue of the sky. She had always loved the strength of his legs, and the raw power of his corded thighs sent a shiver through her, tightening her breasts and heating her in the most unsuitable places. She unbuttoned her coat and tugged at her knotted neckcloth as Lucien hammered, his back muscles shifting beneath his shirt.

Lord, she was beginning to love linen shirts. Lucien had ruined at least half a dozen, and was ruining yet another as she watched. A pity he could cast aside hearts as easily as he cast aside his dirty linen.

He climbed down. "There. That should keep it in place for another hundred years or so."

"I have to refasten that shutter almost every year. The winds blow hard over the cliffs."

"Then I shall just have to refasten it."

"You won't be here." She took the hammer out of his hand. It would be good for her to remember that fact, too.

His brows drew low. "Bella, we need to talk about our past. About what happened before."

"There is nothing to discuss. I made a mistake, that is all."

"It wasn't a mistake, Bella. It was love."

"You don't leave someone you love, Lucien. You stay, no matter how much money you inherit. No matter what lofty title you win."

"You don't understand. You don't know what it was like—"

"Nor do you. You weren't the one left behind, with everyone watching you, wondering what had happened, your reputation in tatters."

His jaw tensed. "Bella, I didn't realize you would pay so dearly when I left."

"How could you not know?"

He raked a hand through his hair. "I suppose I didn't want to think about it, that it was easier if I just imagined you were happy somewhere, married to someone far better for you than I."

Arabella tucked the hammer into the wooden workbox, then hefted it with both hands, carrying it to the front step. There, she set it down and eyed the broken railing as if absorbed. But all the while, she was acutely conscious of Lucien standing behind her.

His voice broke the quiet. "You need to know what happened, Bella. For your peace of mind, if nothing else."

"There is no sense in dredging up a past neither of us can fix." She pulled the vise out of the box and set to work loosening the broken railing.

"I truly cared for you, Bella," he said in a quiet, insistent voice. "More than you know."

She sent him a flat stare. "There was a time when that one sentence would have cured everything. But it has long passed." She managed a casual shrug. "And I don't care to speak of it again."

He grabbed her arm and yanked her to face him, the vise she held clanging to the flagstone. His face was carved in hard lines. "I care, Bella, even if you do not. And I want you to know the truth. I had every intention of returning the next morning and asking for your hand in marriage. But when I returned to the lodge, I discovered my father had been in a carriage accident. I had to return to London immediately. I planned to write once I knew more, but he died within an hour of my reaching London. And then . . ."

He took a long, shuddering breath, as if the memory

haunted him still. "And then I discovered the extent of his folly, the true state of our family affairs." His green gaze shifted across her face. "We were completely ruined, Bella. The house, the lands, all of it was encumbered. Due to his bad management, he'd squandered what investments my grandfather had established and placed everything in jeopardy. And all for his own amusement."

Arabella tried to still the harsh pounding of her heart. Though she wished it were otherwise, she believed every word he said. It all made perfect sense; even to the point of explaining his marriage to an heiress. The anger she'd shored up in her heart still burned hotly, but the tiniest bit of the bitterness dispersed, set loose from a heart that knew all too well the pain of poverty.

If anyone could understand the burden of financial ruin, it was she. How many nights had she lain awake, wondering how to find the money to pay the bills, even put food on the table? More than she could count. Still, she pulled herself free and met his gaze with a direct one of her own. "Why didn't you write to me and tell me that?"

A huge band tightened about Lucien's chest. "I tried to, once or twice, but I couldn't find the words. Then, once I married Sabrina, I knew you'd want nothing more to do with me."

Anger sparkled in her eyes. "So you just left me to wonder? To worry that perhaps I had done something wrong? Left me here to think that I wasn't good enough to . . ." She turned away and grabbed up the vise, setting to work on the loose railing with abrupt, angry motions.

Lucien took a startled step forward. "Good God, Bella! My leaving had nothing to do with you. I was suddenly responsible for my sister and I hadn't a feather to fly with. Worse than that, we owed thousands of pounds."

"You should have written," she snapped. "I deserved that much."

She had deserved far more than that. He longed to touch her, to wipe away some of her pain, but he couldn't. What was done, was done. "I was a fool and I know it now. But I want you to realize that I—"

She dropped the vise and grabbed up the heavy tool-box. "Good day, Lucien. I have work to do." Without sparing him another glance, she marched toward the shed, her body tilted to one side to balance the weight of the tools.

Lucien looked down at his empty hands and sighed. He could fix the railing in an hour, maybe less. But how long would it take to mend Arabella's trust?

The thought made him frown. He would be leaving soon; his contact at the Red Rooster Inn was only a few days from giving him the names he needed. Once he had those, there would be nothing to keep him in Yorkshire.

Lucien watched as Arabella opened the shed door, only to slam it closed behind her. The latch missed and the door bounced against the frame, then swung drunkenly on its hinges. Lucien commiserated with the splintered wood.

Sadly, he had the feeling that this was just the beginning. Somehow, some way, he would set things right with Arabella.

Chapter 12

Dinner that night was grueling for Arabella. Lucien took every opportunity possible to torment her. She could not reach for the cream pitcher without encountering his long fingers placed there just a second before hers. She could neither say a word nor sit in silence without his dark green eyes resting on her, assessing her, caressing in their intent.

To Arabella's chagrin, Aunt Jane seemed pleased, her jovial banter encouraging the duke to new heights of flirtation, to new levels of delicious impropriety. Arabella could only wish she'd had the presence of mind to wear her boots to the table. At least then he'd feel it when she kicked his shins.

As soon as she could, she escaped to the privacy of the library. There, she settled at the desk and opened the ledger. Perhaps if she immersed herself in a sea of figures, the events of the past two weeks would fade away.

She propped her elbow on the desk and rested her chin

in her hand, staring blankly at the page before her. If she closed her eyes, she could still feel the sensuous rub of his chin against her cheek when he'd wrested the shovel from her hands. The memory sparked other, more intimate memories. *Intimacy means nothing to a man like him.*

To make sure she didn't forget it, she repeated the words aloud and added, "He is a duke, and he will never forget that. He is just amusing himself at your expense."

The words sounded much stronger when spoken aloud. But before she could form another bracing statement, the terrace door burst open and Wilson tromped in.

A line of snow skittered across the rug as he pushed the door shut. "Gor', but 'tis as cold as the devil's arse today."

"Just how cold is a devil's arse? I'm curious."

A slow blush rose up his neck and covered his already red-nipped cheeks. "Sorry, missus. That jus' slipped out."

She chuckled and pulled her shawl more tightly about her. "Did you make the deliveries?"

He removed his cap and stuffed it into a pocket, then dug into his coat and produced a hefty purse. "I only wisht we could get as much with every shipment."

Arabella tugged the leather string free. A stream of glittering coins poured into her hand. "Well! Almost twice what we expected."

" 'Tis the cognac, missus. They can't get enough of it."

"Neither can Aunt Emma."

His weathered face creased into a grin. "She has a fine taste fer spirits."

"Indeed she does." Arabella returned to the desk and pulled out a small brass studded box and an iron key. The cask opened with a loud click and the lantern light caught the glitter of neatly stacked coins.

All she needed was seven hundred more pounds and they would have enough to pay Lord Harlbrook's debt in its entirety. She rubbed a fingertip over one of the coins in her hand. That would be a day of celebration indeed. The intolerable man had been a constant thorn in her side since the day she'd taken over Rosemont. She remembered his irritation on discovering Lucien in the coach, and smiled grimly at his outrage when Lucien had so neatly cut the blustering man out. She would have paid twice her debt just to be rid of Harlbrook's obnoxious presence once and for all. Yet something told her that even after she paid the debt, he would try to force his way into Rosemont. Well, she would see about *that*.

"Ye look like the old master when ye smile."

"Pish-posh. Robert inherited Father's handsomeness, not I." She looked more like the portrait of her mother that adorned the morning room—small and unremarkable except for her large eyes, though even those fell short of perfection as they were plain brown, and not a romantic color like. . . . She had an immediate vision of Lucien's glimmering gaze, as green as new grass after a spring rain.

God help her, Lucien was every bit as handsome now as he had been all those years ago. She couldn't count all the times she'd imagined him older; his face lined and harsh, a bit of a paunch to his stomach from his debauched lifestyle, his hair sadly thinning. It had been one of her chief amusements, especially in the years immediately after his abandonment.

She scowled. The least he could have done was to have the decency to grow a few gray hairs.

Wilson pulled out a kerchief and blew his nose loudly. Brought back to the present, Arabella placed the new coins into the box and smoothed the stacks until they were all even. If all went according to schedule, she would have everything paid off within the next twelve months, with the exception of Robert's doctor bills. All she had to do was continue to pad the family coffers a while longer.

A sense of loss seeped into her at the thought. What would she do then? If she were honest, she would admit she was the tiniest bit addicted to the excitement. She loved the smell of the ocean, the unfettered freedom, and the knowledge that she was good at her chosen profession. Good? She smiled; she was better than good.

By God, let other women brag about their embroidery patterns and their ability to render a good watercolor—she was a first rate smuggler. Even Wilson had to admit that much, and he hated her being involved at all. She glanced at the groom who stood before the fire.

He wiped his nose one last time and stuffed his handkerchief back into his pocket. "How is yer duke this evenin'?"

She closed the box with a snap and twisted the key in the lock. "He is not *my* duke."

"Sorry, missus. It was jus' a turn of phrase."

Embarrassed at her overreaction, Arabella crossed to the hearth. "We must order another shipment of cognac. I will—"

"No, you won't," he said bluntly. "If there's more orderin' to be done, I'll do it." He shook his grizzled head. "Ye shouldn't have anythin' to do with this business, missus."

"Nonsense." She reached out and brushed a stray bit of straw from the edge of his collar. "How would you manage without me? They'd talk you into taking poorly turned brandy at twice the price."

"I ran it alone oft enough afore ye discovered what I was doin'," he responded gruffly.

"You were never alone. You had Twekes and Lem with you."

At the mention of his two burly nephews, Wilson snorted. "The only thing those two are good fer is loadin' and unloadin' the wagon. That and drinkin' up any profit ye might have left." He shook his head ruefully. "But I has to admit, Missus, ye are a born smuggler. No one can haggle like ye." At her smile, he hurried to add, "But that don't make it right."

Right or not, Arabella was not about to let Wilson bear such a burden alone. In a way, this profession put her on a par with her ancestor the Captain. She glanced up at the picture that hung over the mantelpiece. Her profession gave her an instant bond with the Captain. She could understand the sacrifice he must have made when he gave up roaming the seas and settled in his rose-colored house high on the cliffs. Arabella noted the arrogant tilt of his head and the fearless light in his eyes, and she wished she possessed even a tenth of his daring.

"Gor', missus, ye are a stubborn one." Wilson shook his head, his brows lowered. "What if the duke finds out what ye're about?"

She scowled. "The duke's presence does not affect our plans."

"He is as sharp as a pin, that one. I could see it in his eyes."

"More like a knife blade than a pin," she muttered, remembering Lucien's gaze in the carriage after they'd rescued him. Nothing got by that man.

"Ye said ye knew him, missus, but I don't recall ever havin' a real duke at Rosemont."

Arabella picked up the poker and stirred the fire higher. "Fortunately for us all, he will be leaving soon." *Please, God.* She turned to Wilson, anxious to put the topic behind her. "When will the next shipment arrive?"

"Not fer another fortnight. But afore it gets here, we need to do somethin' about Constable Robbins." Unease darkened Wilson's gaze. "I ran into him when I was comin' out of the King's Deer."

"What did he want?"

"He seemed mighty suspicious as to why I had traveled all the way to Littledean jus' to wet me thirst. Lord Harlbrook was there, as well. I think he knows somethin', missus."

"Constable Robbins would have already made an arrest if he knew anything of our business. Did they see you make the delivery?"

Wilson looked affronted. "Lawks no, missus! 'Tweren't no but me and Twekes and Lem, and ye know they can hold their counsel."

Wilson's large nephews were notoriously reticent. Despite the fact that they were perennial favorites at every local tavern on the coast, they possessed a natural tendency to silence. Arabella didn't think she'd heard either of them speak more than two sentences a row. "Perhaps we should hold off on the next shipment," she said.

"I hate to do that, missus, especially with the cognac in such demand."

Though she wished it were otherwise, Arabella agreed. She didn't want to disappoint their customers and they still desperately needed the money.

If only the constable hadn't suddenly become so interested in the smuggling trade, she thought resentfully. And that was apparently thanks to Lord Harlbrook's interference. If she could wave a magic wand and turn that spineless toad into the slimy worm he was, she'd do it without thinking twice.

Wilson pulled his hat from his pocket and pulled it low over his ears. "I'll send out the signal tomorrow, missus."

"Fine, and tell them to keep to the schedule. We'll just have to find a way to deal with Constable Robbins." But it was Lucien she was worried about. His constant presence made it difficult for her to slip away and attend to the shipments.

She scowled. He would be gone before the next shipment was due, even if she had to have Lem and Twekes carry him off. She turned to Wilson. "We need to check our stores and see what we have left. Meet me at midnight."

The old groom wrapped his muffler around his throat. "Very well, missus."

Arabella pulled her shawl closer and stared into the fire. "Only twelve more months, Wilson. Then the bills will be paid and we can return to normal."

"Master Robert should be up and about by then, too."

"I think he looks much better, don't you?" she asked eagerly.

" 'Deed I do, missus," replied Wilson in a stout tone. "Very lively, he's been lately."

She managed a very credible smile. "Thank you, Wilson."

The old groom's craggy face softened. "Ye're welcome, missus." He stepped to the terrace door, pulled his coat about his ears, and slipped outside.

Arabella shivered as cold air swirled about her feet and tugged at the edge of her dress. With renewed determination, she returned to the desk and bent over the ledger.

As if to mock her efforts, Lucien's deep laughter echoed down the hall, followed closely by Aunt Jane's boisterous laugh that sounded suspiciously like a horse's whinny.

She fought a sense of ill usage. Here she was, toiling away, trying to keep her family from ruin, and that spendthrift bounder enjoyed Aunt Jane's unalleviated adoration.

It was simply too much. She should march upstairs and tell him just what she thought.

She slapped the ledger closed and marched to the door, but just as her hand closed around the knob, she caught herself. What was she doing? The last place she needed to be was in a room with Lucien Devereaux.

Especially when he was in bed.

Half clothed.

His hair tousled, a lazy gleam in his green eyes, and the most devilish smile ever to grace a—

"Oh, for heavens sakes, stop that!" Arabella stomped back to the desk and dropped into her chair so hard, it slid back almost three inches. It wasn't just dangerous for her to see Lucien—it was lethal. She yanked the chair back into place, propped her elbows on the desk, and rested her chin in her hands. She wished her father were still alive to tease her from her despondency.

She reached into the desk and pulled out the letter he had written the day he'd taken ill, never again to rise from the sickbed. The short missive was filled with her father's broad charm and exaggerated blandishments, concerning a bet he had won—a rare happening in those dark times.

When it came to gambling, James Hadley had not been a lucky man. Of course, no one had been able to convince him of that. He always believed that his big win was just around the corner—only one flick of a card away.

She still missed his loud, joyous voice booming through the house, the feel of his arms crushing her against him when he hugged her good night, and the scent of pipe tobacco that had always lingered on the collar of his greatcoat.

But while James Hadley had loved his family, he had loved gambling more. Her hand tightened over the letter, her fingers creasing the edge.

"Pardon me," a deep masculine voice rumbled into the silence. "I thought I heard a mouse." Lucien entered the room, looking every bit as delectable as in her imagination. He was clad in a perfectly cut black coat that traced the line of his broad shoulders, his black breeches stretched over his powerful legs, his cravat intricately knotted and creased. He looked as if he'd just stepped out of a London ballroom.

Some hurts never faded. Arabella carefully smoothed her father's letter and replaced it in the drawer. "I don't know how you could hear anything over all the laughter coming from the sitting room."

He sauntered to the table by the fireplace and adjusted the decanter on the silver tray. "Robert and I were playing a rubber of whist with your aunts." His green gaze gleamed with sudden humor. "Lady Melwin is a feverish opponent, isn't she? I've never seen anyone more determined to win."

"Did you lose money?"

He made a comical face. "Worse—I won. Your aunt now owes me forty-two pounds."

Arabella tried to smother a pang of worry. She should speak with Aunt Jane about her gambling; the last thing they needed was more debt. Her obligations threatened to pull her under if she faltered for even a second.

But she would not falter. James Hadley may have left his family destitute, but his daughter would not forget her responsibilities.

She opened the ledger and sent a politely chilly smile toward her guest. "I hope you don't mind, but I must finish these accounts before Mr. Francot arrives tomorrow."

Lucien came to stand by the desk. "Mr. Francot? Ah, the stern dandy who fancies himself in love with you."

"Pish-posh," she replied, dipping her pen into the ink and setting to work.

He walked to her side and rested his hand on the edge of the ledger, his thumb smoothing the leather. "I don't wish you to be obligated to a man like that."

"A man like what?"

"A man who thinks he is in love with you."

"It is none of your concern who is in love with me and who is not," she replied sharply, then winced at how inane she sounded. What was it about Lucien that so disturbed her, that made her want to argue his every utterance?

"Hm." Lucien leaned over her shoulder as if studying the accounts. His hand slid down the ledger page as he read, and it was suddenly hard for Arabella to breathe. She stared at his long, well-shaped fingers as they came closer and closer to the bottom of the page. If he lifted his thumb, he would brush her nipple through her dress. A strange quiver passed through her and she had to fight the wild impulse to lean forward.

Lucien pointed to a sum. "Is this how much you owe Harlbrook?"

Arabella nodded, unable to speak for the torrent of emotions that skittered through her.

"I will write a draft to cover it."

"I don't want your money."

"Then consider it a loan. You can repay me when Rosemont is once again productive."

She kept her gaze on the desk. "I will *not* take your money, even as a loan. I already made that mistake with Lord Harlbrook and look where it has gotten me."

Lucien placed one hand on the back of her chair and pulled it around until she faced him. Anger simmered through him. "You cannot compare me to that fool."

Her hands tightened about the arms of the chair, her eyes sparkling. "Why not? At least he is forthright about his reasons for visiting Rosemont, while you pretend to have developed a fondness for Robert, who will be crushed when you leave."

There was no answer but the truth, and he could not share it with her. Not yet. Arabella stared back, her stubbornness showing in the firm line of her chin.

Her skin glowed in the lantern light, the soft blue of her dress making her hair appear even darker. Lucien was assailed with the desire to touch her, to thread his fingers through the silk of her hair. He took the quill from the desk and drew the feather down her cheek and across the soft curve of her mouth. "What if I promise to leave, Bella? Will you take the money then?"

Her lashes fluttered down over her smooth, warm skin. Lucien fought the urge to drop the feather and replace it with his hand, to caress her cheek. Damn, but she was as intoxicating as Aunt Jane's sheep tonic.

"Think about it, Bella," he murmured, sliding the feather over her bottom lip. "You wouldn't have to worry about Harlbrook, or paying Robert's doctor bills." The feather traced the firm line of her chin to her ear and then down the side of her neck to the sensitive area at the base of her throat. "And you could take all the time you wished to repay it. You would be free, Bella. Completely free."

For one brief minute, her lashes dropped and a quiver passed through her. Slow color heated her face and Lucien could see that she was fighting the sensation caused by the feather, fighting him. As he watched, her tongue touched the edge of her lip and Lucien's grip on the feather wavered, his blood heating to an instant boil.

God, but she was luscious, the simplest touch arousing her. Lucien loved that about her—even as he hated himself for using it to distract her.

Arabella took a shuddering breath and caught the quill

in her hand, yanking it from his grasp. "Lucien, *don't.*" A frown marred her smooth brow. "Why would you offer such a thing?"

Lucien shrugged. "I see you struggling and I want to help."

To his surprise, a smile flittered across her face, curving her lush lips, her eyes dark and mysterious. "Perhaps I am more resourceful than you realize."

He frowned. What could she mean? Before he could ask, she leaned over to replace the quill by the ink well.

When she turned, she was at eye level with his breeches, where his aroused state was painfully obvious. She turned bright red, shoved her chair back, and stood, knocking the ledger onto the floor. "I don't want your money and I don't want you here. I just want you to leave Rosemont. *Please.*"

Lucien bent to retrieve the fallen ledger. "Whether you like it or not, I'm staying until you accept my offer. Until then, all you can do is ignore me." Not that he would let her. The air between them was too charged, too hot. Just one spark and they would both be consumed yet again by the flames of their passion. He ached for her, ached for what was and what had been. "What do I have to do to get you to accept the money, Bella?"

She was silent for a long moment, then raised her eyes to his. "I want the truth, Lucien. What were you doing on the moors that first night? Why did you come back?"

For one mad instant, Lucien was tempted to tell her. But until he knew the nature of her connection to the smugglers, he could not trust her with information that could endanger far more than his own plans. "I will tell you when I am able. You have my word on it."

"And what good is that?" she said bitterly.

The words hurt like a saber slash to his heart, and he watched as she gathered the ledger and her papers and walked to the door. There, she turned and looked at him. "I will discover your reason for staying at Rosemont, and I will take great delight in exposing your real intentions to my family. They will never trust you again."

Then, in a whirl of blue, she was gone.

Chapter 13

Sir David Loughton swung out of the saddle. "Damnation," he muttered under his breath as his heel hit the ground.

"Gout a-botherin' ye agin, sir?" asked Wilson.

"It is a damnable thing, getting old." The baron wondered why he'd felt the need to come to Rosemont anyway, and in such weather. Truly he was getting soft in his old age, to be drawn along by nothing more than a mischievous impulse.

Wilson put a hand on his own neck. "Ever' time the wind blows, I get a crick in my neck that feels like one of Satan's teeth. Cook says it will go away if I sleep with a bag of garlic 'neath my pillow, but I'd rather die a horrible, painful death than try to sleep with garlic in my nose."

"Ha! I have to agree with you there. My doctor says spirits cause my gout to act up. But I'd rather put up with the aches than give up my port." He handed his reins to the groom. "Tell me, is there any more of that cognac you brought last month? It was superb." He slipped a coin into Wilson's curiously ready palm. "Bring me a pipe, will you? Two, if you can spare it."

The coin disappeared into the folds of the groom's faded livery. "As soon as it arrives. Ned is on his way to make a delivery this afternoon. Maybe he can find one or two fer ye."

"Excellent, Wilson!" He peeled off his gloves and tucked them into the pocket of his greatcoat. "And how are the ladies this fine morning?"

"Doin' the best they can, sir. The best they can."

The baron nodded. He and Wilson were compatriots in a way, self-appointed guardians of a brace of the stubbornest women to walk the earth. "I take it they are still blessed with their noble guest?"

Wilson's face folded into a scowl. "It's goin' on two weeks now. He's brought a curse on the house, he has. Jus' march on up to that door and ye'll discover how bad 'tis, see if ye don't."

Sir Loughton glanced up at the house, the leafless vines stark against the pink stone. Perhaps he should investigate this mysterious visitor. After all, with the amount of money the spirited Jane owed him, he might own Rosemont one day.

The thought made him chuckle. He had no more use for Lady Jane's money than he did the run-down manor. Unbeknownst to the interested population of Yorkshire, Sir Loughton was a wealthy man. A very wealthy man, although he dressed like a sober country squire and Loughton House boasted only four bedrooms and one decent-sized parlor.

Having come into his inheritance at a young age, he knew the disappointments that awaited those courted for wealth alone. At the tender age of seventeen, he'd barely escaped marriage to an avowed fortune hunter, coming to his senses just in time. Since then, he'd been cautious not to let anyone suspect his wealth and contented himself with short-lived flirtations with safely married women.

But in all of his years of confirmed bachelordom, none had had the power to fascinate him like Jane Hadley. A sudden crease furrowed his brow. It was inconceivable that he could feel such a strong attraction for such a woman. She was not his style at all, far too plain and gangly for his palate, which tended to favor younger, more rounded women. Not to mention that she was self-sufficient to a fault, stubborn to the point of belligerency, and the most thoroughly maddening woman of his acquaintance.

All this, and he hadn't even tossed her addiction to gambling into the equation. It was unfortunate that his less-than-gentlemanly impulses had overtaken him and, in a moment of weakness, he had lured her into wagering a huge sum. It was also unfortunate that he had compounded his error and refused to allow her to gracefully withdraw when it became apparent she could not pay. But her every breath seemed a challenge, and he'd refused to bend his knee to such impulses.

Having reflected over the distress he must have placed her in, though, he'd decided to relieve her of her anxiety and dismiss the wager.

Yes, he decided, feeling magnanimous, he would forgive Jane her debt. She would accept, albeit stiffly and without real gratitude, and that would be that—he could end an association that was showing a deplorable tendency to develop into something more than it should.

He frowned. For some reason, acting with such nobility of character didn't feel as fulfilling as he'd thought it would be. He glanced at Wilson. "Walk the mare a bit, would you? I won't be long."

"Ye don't think it?"

Sir Loughton nodded, annoyed at the knowing gleam in the groom's eye. "I am on my way to town and I haven't time to linger."

"Ye'll stop long enough to see the dook, won't ye? I don't trust him as far as I kin see him."

"After Miss Arabella, is he?"

"There ye are, guv'nor. I've always held ye was as sharp as ye could stare."

Though touched by such unexpected approbation, the baron merely nodded. "I will have a look at your guest. And if there is any question as to his respectability, I will send him on his way."

"If'n the ladies will let ye," Wilson said, suddenly glum.

"Is Miss Arabella favoring his suit, then?"

"It ain't her. It's Lady Durham and Lady Melwin." Wilson wrinkled his nose as he led the horse away. "It's the first time we've ever had a dook at Rosemont."

Sir Loughton glanced at the house. There had been one other time Rosemont had hosted a duke beneath its multi-garreted roof . . . but that had been long before Wilson's arrival, and long before Lady Jane and Lady Emma had come to stay.

He approached the door and knocked. After a prolonged wait, the huge oak door creaked open.

Sir Loughton stepped into the foyer and pulled off his bright muffler. "Hello, Mrs. Guinv—"

Instead of the glum housekeeper, an exceedingly correct individual dressed in somber black faced him. The paragon bowed with just enough depth to indicate his uncertainty as to Sir Loughton's title.

"Who the devil are you?" Sir Loughton asked.

The man looked down his long, thin nose, his sandy

lashes casting shadows across his colorless cheeks. "I am Hastings, my lord. The Duke of Wexford's valet."

"Wexford? So that's who—" He broke off when he encountered the valet's interested stare. Sir Loughton gave a short laugh. "I suppose it makes perfect sense, now that I think about it."

"Indeed," Hastings said, his expression holding just the faintest tinge of boredom. "Shall I take your coat, sir?"

Sir Loughton obligingly allowed the valet to help him shrug out of his greatcoat. He tried to alleviate the awkwardness of the moment with a jovial laugh. "You haven't been forced to pay for His Lordship's lodgings by serving as butler, have you?"

Hastings was not amused. After a lengthy pause that effectively melted Sir Loughton's grin, he permitted himself a small, polite bow. "Hardly, my lord. I am merely making myself useful, as I always do."

The tone implied that Sir Loughton had never done anything so noble. The baron had experienced enough seasons in London to recognize a master servant when he faced one. "It is very kind of you to help the ladies of Rosemont. You are to be commended."

"Of course, my lord," Hastings said in a voice that implied the valet thought the baron was being impertinent in even mentioning such an obvious fact. "May I ask for whom you are calling?"

"Lady Melwin. I came to see if she has a commission for me, as I am on my way to town. I am Sir Loughton, a friend of the family."

"Of course, my lord." Hastings opened the door to the morning room.

The valet waited until the baron had entered, and then he cleared his throat and announced, "Your Grace, Sir Loughton has just arrived for Lady Melwin."

Lucien looked up from where he was writing yet another letter to Liza and assessed his visitor. Tall and athletic in build, the man possessed distinguished white hair and a pair of piercing blue eyes.

Lucien smiled as he rose. "I believe you knew my father."

"Lud, yes. He and I were members of White's."

"Then you probably saw more of him than I." Lucien's father had ever been conscious of his standing, maintaining his memberships in the best clubs despite the wear on the family purse. "He once told me he felt more at home there than anywhere else."

A reluctant smile creased the baron's face. "Heard you'd been wounded, but you look right as rain."

"A minor injury I sustained when I fell from my horse. Miss Hadley found me and kindly brought me here for her aunts to patch up." Lucien sealed his missive and held it out for Hastings. The valet immediately crossed to take it and bowed his way from the room.

Loughton gave a sharp nod. "If you were in Jane's hands, then you were safe. I can't vouch for Emma." He tapped his forehead with a finger and said bluntly, "All wind, no bellows."

Lucien chuckled. "You seem very intimate with the household."

"I should. I hunted with James Hadley every year for fifteen years before he stuck his spoon in the wall." The sharp blue gaze pinned Lucien. "Did you know him?"

"I only had the pleasure of seeing him twice. Once here and once in London." Lucien shrugged. "He was a very well-spoken man."

"Hmmm. I thought you would have known him better than that."

"I wasn't allowed that pleasure," Lucien said shortly.

The door burst open and Aunt Jane swept in. "There you are, Your Grace! Arabella must visit the vicar to deliver some jams. I thought perhaps you could—" Jane came to a sudden halt when she caught sight of the baron. *"You,"* she said, her voice rich with loathing.

Sir Loughton grinned. "Who else, m'dear?"

"You are not welcome at Rosemont."

Sir Loughton chuckled. "Don't be a gudgeon, m'dear. No need to air your dirty laundry in public."

She cast him a dagger glance. "There is nothing we need speak about that cannot be said in front of the duke."

"Very well. If he is such a confidant that I can discuss your losses—"

"However," she continued, her accents as frigid as her glance, "since I am busy today, you may return to see me at another time."

There was such an undercurrent between the two that Lucien found himself wondering what had caused such unrelenting animosity on the lady's part and such keen interest on the gentleman's.

Sir Loughton shrugged. "I am free to discuss our business matters whenever you are."

"That is certainly accommodating of you," she said stiffly.

"It is, isn't it?" He crossed his arms over his barrel chest and rocked back on his heels. "Hm, let me see. I am free on Thursday. Perhaps I shall stop by at dinnertime."

"You cannot just invite yourself to someone's house. Of all the impertinent, rude, overbearing—"

"Arrogant, pompous, and boorish." Sir Loughton gave a wolfish grin. "I believe you called me those names just last night. Pray strive for some originality."

Last night? Aunt Jane and Aunt Emma had retired to

their room immediately after dinner. Could they have gone to Sir Loughton's? But why?

Jane's glare would have sent a normal man into immediate hibernation, but Sir Loughton was made of sterner stuff. "Till Thursday, then." He stared at her from beneath bushy brows, openly challenging her.

Jane's mouth folded in frustration before she finally burst out with a testy, "Oh, very well. Come to dinner. I don't care." She stomped to the door, her color high, her shoulders ramrod straight. "And pray try to find some proper clothing."

Sir Loughton blinked his surprise. He looked down at his sober brown coat. "What's wrong with—"

But it was too late; Jane had already whisked out of the room.

Lucien pursed his lips in a silent whistle. "Well."

Sir Loughton grinned, deep laugh lines appearing to either side of his eyes. "Don't let her bluff you. It is the way of the Hadley women, you know. They don't like to feel dependent on any person." Sir Loughton gave Lucien a long, shrewd look, then stuck out his hand. "I must be going, but I enjoyed meeting you."

Lucien shook the baron's hand, then moved to open the door. "Shall I walk you to your horse?"

"Thank you. I'd welcome the company." Sir Loughton limped out the door, accepting his coat and hat from Hastings and then progressing to the front step. Once there, out of hearing of the servants, he shot a hard look at Lucien. "How long does Your Grace plan to stay at Rosemont?"

"A few more weeks, perhaps. Why do you ask?"

The old gentleman's blue eyes didn't waver. "Just wondered. I heard you were staying only until you'd healed, but you seem fit to me."

"I daresay I would be in worse case, except Aunt Jane happened to have some of her sheep tonic at the ready."

"Good God! Surely she didn't!"

He looked so alarmed that Lucien felt it necessary to add, "Lady Melwin assured me it wasn't poisonous."

"I'm damned glad to hear it. What in the hell was Jane thinking to allow such a thing? That woman needs to be—" He clamped his mouth closed, his brows lowered. "I beg your pardon." He walked silently beside Lucien, a frown on his face. "I say, while you were ill, you didn't happen to hear what was in this tonic, did you? It is the most damnable thing, but Jane and Emma have discovered some sort of sheep . . . I don't know. A sheep love potion, I suppose you would call it."

Lucien choked.

Sir Loughton reddened. "Oh, it sounds foolish, I know. But since they started dosing their flocks, they've tripled the number of lambs."

Lucien stopped. *"Tripled?"*

"Or more." Blue eyes surveyed Lucien from head to toe. "How did it make you feel? I mean, did it . . ." The baron reddened even more. "I was wondering how the potion worked. Supposedly, it besets the sheep with lust."

Lust? Oh, Lucien had experienced lust, all right. Unfortunately, it was the same lust that had flamed him to intemperate actions all those years ago. The sheep tonic had nothing to do with it. "All it does is make one very, very sleepy."

The old gentleman's face fell. "Is that all?"

"Perhaps you should ask for a sample and see for yourself."

Sir Loughton gave a rueful shake of his head. "If I did that, I would have to admit that there's a possibility that this tonic works." A twinkle lit the blue eyes. "Jane would never let me forget it."

From across the stable yard, Lucien watched as Arabella and Ned turned the old cart onto the road. Sensibly clad in a gray coat that would have made a farmer's wife proud, Arabella held the reins and urged Sebastian to a brisk trot. The wind tossed her hair, tugging long chestnut strands free so that they blew across her cheeks and wrapped beneath her chin.

As the cart turned onto the road, its bed came into view. Two large, tarp-covered mounds were clearly visible, with straw sticking out of the sides. The perfect place to hide casks.

Lucien took a step forward. He had to saddle Satan and follow them, discover if they were—

Sir Loughton's voice came from behind him. "An amazing woman, Arabella Hadley. Keeps Rosemont running almost single-handedly."

With great difficulty, Lucien managed to nod politely, his every instinct to race after them. "She shouldn't be going out by herself."

"Ned is with her."

"You obviously haven't had the benefit of speaking with him."

Sir Loughton chuckled. "Bubbleheaded, isn't he?"

"Yes," Lucien said shortly, watching as the cart rumbled from sight. He raked a hand through his hair. "You could as easily tell a dead person to roll over as tell Arabella Hadley to be cautious."

"You seem to know her rather well." The baron's hard blue gaze met Lucien's again. "I hope you don't mind my asking, but as a friend of the family, just what are your intentions regarding Miss Hadley?"

"My intentions are every bit as honorable as yours are toward Lady Melwin," Lucien returned instantly.

Sir Loughton gave a bark of laughter. "I suppose you have me there. It is none of my business, anyway." He held out his hand. "I am glad you came to Yorkshire, Your Grace."

"As am I." Lucien shook the offered hand.

As he watched the baron ride away on a showy chestnut, Lucien cast one last, grim look toward the road where Arabella and Ned had disappeared, then turned and stalked to the stables. He had a sinking feeling that a certain man by the name of Mumferd would know exactly what was happening at Rosemont. Cursing his suspicions, he saddled Satan and rode toward the Red Rooster.

Chapter 14

Night was her favorite time. Arabella loved the endless black of the sky and the wildness of the sea. Breathing deeply of the tangy salt air, she reached the low stone wall that lined the cliff and peered back over her shoulder at Rosemont.

The house was shuttered in darkness, one solitary window gleaming with light.

Lucien. Arabella stared at the light and murmured, "I wonder what you are into now."

Every day, he received mysterious letters, and on one occasion had left the house immediately, setting out on Satan and returning well after dark. She knew where he spent his days, for he was invariably by her side. But his evenings remained shrouded in mystery.

She kicked at a loose rock in the garden path, huddling deeper into her coat. She'd wanted to follow him, but Sebastian was simply no match for Satan.

The wind lifted, cold and unrelenting, and Arabella

began to look longingly at the flicker of the fire she could see reflected on the walls of Lucien's room. Not that she wanted to actually be in *his* room, of course. Any room with a warm fire would do. Still . . . she could just imagine how warm and toasty it would be: the fire flickering in the grate, the huge curtained bed nestled in the corner, the faint scent of candle wax in the air, and Lucien . . . She closed her eyes and imagined him sleeping in the great oak bed, his hair tousled, his jaw dark with the faintest hint of a shadow, his long lashes covering his remarkable eyes.

Asleep, he would look younger and more boyish, though nothing could detract from the air of latent sensuality that hung about him like the heady scent of sandalwood. Even sound asleep, he would have the power to make any warm-blooded woman yearn to touch him, and trail her lips across the line of his jaw.

Stop it, she silently admonished herself. She sank onto the hard, cracked marble bench beneath the oak tree and shook her head. Obviously, the days of working side by side with Lucien were taking their toll. She shivered as a gust of wind rushed across her, bathing her in icy cold and rattling the branches over her head.

She hugged the coat closer and sank her numb chin into the voluminous folds. Here, on the cliff edge, the wind blew stronger than anywhere else. Even on a calm day, a steady current of air sliced up the cliff face and pummeled the oak tree in a constant struggle to see which was stronger. It was a wonder that the old gnarled oak still stood, but it did, huge and craggy, with thick limbs that stretched out to the sea, defiant to the end.

Restless, she stood just as the crunch of gravel alerted her to Wilson's arrival, and she turned to see him emerge from the gate. His face was barely discernible in the dim light.

"Are ye ready, missus?"

"Yes." She took the lantern he proffered and turned to lead the way down the path. The trail was stiff and rocky, filled with treacherous dips and stones, but she walked with the ease of familiarity. The path followed along the cliff face, one side solid rock, the other thin air and deep blackness, filled with the smell and taste of the sea.

As she rounded the last curve, the path angled down a rocky, grass-faced ledge. The wind rose, buffeting the rock face until she thought she could feel it tremble beneath her boots. The moon appeared only periodically between huge black clouds that roiled uneasily over the dark sea.

After what seemed an interminable time, they turned the last bend. They were now almost to the bottom of the cliff and approaching a large boulder. In the light from the lamp, it appeared that the trail went directly to the rock, then stopped. But as they came closer, one could just discern where the path took a sharp left turn and disappeared into a narrow crack in the cliff wall.

Arabella lifted the lantern as she stepped into the crevice. A sudden gust threatened to extinguish the light, but two more swift steps brought her into the damp, still air of a cave.

From behind her came Wilson's heavy-booted feet. "If'n we don't hurry, we'll be caught in the tide. 'Tis harsh tonight."

"Then we'll hurry."

" 'Tain't always that easy when yer dealin' with two numbskulls like my nephews." Still grumbling, he took the lantern from her and led the way. The narrow tunnel was treacherous with low ceilings and broken ground, but to Arabella and Wilson, it was as familiar and unremarkable as the entryway at Rosemont.

They rounded a corner and stepped out into a large cavern. There, the hollow dampness rose bold and bleak. The cavern was only half the size of Rosemont's great hall, but since the lantern shed only a pale circle of light, the blackness left the impression that they had just found the edge of eternity.

She and Robert had found the cave long, long ago. Robert had been certain that this was where the Captain's lost treasure was hidden. They had searched for weeks with the wholehearted zeal of children, but they'd found only a few markings on the wall and some broken pottery.

Wilson took a step into the cavern, bumping his head on the low ceiling of the entryway. He cursed, his rusty voice echoing hollowly. Large black puddles stretched out before them, the edges white with sea foam. When the tide came in, water overflowed the cavern wall, filling the cave with brackish salt water until it resembled a lake.

Right now the lake was only partially filled, barely touching the bottom lip of the ledge. But when the tide was high, both entrances were completely submerged. Then, only one corner of the cave remained dry—a ledge high to the right.

On the ledge were signs of habitation: several lanterns hung on pegs, the remains of a small peat fire, and a cot that had been shoved against the back wall. The rest of the high ledge was covered with barrel after barrel of the new shipment.

Arabella clambered up the broken rocks that made steps to the ledge, Wilson behind her. He went to light the other lanterns as she silently counted the barrels.

She frowned. "I count only eleven. I thought we paid for fourteen."

"We did. Where are those blasted nephews of mine?" growled Wilson, looking around. Nothing met his gaze. Yet before he turned the lantern back to the shipment, a longboat came into view through the opening to the sea.

"Late as usual," muttered Wilson sourly. He lifted his voice to call, "Where have ye been, ye clot-headed shallypin?"

The longboat slipped into the circle of light and Arabella could see the huge, lumbering sailor who rowed. The man was as thick as an oak, every limb seeming wider around than a cask. He nodded a greeting and pulled the boat to the little ledge.

Twekes and his brother Lem were Wilson's only flesh and blood. Huge and simpleminded, they were amiable and good-natured.

Seeing Arabella beside Wilson, Twekes grabbed his cap and gave a respectful dip of his head.

Arabella nodded pleasantly. "Where's Lem?"

"Comin' behind me."

"Why?" Her brow cleared. "Ah, the other barrels."

Twekes nodded.

"Excellent. Did you see Mr. Bolder?"

"Aye," Twekes said. He used his paddle to hook a rope threaded through an iron ring and secured the boat against the ledge. "Smarmy bastard," he added without rancor.

"Twekes!" Wilson sent an uneasy glance at Arabella. "Watch yer mouth!"

The giant pursed his lips, a deep crease in his brow. "I cain't think of no better name fer him."

"Then don't call him nothin' at all," Wilson snapped.

Twekes shook his shaggy head. "Ye'd call him that or

worse if ye knew what he was about. The blighter refused to give us the last three barrels." The huge man gave a sly grin. "Lem and I waited till most of his men were on shore and then we rowed out and took a peek fer ourselves."

"What did ye find?" Wilson asked.

"That smarmy bastard standin' there on his ship, casks stacked as high as his head. When I told him we'd just take the ones he owed us, he refused. Said he had more important people to see to than us and ordered us off his ship."

Wilson's face turned bright red. "We've already paid fer that shipment!"

Twekes nodded. "So we loaded our boat wif what he owed us. He didn't like that none and he ordered his men to shoot us."

"Heavens!" Arabella said, alarm tightening her chest.

Twekes shrugged. "There were only four men on board and they been samplin' the merchandise." His grin widened. "They shot holes in their own sails."

"Good fer them," Wilson said. "That good-for-nothing, cheatin' bast—" He clamped his mouth shut. "Wisht I could get my hands on him. I'd clean his bones and toss him into the ocean fer the fish to nibble."

"Weel, now," said Twekes, "that's a good thing to be sure."

"*What's* a good thing?" Wilson asked.

"That ye want to see him. Once we had all of his men trussed up and our barrels in the skiff, the fool jumped in and wrapped hisself about one of the barrels and refused to leave. At first we were goin' to toss him to the fishes. But then Lem decided that maybe ye'd want a word with him." Twekes nodded slowly. "So we jus' left him in the boat. Lem is bringing him here."

Wilson blinked. *"Here?"*

Twekes nodded, evidently pleased with himself.

Arabella closed her eyes and pressed a hand to her forehead.

Wilson's reaction was louder. "Ye idiot! Ye fool! Now he'll know all about our secret hideaway!"

Twekes rubbed a sausage-thick finger across his nose. "That's what I said to Lem. But he said he'd fix it all right and no one'd be the wiser."

As if summoned, the sound of another boat made its way into the small cave. A skiff cut through the water, three barrels proudly resting in the center. Lem steadily pulled at the oars, while in the bow seat sat a plump man, his greasy hair slicked back from a small, cruel face, a wide muffler tied over his eyes. He gripped the sides of the boat as if terrified of falling over, his throat moving convulsively with each wave.

"Damn idiots," breathed Wilson.

Arabella bit back an agreement. "I'm sure they felt they had to do something. We've four months' profit tied up in this shipment."

He sighed, his shoulders sagging. "Perhaps. Best ye cover yer face, missus. Don't want anyone to be able to identify ye."

Arabella pulled her muffler free and covered her head and most of her face, leaving only a small sliver to see out of.

The skiff pulled up to the ledge and Lem obligingly stepped out. "Ye can take off yer blindfold."

The fat man grabbed the cloth and yanked, sending a furious glare at Wilson before scrambling out of the boat, no small feat for a man of his girth. Neither Lem nor Twekes made a move to assist him, but watched with appreciative grins.

Wilson stepped forward. "Mr. Bolt, ye—"

"That's 'Bolder,' " the man corrected with a black scowl, his shifty gaze darting around the cavern as if trying to memorize every nook and cranny. "I warn ye, if I'm not back with me ship within the hour, me men will come fer me, make no mistake."

Wilson spat into the tide. "How? They don't even know where ye are."

The smuggler's face reddened. "Ye're makin' a mistake, I tell ye! Jus' wait."

Arabella made an impatient gestured toward the barrels. "All we want is our cognac." She nodded to Lem and Twekes and they began to unload the boat.

"Wait!" Bolder started forward, his face flushed a furious red. "Some of that is fer me other customers."

"Nonsense," Arabella said. "We paid for three more barrels. Those belong to us."

"Not these barrels. They are promised to someone else."

"Mr. Bolder, you will either give us those casks or return our money this very instant."

"I don't haf yer money wif me." A nasty smile curved his mouth. "And even if I did, I wouldn't give it to ye."

"Tell me, Mr. Bolder. How long can you tread water?"

His brows drawn, he shot an uneasy glance at the skiff where it rocked gently.

Arabella continued. "Lem will not return you to your ship until we've settled our differences. And this cavern has a most unfortunate tendency to fill with water when the tide is high." She pointed to where the water was already beginning to rise. "With the exception of this ledge, the entire room fills with water."

His face darkened. "Then I will stay on this ledge."

"Lem and Twekes wouldn't like that. There is only one cot, you see."

Lem nodded solemnly while Twekes grinned and flexed his big hands.

The smuggler pointed to the cave entrance that led to the cliff path to Rosemont. "Then I'll jus' find me way out through there."

"You are a very brave man," said Arabella admiringly. "I think that would be an even worse way to die."

"Die?"

"Wandering about the caves with no food, no water, no light, for days on end. Thinking each corner will bring you to the surface, only to find that you've been going ever deeper with each step."

Bolder tugged at his collar. "I'd find me way out if'n I had to."

Wilson snorted. "Ye'd be starved afore ye found the way out. That or the snakes'll get ye."

"There are . . . snakes?"

Twekes nodded. "Bigger than my arm." He flexed his impressive arm for emphasis.

Mr. Bolder seemed unable to look away from the massive sinew. He wiped a hand over his damp face. "I—I'll let ye haf two of the barrels, but no more."

"We paid for three."

Muttering darkly, Bolder grabbed the nearest cask, set it at his feet, and placed his fat rump on it. "I'll let ye have all but this one," he said with a belligerent scowl. "It's me last offer."

Thump. A knife landed blade-down, biting into the hard wood of the barrel beside Bolder's plump thigh. The man jumped up, turning a furious face to Twekes. "What was that fer, ye poxy whoreson?"

Twekes rubbed his jaw, the rough scrape of whiskers loud against his callused hand. "It slipped," he said finally.

"Ye idiot! Ye could have killed me!"

"Now, Mr. Badger—" began Wilson.

"That's 'Bolder.' B-O-L-D-E— Oh!" he broke off, his face dark red. "I'm wastin' me breath on the likes of ye."

Wilson stiffened. "I know my letters, I do. And my numbers, which is more than most can say."

Arabella hurried to intercede. "I'm sure our guest is willing to leave all three of the barrels he owes us. Aren't you, Mr. Bolder?"

Twekes pried his knife loose from the barrel and began paring his fingernails, the innocent expression on his face making even Arabella wary.

Mr. Bolder's eyes never strayed from the knife. "Ye'll pay fer this, all of ye!"

" 'Tis time ye crawled back to yer hole, Bolder," Wilson said. "We'll not be doin' business wif ye again."

"Tide is rising," commented Lem. He lumbered to the small skiff and sat down, grasped the oars, and looked expectantly at Bolder. "Best put yer muffler on and tie it tight. If I thinks ye're peekin', I'll put out yer blinkers and toss ye overboard."

Bolder cast one last furious glance at the cask. "Damn ye all!" he snarled. With furious, jerky movements, he climbed into the boat and retied his muffler.

Wilson pointed a finger at Lem. "Jus' drop 'im on shore and come back."

Lem nodded and Twekes gave the small craft a shove. Mr. Bolder's hands gripped the edges and he yelped nervously as it righted itself. Lem grinned and began to row, slipping past the mouth of the cave and into the sea beyond.

Arabella unwrapped her muffler from her face as she turned to Wilson. "What a repulsive man."

"A pain in the arse. But he don't worry me as much as the constable."

Arabella glanced at Twekes. "Did you have trouble?"

"Well, the constable weren't much help."

"And jus' what does that mean?" Wilson asked, sending a disgusted look at his nephew. "That he didn't assist ye in loadin' up the cart? Or that he was shootin' at ye whilst ye were drivin' away?"

"Neither. But he *was* sittin' on the road from Whitby, watchin' fer us."

"And?" Wilson asked.

"Nothin'. He was jus' watchin'. Lord Harlbrook was wif him, too."

"We will have to keep an eye on him." Arabella took a sheet of paper out of her pocket and smoothed it over the barrel. "You can begin deliveries after Lem returns. Two casks of cognac go to the Red Rooster, one to the King's Deer, and four barrels to the Sad Nun."

Twekes nodded, then slipped the list into his pocket. Water had crept into the far entrance and steadily seeped upward. Only a few more feet and it would reach the mouth of the tunnel that led back to the cliff path.

"We'd best go, Wilson," Arabella said. "The tide's rising."

Wilson and Arabella made their way out of cave, walking quickly to outrun the storm they saw approaching. Arabella's mind churned. The confrontation with the smuggler bothered her. The location of their cave could hardly remain a secret now. It would be difficult, but they would have to find another hideaway.

Wilson and Arabella reached the cliff path without mishap and retraced their steps past the old oak and through the garden. There, they separated without a word,

Wilson crossing to the barn while Arabella hurried toward the marble terrace. Just as she reached the bottom step, the rain broke and poured from the heavens, drenching everything with an icy lash.

She stumbled across the slick marble to reach the library doors, and it was with wet, numb hands that she managed to open the door.

Surprisingly, a gentle blaze crackled in the grate, warming the room. Teeth chattering, she crossed swiftly to the fireplace and stood shivering, water dripping to form a wet ring on the rug around her feet.

"Where have you been?" The voice cut through the silence of the room.

Arabella stiffened and turned. Sitting in a chair, wearing a red velvet robe over his breeches, was Lucien. His skin gleamed golden in the warm light of the fire; his eyes darker, richer. The robe hung open to the waist, exposing his broad chest and a fascinating trail of black hair that narrowed to a point that disappeared behind the belted tie. The draped material across his hips and thighs outlined every hard angle, every corded muscle. The sight sent a pang of heat through her that stilled her chattering teeth.

She cleared her throat. "I was in the barn, seeing to the horses."

He stood with the grace of cat, his mouth thinned with displeasure. The light glinted off his black hair and played across the hard planes of his face. "I looked for you in the barn. You weren't there."

She felt vulnerable, standing there drenched to the skin, her hair plastered down the sides of her face. Vulnerable, yet eager. Lucien circled her, taking in the soaked, shapeless coat, the clinging line of her breeches, and her muddy boots. Both hot and condemning, his gaze devoured her.

Arabella lifted her chin. "I don't have to explain my actions to you."

Lucien grasped the lapels of her coat. Arabella took a hasty step away, but a low stool sent her teetering backward.

He caught her, moving with the swiftness of a predator, his hands catching her just before she fell and pulling her upright. Once she'd regained her balance, he yanked her coat off and threw it to the floor.

"Do you know how cold it is out there?" He exuded a raw anger, and a potent sensuality that stole the last of her breath. "Only a fool would wander around in a winter storm."

She calmed her thundering heart, her numb lips making it difficult to speak. "It wasn't that cold until it rained."

His gaze drifted over her hair, her face, her mouth, to the nearly transparent linen shirt that clung to her breasts. Arabella crossed her arms, an embarrassed flush warming her momentarily. A fat drop of water trickled down her cheek and threatened to spill over her mouth.

Lucien rescued the drop, his finger brushing across the curve of her lip. He lifted his gaze to hers, the thick lashes casting shadows until the green appeared black. "Where were you, Bella? What were you doing outside?"

It was so hard to make her brain work. "I—I went to visit one of the tenants—"

He gripped her arm in a painful grasp. "Don't lie to me."

"Lucien, I—"

He jerked her against him and claimed her mouth with a furious kiss, overwhelming her so thoroughly that she melted, her chilled body instinctively seeking his heated flesh. Desire washed over her, tearing down her resistance, destroying all thought.

His hands molded her to him, his fingers exploring, seeking through the wet material. Arabella shivered from the wild heat of his hands as they stroked her through her wet shirt, pulling her farther into his arms, her thinly covered breasts pressed against his bare chest. She twined her arms about him and opened her mouth beneath his, losing herself to the raw power of his onslaught.

With a muffled curse, Lucien broke the embrace, his breathing harsh in the silence of the room. "God, Bella." He cupped her face in his hands, his fingers sunk into her wet hair. Hungrily, he gazed down at her. "I want you."

He whispered the words as if they were too painful to say aloud. Arabella slid her hands to the opening of his robe and her trembling fingers found the tie at his waist. Slowly, she slipped it loose, the brush of velvet against her bare hands increasing her desire.

The robe slipped from his broad shoulders and fell to pool at his feet. She stepped back to look at him, soaking in the picture of raw male virility. In that instant, she wanted him more than she'd wanted anything in her life. She wanted to feel his arms about her, she wanted to taste the dark sweetness of his sensual mouth. She wanted him naked, fierce and passionate, boldly making love to her as he had done so long ago.

Arabella closed her eyes, remembering how she'd once reveled in passion, welcomed its presence. She wanted to burrow into Lucien's strength and take it for her own. What did it matter if he left tomorrow? She would have the memories of tonight to hold to her long afterwards. This was what she'd wanted, what she'd dreamed of. She opened her eyes and drew his mouth to hers, her fingers tangling in his hair, her hips lifting. She poured herself into the kiss, thrusting her tongue into his mouth in reckless invitation.

Lucien responded hungrily. *This* was the woman he'd lost; her arms wrapped around him, her body plastered to his. It was madness, but it was a heady madness. Like deep sweet red wine, her presence raced through his veins and sent his senses reeling wildly. He needed to have her closer, needed to feel her naked skin against his.

Never breaking the kiss, he placed her hand on his bare chest while he slipped his breeches free. His heart beat hotly against the coolness of her palm. Grasping her wrist, he pushed her hand lower, to his stomach, to his hip. He groaned when her fingers closed over his rigid shaft.

Desire poured through Lucien, heating his skin and swelling his manhood until he wanted to roar in agony. He tasted the salty sweetness of her skin and traced the delicate line of her neck with desperate nips and kisses. She moaned and gripped him tighter, her fingers jolting him with pleasure.

God, but she was so inherently honest in her reactions, every move igniting him further. Growling his frustration, Lucien slipped his hands to her waist and pulled her against him, rocking his hips against hers. He tugged impatiently at her shirt, pushing it aside until he could cup the fullness of her breasts. They filled his hands, the nipples already hardened.

He groaned at the feel of those lush globes. Slowly, he backed her against the settee and lowered her to its cushioned softness. She lay against the pillows, her damp hair curling wildly about her, her eyes slumberous with desire.

He loosened her breeches, then bent before her, rolling her wet clothing down, over her hips, down her thighs, his tongue worshiping each inch of dewy skin as it appeared. When he reached the dark triangle at the juncture of her thighs, he stopped, his breathing harsh.

He lifted his head to gaze at her. She watched him, her eyes passion-glazed, her lips moist and swollen from his kisses. Her skin was flushed to soft shell pink, the flickering light caressing the slopes of her full breasts. She looked like a painting, a luscious portrait of a woman who wanted to pleasure and be pleasured. Excitement glimmered over her bare skin, urging him on.

Lucien bent to the tight curls and carefully parted them, finding the soft folds beneath. Her hands moved convulsively as if for one frantic moment she would stop him. But he reached up to lace her fingers with his, then he bent and blew on her damp curls. A quiver traveled across her body, and she gasped, her hand tightening on his. Lucien lowered his mouth. He tasted her sweetness, her erotic response. He savored the scent of her, the feel of her skin beneath his tongue.

Heaven was here, between her thighs. He strained with the need to bury himself here, to sink into her heat. With a groan, Lucien raised himself and covered her body with his. They lay, legs entangled, her arms about his neck, her breath hot on his neck.

For a long moment he savored the contact, riding the swells of his rising fervor. It felt so perfect, so right. She belonged to him; her body so attuned to his that he could feel her need as acutely as his own. It had felt this way before. But this time, Lucien wanted more. More than Arabella had to give. More, even, than he was willing to ask.

Arabella sensed the change the moment it happened. He stilled, his body suddenly rigid, his face set in unyielding lines. The length of his manhood lay against her naked thigh, so tantalizingly close that she had to use all of her force not to lift her legs and force him to sink into her.

He lifted himself on his arms and looked down at her, his face a mask of frustrated passion. "I want you, Bella. But not like this." He placed a gentle, lingering kiss on her lips. Then he sat back and pulled the lap blanket from the back of the settee over her.

Arabella lay still. The heavy fabric of the settee was rough on her back, and her ankles were bound by the breeches that tangled about her feet. She bit her lip, so confused she didn't know whether she was going to laugh or cry. Her body ached with need, but the hollowness of her heart pained her more. He was leaving again.

Lucien rose to his feet and watched her with a dark gaze, arrogant in his nakedness. "I don't want you to wake in the morning and wish we had not been together." He reached over and brushed a hand over her cheek. "I wish—" He broke off. "But not yet."

He turned to gather his discarded breeches. Without a word, he pulled them on and then laid his robe across her lap. "Wear this back to your room. Your clothes are too wet."

Arabella managed to nod, afraid she'd burst into tears if she attempted to speak.

Lucien tipped her face to his. "We will talk about this tomorrow, when daylight has dispelled this madness." He brushed her cheek with his fingertips and then turned and walked to the door. There, he sent her one last heated gaze. "Good night, Bella." The door closed softly behind him.

The fire hissed, filling the silence that followed. Arabella remained on the couch, wondering blankly what he meant. Her mind refused to respond even as her spirit struggled to absorb his words.

For one instant, she had let her tiredness weaken the barriers she had painstakingly constructed around her heart. Her face burned to realize how close she had let him come, how near they had been to making love. She should be thankful he had stopped when he did.

Sighing, Arabella forced herself to gather her wits and stand, scooping up Lucien's robe. The soft fabric carried his scent and she rubbed it against her cheek. After a long moment, she placed the robe on the back of the chair and reached for her breeches. Somehow, wearing his robe seemed to emphasize her defeat. With nerveless fingers, she struggled to pull her wet breeches over her hips, though they adhered to her skin.

Arabella wanted to blame him, to say that he had lured her, but she knew that was untrue. She had *wanted* him to kiss her, to touch her, to make love to her. And if she were honest, she would admit that she still wanted him to do all that, and more.

She sniffed, her lips trembling as she pulled on her shirt and then buttoned her wet coat to her throat. She couldn't handle honesty tonight. She needed to forget Lucien Devereaux, and focus on making the cognac runs even more profitable.

A deep, bone-weary sigh escaped her. Only one more year, and she would have everything she needed. The thought did little to slow the tears that seeped from beneath her lashes.

Chapter 15

The Red Rooster was unremarkable in that it offered moderately edible fare, contained two damp and drafty taprooms of questionable cleanliness, and possessed an equal number of large, smoking chimneys. What made the tavern such a popular locale was the guaranteed quality of drink it supplied to its patrons in a seemingly endless quantity. To the inhabitants of Whitby, it was the closest thing to heaven.

Lucien took a long sip of the tavern's finest. When he'd first visited the Red Rooster, he'd attracted considerable notice. Now that he'd been to the tavern over a dozen times, no one spared him more than a glance. They assumed that the fine ale brought him back time and again. Normally, they will be right—this quality of spirits could hold the attention of a monk.

But today nothing kept his attention, due to an abundance of hot, sultry memories that continued to dance before his eyes. He took a huge swallow of his drink, hoping his overactive imagination would cool. God knew he couldn't ache worse than he did now.

Every sinew of his body felt pulled, fraught with frustrated desire. Last night, it had taken every drop of will he possessed to walk away from Arabella and go to his cold room. He hadn't slept a wink, but had tossed and turned, his mind and body ablaze.

Yet his unrelenting passion was nothing compared to the realization that Arabella was far more deeply involved in free trading than he'd realized. The evidence was overwhelming, and in his fury at realizing what had been under his nose the entire time, he had allowed his emotions to overcome his good sense.

Last night should never have happened. If Arabella decided to come to his bed, it wouldn't be under a cloud of suspicion. He wanted her to tell him the truth. No, he decided, scowling fiercely. He wanted more; he wanted her to trust him.

Bloody hell. Since when has that become important? So important that he'd hesitated on the brink of making love to the woman he'd dreamed of for over ten years. With a groan, Lucien raked a hand through his hair. He was on edge, his mind and body barely in control. And there was no way free.

It had been a relief that Arabella had been little in evidence all day, having chosen the company of Aunt Emma in an effort, he suspected, to keep from being alone with him. He was grateful for the extra time to gather his defenses.

He stared morosely into his tankard and silently consigned his precipitous passion to the devil. What little ground he had won through assisting Arabella in the past two weeks was lost. Now she would be even more determined to get rid of him.

If she demanded it, Lucien would refuse to leave. His hand tightened about the tankard until the metal bent. How deep was she involved with her smuggling venture? Was she simply dispersing cognac and other spirits? Or had she been seduced by the promise of quick wealth into doing something far more hazardous—like bringing in a shipment of jewels that would provide enough funding to keep Napoleon's regathered forces supplied for months?

Lucien shoved his tankard away, sloshing ale on the wooden table. *No.* Arabella Hadley may have been forced by difficult circumstances to have commerce with smugglers, but she was not a traitor. Hell, hadn't her beloved brother fought against Napoleon? Robert was even now confined to a wheelchair, so affected by the torture and pain he'd seen that his frozen mind would not allow him to walk. No, it was impossible that Arabella had anything to do with the stolen jewels.

The tavern door opened and a furtive-looking man slipped in. Dressed in clothing stiff with dirt and sweat, he blended well with his surroundings. The patrons glanced at him and, finding nothing of interest, returned to their murmured conversations.

Mumferd immediately found Lucien, then made his way to the table. "There ye are, guv'nor. Sorry 'bout the time." The man's eyes focused on Lucien's emerald ring. "I brought ye the information ye requested."

"And?"

Mumferd rubbed a dirty hand across his chin, his little eyes flickering around the room before he leaned forward and murmured, "The auction will be next week."

"Can you get me in?"

"Determined to get yer hands on them jewels, ain't ye?"

"Some people collect relics, some coins. I collect more valuable things." Lucien reached into his pocket and withdrew a small leather bag. He hefted it in his hand a moment before tossing it to Mumferd.

The informant caught it with both hands, pulled the leather tie free, and peered inside. "Gor'!" he exclaimed softly, his eyes wide. "These must be wort' a fortune!"

Lucien reached over and retrieved the bag. "I bought them in Suffolk at just such a sale as is to be held here." He tilted the leather pouch into his palm and a handful of diamonds rolled free, glittering in the dark tavern.

"Easy, gov'nor!" whispered Mumferd hoarsely, glancing wildly around the alehouse. "Don't be flashin' them gewgaws in 'ere! There are some who'd as soon slit yer gullet as look at ye."

Lucien picked out one small, perfect diamond, returned the rest to the bag, and then secured it beneath his coat. "Don't worry; my man is just outside."

"It will take more than one man to protect ye from the likes of this crowd."

"Not when that man is Hastings. My valet possesses some rather unusual skills." Lucien placed the diamond on the scarred table. "Mumferd, I want to be in that auction, whatever the cost."

The man stared at the diamond that winked on the dark table. Lucien carelessly rolled the gem with his forefinger until it came to rest directly in front of Mumferd.

With an almost convulsive movement, the informant's fingers closed over the gem. To Lucien's amusement, Mumferd lifted the stone to the light and squinted at it with an expert eye before stowing it away in the folds of his clothing. "I'll get ye in, guv'nor. See if I don't."

The tavern door flew open and the entryway was filled with the broad form of a man. He stepped into the room, ducking beneath the timbered ceiling, his thick neck rising above shoulders that reminded Lucien of ham hocks.

Behind him came another man, equal in size, with reddish hair instead of brown. They were impressive figures, but it was the person who followed them into the room that riveted Lucien's attention.

Wilson.

Mumferd scowled and spat onto the wood floor.

"Do you know them?" Lucien asked.

"Wilson and 'is nephews? A bunch of troublemakers, if ye ask me."

Lucien watched as the three approached the inn keeper and began a lively discussion. "They seem to be on good terms."

"Aye, they provide the innkeeper wif a barrel or two. To hear him talk, ye'd think they were the only smugglers fer miles. The truth is, they haven't the balls of a goat." He curled a lip, a sullen cast to his face. "A pity, too. 'Tis a job fer real men, smugglin' is. But they let that Hadley woman run the ship, and—" He suddenly recalled himself, clamping his mouth shut and sending an uneasy glance at Lucien.

Nausea settled in Lucien's stomach. Bloody hell, what risks had she taken to ensure the welfare of her family? "What do they run?"

"Brandy, cognac, and such. Nothin' like what ye are lookin' to find." Mumferd grinned, his blackened teeth gaping. "Those I work wif are the only one as can provide that."

At least Arabella wasn't involved with the stolen jewels. Still, each time she accepted or delivered a shipment, she was placing herself in grave danger. And knowing her, she probably thought she had everything well in control. But Lucien knew better.

The problem with Arabella's pretty little neck, he decided, was that she stuck it much too far out for her own good. "I suppose Miss Hadley's involvement is common knowledge?"

"Only to them as is in the know. Why are ye askin'?"

"I have interests at Rosemont," Lucien said grimly.

The informant gave an unpleasant smirk. "Lord Harlbrook will be none too pleased to hear about that."

"I don't care about that pompous ass," snapped Lucien.

"Easy, now! 'Tis common gossip he has an eye on Miss Hadley. Her father owed Harlbrook a hatful of money. Harlbrook's always had a soft spot fer Miss Hadley and he expected she'd marry him to settle the debt. But she wouldn't haf nothin' to do wif him. To make matters worse, I hear she's been payin' him every month, and on time, too."

"And he knows she doesn't have the kind of income to do such a thing," Lucien said grimly.

"Harlbrook thinks 'tis Wilson who has been free tradin' and he's determined to stop him." Mumferd sniggered. "Won't he be surprised when he finds out 'tis his lady love and not just her servant?"

"Harlbrook is a fool." Lucien stood and placed a coin in Mumferd's dirty hand. "Notify me about the auction as soon as possible." Without waiting for a reply, he turned and crossed to the door, his thoughts dark with worry.

Just as he reached the door, it opened and Mr. Francot entered. He stopped on seeing Lucien, an instant flush rising to his face. After a moment, he gave Lucien a quick bow. Lucien nodded and watched as the solicitor made his way to a lone table in the far corner.

The Red Rooster was busy this evening. Lucien wondered if he would have the opportunity to see Lord Harlbrook before the moon set. Jaw clenched against the thought of the pompous lord setting a trap for Arabella, Lucien left the tavern and headed to the stables.

Hastings was just emerging, Satan's reins in his hand. "Ready to leave, Your Grace?"

"Yes, but I am not returning to Rosemont just yet." He vaulted onto Satan's back. "I've something to see to first. Miss Hadley is involved in the smuggling operation at Rosemont."

The valet's gray eyes searched Lucien's face. "You are certain?"

"Her servants were in the Red Rooster haggling with the innkeeper. And apparently it isn't a secret: Mumferd knew all about it, the weasel."

"If he knows, then others do, too. This is quite a quandary, indeed."

It was worse than a quandary, it was a dilemma of gigantic proportions. And Arabella was daily placing herself in danger. The memory of her standing by the fire, drenched and shivering, her lips white from the cold, made his heart ache. *God, what a coil.* He was honor-bound to protect a woman who seemed to thrive on danger.

"Hastings, return to Rosemont and inform them that I will not be home for dinner. Tell them I rode to York on an errand and have not yet returned."

"Very good, Your Grace. What will you do?"

"Follow Wilson and his nephews. I want to know where they keep their store."

Hastings reached into his coat and withdrew a pistol, then handed it grip-first to Lucien. "You may need this. It is already loaded."

Lucien tucked the pistol into his waistband. "Always ready, aren't you, Hastings?"

The pale eyes flickered. "It is my job, Your Grace. Lady Hunterston would expect no less." He mounted his own horse, pausing to say dryly, "Pray try not to ruin your shirt. It is one of the few we have left." With that, he bowed his head, then turned his horse onto the road and was quickly gone from sight.

Lucien sat silently for a moment. He wanted to go to Rosemont and demand that Arabella give up her smuggling venture, but how could he ask her to cease supporting her family the only way she could?

"Damn her pride," he muttered. Somehow, some way, he would free Arabella from her connection with Harlbrook—even if he had to pay off the bastard in secret.

A flake of snow landed on Lucien's arm, followed by another and another. He sighed and turned Satan into a small copse of trees opposite the Red Rooster. As he sat in the dark, images of the dire consequences that lay in wait for Arabella began to form. He could see her imprisoned and alone, held in a squalid cell with no hope of escape.

A knot formed in his stomach and he realized Aunt Jane had been right: His actions ten years ago had set an entire chain of circumstances into motion, circumstances destined to lead to disaster. He stirred restlessly and Satan nickered, moving an uncertain step.

"Easy, fellow," Lucien murmured, patting the glossy neck, thinking of Wilson's less-than-quiet discussion with the innkeeper. With his large nephews hanging over his shoulder, the old groom did not seem intent on keeping his presence a secret. All in all, it was the sign of someone secure in his position, someone unafraid of reprisal.

Lucien brushed at the snow that had gathered on the brim of his hat, his heart easing somewhat. Perhaps things weren't as desperate as he thought.

The door to the Red Rooster slammed open and Wilson scuttled out, followed by his nephews. He dispatched them to collect their wagon and within minutes, they were lumbering down the lane toward the coast.

Lucien followed, staying a discreet distance behind.

They rumbled along to a hidden winding road that followed the slope of the cliff to the shoreline. The path cut steeply, but the cart traveled without pause through the blowing gusts of snow.

The road finally came to the bottom of the cliff and then turned sharply and went back along the shore. The sea winds blew strongly here, masking sound so completely that Lucien no longer worried about staying so far behind.

Finally, Wilson halted the wagon and Lem and Twekes clambered out. Lucien guided Satan to a small stand of brush off the path. As he tied the horse, the distant blink of a mellow gold light caught his eye from up above the cliff. He looked up and gave a grim smile. *Rosemont.*

He patted Satan, then returned to the sandy path and walked quietly toward the halted cart. He came to an abrupt halt twenty feet away—the cart was deserted, its occupants nowhere to be seen.

Lucien frowned. Where could they have gone? Except for the scraggly brush, there was just solid cliff and ocean. Just as he was about to turn away, he caught sight of a small dinghy making its way along the coast. Lem and Twekes rowed, their powerful strokes sending the little craft shooting toward two large black rocks that jutted out of the sea. Wilson sat in the bow and barked instructions.

Were they meeting a ship? But no. The ocean was far too wild, the rocks too treacherous. The small dinghy turned abruptly and headed straight between the rocks and toward the cliff face. The water rose and swelled, slapping at the small craft, but Lem and Twekes rowed steadily.

Lucien watched intently as the boat disappeared into the black rim of the cliff. *A cave.* It had to be. No wonder it had been so difficult to obtain evidence of Rosemont's smuggling. They had the perfect hiding place.

A short time later the boat reappeared just as suddenly as it had disappeared. This time it rode noticeably lower in the water, a brace of casks lashed inside. Moving with powerful strokes, Lem and Twekes rowed to shore, landed the craft, and loaded their booty onto the cart. Wilson's gravelly voice could be heard over the wind, complaining about his nephews' slowness.

Lucien watched from a patch of brush a scant ten feet away, obscured by the falling snow and the black night. He longed to move, his feet numb, his fingers aching with cold even inside his gloves. But he held as still as possible. Soon the cart was loaded. Lem and Twekes hefted the boat to one side and covered it with brush. Dousing their lamp, they set it behind a large rock and clambered back into the cart.

Lucien waited until the cart had turned the first wending curve before he slipped out, placed the lamp into the boat, and then dragged it back into the sea. It was a Herculean job, but he welcomed the struggle, as it warmed his feet and hands.

As soon as the surf lifted the boat, Lucien climbed in and began to row. The steady splash of the oars urged him on. He aimed the boat between the two rocks and headed straight for the cliff, slipping into the dark cave with remarkable ease. The rising tide was quickly filling the opening, though, and he had to duck his head to keep from hitting it on the low-slung rock.

Once inside, he lit the lamp, though the farthest reaches of the cavern remained enshrouded in eerie darkness. Straining to see across the black, roiling water, Lucien found a ledge where a group of casks rested.

Heart pounding, he guided the boat to the ledge and tied it to a waiting post. The remains of a cold fire and a cot sat on the ledge, surrounded by a towering stack of casks that reeked of cognac. He lifted the light and examined each cask.

One caught his attention. Smaller than the others, it sat to one side as if ready for delivery. Lucien rolled it to its side and looked for a marking of some kind, but found none. He pushed the cask upright with his foot and heard a scraping noise, like nails against wood, faint and slight.

He dropped to his knees, his throat tight. *Bloody hell.* Could he have been wrong? He looked about for a way to open the cask, but could find nothing. As he glanced around, he noticed that the boat was closer to the ledge now, the rising tide lifting the level of the small cavern lake until it almost obscured the opening. Another few minutes and he would be trapped inside.

"Damn!" He grabbed the cask and carried it to the boat, then he freed the skiff and jumped in. Cursing, he rowed toward the opening. Only a sliver of light separated the waves from the mouth of the cavern, the small space opened and closed with each swell of brackish water.

Lucien tightened his grip on the oars. He would have to time this carefully. He didn't want to think what would happen if a wave slammed the boat against the rock face.

He maneuvered the skiff to the opening, fighting the tide and struggling to hold it in position. Then, just as a wave hit the rock, he shot forward with a mighty stroke of the oars, throwing himself into the wet floor. The small dinghy caught the back swell of the wave and dipped down, under the mouth of the cliff, and lifted out on the other side, the twinkling of the stars welcoming him.

Lucien struggled upright, grabbed the oars, and rowed as hard as he could. He was frozen, wet, and thoroughly exhausted when he finally dragged the small boat ashore and covered it once again with brush.

Grimly, he picked up the small cask and carried it to a

flat rock by the sea. Lifting it over his head, he smashed it. Cognac gushed out—and there, glittering on the black rock, lay the damnable evidence. His heart sank as he collected twelve brooches and a large ruby necklace, which winked like black blood in the dim light.

Refusing to think about the meaning of his discovery, Lucien tucked the jewelry in his pocket and then collected Satan and began the arduous journey back to Rosemont.

His mind whirled with the harsh reality that Arabella might be involved in the sale of the jewels. Though he'd seen the proof himself, he could not believe it—*would* not believe it. Lucien urged Satan to a gallop as soon as they hit the main road. He had to see Arabella—and this time, he would discover the truth.

As he rounded the final curve of the drive, he saw two riders dismounting at the door. Lucien immediately recognized one of the horses as Lord Harlbrook's. And if it was indeed the stubborn lord's, then the other horse would belong to the constable.

Lucien pulled Satan to a halt, his mouth painfully dry, his heart thundering in his ears. Arabella's pride be damned—there was only one way he could save her now.

Chapter 16

"**D**on't look at me like that," Arabella muttered at the Captain, who smirked at her from the library wall as she paced the carpet. "If anyone has the right to look smug, it would be Lucien. I all but fell into his arms last night."

She brushed a hand over her eyes and wished she could remove the discomfiting memories. She wished that one moment of weakness, brought on by the excitement of a black, starry night, had never happened.

The worst part of it was that she couldn't blame Lucien—she had been a more-than-willing participant. Even now, she could taste the passion that had flamed between them and she longed to feel his hands on her bared skin once more.

But it had always been that way. Despite the gap between their circumstances, the physical pull between them was as hot and passionate now as it had been ten years ago.

How could she face Lucien after such an embarrassing display? No doubt he'd spent the better part of the day congratulating himself on his nobility in stopping their lovemaking when he had. "Damn good of him," she muttered.

She glared at the Captain's portrait. "This may shock you, but it would have been far better if he had finished what he'd begun. At least then I could have gotten some sleep last night without wishing he'd—" She stopped, her face and neck hot. Thank goodness neither Aunt Jane nor Aunt Emma were nearby to hear her make such an admission; they'd probably burst into tears at the thought.

Arabella crossed her arms and resumed her pacing. She *had* to keep firmly in mind the fact that she was the only one with anything at stake in this relationship. For Lucien, Rosemont and everything connected with her was a momentary diversion and nothing more. Once the newness wore off, he would be gone.

The only good outcome from last night was that it had forced her to come to a decision. It was time Lucien left Rosemont, and if he did not leave on his own accord, she'd get Lem and Twekes to do the honor for her. The thought brought her some comfort as she imagined all the ways Wilson's nephews would toss Lucien out on his ear.

The clock chimed a gentle reminder of the hour, and she turned to look at it, frowning. Lucien had been absent from the house since early this morning, not even returning to eat dinner with the rest of the family.

The door opened and Mrs. Guinver entered, a troubled frown on her face. "Sorry to bother ye, missus, but 'tis the constable. He's come with Lord Harlbrook and he demands a word with ye."

The constable and Lord Harlbrook. Arabella smoothed her skirt of sprigged muslin, proud to see that her hands did not tremble. "I certainly hope Lord Harlbrook has not lost another pig."

Mrs. Guinver brightened. "Daresay he has. Shall I show them in here, missus?"

"Yes, that will be fine."

The housekeeper bobbed a quick curtsy. Arabella tried to still the wild thudding of her guilty heart. She knew it was more than another lost pig. Knew it with a certainty that robbed her of lucid thought. She should be afraid of going to gaol and the humiliation of being arrested, but all she could think about was Lucien's reaction when he discovered that she was no more than a common smuggler.

She stiffened, her pride returning in a flood. Who was he to judge her, anyway? She was certain that during the course of his sordid life he'd done worse things than sell a cask or two of unstamped cognac.

A heavy step announced the arrival of Lord Harlbrook. He entered quickly, his small eyes assessing her as he approached. Constable Robbins followed.

"Lord Harlbrook. Constable Robbins." She dipped a swift curtsy. "Pray have a seat."

"We've no time, Miss Hadley," the constable said. "Though I'm glad to see ye looking so well. Ye certainly appear—"

"We've come on business," Harlbrook interrupted. "*Important* business."

The constable shot a frowning look at the lord before turning back to Arabella. "I apologize fer inconveniencin' ye, but I've a weighty matter that needs tendin' to."

Arabella nodded, gripping her hands tightly behind her back. "I trust no one has been injured?"

"No, no," said the constable hastily. "Nothin' like that. We've just' come to—"

The door opened and Lucien walked in. To Arabella's surprise, he was dressed in evening clothes, his hair brushed back from his face, a fresh white cravat tied about his neck in an intricate weave.

His eyes found hers and, in that instant, she realized that he knew everything. The knots in her stomach clenched tighter. How had he found out? *God, what must he think of me now?*

She wanted to explain to him what had occurred, why she had taken such a drastic step, but he turned away and nodded a greeting. "Gentlemen. I trust nothing is amiss?"

"This is none of your concern," Harlbrook said, scowling. "We are here to see Miss Hadley on private business."

Lucien's mouth curled into an insultingly brief smile. "What's wrong, Harlbrook? Indigestion? Try some Italian soda. It is said to be amazingly restorative."

Harlbrook reddened, but before he could say a word, Constable Robbins managed a ponderous bow. " 'Tis good to see Yer Grace in such fine spirits. As old Mr. Hadley is no longer wif us, God rest his soul, and young Mr. Hadley is not in the way of bein' able to advise Miss Hadley, perhaps ye should stay and hear what we've come to say."

"That will not be necessary," said Harlbrook, his stocky frame stiff with outrage. "I will advise Miss Hadley myself."

"Aye, well, I'm thinkin' she needs someone else," said Constable Robbins, sending a dark glance at Harlbrook before returning his gaze to Arabella. " 'Tis bad news I bring ye, Miss Hadley. Bad indeed. A ship was seen off the coast last night."

"I see," Arabella said. "Did it sink?"

Lucien smothered a grin. She was going to make it as hard on them as possible. *Pluck to the backbone.*

"No, it did not sink," Harlbrook said impatiently. "It landed at Robin Hood's Bay in the dark of night and unloaded a considerable shipment of illegal spirits. We have evidence that someone at Rosemont received part of that shipment."

Arabella lifted her brows, her face just a fraction above chilly. Lucien wanted to step between her and the constable, to shield her from the questions, to protect her from Harlbrook's insolence. But she would not appreciate his interference. He had to settle with shoving his hands into his pockets and trying to contain a desire to solidly thump the brash lord.

She said in a quiet, calm voice, "Constable Robbins, surely you are mistaken. I'm certain that no one here is involved in such a . . . a horrendous undertaking."

"Nonsense," Harlbrook snapped. "I've known Rosemont was involved for weeks. And we know who it is, too."

Arabella's only reaction was a slight fluctuation in the color of her cheeks. "Lord Harlbrook, however much you may wish it, you are not responsible for my welfare. And I would thank you to remember that fact."

Harlbrook's face darkened, but before he could speak, the constable stepped in the breech, tutting loudly. "There, now, Miss Hadley. 'Tis a horrible business, this is. And ye'll be jus' as surprised as I was to discover such shameless happenin's here in our quiet little corner of the world."

She placed a hand on her throat and rewarded him with a grateful smile. "I am shocked that anyone would think that free traders would be welcome at Rosemont. I assure you, I will never again travel after dark without both Ned and Wilson in attendance."

"Wilson? Ha!" scoffed Harlbrook. "As soon take the

devil with you, if you look for safety." He sent a dark glare to the constable. "Tell her the whole story."

The constable gave a ponderous sigh. "It appears Wilson's nephews are heavily involved. They were seen rowing away from the ship."

Harlbrook gave a short laugh. "And if Lem and Twekes are involved, 'tis a fact that Wilson is bound to be in it, too."

"Nonsense," Arabella scoffed. "I'm sure there is some mistake. After all, you said it was night when the ship came in. Perhaps it was someone other than Lem and Twekes. Certainly there are many men who could meet their description."

Lucien gave her credit; even facing overwhelming odds, she still managed to latch on to crucial facts and use them to her advantage. But his admiration was tempered with the heavy knowledge that he'd found far more than cognac in the cave.

The constable swung his head back and forth. "We captured one of the smugglers, Miss Hadley. He identified them right and tight."

Bloody hell.

"Which is why we've come this evening," Harlbrook said, taking an eager step forward. "We've come to arrest Wilson."

Arabella paled, her hands closing into the folds of her dress. "Surely you cannot be serious."

" 'Deed, we are," said Constable Robbins in an apologetic tone. "I'm not one as believes ye should track down every free trader ye sees, but in these difficult times we haf to uphold the crown."

"Are you insinuating that *I* have anything to do with free trading? The Hadleys have *never* stooped to illegal trade."

"No, no," said Constable Robbins hurriedly, shooting a pleading glance at Lucien. "We didn't mean to suggest that you—"

"Indeed not!" Harlbrook said in a superior tone. "The thought that a gently bred female as yourself might be involved in something as common as free trading is ludicrous!"

The picture of outraged gentility, Arabella tilted her chin and sniffed. "I should hope not." Though her tone was firm, Lucien noticed a quiver of emotion in her face, a slight crack in the veneer she so desperately presented.

He moved to stand beside her, placing one hand on the small of her back. The muslin clung to his fingers and he had to fight the urge to place an arm about her and hold her to him.

He settled for training a hard gaze on the constable. "I assume you've evidence for this arrest?"

Constable Robbins eyed him for a meditative moment before saying bluntly, "Aye."

Harlbrook snorted derisively. "Enough to hang the old goat."

"Indeed?" Lucien slid his hand in a slow circle on Arabella's back. The warmth of her skin began to seep through the material. "Think very carefully, gentlemen, before you make accusations you cannot prove. You are talking about a servant of the future Duchess of Wexford."

Beneath his hand, Arabella stiffened and lifted her gaze to his face, but Lucien kept his gaze on Constable Robbins.

A look of acute relief spread over the constable's face, but Harlbrook turned a vivid red. *"Wh-what?"* he sputtered. "I don't believe it!"

"Don't you?" asked Lucien in a gentle tone.

"I—I—" Harlbrook turned an angry face to Arabella. "Is it true?"

She clasped her hands, her gaze on the ground.

Lucien waited for her answer, his throat painfully dry. *Forget your damnable pride and say yes,* he urged silently, holding his breath until his ribs ached.

Finally, after an interminable moment, Arabella nodded. Lucien swallowed a sigh of relief.

The constable made a disgusted noise. "Of course it is true! Why would the dook lie 'bout such a thing." He turned toward Arabella and offered an apologetic shrug. "Don't mind Harlbrook. He's not been the same since the innkeeper at the Roarin' Lion refused to serve him, sayin' as how he was havin' to pay double because of His Lordship's interferin' with the free traders."

"That has nothing to do with it!" Harlbrook glowered at Lucien. "When is this marriage to take place?"

"In a week. At Christmas. You are, of course, invited to the wedding." Lucien turned his head away and yawned. "Pardon me. It has been a long day and it is quite late."

Constable Robbins took the hint. He tugged urgently on Harlbrook's arm. "There, now, I don't think we need to be stayin' any longer. The dook has answered all of our questions. Mayhap we should ask some more questions of our witness. It *was* dark when he saw the men leavin' the ship."

Though Harlbrook continued to protest, the constable led him firmly from the room, stopping at the door only long enough to give Lucien a sharp glance. "It will be several days afore we're able to return and ask questions."

Lucien didn't pretend to misunderstand. "Thank you for your assistance."

The constable sent a hard glance at Arabella, then left.

As soon as the latch clicked into place, Arabella pushed away from Lucien and walked stiffly to the fire. She stared into the flames, her arms crossed over her chest as if to ward off a deep, penetrating chill.

Lucien watched her, his mind a turmoil of facts and emotions. "Bella, tell me about the smuggling."

She turned her head slowly, her eyes unfocused. "What?"

"I have seen the cave. In fact, I just returned from there." He sighed and raked a hand through his hair. "I know what you are doing."

Her mouth trembled for an instant, then she drew herself up. "You don't know anything."

Lucien crossed the space that separated them in three wide strides. He gripped her arms and yanked her around to face him. "You little fool! Do you realize the punishment if you are caught? Do you know what they do to smugglers? To traitors?"

"Traitors? I am not a traitor!"

"Don't play the innocent, Bella."

"How could I?" Her mouth curved in a bitter smile. "I lost my innocence ten years ago, Lucien. Or don't you remember?"

Oh, yes, he remembered. He remembered the scent of her hair and how it entangled his hands like a silken net. He remembered the taste of her skin beneath his seeking tongue. He remembered sinking into the very center of desire, his body burning so hotly he'd thought he would die. He remembered every nuance, every shadow, and every perfect inch of her body.

It was the one thing he'd clung to through the years as his life disintegrated, as he realized the price he had paid when he'd married Sabrina, as he struggled to make his own way to save his family from ruin.

Now, staring down into Arabella's upturned face, her wide brown eyes meeting his unflinchingly, he could see her as she was last night: her eyes dark with excitement, her hair damp and curling about a face flushed with passion. She was everything he desired. Everything except his.

He released her and rubbed his neck wearily, so tired he could hardly think. He was emotionally stretched, his body weary, and his arms ached from rowing the dinghy. They had so much to overcome, so much at stake, and the smuggling was only a small facet of the barriers between them.

He sighed. "I am too tired to think about this anymore this evening. Tomorrow we will decide—"

"*We?* Tomorrow *I* will decide what I am going to do. I agreed to say we are to be wed only to remove that fool from my house. There must be a better way to handle this situation."

Frustration, hot and bitter, boiled through him. "Bloody hell! What do you think will happen if Harlbrook discovers we are not to be wed after all? He will see to it that Wilson hangs."

She whirled away to pace, her movements desperate. "I can protect him. All I need is some time and I will—" She came to an abrupt halt, her back stiff. A sob wracked her body and she clenched her eyes closed, pressing a fist to her mouth.

Lucien was beside her in an instant. He pulled her close and held her tightly, cupping her head to his shoulder and resting his cheek against her hair. She stood within the circle of his arms, her head bowed as she cried. Though she made no move to break the embrace, neither did she soften in his arms.

Lucien pulled her tighter, stroking her back, her shoulders. "Ah, love, we'll find a way through this," he whispered, his cheek against her curls. "I promise."

She had borne so much, carried so many people in the only way that she knew how. And now she faced the greatest injustice of all—and it wasn't gaol; it was the thought she might not be able to take care of those who needed and counted on her.

He waited quietly for her to regain control, murmuring words of comfort against her hair. God, it felt good to hold her, her heart beating against his, knowing that for this moment, she was safe and in his arms.

As her sobs quieted to hiccups, she tried to pull away. But Lucien refused to loosen his grip, cupping a hand behind her head and holding her against his shoulder. His shirt was soaked, his jacket wrinkled beyond even Hastings's ability to straighten, but Lucien did not care. All he cared about was that for once, he was right where Arabella needed him to be.

After a moment, he turned her face to his. Tear-spiked lashes framed chocolate-colored eyes full of pain. But he needed the truth, needed it more now than ever. "Tell me, Bella," he whispered. "Tell me about the smuggling."

She stared up at him and her mouth trembled. For an instant he thought she would yield, but her mouth firmed and she jerked herself free. "There is nothing to tell."

Lucien sighed, every ounce of his tiredness returning. He reached into his pocket and pulled out a small bundle. He laid it in his palm and unwrapped the ends of the handkerchief until a small pile of brooches glittered in the lamplight, one long ruby necklace threaded between his fingers. "I found these in the cave, Bella."

Her eyes widened. "You found them *where?*"

Every instinct he possessed told him that she was surprised, shocked even, at the discovery. Lucien closed his hand over the jewels and he retied the handkerchief. "They were inside a cask."

She stared at the small bundle, her breathing ragged, a slight crease between her brows. Finally, after what seemed an eternity, she raised her gaze to his. "I didn't know, Lucien. I swear it."

He accepted her word without question, not knowing if he believed her because she was indeed innocent, or because he couldn't bear the thought that she was guilty. "I need to know about the smuggling."

Arabella swallowed, her throat working before she nodded. "I will tell you everything, but . . . can we wait until tomorrow? I am so tired. I—I need to think."

Had it been anyone else, he would have refused, demanded on the spot to be informed of every last detail. But he was not immune to the shadows beneath the haunted eyes, nor the tremor that shook her ever so slightly. "Very well, I won't tax you anymore tonight. But tomorrow, we will have an accounting."

She nodded, then turned to leave the room, walking slowly, her slippers moving silently on the carpet. She halted as she reached the threshold and looked over her shoulder. "I would appreciate it if you didn't tell my aunts what has occurred."

"About the smuggling or that we are to be married?"

"Both."

Now, more than ever, Arabella needed the protection of his name and title, but all he said was, "As you wish."

Her eyes sought his and she gave an uncertain smile. Then she left, closing the door softly behind her.

Lucien let out his breath in a long, weary sigh. Prickly and defiant, stubborn and unyielding, she would be anything but an accommodating wife. He thought of her frosty demeanor in dealing with Harlbrook and he smiled wearily. One thing was certain—come what may, Arabella Hadley would make one hell of a duchess.

Chapter 17

Arabella closed the barn door and went to pat Sebastian, finding solace in his familiar presence. As if sensing her disquiet, the old horse blew out, his breath frosting the air to a cloud of silver. It was cold this morning, a deep, bitter cold that slipped between her layers of clothing and stole away whatever warmth it found hoarded there.

She sighed and rested her forehead against Sebastian's bony neck, staring out at the white-tinged morning. For the last half hour, snow had powdered the air, falling softly on the harsh edges of the house until it looked fresh and white, like an iced cake.

"I suppose I should just tell him everything and get it over with," she muttered. Did she really have any other choice?

Sebastian shook his head and managed a shuffle that might have been a prance in a younger horse.

Arabella managed a weak chuckle. "Stubborn to the

end, aren't you? He already knows enough to send us all to gaol, but he didn't." She pursed her lips and frowned. He had even tried to help. "Lucien is a surprising man."

Hearing his master's name, Satan dipped his head over the stall door and watched her with liquid eyes.

"I would pat you, too, but I need all of my fingers, thank you. You are as quarrelsome as your owner."

Satan sniffed and then ducked his head back into his stall as if affronted.

Arabella smiled. Last night, after her confrontation with Lucien, she had fallen into bed and slept until dawn. Now, refreshed and dressed in Robert's old clothes, she felt some of her strength returning. She had allowed Harlbrook's malice to shake her confidence. Never again, she decided.

She leaned over Sebastian's stall door and held out her hand. When the horse shuffled closer, she pressed her cheek against his neck. It was so peacefully silent here.

Arabella closed her eyes and breathed in the scent of hay tinged with the fresh smell of new-fallen snow. Sooner or later she would have to explain to Lucien just how and why she'd become a smuggler. Somehow, it had seemed a less disreputable decision when she didn't have to say it aloud.

Sighing heavily, she picked up a shovel and hefted it over her shoulder. Before she met with Lucien, she would reorganize the shed. The task needed to be done, now that the door had been repaired. Besides, it wasn't cowardly to merely postpone a conversation that she was fully committed to having.

Reassured at her reasoning, she walked out of the barn and into the silent snowfall. The shoulders of her coat collected a heavy dusting of snow as she went, each flake a sparkling diamond.

Diamond. Like those that had winked in the palm of Lucien's hand. No wonder Bolder had been so desperate to keep the casks. She stopped and stared at the door of the shed. The brash smuggler would return for his shipment, she was sure of it. With such a priceless cargo hidden in the caves below Rosemont, he'd have no choice.

The thought tightened her throat. *Heavens, what have I gotten myself into?* Bolder was not the kind of man one simply apologized to. He would want more than the return of his merchandise; he would want something to make up for the humiliation of being bested.

She opened the shed door and carried the shovel to the back wall, where all the tools hung in a row. She had just lifted it above her head to hang it in place when a dark shadow flitted across the wall. Images of the weaselly smuggler flashed before her eyes and she whirled around, the shovel falling to the floor, her heart thudding against her ribs.

Lucien stood in the doorway, his hat and black coat lightly dusted with snow. "Sorry to frighten you, but I thought we would have more privacy out here."

He stepped into the shed, the small building instantly seeming half its normal size as he brushed snow from his shoulders. "It looks as if we'll have a white Christmas, after all."

She tried to regain her breath, but all she could do was stare at him.

He crossed the small space that separated them. Looking far too handsome for his own good, he smiled, a strange glint in his eyes. "Where have you been all morning?"

"I am going to clean out the shed. It needs it." But not as badly as she needed to get some room between her and Lucien. She cleared her throat. "I try to keep this place in order, but it never stays that way."

"How inconvenient." He lifted a hoe from a corner where it had been propped for so long that cobwebs clung to it, then he hung it on the back wall. The front of his greatcoat opened to reveal an impeccable black waistcoat, his starched cravat tied in an intricate weave, one lone emerald shining in the folds.

Arabella looked down at the loose breeches she'd borrowed from Robert, her coarse shirt, and dull gray coat. For some reason, the contrast between their stations had never been more obvious. It was the reason he would never think to marry her—unless she were on the verge of being hauled to gaol. *Damn his chivalrous instincts.* They made it all the more difficult to dislike him.

She tilted her chin to a pugnacious angle. "Let's not prolong this. What do you want to know?"

His smile faded, but he shrugged, his gaze intent. "Everything."

Somewhere beneath her embarrassment, she was conscious of a feeling of obligation mingled with a torrent of other, unnamed emotions. She shoved her fists into her coat pockets. "When my father died, he left us with bills we could not pay. We were destitute. Unknown to me, Wilson had been dabbling in free trading. When I found out, I helped him."

"How?"

She glared at him. "Within three months of my becoming involved, we began to supply twelve more inns, added almost eighteen casks per month to our shipping total, and tripled our income."

He swore softly. "Which would only make you more visible to the authorities."

She'd known that, of course. But by that time she'd been struggling to pay Lord Harlbrook and the risk had seemed worthwhile. Still, those were things she'd never admit, especially not to Lucien. "We had no trouble until *you* came."

The hard line of his jaw told her what he thought of such poor reasoning. "What of the jewels?"

She frowned. "I don't know. How did you find them?"

"The cask was separate from the others, and it was somewhat smaller, too."

Her brow cleared, the corners of her mouth turning downward. "I should have known. We had a dispute with our supplier and we ended up with part of someone else's shipment." She looked up at him. "Lucien, I didn't know about the jewels until you showed them to me. I swear it."

His gaze flicked across her, then he sighed and yanked off his gloves and stuffed them in his pocket. "Who else is involved besides you and Wilson?"

"His nephews, Lem and Twekes."

"Anyone else?"

She shook her head. Embarrassment heated her cheeks; her throat clogged with unshed tears. But she would not cry. She wouldn't give Lucien Devereaux that much satisfaction, damn his judgmental soul. What did he know about true poverty? About the pain of trying to provide for loved ones who were unable to provide for themselves? When his pockets had been to let, all he'd had to do was ride to London and sell his title to the first heiress who came along. She hadn't had such a luxury.

Her clouded gaze fell on the dropped shovel and she bent to retrieve it just as Lucien did. His large, warm hand brushed Arabella's and for one burning instant they stood, fingers overlaid.

Arabella withdrew her hand and tucked it behind her. "Why do you want to know about the smuggling?" She managed a tiny smile. "Thinking of going into the trade yourself?"

He was slow to answer, his gaze touching her brow, her eyes, her mouth. "Let's just say that I have interests." His lips quirked in a lopsided grin. "We are betrothed, you know."

"A betrothal is a commitment." She let her disdain show. "What do *you* know about commitment?"

His face closed. "Neither of us have led blameless lives, Bella."

"I want you to understand, Lucien: my family was destitute. Rosemont was crumbling about our heads. *I had no choice.*"

"Then we are even: neither did I." Lucien watched as she frowned, weighing his words, wondering if he told the truth. He reached out and gently brushed a stray tendril of hair from her forehead. "But we both have a choice now. Arabella, marry me."

A fierce, almost martial light brightened her gaze. "I do not need your charity. Unlike you, I will not sell myself."

Lucien hated it when she was like this, all outraged fury, her eyes blazing contempt. He especially hated it when she was right, in the bargain. "Had I been more prepared to assume the duties of my title and less swayed by the opinions of others, I might have found another way out of my difficulties just as you did."

"Others? What others?"

He didn't reply; the answer would only infuriate her. But he'd had enough—enough accusations, enough useless anger. And enough hurt. Every time her brown eyes flashed with pain, his own heart bled. He'd just offered to share his fortune, his home, and even his name with her, and she'd scoffed as if he'd tried to pass a false coin.

But no matter her feelings, she couldn't deny their passion. It was the one weapon he possessed. Lucien reached out and pulled Arabella against him, lowering his mouth over hers before she could protest. Her mouth was berry-sweet beneath his; her swift breaths mingled fury and raw need.

Heat built between them and her arms crept about his neck. Lucien moaned against her mouth, his hands moving over the curve of her back, her hips, and lower. God, but she tortured him with the potency of her ardor, her unrestrained responses pushing him higher and higher, until he lost his own control.

Behind them, a loud bang rang out and then the shed was plunged into darkness. Lucien raised his head to look at the shed door.

"What was that?" Arabella's voice trembled the tiniest bit.

She tried to step away, but Lucien tightened his hold. He could just discern the oval of her face in the darkness. "The wind must have blown the door closed."

"Perhaps it was the illustrious Captain," she said, a quirk to her lips that made him want to kiss her yet again. "Aunt Jane seems to think he is a bit of a matchmaker."

"Aunt Jane also thinks he can eat," Lucien returned roughly. She still stood within the circle of his arms and he was afraid to move, afraid she'd never return. "We need to talk about the smuggling, Arabella. It must stop."

For a moment he thought she'd deny him, but she nodded. "I know. I let it continue far too long. I will tell Wilson today."

She removed her hands from his shoulders and Lucien reluctantly allowed her to step away. "Who is your supplier?"

"A little weasel by the name of Bolder."

"How can I find him?"

"We contact him by leaving word at the Red Rooster with a man named Mumferd."

Things suddenly became all too clear.

Unaware of his thoughts, she continued, "He is a cringing little creature. Lem and Twekes dislike him."

So Bolder was the mastermind of the smuggling outfit, slipping in whatever illegal merchandise he could, while Mumferd bated well-monied purchasers to the sale.

Arabella's gaze narrowed on his face. "What is it? You look upset."

Before Lucien could answer, an acrid odor wafted upward. "What's that?" Arabella asked.

The darkness around them thickened with a ghostly gray haze as a crackling sound began.

"Bloody hell!" Lucien whirled to catch a glimpse of a dull red glow. Someone had stuffed hay beneath the shed door and set it ablaze.

He crossed to the newly built door, lifted a booted foot, and kicked with all his might. It didn't budge an inch.

The fire lapped hungrily at the walls. The ancient boards creaked and popped, surrendering themselves to the blaze until the flames climbed to the framing above.

Within minutes, one whole wall was aflame. Smoke boiled through the tiny room, burning their eyes and lungs.

Coughing, Lucien grabbed Arabella and pulled her toward the back of the shed. He slammed his hand along the wall, looking for a weak spot. But like all of the buildings at Rosemont, it was solidly built—there was no breaking free.

Each breath was a labor, the heat searing the air with a fiery haze. Like malevolent fairies, the fire danced across the dry wood, crackling with evil laughter. Smoke billowed white and thick, visible even in the darkness of the shed. Lucien pulled Arabella to the floor and unwrapped the muffler from his neck and looped it about her own. "Put this over your mouth."

"No," she cried hoarsely. "You take it!"

"Damn it, Bella! Don't be a fool! I can—"

With an almost human roar, the thatch roof burst into flames, bits of burning twigs showering them. Arabella screamed in pure terror. Lucien was glad she was wearing breeches and not a dress with yards and yards of material. The idea of flames curling about Arabella's legs fanned Lucien's fear. He pulled her against him and covered her body with his.

She pushed at him and tried to say something, but the smoke choked her words. The smoke roiled thicker and Lucien cursed his luck, cursed his poor timing, cursed everything and everyone that seemed determined to keep Arabella from him. But he would beat this. Beat it as he had beaten everything else.

Eyes burning, his throat afire, he reached across the dirt floor, his fingers grasping for something to use to break through the wall.

"Lucien." Arabella's raspy voice cut through the maniacal crackle of fire. "The shovel."

"What?"

A cough raked her and she barely managed to croak, "Get the shovel."

Of course. He leaned farther out and his fingers brushed something cold and hard. With superhuman effort, Lucien grabbed the shovel and scrambled to his feet. He turned to the wall and swung it over his head like an ax, hitting the wall with all his might.

The welcome sound of splintering wood greeted him and he swung the shovel again and yet again. A small opening appeared in the wood, the smoke pouring out.

Lucien threw the shovel aside and kicked the loosened wood until the boards split wide. But still the opening was not wide enough.

He took two steps back, fighting for breath. Then, head bowed and teeth clenched, he threw himself against the weakened boards. Pain shot through his shoulder as the wall gave way with a splintering crash. Lucien fell to the blessedly cold ground and gulped frozen air into lungs that burned, then, staggering to his feet, he headed back into the fire.

Strong hands stayed him. Lord Harlbrook's red face appeared through a tear-stained blur. "Easy, Wexford! You've had too much smoke."

"Bella!" Lucien gasped, wiping his streaming eyes. "I must—"

"Francot's already gone for her."

Lucien turned to see the solicitor pulling Arabella from the opening. Francot assisted her to where Lucien sat and gently laid her down on Harlbrook's spread coat.

She curled onto her side, gasping for air. Oblivious to their audience, Lucien gathered her close. She grasped his shoulders, her face smudged with soot, tears streaking from eyes reddened by smoke.

Never had he seen a more beautiful sight. He brushed some of the soot from her face, watching as the snow gently fell to wash her black-streaked skin.

Harlbrook rocked back on his heels, his brows lowered. "Good thing for you that Francot heard Miss Hadley shouting for help."

The solicitor shuddered, his face pale. "I—I heard her scream and I . . . Oh, my God. It was horrible." He dropped to his knees beside her. "I was afraid . . . so afraid I might be too late."

Harlbrook placed a beefy hand on the solicitor's shoulder. "There, now. She's fine, as you can see."

Mr. Francot nodded, his eyes wet.

Air had begun to return to Lucien's lungs and he lifted

himself on one arm and looked down at Arabella. "Are you hurt?"

A glimmer of a smile touched her lips and she managed to say between breaths, "Just . . . my pride."

Lucien chuckled. "I rather thought I heard it crack." He stood, then reached down and helped her to her feet, wincing when an unexpected pain shot up his arm.

Her eyes searched his anxiously. "Your shoulder?"

"I seem to have the devil of a time staying in one piece around you, sweetheart."

An unexpected gurgle of laughter spilled from her lips.

The sound of a harness jingling to a halt made Lucien turn. Wilson hopped down from the cart, his shocked gaze going from the shed to Lucien and Arabella. "Lord, what's happened now, missus?"

"The shed caught on fire," Arabella said. "We have Mr. Francot to thank for his timely intervention."

The solicitor's face reddened. "No, no. It was nothing. Really."

Arabella stepped forward and caught his hand, holding it between hers. "We owe you our lives."

He almost snatched his hand away. "No, I didn't do anything. Really I didn't. I—I should never have—I must leave." He gave a jerky bow, spun on his heel, and ran to his horse.

Lord Harlbrook sent a hard, puzzled look after the solicitor. "Strange. When I arrived, I thought . . ." He stopped, then shrugged and placed his hat on his head and gathered his coat. His small eyes darted uneasily at Arabella. "I came to tell you that Constable Robbins is questioning each and every innkeeper. We will have proof enough for an arrest by this evening."

Lucien had to admire the way Arabella's gaze never wavered. She even managed a smile as cold as the snow that drifted all around them. "Thank you for the information, Lord Harlbrook, though I'm not sure why you think we would be interested."

His face tight with disapproval, he gave a short bow, then strode to his horse.

Arabella watched the scowl deepen on Lucien's face. The scent of wood smoke clogged her dry throat with tears. It had been so close. Too close.

"I think ye'd both best come and flash yer peepers at this," Wilson said from near the shed.

Lucien released Arabella and she shivered. An instant later, she was enveloped in his greatcoat, the warm wool covering her from neck to heel. Lucien smiled down at her, his fingers brushing against her neck as he pulled the collar tighter about her neck.

She swayed toward him, burrowing her face into his shoulder. She had found him, only to come so close to losing him again.

Wilson's voice drifted through the snow. "I don't know what ye are goin' to think of this."

Lucien's hand strayed from Arabella's collar to her chin. He lifted her face to his and smiled down at her, his teeth white in his soot-streaked face. "Easy, love," he whispered. "Come. Wilson is calling for us."

She managed a shaky smile and, hand warmly enveloped in his, followed him to where Wilson stood by the remains of the burning shed. It had collapsed inward and only parts of each wall remained standing, flames still crackling among the smoking pile.

Lucien stared where Wilson pointed. "Bloody hell."

"What is it?" Arabella asked.

Wilson spoke over his shoulder. "The door was blocked shut from the outside. Whoever it was pushed a cart against it."

"Maybe it rolled there by accident."

Lucien's green gaze flickered to her. "Whoever moved the cart also stuffed straw under the door to make sure it would burn quickly."

The old groom spat, then cast a sideways glance at Lucien. "Looks to me as if someone was tryin' to kill ye."

"Why would anyone want to kill the duke?" asked Arabella.

Lucien frowned. "I don't know."

Arabella looked at the blackened hull of the shed and a tremor shook through her. "Perhaps they were not trying to kill the duke. Maybe they were trying to kill me."

Wilson's mouth opened, but no words came out.

"Who would want to kill you?" Lucien asked, his brows drawn.

"Bolder. He was so angry when we made him renegotiate the shipment, and—"

"Here, now, missus," said Wilson, sending a startled glance at Lucien. "There's no need to tell everythin'."

"I already know about the smuggling," Lucien said. "I followed you and your nephews from the Red Rooster two days ago."

"Ye did, did ye?" Wilson said, obviously affronted.

"The duke is not threatening to turn us in, Wilson. He wants our help in discovering something else. There were jewels in one of the casks."

Wilson's eyes widened. "Jewels?"

Lucien nodded. "Apparently Bolder has been dabbling in something far more serious than cognac. From what I can discover, he plans on selling them to fund an effort to free Napoleon."

"Gor'! No wonder he was so brash wif us."

"Wilson," Arabella said, "we must stop free trading."

"Oh? And jus' what made ye decide that?"

Arabella tilted her head toward Lucien.

Wilson eyed Lucien with new respect. "I've been tryin' to tell her it ain't the thing fer a gently raised lady, but she'd none of it. If ye've got her to agree, ye're a better man than me."

Arabella sniffed. "I am not admitting any such thing. But with things the way they are . . ." Her gaze drifted to the smoking shed and she shivered.

Wilson rubbed a gnarled hand along his unshaven jaw and sighed. "These are havey-cavey times, they are." He sent a concerned look at Lucien. "But there's more. Someone found the cave last night and took every last cask."

The news just got worse and worse, Arabella thought bleakly. Not only was her profit gone, but her entire business. How would she ever make Harlbrook's last payment? She dashed a hand across her eyes and turned to Lucien. "I need to go. I promised Aunt Jane I would visit one of the tenants today."

Lucien nodded. "I've an errand to run this morning, but I should return by noon. We'll go then."

"I'll be fine. I'll take Wilson with me."

He slid a hot green gaze across her. "We'll go when I return."

Without quite knowing how, Arabella found herself bustled into the house and delivered into the safety of her aunts' arms. Aunt Jane took one swift look at Arabella's soot-covered face and ordered a long hot bath. Aunt Emma bustled to the kitchen to see to the preparation of some nice hot soup. Arabella was too shaken to do more than agree, her mind churning as she sat in the gently steaming water.

No indolent lord would bother to investigate a smuggling operation, especially one as small as the one she and

Wilson ran. No, Lucien had been after something more valuable.

Arabella soaped one of her legs, her movements slowing as her tumbled thoughts finally locked into place. *He put the answer in front of me last night. The jewels.* It was the only thing that made sense.

Perhaps they were also the reason someone had tried to kill her and Lucien. But how had Lucien known to look for the jewels in Yorkshire? Perhaps he was helping the owner? The thought reassured her and she almost smiled until she remembered where he had found the gems—in *her* cave.

She slid further into the tub and sighed heavily. A month ago, she had been ready to swear everything in her life was finally heading for the better. Now . . .

Damn Lucien. Whatever his reason for returning to Yorkshire, he wasn't leaving until he'd thoroughly explained himself to her. That decided, she rose, dried herself, and dressed.

Chapter 18

Arabella rested until noon, waiting impatiently for Lucien to return. Her mind too fraught with the occurrences of the day, she finally rose and went downstairs. After assisting Mrs. Guinver darn linens for a desultory half hour, she went in search of her aunts to see if they had any commissions for her while she was visiting the tenants.

Lucien had told her to wait until his return, but she had a pressing need to do something, *anything*. She was just walking through the vestibule when the murmur of voices halted her. Low and feminine, they drifted up the steps from below.

Strange. What were Aunt Emma and Aunt Jane doing in the storage hall? Frowning, Arabella descended the stairs, pausing on the last step when she heard Aunt Emma speaking.

"Oh, Jane! What will you do now? We are sunk. Not even the Captain can help us now."

Arabella peered around the corner to the old store-room. Emma was perched on a barrel of flour while Jane paced up and down the narrow aisle between the salted pork and dried herbs.

"I hate Sir Loughton!" exclaimed Jane, her arms crossed beneath her sparse bosom as she marched. "The lecher."

"It was most ungentlemanly of him," agreed Emma, swinging her feet to and fro, her heels thudding against the wood.

"I've known that bounder was not a gentleman from the first day I met him." Jane's booted feet clipped a steady beat as she paced. "That . . . rapscallion! If I were a man, I would call him out."

"Yes, but if you were a man, he would not have offered to dismiss your gaming debts for a quick roll in the hay."

Arabella almost lost her balance, catching the railing just in time. Gaming debts? A roll in the hay? She tried to imagine gruff Sir Loughton making such an improper proposition, but could not.

"Ha!" Jane's voice rang out. "If that man thinks I will allow him to so much as kiss my hand after such a request, he has another think coming."

"There's no need to get so upset," Emma said, tilting her gray head to one side, her face taking on a dreamy look. "If you feel you cannot make such a sacrifice, then I will . . ." She stopped and cleared her throat before saying in a brave voice, "Jane, if you think it will help, *I* will sleep with Sir Loughton."

Jane halted in her tracks. Arabella could not see her face, but her back was ramrod stiff. "And just what," said Jane in a thinly stretched voice, "do you mean by *that*? You have a tendre for that lecher, don't you?"

"Oh, no! Please, Jane! I can see that you are upset. If I

had realized you meant to accept him, I never would have said a word."

"Of course I am not going to accept him! Do you think I have taken leave of my senses?"

"If anyone has taken leave of their senses, it is Sir Loughton," said Emma stoutly. "*You* are perfectly sane."

Jane resumed her pacing. "I was a fool to think I could talk that man into coming to a genteel settlement on the notes he won from me last month."

Arabella leaned her head against the wall and closed her eyes. Just how much did Jane owe?

"Yes, but . . ." Emma's voice clouded with doubt. "Do you think it was wise to wager him double or nothing on a single card?"

"You do not understand the rudiments of the game," Jane said in a haughty voice. "Furthermore, you do not understand the code of conduct expected in such circumstances. I could not, in all honor, refuse such an offer. I mean, double or nothing!" She slashed through the air with her hand. "I could have wiped out the entire debt in one fell swoop."

"Yes, but now we owe twice as much and I don't know where we are to get it. Ten thousand pounds is a great deal of money."

Ten thousand pounds. Arabella sank to the top step, dazed.

"Maybe there is *one* thing we can do," Emma said. "What does Sir Loughton want more than anything else?"

Jane stiffened and Emma added hastily, "Besides you."

"I'm sure I don't know."

"The sheep tonic. Maybe he would trade us your notes for the sheep tonic."

For an instant, Arabella's heart took flight. But then Jane sighed and resumed her pacing. "No, we cannot.

While I don't mind making a small batch of tonic now and then for our particular friends, it would be an error to think of Sir Loughton in such a way. His sheep compete against ours at market. If both of our farms produced an excessive amount of lambs, the prices would fall immediately."

"Then we would be right back where we started from." Emma gave a heartfelt sigh. "I suppose our only hope is that the duke will see his way to win Arabella."

"It is just a matter of time," Aunt Jane said firmly, "before they realize what nodcocks they've been. I'm sure of it."

Blindly groping for the railing, Arabella rose and made her way back to the foyer. Once there, she sank into the first chair she found and sat staring straight ahead. *Ten thousand pounds.* Arabella pressed her hand to her forehead. It was yet another care, another impossible feat she had to accomplish. But whatever happened, she could not allow Aunt Jane to exchange her virtue for a few notes.

Within the space of one short day, her smuggling venture had collapsed about her ears, threatening Wilson's welfare, if not her own; someone had tried to kill her and Lucien by setting the shed on fire; and now Aunt Jane had been lured into wagering a staggering sum to Sir Loughton. Arabella rested her elbow on the arm of the chair and covered her eyes. What on earth was she to do now?

A knock sounded at the door and Mrs. Guinver bustled forward from the hallway. She stopped when she saw Arabella. "Heavens, missus! What are you doing sitting here in the foyer?" Concern shadowed the housekeeper's plump face. "Are you ill?"

Arabella gathered herself as best as she could. "No, I'm fine, thank you."

"You don't look fine to me. You look as pale as snow,

which isn't to be wondered at, considering all of the excitement we've had this morning. Perhaps you should come into the library and settle yourself on the settee whilst I fetch you a nice pot of hot tea."

Arabella was long past the point where a cup of hot tea could solve anything, but perhaps if she sat quietly and mulled over her predicament, an idea would come. She managed a weak smile. "Thank you, Mrs. Guinver. I will—"

The knocking sounded again, this time more insistent. Mrs. Guinver made an exasperated sound. "You run along, missus, and I'll get the door." She bustled away before Arabella could get to her feet.

Mrs. Guinver opened the door and Arabella heard Mr. Francot say, "I need to see Miss Hadley at once. Is she—" He caught sight of her at the library door and took an impetuous step forward, crowding the housekeeper out of the way. "There you are! I hope you are feeling better."

"I'm quite well, thank you." She wished him to perdition at the moment, but at the relieved look on his face, Arabella softened. "I was going to have some tea. Would you join me?" Somehow, she didn't really want to be alone just now.

His face brightened. "Of course."

Mrs. Guinver shut the door and took the solicitor's hat and gloves. She favored him with a sour glance and said, "I'll bring ye some tea and cakes, but ye can only stay a minute. Miss Hadley needs to rest."

He sent a sharp glance at Arabella and must have concurred with the housekeeper, for he nodded once and said, "I won't tax her, I promise."

The housekeeper gave a satisfied nod and left as Mr. Francot followed Arabella into the library.

She waited until he had seated himself before she

perched on the edge of a chair. "Mr. Francot, I'm glad you returned. I need to speak with you."

Twin spots of color appeared in his cheeks. "Indeed, I *had* to come. I wanted to see for myself that you were not harmed this morning."

Arabella waved an impatient hand. "I'm fine, thank you. Mr. Francot, at one time you—" The words clogged her throat, but she swallowed and continued. "You mentioned you knew someone who might be interested in buying Rosemont." She lifted her gaze to his. "Do you think the buyer would be willing to renew his offer?"

A brief look of surprise crossed his heavy face. "Of course. I'm sure he would. May I ask what has happened to make you change your mind?"

"I just . . . I want to sell the house, and as quickly as possible. Would you speak with your acquaintance?" Each word tasted of metal, bitter and cold. "I will need the offer in writing."

"Yes. Yes, of course." He placed his hands on his knees and leaned forward. "Miss Hadley . . . Arabella, I hate to see you in such a taking. If you could but see your way to . . . if there is anything you need, I hope you will . . ." His face turned a bright red, his emotions seeming to grow stronger by the minute. "I—I care for you, and I would do anything in my power to offer you some relief from these horrible circumstances."

"Thank you, Mr. Francot," Arabella said, wishing miserably she could think of some other way out of her predicament. But no brilliant idea came forward.

"Yes, but I—"

He stopped and delivered such a look of burning passion that Arabella slapped a hand over her eyes. "Mr. Francot, please don't—"

It was too late. The solicitor had already dropped awkwardly to one knee in front of her. He reached over and took her hand from her eyes, holding it tightly. "Miss Hadley, I know I am not worthy of you—"

"No, you are much too worthy." And that was the problem. For some reason she was unable to fall in love with sane, logical men, but must expend her passions on reckless dukes who would soon be comfortably on their way back to London.

"Mr. Francot, please get up." She tugged to get her hand back, but his grip just tightened until she winced.

"Arabella, just hear me out. I haven't much to offer, but one day soon, I will be able to buy you anything your heart desires."

She jerked her hand free and then stood. "Mr. Francot, please get up. Though it is a very generous offer, I cannot marry you. I have my brother and my aunts to think of, and—"

He climbed ponderously to his feet. "I would care for all of your family as if they were my own."

For one brief, horrible moment, she considered his proposal. Marriage to him would mean a life of normalcy such as she'd never had; her own home without the worry or repairs or bills, a garden she could tend, maybe even children. Her heart twisted painfully. She'd spent so much of her passion and effort on Rosemont, she hadn't allowed herself the luxury to think about children.

Arabella raised her gaze to his. Though his passion shone brightly, the only feeling she could discover within the depths of her own heart was a mild disappointment that his eyes were not green. Like Lucien's.

It wasn't a fair comparison. Lucien was ten years younger and possessed all that came with good birth and fortune. Or he had, until his father had mismanaged the estate and then left Lucien to deal with the consequences. In a way, his case was much like Arabella's.

For an instant, she wondered if *this* was what it had been like for Lucien. Faced with pressing obligations, a failing estate, a sea of debt, and the care of his little sister, he must have thought he was in the grip of a relentless nightmare. To a desperate twenty-year-old, Sabrina and her fortune must have seemed like an answer wrought from God. A tightness settled in Arabella's chest as she remembered the stark desolation on Lucien's face when he spoke of Sabrina. Some things were far more important than security. "Mr. Francot, I cannot let you sacrifice yourself in such a way. I must refuse."

His brow lowered. "Please, it wouldn't be a sacrifice."

"You may not think so now. But later . . . No, it wouldn't do for either of us."

His hands dropped to his sides and for a moment she feared he would cry. But when he lifted his head, his eyes shone with a bright eagerness that made her take a step backward. Her retreat seemed to fuel him, for he reached out, grabbed her to him, and then planted an awkward kiss on her lips. Arabella struggled to free herself, but he only tightened his grip, his wet mouth moving over her lips with bruising force.

"Mr. Francot!" Mrs. Guinver's voice whipped across the room.

He release Arabella so suddenly that she fell back against the cushions.

The housekeeper slapped the tray on the table so hard that the plates jumped, then she pinned a glare on the solicitor. "I'm going to get Ned." With that, she turned and marched out the door.

"No!" Mr. Francot said, but she was already gone. He raked a shaking hand through his hair. "Good God, what

have I done? Arabella, I didn't mean to upset you. I love you too much for that."

"Please just go." Arabella wiped her mouth with the back of her hand. "And do not return to Rosemont."

The front door opened in the foyer and Arabella could hear Ned's booted footsteps as he crossed the vestibule. His mouth white, Mr. Francot bowed and, with one last anguished look, he left.

She watched him go, angry tears slipping past her lashes. "This must be the worst day of my life."

As the steps came closer, Arabella patted her face dry and turned to welcome Ned with a pacifying smile.

But it wasn't Ned. Lucien stopped on the threshold, looking darkly handsome in his greatcoat and riding boots. "There you are," he said. "Are you ready to—" He stopped, his brows suddenly drawn. "What's happened?"

It was strange, the way her stomach warmed at the sight of him. Strange and disturbing. She managed a watery smile. "Nothing. I was just discussing some business matters with Mr. Francot."

Lucien's face darkened and he crossed the room until he stood directly in front of her. "You've been crying."

For one mad moment, she thought about tossing her crumbling pride to the winds and throwing herself in his arms. But all that would win was momentary comfort and a lifetime of regret. So instead, she applied herself to the task of tucking her handkerchief away. "I am still distressed by the events of this morning and it has made me weepy. I'll be fine in a moment."

Lucien looked down at her bent head as she slowly restored her handkerchief to her pocket. Though she managed the words very credibly, there was an air of tragedy about her that tightened his throat and made him want to bury his fist in the face of whoever had caused her to cry.

An image of Mr. Francot's strained expression as he passed Lucien in the doorway suddenly came to mind. "Did that popinjay insult you?"

"Which popinjay?" she asked, her voice strained.

"You know exactly which popinjay I am talking about."

"I have already told you that I'm fine. Are you ready to leave? I really must deliver Aunt Jane's basket to the March family before the weather breaks."

Lucien placed his finger under her chin, very gently tilting her face toward his. Her eyes were damp, the lashes spiky with tears, but it was her mouth that caught his attention. Swollen and bruised, it told its own story. Lucien swore and turned on his heel, hot anger flooding through him. He would find that opportunistic bastard and thrash him within an inch of his life.

Arabella caught Lucien's arm before he reached the door. "Leave him be, Lucien! He's already apologized and he is very sorry."

"He hasn't begun to be sorry."

She planted her feet firmly and refused to budge an inch, her hands tight about his arm. "Leave him alone. I owe him so much. And today . . . today was just a mistake."

It angered Lucien that she could so easily forgive Francot, but could dredge up only tolerance for him. He snarled, "That arrogant fool wants you in his bed, and nothing more."

"And you?" she snapped, releasing his arm to glower at him. "Why are you helping me, Lucien? Why did you fix the steps and the fence and the shutter and all the rest? Because you wished to see Rosemont returned to her former glory?" Her mouth tightened. "Or because you found it convenient to hide here while you hunted for your jewel thieves?"

She was too sharp by far, Lucien thought with grudging admiration. "I admit that I knew the jewelry was being brought to auction somewhere nearby. But I didn't have to stay at Rosemont, Bella. I could have lodged at any of a dozen inns along the coast."

"Then why *did* you stay here?"

"Because you needed me."

Her eyes flashed. "I am not a charity case."

"No, you are not, and neither am I. What matters is you, Bella. You, and Robert, and Aunt Jane, and Aunt Emma, and Wilson, and everyone else at Rosemont. I don't wish to see any of you harmed."

"And that's why you stayed?"

Lucien nodded once. "And because I know I wronged you. I thought perhaps I could make it up." She made a move to turn away and he held up a hand. "I know I can't, but I wished to try. Surely that is worth something."

"I'm sure it would have been, had it occurred ten years ago. As it is, it's nothing more than a careless afterthought. And I have more than enough afterthoughts of my own without borrowing yours."

Lucien took a step closer, caught by her words. "You are having afterthoughts? About what?"

She made an exasperated noise, though her cheeks colored hotly. "I have afterthoughts about why I ever let you stay here. About how you have done nothing but plague me since you arrived. About how I wish to heaven I had left you in the road where I found you."

"So all of your afterthoughts have been about me. Interesting." He captured her hand so she could not back away. She bit her lip, but didn't attempt to free herself.

Lucien smiled at the small victory. "Tell me more about these dreams you are having," he said, his voice warm.

"Afterthoughts," she corrected, her gaze fastened on his thumb where it rubbed a warm circle on the delicate skin of her palm.

"Ah, yes." Lucien lifted her hand to his lips and kissed the tips of her fingers, one at a time. She watched, her lips parted, seemingly fascinated. But it wasn't enough. He wanted to erase the pain he'd witnessed when he'd entered the room, and restore some measure of her pride. He carefully curled her fingers over his. "Tell me, Bella. In these . . . afterthoughts, am I naked?"

Her gaze flew to his and an unmistakable quiver of amusement crossed her face, though she quickly contained it. "You were fully dressed. In fact, you were bound and gagged, lying in the road where I found you," she said defiantly.

"Ah, and then I suppose you rode up on a gallant horse and rescued me. Like in a fairy tale."

She showed her teeth. "No, I was in a farmer's cart. But after I ran over you, I did back up to make sure you were dead."

"How . . . how thorough of you, my dear."

Her lips quivered with laughter and Lucien knew he had succeeded. She pulled her hand from his and managed a very natural grin. "You are absurd. But we should leave now if we are still going to visit the tenants."

Lucien bowed. "I am at your disposal, Miss Hadley."

Her lips twitched. "Thank you. If you will excuse me, I must go and put on my boots. Please see if you can find Aunt Jane and get the basket we are to deliver."

Lucien watched her go, his heart lighter than it had been in days. She was warming to him, though it would take time before she completely trusted him. Unfortunately, time was the one thing he did not have.

He wished he could plan a gentle wooing, one of kisses and candles, of whispered compliments and heated touches. But with Harlbrook pushing the constable toward an arrest, and the mysterious Mr. Bolder out to seek revenge, it would be madness to consider such a thing. Lucien had to find a way to get Arabella to marry him, and quickly.

But how? How could he gain her acquiescence? Winning a smile was one thing; winning her hand in marriage, another. He turned toward the door, his gaze drawn to the portrait over the fireplace. The Captain's roguish smile seemed like a challenge.

Lucien found himself grinning back. "Easy for you to say. In your day and age, all you had to do was toss the woman of your choice over your shoulder and she was yours. Today—" Lucien raised his brows, a sudden thought occurring. *Today it might be even simpler.*

With a renewed sense of purpose, Lucien strode from the room, calling for Aunt Jane as he went.

Chapter 19

Arabella frowned at the snow-covered road. "This isn't the way."

"No?" Lucien slanted her a glance. She sat in the cart beside him, neatly gowned in an outmoded dress of faded blue wool, her feet encased in worn boots, a shabby fur-lined hat framing her pink-cheeked face. With her chestnut curls tucked beneath her bonnet, her pelisse buttoned to her throat, and her hands tightly clasped around a basket filled with jams and jellies, she appeared as annoyingly respectable as a governess.

But there was nothing respectful in the look she shot him. "It will take us an extra thirty minutes to reach the tenant's cottage by taking this road. It goes all the way through the forest."

"This is the way Aunt Jane instructed. She said the view was remarkable." Lucien peered through the thick foliage. Somewhere off this path was a deserted crofter's

242

cottage that was, according to Aunt Jane, abandoned and *very* romantically situated.

Simply compromising Arabella wouldn't be enough to convince her to marry him; she was far too strong-minded to succumb to such a pale ploy. It would take a full-fledged seduction of mind, body, and reason. He would have to answer her on all levels, meet her parry for parry, argument for argument, and passion for passion. She would not be satisfied with less. And, strangely, neither would he.

Aunt Jane had conveniently remembered the cottage, packed a basket full of tempting food, placed warm blankets in the box on the cart, and had Arabella ready to go within a half hour. She'd done everything but toss her niece into his arms.

The cart rumbled around a bend, and Lucien caught sight of the cottage. Thick ivy grew up the hand-hewn stone walls. Broken, rotting shutters hung in disrepair and part of the thatched roof lay open, allowing access to the room below for whatever animals and weather could fit through the hole.

Lucien grimaced. There was nothing romantic about a sagging roof and broken shutters. He only hoped it would provide sufficient cover for the night.

"The other road would have been much shorter," Arabella said, a frown between her brows. "Aunt Jane should have known that."

"I'm sure she thought we'd enjoy spending more time together." He grinned. "You may not have noticed, but she has developed a fondness for me."

"That is just because she still harbors the notion that you and I—" She broke off, and stared fixedly ahead.

"That we what?"

"Nothing," Arabella said hastily. "I simply wish we'd taken the shorter path—I've things to do today."

"Carrying Christmas jams to the tenants won't take long."

"You don't know how much work I have to do. I left Wilson repairing the broken door in the stables, and Ned still has to rescue what he can from the shed." She straightened her shoulders, her hands tightening on the basket. "I am a very busy woman."

And a very intriguing, very beguiling woman, at that. "Then admit it is getting warmer."

"It will probably rain before dark."

"At least admit that you are happy to escape for a little while."

"Escape? From what?" she asked, all indignant pride.

"From a daily drudgery that must be as tiresome as it is exhausting."

"Helping one's family is not 'drudgery.' But then, you wouldn't know that."

"Wouldn't I? Who do you think has been tending Liza since she was a seven-year-old brat with two front teeth missing?"

"Your aunt, most likely."

"Aunt Lavinia had neither the time nor the heart to raise a seven-year-old, especially one as precocious as Liza." He smiled, thinking of Liza's tumultuous childhood. "She was a handful. I taught her to ride and shoot, helped her select her governess—"

"You let her choose her own governess?"

"Of course. How would I know whom she did or did not like?"

"I'm sure her Latin is irreproachable."

"No, it is execrable, but her Greek is nearly flawless. She loves philosophy and can debate it for hours."

"Any sister of yours is bound to be good at arguing."

Lucien laughed and was rewarded with the faintest twitch of Arabella's lips. His mouth went dry, his body leaping to the ready. *Steady*, he told himself. *Now is not the time.*

If Aunt Jane did as she had promised, then by this time tomorrow, he and Arabella would be wed. Despite the circumstances, Lucien felt a dizzy excitement.

Arabella's gaze narrowed. "You look very smug. Did you find Bolder? Was he at the Red Rooster?"

If they were to become partners in truth, there could be no more secrets between them. Lucien shook his head. "I rode for miles this morning and he wasn't anywhere to be found. I went as far as Bridlington before anyone had even heard of him, and that was to little avail. No one seems to know where Bolder comes from or where he stays."

"That's because he lives on his ship."

He frowned. "How do you know that?"

"Lem. The tavern maid at the Sad Nun fancies him. She heard Bolder complain about having to live in such close quarters, and say that he would be glad when this job was done so he could live on solid ground once again."

A man who slept on a ship could escape at a moment's notice. Lucien would have to send word to the Home Office to keep a fast ship ready should he need it. He had no intention of letting the smuggler escape. "Do you know which ship?"

"The *Grande Marie*. She's docked at Aylmouth now, but she's moving soon. She never stays in one place longer than a few days at most."

No wonder he'd never been able to locate the smuggler. Perhaps the auction would be held on board, too. "That is very useful information."

"I thought you would be interested."

She was fishing for more information and he knew it. To turn her mind to other topics, he asked, "How did you establish your contact with the taverns?"

"Wilson was already supplying several of them himself. It was backbreaking work and he wasn't getting paid well. Now Lem and Twekes haul the barrels, make sure everything is sorted properly, and watch over the shipment until it is delivered, while Wilson takes orders and makes sure everyone gets what they need."

"And you?"

"I handle the money, decide how much to reinvest, and hold back a certain percentage for emergencies. I keep forty percent of our initial investment on hand in case we ever stumble on an opportunity. Just last year, Bolder came up with an astounding bargain on some brandy that was too good to pass up."

He looked down at her. "You are remarkable, did you know that?"

"It doesn't matter what I am, if I cannot protect Wilson." Her gaze darkened. "My decision to increase our shipments put him in more danger than he ever was when he worked on his own."

"You did what you had to, Bella. No one could ask more."

Arabella bit her lip. There was something different about Lucien today; something that heated his gaze with an intensity that made her exceedingly uncomfortable. She had the feeling he was watching her, waiting for something. Well, she had a few telling questions of her own. "Lucien, the jewelry you found in the cask, where did it come from?"

His gaze flickered just a second before he shrugged. "It was stolen."

"Obviously," she said dryly. "But why was it in the cask?"

"That is exactly what I want to know." The cart turned onto a wide lane that bordered a sturdy cottage set at the edge of a clearing. Lucien regarded the small house with apparent interest. "Who are these tenants Aunt Jane was so adamant we visit?"

"The Marches have been here for almost twelve years. Mary is Cook's niece, and she and her husband, John, produce almost half of the sheep we take to market."

The cart lumbered closer. Though small, the cottage was strong and sturdy, the thatched roof thick, the wattle walls free of holes. Arabella surveyed the home with satisfaction. "Wilson and I keep all of the tenants' homes in the best repair we can."

The corner of Lucien's mouth lifted in a half smile. "It seems the only person at Rosemont that you don't take care of is yourself."

The door to the cottage burst open, and a swarm of blond children tumbled out. Within minutes Arabella was standing by the cart and trying to carry on five different conversations at once.

Giving it up as a lost cause, she laughed and cast a glance at Lucien. He watched her, his mouth curved in a smile, that strange light in his eyes. For an instant, he shared her amusement, and it was as if their thoughts touched, their minds so of one accord that there was no need for words. Blushing furiously, Arabella looked away.

Mrs. March came outside, her hands covered with flour, the scent of nutmeg and cinnamon whirling about her. "Now, children, leave Miss Hadley be. I'm sure she didn't come to be mauled by the likes of ye."

Arabella laughed. "Oh, Mary, but I did! I assure you, I have thought of nothing else. Christmas at Rosemont is sadly lacking without any children."

"Ye're welcome to some of mine anytime ye wish it,

and well ye know." Mary's bright gaze found Lucien. "And who is this, takin' Wilson's place?"

Arabella hurried to make introductions. "Mary, this is the Du—"

"Devereaux," he interjected smoothly. "Lucien Devereaux." He climbed down from the cart, lifting the heavy basket of jams. "I am charged with carrying the basket. That is my sole purpose."

Mary's broad face split into a grin. "If ye got Miss Arabella to let ye do anythin' fer her, then ye are also a wizard, make no mistake."

He slanted her a smile and Arabella was instantly aware of how broad and handsome he looked, standing by the cart. He handed the basket to one of the boys who stood on the stoop. "Here, you look like a strong lad. Carry this inside for your mother."

"Aye, sir," said the boy, clasping the basket with both hands and casting a triumphant glance at his younger siblings.

Mary stood aside as her son marched into the house. "There, now, Miss Arabella. There's no need fer ye to bring us anythin'."

"Oh, don't blame me for that shocking basket. Aunt Jane knitted socks for each of the children and Aunt Emma bought them sugarplums. All I did was help Cook pack the jams."

"And brought them out on such a cold, damp day." Mary nodded to Lucien. "Ye can put the horse under the shed if ye'd like. There's some hay in there, too. James has no but one horse and he's out on her today." She turned to Arabella. "Lost a sheep, we did. Wandered off durin' the snow. Now come in by the fire. Ye're like to freeze out here."

She led the way into the house. "Ye are jus' in time. I

was bakin' the Christmas cake, and we've pudding as well."

Arabella followed Mary. The inside of the cottage was as homey and warm as the outside appeared. In front of a steadily burning fire sat a long, low table filled with little round cakes that made Arabella's mouth water. A brightly braided rug covered most of the floor and several sturdy chairs were placed about the room.

Arabella sighed. She loved coming here. The house was always full of warmth and comfort, and everyone worked together. Mrs. March gathered a large bowl and prepared to make plum pudding and Arabella immediately set about helping her.

They had just begun when the door opened and a large, burly man walked in. His hair was as blond as Mary's was red, his skin pink from the outdoors. The children immediately converged on him, laughing and talking at once until he gruffly ordered them to cease their squealing or he'd think they were Christmas pigs come for supper. Undaunted, they laughed, but soon turned to the sugarplums Aunt Emma had sent them.

He sniffed the air, coming to an abrupt halt. "Is that plum puddin' I smell?"

Mary watched him with a fond smile. "Ye know what it is, ye silly lummox. Did ye not tell me ye wished fer some today, jus' before ye left?"

John smacked his lips. "Aye, 'tis the best in all of England."

"Ye say that every year, and every year I have to remind ye that ye haven't tasted all of the plum puddin' in England. There might well be some that is better."

"But not sweeter," he said, swinging her into his arms and bestowing a loud kiss on her cheek. "I'd wager me last farthin' on it."

"Lawks, John! Not in front of the guests." Red-cheeked but clearly pleased, Mary pushed him away and nodded to Lucien. "This is Mr. Devereaux, who brought Miss Arabella fer her visit."

John immediately crossed to Lucien. "There, now, are me boys drivin' ye to distraction?"

To Arabella's amazement, Lucien replied easily, and within minutes the two men were engrossed in conversation, discussing everything from hunting to horses.

While assisting Mary, Arabella watched Lucien. It was strange, seeing him sitting on the rough-hewn chair, a child hanging on his knee, another sitting in his lap, as he talked with John. Stranger still was the way he was so completely at ease, as if hearth and home were his usual setting, and not the glittering ballrooms and clubs of London.

Lucien caught her puzzled gaze and grinned. Arabella smiled back, her spirits lifting. Suddenly her burdens didn't seem so heavy.

Mary shot a sly glance at Lucien. "Yer gentleman friend needs to eat before he takes ye home."

"I wish we could stay," Arabella said. It was lovely being here, and she knew that some of the ease she and Lucien had established would disappear once they returned to Rosemont. "But we must get back before dark."

"A pity. Still"—Mary leaned forward to whisper— " 'tis a handsome man ye've found. And the children love him."

It was true, and Lucien seemed equally taken with them. As she watched, Lucien's gaze came to rest on little William, the youngest of the March brood. A toddler the age of three, he had a round, plump face topped by a headful of angelic blond curls.

He was too shy to sit with the stranger, but that didn't

stop him from hiding behind a bench and watching Lucien with large blue eyes. Lucien solemnly returned little William's stare but made no motion toward him. Eventually the little boy edged closer, first rubbing his shoulder on Lucien's knee and then leaning his full weight.

Lucien winked at William and the boy grinned around his thumb. Soon he was sitting in Lucien's lap, playing with the emerald pin and hopelessly mussing his cravat. For an instant, Arabella wondered how Lucien would react to a child of his own. But try as she might, she could not conjure up an image. Though he reveled in playing with the Marches' children for a brief hour or two, he was not the kind of man to wish to raise a family. He'd shouldered that weight once already; he wouldn't be willing to do so again.

Arabella sighed, her heart aching as John reached over and plucked William out of Lucien's lap. "Here, now, Willie. Don't ye mess up the gentleman's fine clothes." He shot a narrow stare at Lucien. "Do you live here?"

"No, I live in London most of the time."

"Ah, that's a fine town. I went once when I was a lad. Will ye be returnin' anytime soon?"

"Next week."

Arabella felt as if the air had suddenly grown too thick to breathe. She should not have been surprised; still, some part of her felt betrayed. When would she learn? For her, Lucien Devereaux was a heartbreak waiting to happen. She picked up some wooden trenchers and set them near the table, trying desperately to keep her face from revealing too much.

Mary came to stand beside her. "He looks like a lovely man."

"He can be," she said shortly.

"Oh, lud, child. None of them are perfect. Ye has to

make 'em that way." She set Arabella a sharp glance. "Does he treat ye well?"

"No. He is bossy and interfering." *And then he leaves me.* Arabella picked up a rag and began to clean the wooden table, attacking every uneven place as if it were a grease stain.

"Ye can tell he holds ye in respect. He's not stopped starin' at ye since ye came in."

Arabella refused to look his way, afraid her shock might show in her eyes.

"Ye has to have respect fer each other if ye want a solid marriage. 'Tis the only thing that gets ye through the hard times." Mary nodded toward her husband. "Ye need someone who'll stand by yer side, Miss Arabella. Someone who'll take care of ye and let ye take care of him."

"I don't need anyone to take care of me."

"Of course ye don't. But 'tis nice to have another pair of shoulders to help bear the burdens, especially when ye've wee ones."

John sat with a child on each knee and one leaning over his shoulder. Though he spoke with Lucien, his hands were forever patting the head of this one or ruffling the hair of that.

"He do love them, don't he?" Mary said with a satisfied sigh. " 'Twill be the same fer ye, when ye marry. And 'tis past time ye did. Why, Master Robert'll take a wife soon, and then where will ye be?"

Robert take a wife? She had never given it any thought, but when Robert married, she would no longer be needed. A lump the size of a boot lodged in her throat.

Mary placed a pudding in the now-empty basket. "There, take this with ye." She glanced out the window and frowned. "If ye're goin' to leave before dark, ye'd best go now."

"What's that?" called John from his seat by the fire. "Ye can't leave before supper. 'Tis too cold to travel without something to warm yer stomach." He looked at Lucien. "Don't you agree, Mr. Devereaux?"

Lucien's gaze brushed over her face. "It won't hurt to stay another few minutes."

Arabella murmured a protest, but Mary would have none of it. Before she knew what she was about, they were all seated at the long table. Mary served a shepherd's pie rich with gravy and topped with a flaky crust that would have made Cook green with envy. Conversation never ceased and Arabella's heart eased somewhat.

It was different this time; Lucien hadn't promised her anything. All he'd done was offer his assistance. If she'd become dependent on him in some indefinable way, well, that was her fault. Coming to such a reasonable conclusion helped her to put on a cheerful face, and she was even able to laugh aloud at some of the antics of the children.

Seated by Lucien's side, his thigh pressed against her, his warm gaze turning to her frequently, the half hour flew past and lengthened. Arabella found herself lingering more and more. By the time she and Lucien had climbed into the wagon, ready to depart, it was already getting dark.

John stood by the cart and cast a frowning glance at the sky. "It looks like rain."

"Or sleet," added Mary, *tsk*ing. "It gets cold so quickly. Perhaps ye should stay the night."

Arabella stared up at the gray sky, where the moon peeked out from behind swirling dark clouds. "Surely we can make it if we hurry."

Lucien must have agreed, for no sooner had she said the words than he thanked their hosts, tucked a warm blanket across her lap, and set the horse in motion. With a final wave at the Marches, they were soon traveling down the road, Sebastian holding to a steady walk.

The air was crisp and fresh, promising rain before morning. Barren branches rose toward the moon, which slipped between the clouds, casting eerie shadows that seemed to aggravate the rising wind. Arabella found herself leaning closer to Lucien.

He pulled her against him. When she tried to move away, he held her tighter, saying curtly, "Just to keep warm."

She relaxed and let his heat seep through her pelisse. Though she knew it was only imaginary, the feeling of belonging, of being loved and cherished, was too lovely to let slip away. Next week, when he left, she would deal with her loss. For now, it was enough just to sit beside him.

She must have dozed, for she woke when he pulled her closer, opening his coat and draping it over them both. "In case it rains," he murmured.

She tried to straighten, but his arm held her close. Sometime while she'd been sleeping, her bonnet had fallen loose and lay on the seat beside her.

"Go back to sleep, Bella. Sebastian and I will take care of everything."

His voice rumbled beneath her cheek, lulling her. "I am not sleepy," she said, though she didn't make a move to sit upright. She closed her eyes and relaxed against him, savoring the feel of his broad chest against her cheek. Had it been anyone other than Lucien, she would never have allowed such impropriety. But he would be gone soon. And she would be alone once more. For now, though, she enjoyed the luxury of being completely enclosed in his arms.

She was just slipping back to sleep when a sudden jar of the cart made her open her eyes and grab the seat. They were standing stock-still in the middle of the forest, the cart tilted to one side. "What happened?"

"The cart slid off the road." Lucien urged Sebastian on. The horse laid his head low and pulled, but the cart didn't move.

Arabella looked around, noting the thick trees. "Where are we?"

"On the road to Rosemont."

"But this isn't . . ." She frowned. "You took Aunt Jane's shortcut."

"It was the only way I knew," he said curtly. "And you were asleep."

"You should have wakened me." She looked over the side of the cart. "How on earth did this happen?"

"Ice formed across the road, and we slid sideways. I tried to pull on the brake, but it stuck."

Her heart sank. "We'll never get out of here now."

"Surely I can yank it loose," Lucien said, his strong hands already closing over the brake.

"The only way to loosen it is to—"

Crack. The handle broke in half. Lucien looked at it for a long minute before raising his gaze to her. "You were saying?"

Irritation built. "I warned you!"

"So you did." He glanced up at the sky and dropped the broken handle into the floorboard. "Well, there's no way we can fix this tonight. It is going to rain any minute. I saw a cottage near here on the way in."

He assisted Arabella out of the cart, unhooked Sebastian, and then loaded the horse with items from the cart. Before he had finished, large, soft drops of rain began to plop onto the cart in a steady tattoo.

Arabella shivered. "Perhaps we could walk to the Marches'. Surely we could find our way there."

"And if we don't? I, for one, do not fancy freezing to death."

As much as it galled her, he was right; the night was already frigid. The rain that fell was cold, almost freezing. It would swiftly turn to sleet and then snow. As she followed Lucien into the woods, the skies opened and the light rain became a furious storm, drenching her completely in the first minute.

"This way!" Lucien yelled above the roar. He grabbed her hand and pulled her along until they stumbled through the door of a dark and damp cottage. Lucien immediately went back out, and returned carrying a bundle under his coat.

Lightning lit the interior of the cottage, followed by a crack of thunder. The ground vibrated from the tumultuous crash. Arabella glimpsed their haven and it chilled her as much as the sleet. Half the roof had fallen away, the opening allowing a steady pour of rain that made a small river out the door. Broken tables and a chair lay on the dirt floor, and a single fireplace filled one small wall.

Within an amazingly short period of time, Lucien had started a fire using the broken chairs, adding wet wood that sent smoky swirls up the chimney and puffing into the cottage. Digging through the corners of the hut, he found an old cot, barely wide enough for one person. He turned it upright, draped a wool blanket over it, and pulled it close to the fire. Arabella sat huddled on one end, her arms clasped together, shivers racking her body.

Outside, the whole world seemed to be awash in dull, cold gray, but inside the stone and wattle walls, the fire radiated a welcome heat. "I should have known it was going to rain," Arabella said in a hoarse voice.

Lucien turned from stoking the fire and caught sight of

Arabella's pale face. With a muffled curse, he strode to her side and hauled her against him. As if it were the most natural thing in the world, he lifted her into his arms, sat on the cot, and opened his coat around her.

Enveloped by warmth, Arabella pressed her cheek against his shirt. The heavy wool of his coat had protected him better than her thin pelisse, and his shirt was still warm and dry against her cheek. Gradually her shivers abated.

He rubbed his cheek against her hair. "You are soaking wet. We must get you out of those clothes."

She shook her head.

Lucien held her tighter. "You will become ill."

"No. I just need to get warm." She pushed closer still, hiding her face against his neckcloth.

He didn't move. He just sat, holding her as the flames crackled and the thrum of rain pitter-patted through the hole in the roof. The only light came from the flickering fire. A slow tremor of awareness trickled down her spine.

"Bella," Lucien whispered against her temple.

She tightened her grip, unable to release him, unable to forget next week, when he would leave once more.

Lucien cupped her face with a warm hand and turned her face to his. "This morning, during the fire, all I could think was that I would never get the chance to do this." He touched his lips to hers.

Heat exploded and all the feelings she'd been stifling burst to the fore. She wrapped her arms about him and held him closer, opening her mouth beneath his. Somehow, she was no longer sitting on the edge of the decrepit cot, but lying across it, Lucien's broad form blocking out the heat of the fire.

But she had no need of the fire now. Her insides burned

with a deep heat all their own. His hands slipped down her shoulders to her breasts and beyond, caressing the entire length of her body.

His hand cupped her ankle and she stiffened, cold reason returning. *What am I doing? He will leave and I will still be here, alone.* The thought banished the last vestige of the spell he'd woven. She pushed him aside. "No."

He stopped, his gaze meeting hers. Green fire sparkled in the depths of his eyes, but he removed his hand, rocking back on one elbow to look down at her. "Why not?"

Lucien trailed his fingers near the corner of her mouth and she tried to move away. Her heart pounded a furious beat, but she managed to say in a credibly even tone, "It might snow if this continues through the night. We should leave now."

He dipped his head until his lips were but an inch from her ear. "It would be a pity if we were trapped here. For days. And no one knew where to find us." The low sound brushed across the delicate lobes of her ears like raw silk.

She rolled to her side, almost falling off the cot in her haste to get away. Tripping a little over the edge of the blanket, she went to the window and peered out into the swirling darkness, shivering at the cold. "The rain will stop soon and it will—"

"Begin to snow." In a deep, rich voice, he said what she both wanted and feared to hear. "We have no choice but to stay until morning."

Arabella looked over her shoulder. A slow smile curved his lips. He rolled up on one elbow and lifted the corner of the blanket in invitation. "Come back to bed, Bella. It's much warmer here."

She looked at him, at the finely muscled sinew of his arms, at the bronze column of his throat. He was right: It did look warmer. So warm that she wondered if she would melt if he took her in his arms again.

But her other option was to freeze to death by the inadequate fire, alone and cold during an interminable night. *Some choice: death by ice or death by fire.* The only problem was, she wasn't sure which would hurt the least.

Chapter 20

Arabella turned back toward the fire, afraid to look too long at the tempting picture of Lucien in bed, waiting for her. "Surely this weather will clear and we'll be able to find someone who can help us. . . ."

The closest cottage was much too far away to attempt in the middle of a cold black night. The freezing rain continued to pound on the broken roof and drip steadily into the little stream that flowed out the door.

Lucien met her gaze, a slow, almost slumberous smile curving his lips. "What's wrong, Bella? Afraid?"

She clenched her hands into fists. She could not deny that she was aware of him, of his every move, of his scent, the strong line of his jaw, the burning shimmer in his green gaze. Lying in bed, his hair damp, his gaze fastened on hers as if she were the only woman in the world, he appeared a fallen angel, darkly handsome and intent on gratifying her every desire.

Arabella fought a wave of hot excitement. She plucked

nervously at her buttoned pelisse. The thin wet wool hugged her body and made it difficult to breathe.

She sent a careful glance at Lucien, caught by the sensual line of his mouth. She knew that mouth, had tasted it and felt its heat. She ran a nervous tongue over her own lips. Every part of her yearned for him, craved his touch, desired the feel of his lips sliding over her mouth, her cheek, her neck, her breasts.

A rumble of thunder shook the cottage. Arabella shivered, fighting off the sensation that she was drowning in a swell of desire.

"You are cold." Lucien rose from the cot to pull his coat snuggly around her shoulders. He gathered the front, his hands brushing against her throat. He smiled when she sent a glance up at him, and for an instant his gaze darkened. Arabella couldn't breathe. She just waited, awareness stretching, her lips tingling with imagined pressure. . . .

Muttering a fierce curse, he turned away and bent to tend the fire.

Disappointment washed over her in waves. Arabella sank onto the edge of a broken chair and hugged the heavy wool coat to her. It enveloped her with his warmth, even as the intriguing scent of his cologne rose to envelop her senses. Arabella pulled the material closer, dropping her chin into the rough wool so she could savor the feeling of his presence. But that was all she would have; he was leaving in a week. "Perhaps I can ride Sebastian home."

He turned to look at her, his brows slightly raised. "What?"

"I could ride Sebastian—"

"You aren't going anywhere. Someone tried to kill one of us this morning, and I'll be damned if I let you go jaunting about by yourself. We will stay here, where we are warm and safe."

She wanted to argue, but the memory of the fire was too fresh. She couldn't shake the feeling of helplessness that had gripped her as she lay on the floor of the shed, choking for breath. What would Robert do without her? And Aunt Jane and Emma? Lord Harlbrook would waste no time in presenting his notes, and all would be lost. And now, with Aunt Jane's gaming debts, Sir Loughton would also have a claim to the estate.

She didn't know how long she'd sat there, staring into the fire, when Lucien stooped beside her. He put his arms about her and gently turned her to face him. "We don't need to think about what happened this morning, Bella. Or last night or ten years ago. We are here, tonight. Just us." His voice ran along her senses, melting everything in its path. "Kiss me, Bella."

She shook her head.

"Then let me kiss you." He brushed the tips of his fingers along her cheek, leaving a trail of delicate fire. "Just say the word, Bella *mia*. Tell me what you want."

What *did* she want? She swallowed, aware that he was deliberately seducing her. *And why not?* a voice inside her whispered. *Why not let emotion overtake you just this one, last time?* Perhaps this was her last chance to experience again the heat of true passion, the pleasure of true . . . She caught herself a moment before she committed the worst sin of all—believing herself in love once again with Lucien Devereaux.

It was a good thing she was older and wiser, and had far too much sense to get emotionally entangled with a man who did not know the meaning of the word *commitment. Which,* a naughty voice whispered to her, *is why it makes such perfect sense to succumb now.* Only with

Lucien did she feel the wild surge of excitement, this heady power, as if she could do anything she wanted. And it was time she did something just for herself. Something so sinfully selfish that it would warm her memories forever.

"Bella," he murmured. He took her hand and placed the pad of her forefinger against his lip. With the tenderest of touches, he bit the pink end of her finger, swirled his tongue over the imaginary wound, and then gently closed his teeth over it again. Jolts of shocked desire traveled through her.

His eyes darkened and he slipped her finger into his mouth. Heat swelled as his tongue stroked her flesh. Need pooled between her thighs, and she clenched them together to still the ache.

He withdrew her finger and placed a reverent kiss on it. "I want you with me, beneath me," he whispered. "Do you want me, Bella?"

In answer, Arabella twined her arms about his neck and pulled his mouth to hers. His lips were hot and demanding, his hands cupping, stroking, exploring her as if he'd never touched her before. He groaned as she raked a hand through his hair, holding him to her.

The coat dropped to the floor and suddenly touching him was not enough. She wanted to taste him, to fill her senses until there was nothing but Lucien. A wave of longing slammed into her heart, and the walls she'd built to protect herself began to crack. Lightning flashed across the skies and thunder shook the ground as Arabella lost herself in the taste of him—his mouth possessing hers, the hot feel of his lips on her skin, the sensuous thrust of his tongue in her mouth.

The edge of the cot pressed against the back of her legs, and Lucien broke the kiss long enough to look down at her. "I want you," he whispered hoarsely. "I've always wanted you."

"And I want you." So badly that she didn't care anymore what anyone thought or would say. All she cared about was the feel of his hands as he molded her to him. His fingers slid through her hair, down her throat, to the top button of her pelisse. He tried to unbutton the wet wool, but it fought him. Cursing, he yanked at it, ripping the material.

Arabella reached to help him. Together, they tore the clinging wool away, revealing her wet gown beneath. Lucien's hands closed over her shoulders and he held her away, his gaze brushing over her body where the gown was plastered to it. "Beautiful," he murmured. "So beautiful."

A flush of power surged through her. With trembling fingers, she undid the lacing on her gown, her breasts pushing against the cold material, her nipples hardening.

His face was a mask of torment and she reveled in it. His breath harsh, he reached for her, but she stayed him with a single word. Slowly, never unlocking her gaze from his, she undid her lacings and pulled the gown off, dropping the petticoat to the floor. Nothing remained but her thin wet chemise. It clung to her, hiding nothing.

Lucien moaned, his hands fisted at his sides. "Damn it, Bella. I can't take this much longer."

Neither could she. Her whole body throbbed with desire and if he didn't touch her soon, she would explode in a whoosh of heat. "Undress me," she commanded, excited by her own brazen behavior. It would be a night *they* would never forget.

Lucien knelt on the dirt floor. He looked up at her, his head even with her chest. The sight of his sensuous mouth so near her nipples caused them to pucker as if he had touched them. He lowered his hands and placed them on her calves. Slowly, ever so slowly, he slid them up, over her knees, to the swell of her hips, past her waist, over her breasts, and to the thin straps of her chemise. With hands that trembled slightly, he pushed the straps aside. The air brushed her with cold tingles.

As he exposed her bare skin, he kissed each spot until his tongue trailed a heated path between her breasts. She tangled her fingers in his thick hair, pulling him closer. He shoved the material down, baring her breasts to the chilled air. Lucien's unsteady breathing aroused her further, causing the damp place between her thighs to ache.

His mouth closed over one peak and heat sluiced from her breast to below. Arabella gasped as he pushed the chemise down to her hips, his mouth again following the skin he now laid bare.

She writhed against him, her hands moving wildly over his neck and shoulders. His tongue played along her stomach—and then her chemise dropped to the floor.

For an instant, neither moved. Then slowly, ever so slowly, Lucien leaned forward and placed a kiss in the tangled curls that beckoned. Arabella moaned, her entire body rigid.

He gently pushed her back onto the bed and placed his hands over the top of her stockings. Slowly, deliberately, he rolled them down, his hands warming the chilled skin as he went.

"You are so beautiful," he murmured. "So incredibly beautiful." He reached up and gently touched her nipple.

Arabella clenched her hands into the wool coat that lay beneath her. "Don't," she managed to get out through her parched lips.

"Don't what?" His mouth curved in a devastating smile. "Don't do this?" He flicked the tip of his finger across her breast. "Or don't do this?" He bent his head and laved her peak, his hot tongue flooding her with sensations. His eyes glinted as he moved back, his chest rubbing across her belly, his shirt rough against her skin. His hands trailed over the delicate skin of her thigh. "Or perhaps you don't want this."

He dipped his head low, then lower still, until his tongue touched her very core. Arabella gasped and involuntarily thrust her hips forward, pressing his mouth further against her womanhood. He moaned, his hands closing over her bottom as his tongue danced in and out, sending her spiraling madly out of control.

"*Lucien!*" The world exploded in a thousand colors and pushed her over the edge of passion and into a whirlpool of melted desire.

Hungrily, Lucien watched as she found her release and her breathing returned to normal. Then he stood to remove his boots and undo his breeches. Arabella's warm brown eyes never left his. She lay completely naked, her thighs slightly parted, her skin pink and passion-kissed.

It was like a dream, one he'd had a thousand times since he'd left her all those years ago. Yet this time, there would be no leaving. There would only be him and Arabella, forever.

Like a man starved, he yanked off the rest of his clothing and leaned down to join her on the narrow cot. He expected her passion to be spent, to have to seduce her back to the point of excitement, but he had no sooner put his lips to hers than she pressed herself against him, thrusting her tongue into his mouth in invitation.

He'd meant the kiss to be gentle: his promise to care for her always. But she was beyond gentle. Arabella threw her arms about his neck, pressing against him, fanning his lust to flames. The kiss deepened and she moaned against his lips, begging for more, begging for release.

He rolled her to her back and positioned himself over her, straining against the fierce desire that urged him on. Slowly, carefully, he lowered himself into her, keeping her eyes locked to his. Her lips parted as her breath tore between her lips. Her fingers curled, her nails biting into his arms. "I want you, Lucien," she whispered hoarsely. "Please. . . ."

He thrust home, plundering her depths. She gave a startled cry, her head thrown back, her hips arching to meet his. Again and again he thrust, each stroke ecstasy, each departure an agony.

She lifted her legs and clasped his hips tightly, her body writhing in a sensuous dance beneath his. He could feel her need building as she arched into him, his own emotions barely under control, his body aching with the torture. *One more time,* he pleaded wordlessly. As if she heard him, she stiffened beneath him, her body arching so wildly that Lucien had to wrap his arms about her to hold her to him.

Pleasure crashed through her and across Lucien and his passion finally exploded to meet hers. He collapsed against Arabella, cradling her to him. God, but she could drive him to heights no other woman could. He didn't know what it was—her natural warmth, the passion she embraced life with, or the completely uncontrolled way she reacted to his touch—but it was almost more than he could handle.

He turned his head and met her gaze. Her lips were still parted, her breath gasping and uneven, her eyes soft and unfocused. Yet she managed a small, soft smile, so tender that he gathered her close and placed a kiss in her hair.

Lucien savored the warmth of her breath against his

chest, the feel of her hair where it tumbled over his arm. Time slipped by and her breathing settled into the deep rhythm of sleep. Lucien looked down where she lay curled so trustingly against him, her lashes shadowing her cheek, her soft, pink mouth parted in sleep.

Something shifted in Lucien's chest and he brushed a curl from her forehead. Come what may, she was his. His to have and to hold. His to protect—with his life, if necessary.

His stomach tightened at the thought. This time, he would not fail her.

For a long, long time, Lucien lay with Arabella in his arms, his face drawn and set.

What was it about her that touched his heart? He pulled the blanket over her shoulder and tucked it about her as if she were a child. But there wasn't anything childlike about Arabella. She had taken on the care of her brother and aunts without hesitation or any self-pity. She was strong and capable, one of the most independent women he knew.

Though he appreciated her good traits, he was not blind to her faults. His Bella was too quick to anger and far too stubborn—just like her brother.

Lucien rested his cheek against her hair, the wild, silky curls brushing his chin. But of all her family, Arabella had inherited the Captain's pirating spirit—she thrived on the excitement of a livelihood that would have left many men weak-kneed with trepidation.

As if aware of his thoughts, she murmured an incoherent word, and then turned to burrow against him, one hand resting on his chest. Lucien held her tighter, a band constricting about his heart.

Before he could devote himself to Arabella, he had to let the past go. Somehow, he'd let Sabrina's tragedy keep him from living. He needed to move forward and face the future—a future that included his Bella.

The thought held him for some time, until finally, too tired to do more, he drifted off to sleep.

Chapter 21

A brisk rap awoke Arabella from a deep, languorous sleep. The dim light meant it was early—much too early to rise. Yawning, she stretched and then shivered as a finger of cold air wafted over her bare skin.

Her eyes flew open, memories of the night yanking her awake. She started to sit up, but a warm, masculine leg moved over hers, pinning her to the bed. *Lucien.* She turned her head and gazed at him. His thick, black hair fell across his forehead and softened the lines of his face. Just seeing so much male beauty asleep beside her made Arabella sigh. And last night, for a short while at least, he had been hers. The thought curled up to warm her.

The sharp rap rang out again. Startled, Arabella turned toward the heavy oak door and caught sight of Aunt Jane's favorite blue bonnet through the vine that covered the window. She gasped and dove under the covers, slipping an arm out to search the floor for her lost clothing.

A lazy voice drawled in her ear. "Hmm, a sprightly

270

maid, to awaken me by burrowing 'neath the covers."
Lucien pulled her closer and pressed her other hand to his
manhood, now soft and warm between his legs. "Is this
perchance the treasure you seek so eagerly?"

She jerked her hand away. "Will you stop that? Someone is at the door."

"Let them find their own amusement." His hands wandered over her hips, her breasts, instantly rousing her. "I
have plans for you, milady. And they include only ourselves."

"Aunt Jane is here!"

That stopped him. He lifted his head. Outside came the
faint murmur of voices, as if someone were holding a
meeting.

"How did they find us?" Arabella asked desperately.
She knew what would happen, and she was not about to sit
idly by as her aunts tried to shame Lucien into marrying
her. She fought an overpowering desire to crawl under the
cot and hide.

Lucien seemed impervious to the danger. He regarded
her with a smiling gaze, his attention focused on her lips.
"Maybe if we ignore them they will go away."

Or burst through the door and stumble in to see their
niece naked in bed with a duke. Aunt Jane would think
she'd died and gone to heaven. The idea sent a wave of
panic through Arabella, and she jerked upright and swung
her legs over the side of the cot.

Lucien's muscular arm encircled her waist. With a
smooth, easy motion, he hauled her back beside him,
tucking the blanket back over her. "Stay here." His
whispered command tickled her ear. "It is too cold to
rise."

"What if they come in?"

"Then you will have to tell them."

"Tell them what?" she asked, stung that he would put the entire burden of confession on her shoulders.

"That there isn't room in this cot for anyone else. In fact"—he nuzzled her neck—"there's barely room for us."

"Lucien, I will not say anything so improper!"

"You'll have to," he whispered into her hair. "I'm going to be much too busy touching you, kissing you, tasting you." He nipped her shoulder, sending a tremor of awareness all the way to her toes. He rubbed against her, the hardness of his manhood telling her he was more than ready to resume their lovemaking.

"Will you stop that?" She pushed at his arm. He was making it pure hell to even think. "Lucien, Aunt Jane was peeking in the window—she may already know—I will have to tell them. . . ." She trailed off miserably.

He stilled for an instant before threading his hand into her hair and turning her face toward his. He held her there, his eyes sparkling and hard. "What will you tell them, Arabella?"

"That you and I did not . . . that we just slept here because of the snowstorm and . . . and nothing else."

He regarded her for an intense moment. *"No."*

She gritted her teeth in frustration. Even now, her aunts would be deciding what color of wedding gown she should wear. Panic seared her lungs. "We have to get dressed!"

She scrambled to untangle her legs from the blanket, but Lucien held her tight, his voice warm against her neck. "It is too late, sweet."

"But they could open the door any minute and find us."

He nuzzled her neck. "Hmm. You smell like cinnamon."

"That's from Mary's plum pudding, you lummox! Don't you understand—"

He cut her off with a kiss, his mouth demanding, insistent, his hands moving rapidly over her breasts, her stomach. She was lost before she could even fathom his intent, her body instantly arching against his.

Lucien reached down to let his fingers begin a leisurely journey across the curve of her knee, to the inside of her thigh, coming to rest just inches away from the tight sable curls. From there, it was but a second of heart-rending pleasure as he cupped her intimately, his long fingers stroking ever so lightly, bringing her to an instant state of arousal that was so strong, she forgot about the murmur at the door, forgot she was in a cottage in the middle of the forest. She forgot everything but the fact that she was naked and in his arms.

The door suddenly burst open and Aunt Jane stood silhouetted in the predawn dimness, a lantern in her hand. Arabella gasped, yanked back to reality by the sudden glare.

"Behold," murmured Lucien into Arabella's ear, "so cometh Justice holding aloft the lantern of Truth."

She elbowed him, hard.

"Oh, my . . ." Aunt Jane sputtered. "I—I never thought . . . I didn't realize . . . this isn't what we had agreed—"

Behind Aunt Jane stood Aunt Emma, her eyes wide, her mouth drawn in a perfect O.

Vicar Haighton strode into the cottage, his nose red from the cold. "Here we are, ladies. I tied up the cart. I trust you have found our missing—" His gasp of shocked outrage could have been heard in the next county.

Arabella dropped back onto the makeshift pillow and yanked the covers over her head. *Please, God, I will never again ask for anything. Just make them all go away.*

After a moment of stilted silence, Lucien said, "Uhm,

pardon me, Lady Melwin." Without waiting for an answer, he burrowed beneath the blanket, his voice brushing across Arabella's ear. "I hate to bother you, sweet. And I know you must be tired from our exertions, but we must get up."

"Then go," she hissed, turning to glare at him. The lamplight shone through the blanket and bathed everything with a soft yellow glow. "I am not stopping you."

His eyes lit with a strange light. "No?"

"No. Do whatever you want to do; I am staying here."

"For how long?"

"Forever, if necessary."

"You will die of starvation."

"So be it," she snapped.

Aunt Emma coughed loudly, but Aunt Jane was not so circumspect. She harrumphed and said loudly, "Vicar Haighton, how quickly can you marry them?"

While the vicar sputtered an answer, Arabella turned to Lucien. "It is rather dark in here. Perhaps they didn't get a good look at me."

He raised his brows and she continued, "You could tell them that I'm not here, that you left me at the Marches, and that the woman under the blanket is someone else. They would believe it, because you aren't exactly an angel, and—"

"*No.*" Lucien cupped her face and rubbed the pad of his thumb over her full bottom lip. "Arabella, you cannot expect me to tell your aunts that I met some chance woman in the forest and seduced her."

"Why not?" she demanded. Her fingers closed over his wrist and she pushed his hand away.

"Pardon me!" Aunt Jane's voice came from directly above their heads, as if she had bent down to yell through the blanket. "Vicar Haighton and I would like a word with you both. Could you please come out from beneath that blanket?"

Arabella clenched her teeth, her body stiffening like a board. She looked at Lucien and he noted the swell of tears in her eyes. "I can't," she whispered, her voice breaking. "Not now. Not like this."

He brushed a curl from her forehead. "No?"

She shook her head, the tear dislodging and rolling down her cheek.

Lucien kissed away the tear, a feeling of regret shading his good humor. It really was for the best, and the sooner she realized it, the better. "Do you want me to speak to your aunts?"

Arabella nodded miserably, another tear slipping out to join the first.

"Very well." He placed a quick kiss on her cheek and then lifted the blanket, careful to uncover only his own head. "Ah, Lady Melwin. Arabella and I would like some time to compose ourselves."

"Compose?" Aunt Jane's gaze sharpened and she lifted a hand as if to reach for the blanket. "What's wrong?"

"Nothing." Lucien curled an arm about Arabella's still form and pulled her closer. She turned toward him, hiding her face against his chest. "We are just a little, er, over-whelmed by so many guests."

Aunt Jane stared at him, her eyes hawkish. Whatever she read in his face must have reassured her, for she relaxed and gave a brief nod. "I suppose you should dress before speaking with the vicar."

Arabella murmured a protest against Lucien's chest, and the warmth of her breath against his bare skin made his breath quicken. He cleared his throat. "Yes, well, we will need more time than that. We would like time to er, prepare before meeting with the vicar."

Aunt Emma tugged on Aunt Jane's lace sleeve. "Jane, for heaven's sake, leave them alone long enough to put their clothes on!"

"But we can't leave them here!"

The vicar pursed his lips. "Lady Melwin is right. We should not leave them alone in such a manner. It is most improper."

Aunt Emma gave an inelegant snort. "Why not? They cannot fornicate worse than they already have."

Lucien choked back a laugh, drawing the vicar's stern gaze.

The portly man gave a disgusted sigh, then strode to the door, saying gruffly over his shoulder, "We will see Your Grace at Rosemont within the hour, if you please."

"Yes, sir," Lucien said meekly.

"Oh, stop that!" Aunt Jane snapped. "We brought Satan; we'll tie him up outside." She stared hard at the blanket where Arabella lay hidden before letting out a long sigh and marching from the cottage. Aunt Emma followed, smiling apologetically at Lucien and thoughtfully closing the door behind her.

Lucien sighed, then lifted the blanket back over his head and joined Arabella in their makeshift tent.

Arabella looked up at him, her hair a nimbus of curls about her face, her nose red. "What will we do?"

"It appears, my love, that you and I are to wed."

"No."

The vehemence of her denial made him wince, even though he had expected it. "And why not?"

She turned away and covering her face with her hands.

Her muffled voice answered, "You don't want to marry me, and I have no wish to marry you."

"I don't know about that." Lucien's gaze trailed down the delectable slope of her back, all the way to the rounded swell of her bottom. "Perhaps your aunt is right. This may not be exactly what we planned, but there are many reasons we should marry."

"Name one," she said over her shoulder.

"Well, for one—you are ruined. You have to marry."

"No, I don't," she said, sounding so sure that he slipped an arm around her waist and turned her onto her back so he could see her face.

"Why not?" he demanded.

"Because I was ruined when I was sixteen. You can't be ruined twice."

"I would like to try," he murmured, kissing her shell-pink ear.

She swatted at him. "Stop that. This is serious."

"Yes, ma'am," he said meekly, grinning when she glared at him. "There are other reasons we should consider an alliance, too. For example, think how embarrassed your aunts will be if the vicar sees fit to mention to anyone what he saw here."

That struck home, for she turned a bright red before rallying. "My aunts are more likely to be distraught that I missed a chance to be a duchess."

"That is yet another reason: You'll be a duchess. Think of how much enjoyment you could glean from that." He rested his cheek against her hair. "Just imagine Lord Harlbrook's face when he has to call you 'Your Grace.' "

She bit her lip. "He would hate that, wouldn't he?"

"With every breath in his body."

She lingered on the image for a while, then sighed heavily and shook her head. "No, I don't want to be a duchess. I have far too much to do here."

Lucien shrugged. "As you wish. But I happen to be a very wealthy duke, Bella. Think of all the improvements you could make at Rosemont if you had considerable funds at your disposal."

She turned to look at him, a serious expression in her wide brown eyes. "Lucien, if we were married and I told you I needed a certain sum of money, would you give it to me without asking any questions?"

"Yes," he replied without pause. *What in the devil had she gotten herself into now*?

"Even if I asked for ten thousand pounds?"

Ten thousand? At her steady, pleading gaze, his lips twitched. "We will consider it a bride gift."

She brightened. "You would?"

"Anything you desire." He brushed the end of a strand of hair across the delicate line of her cheek. "You know, I like the idea of having you as my duchess."

She frowned and shifted to face him directly. "Lucien, you've given me so many reasons to marry you, but what possible reason would *you* have to marry *me*?"

Because I love you to distraction. The words burned on the edge of his lips, begging for release, but he hid them behind a casual smile. "I am getting older and it is time I settled down."

A frown curved her brow. "You did say that your aunt was forever pressing you to marry."

"I believe the word I used was *hounding*. If I marry, she will cease to bother me." He traced the line of her brow with his finger. "Especially if we produce an heir within the next year."

He saw a flash of something in the back of her eyes, but

he held his ground. Their marriage would be as passionate as he could make it. She would be his wife in every sense of the word.

Lucien slid the back of his hand down her cheek. "I watched you at the Marches', Bella. You want children."

"Yes. Someday."

"You dream of them, as do I."

"I . . . I suppose I do. I just never thought to have them this way."

Married to a man I do not love. She didn't say the words, but Lucien heard them nonetheless. His heart ached at the thought. He'd failed at love before, and he could not bear the thought of disappointing her yet again. It would be better for them both if he kept his heart firmly under control.

He swallowed the tightness in his throat. "There are other reasons we should marry. Constable Robbins would never dare accuse the Duchess of Wexford of smuggling."

"No, but he might still accuse Wilson."

"We'll send Wilson to one of my estates in Derbyshire. The constable won't know where to find him." He leaned over to place a kiss by her ear. "Bella *mia,* think of it: no more freezing cold caves, no more dealings with men like Bolder to provide a home for your aunts."

He knew he'd scored a mark with that one, because a dreamy expression softened her face. Lucien swooped in for the kill. "And there are doctors in London," he murmured softly, running a finger up and down her arm. "Doctors who have experience in dealing with cases like Robert's."

She turned to look at him then, her face alive with hope. "Oh, Lucien! Do you think they could cure him?"

"I don't know, sweet. But as soon as we are wed, we will find out." He prayed he could find one who knew something about Robert's peculiar paralysis. If he had to turn over every brick in London, he would find someone to cure Arabella's brother.

She stared at him, clearly caught between fear and hope. For an instant, Lucien felt like the biggest heel on earth. *It's a necessary deception,* he told himself.

Finally, she let out her breath in a long sigh that sounded suspiciously like defeat. "Very well. I will marry you."

Lucien laughed softly, catching her against him and burrowing his face in her neck. God knew, it wasn't perfect, but it was a beginning.

And it was far, far more than he deserved.

Chapter 22

Lucien and Arabella rode up to Rosemont on Sebastian and Satan an hour later than they'd promised Aunt Jane. Lucien had refused to rise without taking advantage again of the privacy of their makeshift bed.

Their lovemaking had been different this time. Still hotly passionate, but there had been an undercurrent of tenderness that had astounded Arabella as much as it had confused her. It had been as if Lucien were taking an oath every bit as serious as the wedding vows Aunt Jane dreamed of.

Arabella had chided herself severely for succumbing to such fanciful ideas. Lucien was marrying her for pragmatic reasons—reasons he had spelled out in such a deliberate, calm way that there could be no mistake that it was to be a marriage of convenience only. His heart was not engaged, and neither was hers. Wrapping her mind firmly about this cold, logical fact, she resolved not to allow her uncertain emotions to lead her into reading more into

Lucien's proposal than what it was—the only answer to an unfortunate situation.

The ride home had been quiet, filled with a strange kind of peace. Despite Arabella's protests, Lucien had again wrapped his greatcoat about her, pointing out that his clothes were drier than hers. Surrounded in blessed warmth, she felt cherished and protected. It was a new and heady experience, and she selfishly didn't want the illusion to end.

She gave a contented sigh and reflected that most of the reasons that Lucien had put forth for their marriage were inconsequential. She was sure she could protect Rosemont; she had single-handedly done so for almost six years now. True, the complications with Constable Robbins were an inconvenience, but she could shield Wilson and his nephews if she had to. If nothing else, she could fall back on her long friendship with the constable, though she was loath to do such a thing.

But she could not turn away from the chance to give Robert back the use of his legs. It was her dearest wish and she was eager to get to London and discover which doctors should be consulted.

Lucien's voice broke the quiet. "Tell me about Vicar Haighton."

"There's not much to tell. He has been our vicar since last year, when old Vicar Peeples died." She turned to regard Lucien with a frown. "Why?"

"I was just wondering about the topic for this week's service." Amusement glinted in his green eyes. "I hope he doesn't use specific examples."

She chuckled as they made the last curve in the drive. "Aunt Jane will see to it that we are not mentioned by name, at least. She tithes very heavily whenever she is on a winning streak."

"What a relief." Lucien drew Satan to a halt. "You have visitors." He nodded toward a fashionable carriage that sat at the door, looking out of place in front of Rosemont's shabby front step.

"I wonder who that is?" Arabella asked.

Ned and Wilson were struggling to transfer a hefty trunk to an already considerable pile of luggage.

"Another aunt, perchance?"

"No, Emma and Jane are the only two—" She broke off, her gaze still fixed on the carriage.

Lucien turned as a tall, fashionably clad young woman climbed down from the carriage. Even at this distance, he recognized the auburn tresses cut à la Sappho that complemented her high, wide brow and bold, autocratic nose. "Bloody hell," he cursed beneath his breath. "Liza."

"Your sister?"

"In the flesh," he answered grimly.

"I thought she was in London getting ready for the season."

"No doubt she has given my aunt the slip." Lucien's jaw tightened in frustration; his sister's active curiosity guaranteed that she would meddle in what didn't concern her. "It looks as if she plans on a prolonged stay. I wonder how she managed to escape Aunt Lavinia."

"Escape? From a season?" Arabella's sable brows rose. "Why would she do such a thing?"

"My sister prides herself on being unconventional. She dislikes the idea of being puffed off on the marriage mart."

"Ah, a woman of character." Arabella turned a wide, innocent stare his way, a quirk to her mouth that instantly melted some of his irritation. "I suppose you fight rather frequently."

"No," he said briefly, answering the twinkle in her eyes with a grin. "I only see her once or twice a month."

"That saves you, then."

A quiver of laughter warmed Arabella's voice and Lucien chuckled with her. His greatcoat looked huge on her small frame, the cuffs dangling well over her hands, the hem draping past her feet. A smudge of dirt marred the creamy texture of her left cheek. She looked healthy, happy, and as mischievous as an imp. Lucien had to fight the desire to lean over and plant a kiss on her smiling mouth.

"You should not be laughing, madam," he said, reaching out a finger to touch the end of her nose. "Liza will ruin her chances if she continues with such hoydenish ways."

"Just by visiting her brother in the country? Surely not."

"I would wager there is no chaperone in that carriage." He shook his head. "She has already gotten into more scrapes than I can remember."

"Is it important that she marry? Marriage without love would be horri—" Arabella broke off, a red stain appearing under the smudge of dirt on her cheek.

Lucien turned back to the door so she would not see his disappointment. She may not love him now, but perhaps, with time . . . He could only hope.

"Liza may marry whom she wishes, so long as the man is of good character. But first, I expect her to take her place among the ton, as is her right. My father would have wished her to do at least that much."

"I see." Arabella watched as Liza stood arguing with Wilson about the handling of an especially large trunk. "I always wanted to be presented at court."

Lucien caught the wistful note in her voice. "Why didn't you?"

"The money, for one thing. And for another, there was

no use in being presented when—" She stopped, her cheeks flaring with color, but not before he'd caught the mortified glint in her eyes.

"When you had already been ruined by a thoughtless cad." What he would give to redo those few hours of his life. He started to turn Satan toward the house, but she laid her hand over his.

"I didn't say that. By the time I was of an age to be presented, we were badly strapped for funds. My father was not a frugal man."

"No, but he loved his daughter very much." Lucien turned her hand palm up and pushed the coat up, exposing the inside of her wrist. He pressed his mouth to the delicate skin. God, but he loved her skin, every smooth, soft inch of it.

Color bright, she pulled her hand back and Lucien could feel her withdraw as surely as if she'd ridden off.

Arabella cleared her throat nervously. "You should see to your sister. Something might be amiss."

"Perhaps," he answered shortly, turning his gaze back to his sister's carriage. If Arabella ever suspected his deception in arranging their marriage, it would forever destroy any chance he had for their future. Fear lodged against his rib cage and ached like a wound.

"I shall ask Mrs. Guinver to prepare a room for Liza." Arabella's voice seemed unnaturally loud.

"Don't bother; she won't be staying."

"Of course she will—just look at all those trunks. You go and speak with her. I have to change before we meet with the vicar." With a slight smile, she turned Sebastian toward the stable.

Lucien sighed and rubbed a hand across his face. Though he had won her acceptance of their marriage, he felt hollow inside. His marriage to Sabrina had been a public show, welcomed at the time by them both. She had desired his title and social connections, and he had been desperate for her fortune. But Arabella wanted more. He saw it in the way she looked at him, her dark eyes wistful, as if seeking something he could not give. Something he dared not give for fear of overwhelming her with his passion.

Quelling a fierce swell of emotion, Lucien wheeled Satan about and galloped to the carriage, pulling the horse to a sliding halt.

Liza turned in surprise, her face brightening. "Lucien! I am so glad to see you. This stupid man refuses to—"

"What are you doing here?" Lucien demanded, his irritation finally finding focus. At any other time, he would have been happy to see Liza. But today, with Bolder free to cause more mischief and Arabella only hesitantly committed to marrying him, Lucien wished his sister anywhere but at Rosemont.

Liza drew herself to her full height. At six feet in her stocking feet, she still had to look up at her brother, a fact she found unnerving, as he had an unfortunate tendency to scowl. It was disconcerting, to say the least. Swallowing hard, she managed to keep her smile. "I have come for a visit."

"How nice," he said in a tone that implied something entirely different. "Didn't you think to notify us?"

"I wrote you a letter telling you when I was to arrive."

"Just when did you send this missive?"

She brushed a flake of snow off her ermine muff with a gloved hand, careful not to meet his gaze. "Yesterday."

"Yesterday. By post, no doubt."

"Perhaps."

"And I suppose it will arrive sometime next week. Just as you planned."

She had the grace to look shamefaced.

He gave a disgusted sigh. "Where is our estimable aunt?"

"In London, at Wexford House."

"And I suppose she has no idea where you are."

"Of course she does. I left her a note."

"How obliging of you."

Liza clenched her hands into fists deep within the ermine muff and waited. When he didn't reply, she peeked through her lashes and winced at the stiff anger she saw in his face. "Lucien, you have to understand. I simply could not stand it any longer."

"We've had this conversation before, Liza. One season is all I asked. You promised you would give me at least that."

"The season doesn't start for months."

"Yes, but Aunt Lavinia wanted to get Wexford House in order. You knew that was part of the arrangement. Besides, she assures me that there are a remarkable number of people still about, since the weather has been so mild."

"Yes, and all of them are over eighty and think dancing is a great waste of time. Aunt Lavinia has had so many card parties, I am near to screaming from boredom."

"Liza, I hope you have been polite."

"As much as possible. I really cannot believe you are defending Aunt Lavinia. You dislike all that pandering and mincing even more than I." She lifted her chin and said in a lofty tone, " 'Riding is such a fatiguing exercise. No truly genteel woman would do more than take a short turn about the park, and only on the veriest slug.' "

"Our aunt would never say anything so asinine."

"All of it except the part about the slug. I believe her words were 'a calm, older mount.' But that wasn't the worst of it." Liza drew herself back up and pursed her lips into a severe frown. " 'Elizabeth, do not walk so quickly. A gentle lady does not dash about; she glides like an angel.' "

A reluctant smile curved his mouth. "An angel, eh?"

"Lucien, it was not to be borne. She is a pompous fluff-head and I couldn't take another minute."

"Aunt Lavinia is well established and could do you an immense amount of good if you would but let her."

"You don't know how confining it is, to stay with her day and night. All she ever does is shop and talk and visit. That and take naps, though why she would be tired, I'm sure I don't know. She doesn't do a thing that might fatigue a person." Liza made an impatient gesture. "I vow, it is a wonder I did not pull out all of my hair after the first week."

"You must return."

"I know," she said, heaving a sigh. "But at least let me stay here until Christmas, and then I'll—"

"No." He turned to the wizened servant who'd been unloading her trunks. "Wilson, load Miss Devereaux's trunks back on the coach. She is leaving."

"You can't do that!" Liza cried, all of her hopes shriveling. "Lucien, please don't make me go back." To her chagrin, a great tear welled in her eye. Drat it all, she was tired and hungry and worried to death after sitting in the coach and wondering how to explain her presence to her stern brother.

She'd consoled herself on the trip up with the reflection that no matter how displeased he would be that she had left London, he would at least be glad to see her. They had always been close, especially after Father's death. But Lucien did not look pleased. He looked as if, for two pence, he'd kick her out in the cold with nothing more than a stern order to rejoin her aunt.

Another tear joined the first, coursing slowly down her cheek. Before Liza knew what she was about, a choked sob broke through and there was nothing for it but to give in to the tears.

Lucien gave a muffled curse. "Stop that," he commanded gruffly. When his order was met with yet another sob, he sighed, reached out, and gathered her close. "I'm sorry, Liza," he murmured as she pressed her face against his damp coat. "I didn't mean to yell. It has just been a difficult day."

She pulled back, searching through her reticule for a handkerchief. Finally locating one, she mopped her face. "At least let me stay for one week, until Christmas. I promise I will return to London without one word of complaint, and I will be so good. I will even learn to glide like an angel, if that is what Aunt Lavinia wants."

He gave a reluctant smile. Christmas was indeed coming upon them. He had been so wrapped up in Arabella that he hadn't remembered.

Liza placed a hand on his lapel. "Just for a little while. Please, Lucien. *Please.*"

"Bloody hell, why I let you talk me into these things—" He broke off and sighed heavily. "Oh, very well. I suppose if I say no, you'd just conjure up another excuse to stay."

Her smile blossomed. "Oh, thank you, Lucien! It will be wonderful having Christmas here, and in such a lovely house." She turned and stared up at Rosemont, happiness lifting the corners of her generous mouth. Without waiting for Lucien, she walked up the front stairs and to the door, where Ned struggled with two overstuffed valises.

Shaking his head, Lucien turned back to the carriage. "Wilson, I'm afraid Her Ladyship will be staying after all."

The gnarled groom stopped where he was struggling to push a huge trunk back onto the carriage. "Ye has to be roastin' me."

A wry smile twisting his mouth, Lucien shook his head. "My sister has decided to stay."

Wilson stepped back and allowed the trunk to drop onto the drive with a thud, dangerously near Lucien's foot. "I'll be a cankered wisternole if I'll load these bags again."

Lucien didn't blame him. "If you will take Satan to the stables, I'll finish up here." He hefted the trunk to his shoulder and carried it inside, the sound of Wilson's grumbling following him.

Hastings stood in the foyer, Liza's pelisse and muff carefully laid across his arm. He blinked when he saw Lucien carrying the huge trunk, then turned to Liza. "One must wonder what vail should be bestowed in an instance like this. He is, after all, carrying your trunk. But then again, he is also a duke. A very perplexing case."

"Quiet, Hastings," Lucien growled, staggering a little under the weight. Heavens, how much clothing had Liza brought with her? He set the trunk in the corner just as Aunt Emma came bounding down the stairs, her mobcap askew, the unmistakable whiff of cognac in the air.

She skidded to a halt when she saw so many people in the foyer, and her round eyes widened as she took in Liza's tall, fashionable form. "Oh, my! You look like you just stepped from the *Ladies' Magazine*! What a lovely traveling gown."

Liza blushed and dropped an awkward curtsy. "I beg your pardon, madam, but there has been a mistake. The letter I wrote to my brother asking if I may stop by for a day or two has been delayed, and I—"

"So you are come to stay? What a pleasant surprise!" Emma bustled forward. "You *must* be Miss Devereaux, the sister of our dearest duke!"

Liza glanced over her shoulder at Lucien, her eyes wide. To his intense annoyance, she mouthed the words, *Our dearest duke?* and gave him a droll look.

Clearing his throat, he turned to Emma. "Lady Durham, this is my sister, Miss Devereaux. Liza, this is—"

"Oh, call me Aunt Emma! Everyone does. And of course you are welcome to stay at Rosemont, my dear. You must be famished after such a trip." She glanced around, her gaze falling on Hastings. "Oh, Hastings! Could you ask Mrs. Guinver to bring a tray with some tea and cakes to the morning room?"

The valet bowed. "Shall I have some of the marmalade brought as well?"

"No," said Emma with a thoughtful frown. "But you can ask what rooms are available for our guest." She waved a vague hand. "I'm sure something is ready."

"Of course," said Hastings, not betraying by so much as a quiver that he thought something far otherwise.

Liza smoothed a nervous hand down her dress. "I really do not mean to impose. Perhaps I should find lodgings elsewhere."

"Nonsense! Rosemont is renowned for its hospitality. We could not allow you to stay anywhere but here."

"You are much too kind."

Emma waved a cheerful hand and smiled, her eyes huge behind her spectacles. "I'm sure it is no wonder you wish to stay, my dear, what with the wedding and all. We've much to plan, you know. Food, greenery for the mantel places, invitations to write—"

"Pardon me," Liza asked politely, "but whose wedding is it?"

Emma blinked. "Why, I suppose you don't know yet. How delightful! Your brother is to marry my niece, Miss Arabella Hadley." She took Liza's limp hand and patted it. "You will just love her. Everyone does."

"My . . . my brother is to marry? Surely you are mistaken."

"Oh, no!" said Aunt Emma. She looked at Lucien. "Am I not right, Your Grace? Aren't you to marry my niece?"

He nodded once, his face grim.

Liza swallowed. "B-but you never said a word . . . you never wrote or—"

"I didn't have time."

"Oh, yes," Emma said, a vague smile on her plump face. "You see, we only just found out they were to be married this morning, when we walked in on them while they were—"

"I don't think my sister needs to know all of the details," Lucien said firmly. He sent a brief glance at Liza, his face suspiciously red. "I suppose it is a good thing you arrived when you did. At least you will be here for the ceremony."

"You are getting married before Christmas?"

"Tomorrow, if I can arrange it."

"But—"

"We'll discuss it later," he said, glancing meaningfully at Emma. "In the meantime, I had best get the rest of your trunks."

Before she could protest, he left. Liza's fingers curled into her palms. It all became very clear to her. Somehow, some way, Arabella Hadley had tricked her brother into marriage. No wonder he'd been so upset on finding her on his doorstep. He was a proud man and he would not wish for anyone to witness the indignity of his marriage to such an odious schemer.

Liza's heart swelled with righteous anger. "Where is Miss Hadley? I would like to meet her."

"Oh, she will be down soon. Mrs. Guinver is drawing a bath for her right now." Lady Durham took Liza's hand in hers and inexorably led her to the morning room. "Come and have a bit of tea while we are waiting for your room to be readied, and tell me all about your trip here."

Left without any recourse, Liza followed. Much later, refreshed after a plate of cold meat, bread and butter, and some of Mrs. Guinver's special restorative tea, Liza stood at the window of her bedchamber. Aunt Emma was as talkative as she was naive, and it had taken very little to discover the full circumstances of Lucien's wedding. Liza scowled, thinking of all the times her brother had warned her against the attentions of men who might be interested only in her fortune. Now some brazen harpy had come along and neatly tricked him into the very same trap.

Liza sniffed. It was a good thing she had come to Rosemont when she did. She would find Miss Hadley and see for herself what kind of a woman would behave so dishonorably.

Girded in righteous anger, Liza sailed from her room and down the steps. The door to the morning room was closed, but the low murmur of voices escaped through the wood panel. She hesitated, one hand ready to knock, wondering if she dared burst in. But the thought that the occupants might be someone other than Lucien and the unscrupulous Miss Hadley stayed her hand.

Just as she turned to retreat to the stairs, a sliver of light from beneath a tall door down the hallway caught her attention.

She quietly tiptoed over and listened, but no sounds came from within. Curious, she opened the door and came to a sudden halt. A man sat in a wheeled chair by the fireplace, a huge tome in his hands.

Liza cleared her throat. "Pardon me. I didn't realize anyone was in here."

The man turned his head and she saw he was much younger than she'd at first thought. His hair was a true chestnut, dark brown with red lights, and curled over his forehead, showing signs of needing a cut. Had he dark eyes instead of silver-gray, he would have looked exactly the way she always pictured one of Byron's tortured heroes.

She dipped a curtsy. "How do you do? I am Miss—"

"I know who you are," he said unpleasantly. "You are Wexford's sister."

While Liza was not one to be immersed in her own self-worth, it was unusual to meet someone so patently unimpressed with her title. Worse, he continued to stare at her in a bold, rude manner, looking her up and down as if she were a horse.

Liza's temper flared. "Well, you know me, but I don't know you," she said ungraciously.

"I am Robert Hadley. This is my house you are standing in." Then, apparently thinking his discourteous introduction sufficient, and deeming her of no more interest, he turned back to his volume and ignored her.

Liza didn't know what to think. She had never been spoiled or used to getting her own way at every turn, but she had been brought up by an aunt who clearly believed that the world owed some deference to the prestigious Wexford name.

Gathering her scattered courage, Liza stepped forward. "I understand that your sister has entrapped my brother into marriage," she said sharply.

"Entrapped?" He gave an inelegant snort. "That shows how little you know about it. If there was any entrapment, it was your brother who orchestrated it. He has been hot on her trail since he arrived. Any fool could see that."

"Lucien would *never* stoop to such a thing! May I remind you that my brother is a duke, and the handsomest man in London. Women chase him in swarms."

"That explains why he is so enamored of my sister, then," Robert said with a superior smirk. "Men don't like forward females."

Liza's hands balled into fists. "*Real* men like women who are their equals and do not pander to their every whim and whimsy."

"What do you know of real men? Unless London has changed drastically since I visited it, there *are* no real men in London."

Having spent the last two months there, Liza was inclined to agree with him, but she was not about to bow so tamely. "Your manners are intolerable. You are arrogant, rude, and—"

"Rude? What about people who come unannounced for a visit and demand the best guest room? What do you call that?"

"I sent a letter, but it has apparently been mislaid. Besides, I did not ask for the best guest room. I would have been happy for a pallet in the attic, if that had been all that was available." Anything to escape Aunt Lavinia's stifling presence.

"Ballocks."

"I beg your pardon?"

"You heard me," he said impatiently, sending her a silver glance. "Please don't tell me you do not know what ballocks are."

"I do indeed know what they are," she said acidly, wondering if it was a special crime to kick a crippled man in the knee. "I am no missish female, Mr. Hadley. I am quite familiar with the term *ballocks*. In fact, I use the word quite frequently myself."

His brows rose. "I don't believe you."

"Well, I do."

"Let me hear you, then."

That gave her pause, but she hid it behind a scowl. "Very well. Ballocks. There, I said it."

He snorted. "I would hardly call that using a word. If you are going to use a word, then grab it with both hands, don't just fondle the damn thing."

His needling pricked her anger, and she seethed with the desire to put him in his place. "Very well, damn it. *Ballocks to you!*"

"Oh, dear," said a soft voice from the doorway. Aunt Emma stood with her mobcap askew, wringing her hands and looking from one to the other. "Is . . . is there a problem?"

"No!" said Robert and Liza in unison. Liza glared, but Robert seemed amused, a smile lifting the corner of his mouth.

"Oh. I see," said Aunt Emma, plainly bewildered. Her brow furrowed for a moment, then cleared as she brightened. "I know! Perhaps you would like some nice tea and cookies."

"Thank you, Lady Durham," said Liza stiffly, "but I find that I am more tired than I realized. I wish to retire to my room, if you don't mind."

"Coward," murmured Robert, watching her with eyes strangely alight.

She sent him a quelling glance, her head held at a proud angle. *"Fool."*

"Oh, dear," said Aunt Emma again, looking uneasily from Robert to Liza. "I hope you found everything in your room satisfactory, Miss Devereaux. Was . . . was the bed not made?"

"The room is lovely, thank you."

Robert *tsk*ed. "And to think you would have been happy with a pallet in the attic."

With a frigid glare that caused its intended victim to grin even wider, Liza stormed out the door, pausing only to offer the tiniest curtsy to Aunt Emma as she went.

"What will Jane say?" Aunt Emma said. "We had such hopes that perhaps—"

"If you will excuse me, I am going outside," Robert said shortly, though a smile lingered on his mouth. With a last glance at the doorway through which Miss Devereaux had disappeared, he pushed himself onto the terrace and slammed the door behind him.

Aunt Emma pulled her medicine from her pocket. Rosemont couldn't handle any more upsets. She took a long sip and looked up at the portrait of the Captain. With a quick glance over her shoulder to make sure she was alone, she turned to the portrait and said in a loud voice, "I wish you would at least make a push to help us. Jane and I can only do so much, you know."

To her astonished gaze, it appeared as if the Captain's gentle smile broadened, his blue eyes twinkling. Emma took a hasty step back, her mouth wide open. Then she turned and ran from the room, calling for Jane as she fled.

Chapter 23

Aunt Jane was determined that the wedding would be the social event of the year, and since she had less than twenty-four hours in which to plan it, she was in something of a tizzy. Arabella could have cared less for the type of cake that was served, the amount of greenery to be used in adorning the church, or the color of cloth hung over the old settee. It was fortunate for all involved that her aunts' boundless excitement made up for her own lack of enthusiasm.

By midafternoon, the morning room was already covered with Christmas greenery, the carpets beaten and replaced, the chairs arranged to hide the faded and worn spots, and every bit of silver that had spent the last ten years collecting dust in the Rosemont cupboards was on display. All in all, it was an impressive sight that would greet their guests after the wedding tomorrow.

Arabella sat near the open door of the morning room and listened with half an ear to her aunts' endless quibbling over the arrangement of the extra chairs, and wondered how Lucien was faring with the vicar. She didn't have long to wait. He emerged from the library a short time later, looking suspiciously white about the mouth and ready to murder someone. Arabella slipped unnoticed from the room and joined him in the foyer.

He stood staring with an unseeing gaze at the front door, as if he longed to pass through and never return. The sight made her spirits sink even lower. She wished she knew how to set him at ease and convince him that all would be well, but she couldn't find the words.

She had just decided to leave when he muttered a curse and turned, coming to an abrupt halt when he saw her standing so near.

His face softened and some of the tension left his shoulders. "I was coming to find you. I must leave to get the license."

Arabella's mouth went dry. Part of her wanted to offer him his freedom and point the way to the door, while the other part longed to burrow in his arms and never let go. She clasped her hands behind her back. "Then we are to be married." Perhaps if she said it aloud, it wouldn't seem quite so preposterous.

"Yes," he said in a firm voice, as if daring her to contradict him. "Tomorrow morning. All I need to do is get the license from the bishop. In the meantime, you should rest." A sudden smile warmed his eyes and he crossed to stand in front of her, his shoulders blocking the light from the window. "You look a bit pale this morning. I should have let you sleep more." He brushed his fingertips over her cheek, his touch warming all the way to her stomach.

Arabella closed her eyes and wondered what he would do if she placed her head against his broad chest and listened to the steady beat of his heart as she had done in the cottage. But somehow, the intimacy of the cottage seemed far away, the spell broken by the cold, stern necessity of their circumstances. She raised her gaze to his. "Lucien, perhaps we should reconsider—"

His hand touched her lips, silencing her. He regarded her somberly, his green eyes dark with some emotion. "We are set in our course, Bella." He dropped his hand to capture hers. Smiling, he brushed a soft kiss across her fingers and gave her hand a comforting squeeze. "Don't look so worried. This is best for us all."

Arabella looked down at his large hand as it enveloped hers, and she wondered at the sense of security such a simple touch could convey. She only wished it were more than an illusion, something stronger than just her desires. "Lucien, I hope you—"

"Ah, Wexford! There you are," Aunt Jane said, emerging from the morning room, an ominous list in her hand. "We must discuss the exact time of the wedding. Wilson is ready to deliver the invitations, and we must get them written before another minute advances."

Lucien gave Arabella's hand one last squeeze, and then he followed Aunt Jane into the morning room. Arabella started to follow, but Cook appeared, complaining about Wilson's refusal to go to town at her bidding. By the time Arabella returned to the foyer, Lucien had already left.

The rest of the day passed in a blur, with Aunt Jane or Aunt Emma always hovering just around the corner, keeping her busy with seemingly useless tasks. Arabella thought that if she stayed occupied it would ease her mind, but everything reminded her of Lucien and the awful predicament their untoward passion had placed them in. She could only hope he would not come to regret the hasty events of this day.

The sun sank lower on the horizon behind a bank of

thick black clouds that rumbled louder as night approached. Arabella found herself starting at every noise, imagining that Lucien had returned, but each time it was one of the servants passing through the hallway, or the wind rattling the shutters. With each disappointment, her uncertainty grew.

Dinner only made things worse. Lucien's sister seemed disposed to glare until Arabella felt acutely uncomfortable. Even Robert was in a strange mood, making cutting remarks to Liza and then laughing whenever she retaliated.

Their bickering quickly became more than Arabella could bear, and she pleaded a headache and escaped to her room. There, she fought against a looming sense of failure as she paced the floor, her thoughts as depressed as the driving rain that pelted the countryside.

After an hour of relentless examination, one undeniable fact remained—she could not marry Lucien. While there were innumerable benefits for her, he gained nothing in the bargain. She would find a way to deal with her own difficulties—she always had.

The ugly truth was that there was nothing to keep Lucien at Rosemont. He didn't care about her—he'd made that fact abundantly clear when he'd listed all of the reasons why they should wed. Not one had anything to do with love.

Her eyes watered and she was forced to find a handkerchief before she could resume her pacing. It was better this way. No declarations of love, no pretense at emotions, just a calm, orderly arrangement—rather like a business deal. Strangely, the thought made her heart sink even lower.

Night crept in and the clock ticked away the passing minutes. Arabella was finally too tired to pace any longer, so she sat before the dying fire, her arms wrapped around her stomach, her hands damp and quaking. *God, what am I doing?*

Outside, the rain increased in tempo, beating against the house as if desperate to gain entry, but Arabella didn't hear it—she was too busy trying to decide how to tell Lucien that there would be no wedding.

The rain sheeted across the inn yard, rivulets of muddy water sluicing into the road. Standing under the dripping eaves, Lucien stared grimly at the rain and clenched his jaw. *Bloody hell, will this torrent ever end?*

His greatcoat was soaked, his boots crusted with mud, and his temper frayed. Gritting his teeth against his impatience, he took off his hat and shook it. A shower of fat, cold droplets sprinkled across the mud-smeared threshold.

It had taken two hours to locate the bishop's place, only to discover that the man was not home and wasn't expected anytime soon. After kicking his heels for the better part of an hour waiting for the blasted man to return, Lucien had finally set out after him, locating the rotund clergyman at his sister's house. It had taken an earnest plea and two gold sovereigns before the bishop could be persuaded to drive his cart back to York to issue the license.

Then, mission completed, Lucien had set out for Rosemont, only to be halted by the storm. Lucien replaced his hat and pulled the brim low, thinking of Arabella's pale face as she stood in the vestibule this afternoon. There was no mistaking the doubt lurking in her eyes. But Lucien knew there was a way to chase away her haunted look. He remembered her after they had made love, her smile softened with pleasure, her eyes glowing with happiness. He moved impatiently. *Bloody hell, I have to get home.*

The thought held him. Since when had he considered Rosemont home? The leaky old manor house was special only because it was where Arabella lived. Maybe that was it—it wasn't the house, but his Bella. Lucien pulled a cheroot out of his pocket and lit it, liking the thought of calling Rosemont home, of calling Arabella wife.

A carriage pulled into the muddy yard and came to a splashing halt. A heavily wrapped coachman jumped down and trudged through the rain to open the door. Amid a flurry of preparation, the occupant of the coach stepped out. Lucien noted absently that the man's greatcoat possessed such a preposterous number of capes that the owner appeared to be every bit as wide as he was tall.

"Blasted rain," the young man muttered as he hopped his way through a maze of puddles toward the door where Lucien stood. Once he reached the safety of the overhang, he carefully examined every inch of his clothing for additional mud, removing his wide-brimmed beaver hat so that the dull light from the window fell on a head of mussed golden curls. "Demme! Ruined my new boots, too, blasted rain. That's the last time I ever come to Yorkshire. Never saw such a plaguey, wet place in all my—" He glanced at Lucien and broke off. "Luce? Is that you?"

Lucien straightened in surprise. Edmund Valmont was one of the few people he considered a friend. Though the younger man was naive and possessed far less common sense than he needed, his heart was every bit as soft as his head. "What brings you here, halfling? Is there a race about?"

The plump young peer grabbed his hand and shook it with enthusiasm. "Lud, no! I came looking for you. I've got a message from your aunt and I was determined to locate you and—" Edmund tilted his head to squint up at the swaying inn sign, the rain from his caped greatcoat dripping onto Lucien's boots. "Is this Rosemont? My footman said this was a posting house."

"Your footman is correct. Rosemont is located on the coast just north of here."

Edmund's brow cleared. "Couldn't imagine you would stay at a common posting inn. A duke should—" He broke off, a look of concern crossing his face. "Luce, you aren't on your way to London to see Liza, are you? I mean, if you are, you should know that . . . well, she isn't pre- cisely. . . ." He stopped and drew himself together, eyeing Lucien with a suddenly wild expression. "Luce, I don't know how to tell you this, but—"

"Liza arrived at Rosemont this morning."

Edmund almost sagged with relief. "Thank goodness. Deuced uncomfortable business, having to tell you your sister had disappeared, even though we all know she is more than capable of taking care of herself, and I—" He frowned. "I say, if you aren't going to London, what are you doing here?"

"I had an errand," Lucien said succinctly. "I was returning to Rosemont when the rain began and I didn't wish to risk Satan slipping in all this mud."

"Oh! Well, if you mind waiting until Dotson has the horses changed, I would be glad to take you to Rosemont in my carriage. You can send a man after Satan tomorrow morning."

Lucien looked toward the stables. "How quickly can he get it done?"

"Oh, Lud, he'll be out in the wink of an eye, see if he don't. I told him to make haste—wanted to reach you as soon as possible."

True to his word, the carriage returned a remarkably short time later and, after exchanging a few words with the innkeeper about Satan, Lucien climbed into the carriage behind Edmund.

"Lud, but I'm glad I found you." Edmund settled into his corner of the coach, withdrew a handkerchief, and began wiping the mud from his boots. "Poor Bottle will be in the sulks for weeks if I ruin these."

"Bottle?"

"My new valet. Won him in a card game from Chambers. The fool bet his whole allowance and Bottle's services that he could shoot a cigar out of someone's mouth. He missed and put a bullet right through the window at White's."

"Chambers is not as much a fool as the person who held the cigar for him. Who was the idiot?"

A flush touched Edmund's plump cheeks and he said defensively, "We'd been dipping rather deep, and I . . . well, it don't signify. Bottle was worth getting shot at. I tell you, Luce, I've never had such a correct valet. Almost as bad as being married, only he doesn't cry." Edmund stuffed his muddy handkerchief under his seat and straightened with a relieved sigh. "There, that's the dandy. I tell you, Luce, I'm deuced glad Liza made it here without mishap. Your aunt was in quite a taking when I left."

"I'm not surprised; Aunt Lavinia has a tendency for melodrama. I should have written her as soon as Liza arrived, but I was distracted. I am indebted to you for coming such a distance."

"Don't be. I had other reasons for leaving town, you know."

"Oh? The watch after you again?"

"No. Something worse." Edmund shook his head sadly, his round face puckered in a frown. "*Much* worse."

"Ah. A woman, no doubt. With an angry husband, perhaps?"

"Worse. It's Aunt Maddie; she's lost her mind and I'm to be made to pay for it."

Lucien hid a grin. Edmund's Aunt Maddie was a bewigged harridan who loved nothing more than to shock those who loved her most. "What's Mad Maddie done this time? Embarked on a torrid affair with the Prince Regent?"

Edmund shuddered. "Lud, Luce! Don't even suggest it." He raked a hand through his hair, mussing the golden curls until they made a halo about his head. "My aunt's decided it is time I was married."

"So you are on the fly, eh?"

"You know what Aunt Maddie is, Luce. I had no choice. It was either that or marry some fudby-faced female with a mustache."

"Surely not!"

"I ain't lying, Luce. She wanted me to court Marie Halford. Kept thrusting her in my face till I was afraid to leave my lodgings. When it wasn't the Halford chit, she was forever inviting Margaret Yarrow to sit in the carriage with us, and you know what she is."

"I cannot seem to place . . . Oh, wait. A rather rotund female, if I remember, with brassy yellow hair."

"That's her," Edmund said glumly. "And she has a gap between her front teeth that gives me the shudders."

"Why on earth would Aunt Maddie want you to marry her?"

Edmund flushed. "It ain't polite, but you're almost family, so I'll tell you—m'aunt thinks the Yarrow chit has broad hips and would breed well."

"And often, most likely."

"Not with me for a husband, she wouldn't. Lord, Luce, I'd rather put an end to my existence than have to look at that face across the breakfast table every morning. I tried to reason with Aunt Maddie, she just kept making remarks about how I was getting older. . . ." Edmund turned an anxious face toward Lucien. "I am *not* getting older."

"Of course not. You look exactly the same now as you did five years ago when I met you."

That seemed to satisfy Edmund, for he subsided, only grumbling now and then. As they neared the long coastal road that led to Rosemont, he turned to Lucien. "I say, Luce, come with me to Bath. Aunt Maddie will never think to look for me there."

"As promising as Bath in the winter sounds, I cannot leave right now. I've plans for the next few weeks." And the years following that. A strange desire to smile gripped Lucien, and all of his earlier impatience returned.

Edmund looked at him and frowned. "Luce, been meaning to ask you, what brought you to Yorkshire?"

"I came to look into a purchase."

"What? More land?"

"No, a gem."

"I should have known. Only a sparkler could send you running out into the countryside. Did you find anything worthwhile?"

"The trip has been most productive." More than Edmund could imagine. Lucien glanced at his friend. Perhaps now was the time to announce his marriage. He intended to send a notice to the *Gazette* by the end of the week, but it would make Arabella's entry into society smoother if the worst of the gossip died out before they arrived.

Fortunately, there was no quicker way to spread word throughout the ton than to admit a secret to a Valmont; the whole family was known for their inability to keep a secret. Smiling to himself, Lucien said, "Edmund, I have found a wife."

Edmund's jaw dropped. "But who—why didn't you—where did you—I can't believe—"

"In fact," Lucien continued in an inexorable tone, "I've just returned from procuring the license."

"License? When are you getting married?"

"Tomorrow."

"*This* tomorrow?"

Lucien stifled a sigh. "I am to marry Miss Arabella Hadley tomorrow at ten."

Edmund leaned forward to grip Lucien's arm. "Don't do it, Luce! Ride with me to Bath. They won't even know you are gone until—"

Lucien shook off Edmund's grip. "I have no wish to run away."

Edmund sagged against the squabs. "I would never have credited that you, of all people, would get caught in the parson's trap. It's almost enough to send a man to the brink."

"I was not *caught* in anything. It is simply time that I marry."

Edmund nodded wisely. "Being chivalrous, are you? Daresay you don't want it breezed about that your wife caught you on the downside. But never fear, I won't say a word to anyone, though this does remind me of poor Haversham. His wife—well, it wasn't his wife then, but Lucinda Truckle. You remember her, don't you? Red hair, sadly freckled? Bit of a squint in one eye? Well, she invited Haversham on a picnic to Faulk Downs and then lured him into the maze and pretended to twist her ankle. He had to carry her for miles and got blisters because he'd had on his good riding boots. Then, when he finally staggered to her carriage, there stood her father, looking like a thundercloud and ready to slap the wedding shackles on him. Poor Haversham was so knocked up by the whole episode that he stayed in bed a week. We all feared he might put a period to his existence, but once he was wed, he rallied quite well and now he's got a pretty little ladybird who can—"

"Damn it, Edmund," Lucien burst out. "You cannot go about telling such tales. This case is entirely different. In fact, if anyone has been tricked, it is Arabella, because I—"

A look of astonishment dawned on Edmund's face. "*You* tricked her?"

"I didn't trick her, precisely, but her aunt and I decided the marriage needed to take place."

"But . . . why?"

"Because I compromised her," Lucien said grimly.

Edmund gawked.

"Ten years ago," Lucien said, "just before my father died, I met Arabella Hadley, and I was . . . well, I was a fool. But now I am going to set things right. Tomorrow she will become my wife."

After a long moment, Edmund let his breath out in a whoosh. "So that's how it is, eh?"

Lucien nodded.

"Don't worry, Luce. I'm sure there is a way out of this fix."

"I don't want out. I *want* to marry Arabella."

"Of course," Edmund replied with a broad wink. "Well, I'll put m'mind to it and see what I can come up with. Ain't the most brilliant thinker, but I'm steady." He scrunched his eyes closed and leaned back in the corner.

After a few moments, his soft snoring filled the carriage and Lucien was left to watch in frustration and amusement as his friend slept the rest of the way to Rosemont.

When they arrived, Lucien stopped only long enough to invite Edmund to the wedding, before he jumped out of the carriage and waved the coachman on.

It was now well past midnight and the house was shrouded in darkness. Only one light gleamed in the upper windows, and Lucien took heart when he realized it was Arabella's.

Hastings opened the front door the instant Lucien set foot on the front step. "There you are, Your Grace. Did the weather catch you?"

"Yes, you'll need to send Wilson after Satan."

The valet took Lucien's wet coat and hat. "I will do so first thing in the morning."

Lucien sat down on a small chair and yanked off his muddy boots, his gaze drawn to the stairs. "Is everyone abed?"

"I believe so. Master Hadley retired to his room but a few moments ago."

"And Miss Hadley?"

Hastings paused delicately. "Miss Hadley is not feeling well. She retired directly after dinner and has been in her room ever since."

Just as Lucien had suspected; Arabella had succumbed to an attack of prewedding jitters. Fortunately for her, he knew just the cure. Lucien stood and handed his boots to Hastings.

"Will you be retiring directly, Your Grace?"

Lucien nodded and turned toward the stairs, untying his cravat as he went. "I plan on being in bed within the minute, Hastings, if not sooner."

"Very good, sir. I shall bring a hot brick to warm the sheets."

"That won't be necessary." He had his own plans for

warming the bed. And warm it would be. And passionate. And thoroughly exhausting. Oh, yes, they would both sleep well tonight.

Smiling, Lucien took the last steps two at a time.

Chapter 24

A soft knock sounded. Startled, Arabella sat bolt upright in her chair, her heart pounding. Surely Lucien wouldn't come to her room. Surely he wouldn't— *Stop that*, she told herself severely. *He isn't even here. It is probably just Aunt Emma, wishing for some company to raid the larder.*

Sighing, Arabella stood and pulled her robe over her gown as she crossed to the door. Before she reached it, it was thrown open and she was enveloped in a warm, masculine embrace.

"Bella *mia,*" a rich, husky voice whispered in her ear, "I couldn't wait."

"Lucien! What are you—"

He kissed her hungrily, his mouth plundering hers so thoroughly that she would have fallen if he hadn't held her so tightly, his hands cupping her against him. Time swirled to a halt as his mouth covered hers, his tongue teasing her lips open and sending shivers of hot fire through her. As he kissed her, he was pulling at his shirt, loosening the ties. He broke the kiss only long enough to yank his shirt over his head and then he was against her again, his familiar warm skin heating her through her robe and gown.

His kiss deepened and she felt as if he devoured her with his passion. Unable to stop herself, she returned his embrace, threading her hands through his damp hair in a desperate bid to get closer.

He broke the kiss with a moan, his breathing harsh as he whispered in her ear, "I have thought of nothing but this all day."

He lifted her in his arms and buried his face in her hair. "Did you miss me?" he asked unsteadily, his rumbling voice sending tremors through her body.

She was lost and she knew it, her carefully planned speech fading with every touch. Desperate to say the words before she forgot them, she tried to draw back. "Lucien, we must talk."

He tightened his hold, smiling down into her eyes. "Then talk. But first . . ." He turned and kicked the door closed, then lifted her and carried her to the wide bed.

"I can't talk in bed!" she protested.

Lucien quirked a brow and laid her gently on the cover. "I won't ask you to."

She clutched at the throat of her robe with nervous fingers. "This is very important, Lucien. Perhaps if we—"

The bed sank as he placed his knee on the side and leaned over her. A sensual curve to his mouth, he took her hands and pulled them over her head, the movement thrusting her breasts against the thin material of her wrap. His gaze deepened as her nipples peaked. She could feel the heat of him through her robe, through the gown beneath, seeking, searching, touching her as surely as his hands.

"What are you doing?" she asked, trying desperately to collect her thoughts.

"Listening to you." He slid a hand to cup her breasts, his thumb swirling along the crest of her nipple, teasing it mercilessly. He trailed his mouth across her cheek, past her ear, his breath hot and sweet.

"Lucien," she said, finding it difficult to breathe, "I want to talk about tomorrow."

"Hm," he murmured, sliding down so that he could taste her neck, his tongue leaving a trail of moist tingles.

"We are making a mis—" She gasped as his teeth scraped along the delicate skin below her ear. His mouth moved lower, over her robe, as he found the beaded point of her breast. His tongue laved the material, wetting it until the cold-hot sensations sent her writhing against him, the heat in her belly building with each stroke.

He tormented her more before he lifted his head and used his teeth to pull free the ties that held her robe. Then he slowly undid each button of her gown, pushing the material aside bit by bit. She watched him, breathless with need when he shot her a look brimming with promise. She twisted restlessly, wanting more, seeking more.

"Easy, love," he murmured, his eyes glinting green fire in the candlelight. "We have all the time in the world."

His words reminded her of why she had to talk with him now, before it was too late. "Lucien, I must tell you—"

He released her hands to push open her gown and free her breasts. "So beautiful," he breathed. With one swift move, he cupped her breasts in his hands, his thumbs flicking the vulnerable peaks. Arabella's fingers sank into the counterpane on either side of her as sensations exploded through her. Her breasts swelled in response to his onslaught, the nipples puckering to a delicate point.

"You can have anything you want," he whispered, his gaze locked with hers. "Just tell me."

She thought she would drown in the passion she saw reflected in his eyes. One of his hands slid down past her breast, down the slope of her stomach, over her hip. There, he began pulling her gown upward. Steadily, without moving his gaze from hers, he gathered the cloth until his fingers grazed the top of her thigh.

She caught her breath. "Lucien, I . . ."

He smiled as her voice trailed away, her eyes glazing as his fingers found the damp sable curls. He parted them gently, looking for the folds beneath. She was so ready for him, responded so quickly, that it was all he could do to rein in his own emotions, his own passions. But rein them in he would.

Moving slowly so as not to startle her, he found her center and pressed gently. She moaned and tossed her head, trying to deny him even as her hips writhed in rhythm with his light touch. God, but she was beautiful, so curved and womanly. Every inch of her begged to be explored, tasted, worshiped.

Lucien's lips met hers, and his tongue entered her mouth. She opened wider and gently sucked him, urging him on as her hips lifted and her thighs spread ever so slightly. She wanted him, desired him. It was the one thing she could not deny.

And it was almost more than he could take. He withdrew his hand to undo the buttons of his breeches, keeping his lips on hers. She moaned into his mouth, the sound as sweet and wanton as her hands that threaded through his hair, stroked his shoulders, ran lightly over his arms and chest. Each touch was as delicate as the brush of a feather.

Lucien returned his fingers to her, bringing her closer and closer to the pinnacle of desire, but he stopped just short of allowing her release.

He lifted himself on his elbow to stare at her flushed face, her kiss-swollen lips. "Tell me what you want, Bella. I want to hear you say it."

She shook her head and turned away, fighting him with every move. He looped an arm about her waist, pulled her against him, and turned, lifting her. She gasped when she realized she was now astride him.

He tightened his hold on her waist and slowly lifted her higher. She stiffened, throwing back her head, her breasts, full and rounded, pressed outward. Her mouth parted and her hands clutched at his arms as he lowered her down onto his shaft, her moisture heating him to rigid hardness. Lucien sank into the softness, clenching his teeth against the onslaught of sensation.

Arabella gave a sound that was half sob, half cry. Lucien pushed her up until the tip of his manhood stood poised once again, ready to invade, ready to take. Their gazes locked and her lips moved silently, her breathing as harsh as his. "Please, Lucien."

The words were like sweet music, a request he could not ignore. He pulled her hips down to his, thrusting himself into her moist heat. She cried out, her face a mask of bliss, her nails biting into the back of his hands. He held her there, feeling the building quiver as she gasped, and then lunged forward, crying out his name as pleasure overtook her.

He wrapped his arms around her and held her close. The clench of her passion pulled him to the edge and he fought it, tried to resist the waves that tugged so deliciously. But the clutching heat undid him, and he roared past the edge.

Slowly, their breathing returned to normal. Arabella made as if to rise, but Lucien refused, pulling the sheet across them. He held her there, her head on his chest, still joined, still mated. It was the way they were meant to be.

A light rap came on the door. Before either could move, the door opened and Aunt Emma stood, her candle held aloft. Her hair was tucked beneath a beribboned and frilled sleeping cap, her stout body encased in yards and yards of ruffled muslin.

She blinked at the sight of Lucien and Arabella in each other's arms. "Oh, my! I thought I . . . ah, I thought I heard a cat . . . dying . . . or something. . . ." Her voice trailed off and Emma stood frozen, her gaze wide.

"Go back to bed, Aunt Emma," said Arabella in a stiff voice.

Emma nervously adjusted the lace at her throat. "O-of course, dear. I suppose you were just having trouble sleeping." Her color deepened. "No, no. Probably not. You weren't sleeping, were you?"

Lucien chuckled, and Arabella pinched his leg. He jerked with surprise, but he managed to contain his laughter after that.

Emma waved a hand. "I'm going back to bed now. I will see you in the morning. Don't . . . don't . . . oh, it doesn't matter. You are getting married. Do whatever you wish." She backed out of the room, bumping into the doorframe and almost tripping over her own robe. Finally the door shut behind her.

Lucien turned to look at Arabella. She had covered her eyes with both hands. Concerned, he lifted one free.

"W-we don't have a cat," she sputtered, then gave a gurgle of laughter.

Relieved, Lucien grinned. "Then we'll have to get one."

"I don't think we should," she said, snuggling beside him and closing her eyes with a contented sigh. "Every time we make love, Emma will be out in the hallway, worried someone is trying to kill it."

Chuckling, Lucien pulled her to his side and gathered her close. "You said you wanted to talk about something, love. What was it?"

"Hm?" she murmured.

He lifted himself on an elbow to look down at her. The flush of passion still touched her skin, and her hair was wildly spread across his pillow. Lucien ran a hand across the tangled skein. "When I arrived you said we needed to talk."

"Oh, yes. That." A huge yawn overtook her. "I can't seem to remember. . . ." Her voice faded as she spoke, and her eyes drifted closed.

"Maybe you will remember tomorrow."

She smiled her answer and within minutes she had fallen asleep.

Lucien stayed awake for a long time afterward, watching her face in repose. She had the most fascinating mouth he had ever seen—the full bottom lip seductive even in sleep. The length of her lashes fascinated him and he brushed the tip of his finger across the delicate ends until she muttered in her sleep and turned away, snuggling into her pillow.

Feeling cheated, Lucien wrapped his arm about her waist and pulled her against him. They fit perfectly, like matched spoons. As if hearing his thought, she curled into him and gave a sigh of pleasure. She was right where she belonged . . . in bed, with him. Content at last, Lucien rested his cheek on her hair and closed his eyes, a smile on his lips.

Chapter 25

There had never been a lovelier bride, decided Aunt Jane, surveying her niece with pride. With her hair piled high on her head, the chestnut strands cascading in fat curls over her ears and across one shoulder, Arabella looked beautiful. The only regret Jane had was that, seen in the light of day, the gown she and Emma had so carefully constructed for their niece appeared to be somewhat . . . overadorned.

Jane tilted her head and regarded the gown critically. Covered with rows of beading, flounces, and rosettes, it was perhaps a trifle ornate. But the sheen of the silk complemented Arabella's flushed cheeks and the long skirt trailed beautifully behind the blushing bride.

Overall, the wedding had gone without a flaw. Outside, a fresh snow powdered the garden and gave the whole world a magical air. The church had been filled with well-wishers and almost all of them had come to participate in the reception.

Jane looked around the morning room and felt a swell of satisfaction. The hundreds of candles bathed the room with a warm golden glow. The scent of fresh Christmas greenery wafted through the air and mingled with the hot brandy punch and cinnamon tarts.

The only flaw in an otherwise perfect wedding was the slightest suggestion of fatigue on the bride's face. Jane noted the circles beneath the brown eyes, but said nothing. Emma, on the other hand, could not look at her niece without turning bright red.

The groom seemed perfectly rested, his attention never straying from his bride. Darkly handsome, dressed in a formal black coat and knee breeches, Lucien was a sight to behold. He exuded a raw masculinity that had most of the women in the room in raptures. Even staid Miss Pipton stared at him so hungrily that her father pinched her and made her cry.

Jane was nearly bursting with pride. The best part of the day was the moment she realized that Arabella was now a duchess. Pride filled Jane's meager breast, and she had to search for her handkerchief through eyes blurred with tears.

Someone thrust a handkerchief into her hand, and Jane mopped her eyes. "Aren't they a lovely pair? Just perfect for each other."

"Balderdash," said Sir Loughton.

Jane jerked her head up to glare. "What are *you* doing here? You were not on the guest list."

Amusement glimmered in his blue gaze. "How do you know?"

"Because I wrote it."

A smile lifted one corner of his mouth. "What's the matter, Jane? Afraid?"

Her back stiffened. "I am not afraid of anyone, Sir Loughton. Least of all you."

His azure gaze darkened. "I've been thinking about you. Every night, in bed, I think of what you will feel like beneath me—"

"Sir Loughton, *please*." Her heart pounding, face heated, Jane glanced around, but everyone seemed focused on the bride and groom.

"I can't help it, Jane. I've had my fair share of soiled doves and done my part to make the women of England happy." He ignored her outraged sniff and bent to whisper in her ear. "But no one has ever intrigued me as much as you."

Jane cursed her weakening knees. It took every ounce of strength she possessed not to sink into a chair. Now that Arabella was married, her luck would change. She would be able to focus her energies on the cards and, if all went according to her plan, she would be out from under Sir Loughton's odious power and able to provide for the family.

Feeling noble, Jane sniffed. "This is hardly a proper conversation."

"Who gives a damn about proper?"

"There is no reason why we need to discuss this now," Jane said hastily, seeing Emma coming their way. "You and I will never be together."

"Never?" His hand slipped to the inside of her elbow and he pulled her closer, his breath warm against her ear. *"Never?"*

Jane didn't have the strength to turn away. It had been years since a man had looked at her with such passion. For some reason, she wanted to turn into his arms and bury her face in his jacket, breathing deeply of his scent, a comforting mix of bergamot and mint.

He tightened his grip. "Jane, come to me tonight. Let me—"

"There you are!" called Emma, finally reaching them. "Isn't it a lovely turnout? And in such weather, too. Mrs. Poole was just saying that it was a sign of our standing in the neighborhood that so many of our friends came today."

"More likely it is a sign of Cook's standing," Sir Loughton said. "I'd run naked through the snow for a slice of her ham. I've often thought about stealing her from you." His gaze flickered to Jane. "I may yet."

Jane bit back an angry reply.

"Oh, Sir Loughton, you are so naughty," Emma said, tittering giddily until she became aware of Jane's fiery glance.

Mr. Francot approached. Though he was dressed in his usual somber fare, his eyes burned in his pale face. He made a ponderous bow and took Jane's hand. "Lady Melwin, I hope I can speak frankly with you. I can only hope Arabella will not regret her actions today."

Emma frowned. "Did she spill some orgeat on her gown?"

Mr. Francot shook his head. "I fear it is something far more serious than that. I should not speak, but I feel . . . Miss Hadley is an innocent. Her whole life has been devoted to helping others. And now, after barely four weeks of acquaintance, she has sold herself to that . . . that . . ."

"There, now," said Jane sharply. "You've greatly mistaken the matter if you think her unhappy. She welcomed this match, and indeed, she and the duke have something of a history together, so it isn't as sudden as you may think."

Sir Loughton snorted and Jane elbowed him sharply.

His startled "Oof" settled her irritation and she was able to say to the solicitor with tolerable cheerfulness, "I know this has been a terrible disappointment for you, Mr. Francot. Just give yourself a week or two and you'll be fine."

Mr. Francot nodded, though the tension about his mouth did not lessen. After a moment of awkward silence, Mr. Harlbrook strode up to offer his stiff congratulations. Jane watched him narrowly, but other than wearing a slight air of resignation, the pompous lord didn't appear to be overly affected by Arabella's marriage. It was with a great sigh of relief for all concerned when Harlbrook bore Francot off to partake of some of Cook's apple tarts.

Jane immediately dismissed them from her mind. Looking around, she noted that every person in the room seemed pleased and happy. Except Miss Devereaux.

Liza stood by the fire, her gaze fiercely fixed on Lucien, her mouth turned in a scowl. Really, the girl would be quite pretty if she smiled, though her height would never allow one to call her a beauty. Jane supposed it was too much to ask a fond sister to stand by and watch her brother marry; it had been a difficult thing for her when James had wed.

She watched as Robert wheeled his chair up to the new couple and talked with Lucien. A genuine smile curved the younger man's lips and for an instant he looked untroubled, the way he had before he'd left for the war.

Jane clasped her hands together and smiled. It really was a lovely day. Soon, all of the guests would leave and scatter about the countryside to regale their less fortunate neighbors with news of the wedding of the year and her happiness would be complete. Except for the money she owed Sir Loughton.

Perhaps it was time to deal with that unfortunate circumstance, as well. After all, with Arabella's marriage to the duke, Jane's luck would be back in force.

Smiling, she placed her hand on Sir Loughton's arm and glanced at him through her lashes. "Could I interest you in a game of cards?"

After a surprised moment, his hand covered hers. "I am interested in anything having to do with you."

She pulled her hand away. "This is a business proposition, sir. Nothing more."

"To you, perhaps. But to me . . ." He lifted his shaggy brows, his blue eyes vivid. "I will play you one last time, Jane. But this time, I get to name the stakes."

"I can only imagine what depraved things you are planning." For some reason, instead of frightening her, they sent a pleasant glow throughout her entire body. Jane wondered if she'd imbibed a touch too much punch.

Sir Loughton flashed an unrepentant grin. "This evening, then. At ten. I shall be waiting." He bowed over her hand and looked into her eyes. "And this time, Jane, leave Emma at home. We won't need a chaperone."

Delicious heat rose in Jane's cheeks, and she nodded.

Looking pleased, he left, stopping only to say a word to Lucien and place a quick kiss on Arabella's hand. As Jane watched him stride out the door, a slow, secret smile curved her lips. After tonight, her debts would be paid in full. One way or another.

Chapter 26

Lucien heaved a heavy sigh of relief as the door shut behind the last guest.

"Tired, Your Grace?" Hastings asked. "Sincerity can be most wearing."

"Very. Have you moved Her Grace's things into my room?"

The valet bowed. "May I ask why you didn't use Her Grace's chambers? They are considerably larger."

"I like the view from my room." Lucien wanted Arabella to realize that she was married. It was time to move forward, for both of them. He only hoped that the memories that he'd created for her last night would help.

Hastings glanced about the vestibule as Arabella emerged from the library with Robert, then leaned forward to say in a low voice, "Sir, a sealed missive arrived for you just before the ceremony." He pulled a letter from his pocket and handed it to Lucien.

Lucien looked at the greasy paper. *Mumferd.* Finally,

the information he'd been seeking. Once he'd put this last detail to rest, he could spend all of his time doing more productive things—like locating a physician for Robert and reminding Arabella every night of all the pleasures in store for her.

He impatiently tore open the missive. "Bloody hell."

Hastings raised his brows.

"The sale is this afternoon." Lucien crushed the note in his hand. "I will have to leave immediately."

"Does your informant mention where, Your Grace?"

"No, I'm to meet him and he will take me there."

Hastings frowned, his lips folded in disapproval. "I don't like that."

"Nor I."

"Your Grace, perhaps I should accompany you. It would be a pity if something were to go awry and you were forced to leave Her Grace alone so quickly after the ceremony."

Lucien fixed a stare on his valet. "Playing on my new-found sensibilities, Hastings?"

Faint color touched the valet's face. "I only thought it prudent to remind you that you have much more at stake now."

Lucien glanced over his shoulder at his wife. In the place of a veil, Aunt Jane had pinned a lace mantle to Arabella's curls. The patterned texture made the chestnut curls appear a warm golden brown and complemented her creamy skin. Hastings was right—he did have more to lose. A lot more. It was yet another reason to bring an end to the jewel smuggling once and for all.

Stifling an impatient sigh, he turned back to Hastings. "Very well. You may go with me. We'll leave as soon as possible."

An expression of relief crossed Hastings's thin face.

"Certainly, my lord. I shall have the horses saddled imme- diately." He gave one final bow and hurried off as if afraid Lucien would change his mind.

Lucien turned to regard his wife. She stood by the library door, talking with Robert. They were laughing, her hand resting gracefully on his shoulder. The sun glinted off her hair and warmed her skin to cream. Below the overtrimmed bodice of her wedding gown, the skirt flared in soft folds to the floor. Lucien could not look at the full skirt without imagining himself untying the ribbons and letting the yards of silk drop to the floor, pooling at her naked feet.

He was damn glad the ceremony was over. It had been hell standing so close to Arabella, unable to touch her or kiss away the uncertainty he saw in her eyes. He needed to prove to her with more than words what she meant to him, what he wanted to mean to her.

Of course, if she ever realized he had purposely tricked her into marrying him, there would be no reconciliation. Lucien rubbed a weary hand to his neck, the thought weighing heavily. The hard truth was that if he wanted Arabella to trust him, then he had to start by trusting her.

And that meant admitting the falsehood behind their marriage.

But what if it turns her against me all the more? Lucien watched her bend down to hug Robert, her eyes shining with laughter.

It didn't matter. Once he told her the truth, all that would stand between them would be her pride, but it was as solid and immovable as a stone wall. Lucien was deter- mined to win his way over those walls. Like the constant fall of water, he would wear away her defenses so gently she wouldn't even know it had happened.

But for now, he had to deal with Mumferd.

Arabella held the door open for Robert as he made his way back into the library. He seemed anxious to return to his books, but she suspected otherwise. Oblivious to onlookers, Robert had watched Lucien's sister all morning, a strange glint to his eye.

Liza was a puzzle, Arabella decided. The girl regarded her with barely disguised animosity, and for the life of her, Arabella could not figure out why.

She turned on her heel, just in time to see Lucien pull on his gloves. She stopped to watch him through her lashes, unable to still a thrill of pride that this man, this impressive, handsome, virile man, was all hers. At least in name. But perhaps that was enough.

Still . . . she couldn't rid herself of the idea that he didn't really belong in this setting. Dressed in his usual black, his coat fitting tightly to his broad shoulders, the blinding white of his cravat a sharp contrast to his golden skin and black hair, he looked as out of place standing in the foyer as a lion in a rabbit hole. He belonged in London among the ton, where he was welcomed and admired. She wondered how she would fit in there, and decided it didn't matter. She would make her way; she always had.

A strange sense of unreality hung over her. All day, she'd had the strangest feeling that the marriage had been a dream—from the night of passion they'd shared and the warm intimacy of waking in each other's arms, to the cold realization that she was standing before Vicar Haighton and pledging away her life.

It was a dream that she'd had many times before— Lucien riding back into her life and demanding to marry her. She gazed at him, noting the determined set of his mouth and the strong line of his jaw.

She swallowed. *Please, God, whatever you do, just don't let me wake up.*

Lucien set his hat on his head and turned, coming to a stop when his gaze fell on her.

She colored. "You are leaving?"

He glanced down at a crumpled missive he held in his hand, a slight frown creasing his forehead. "There is some business I must attend to."

"Now?" Not that she cared, she told herself. After all, this was only a marriage of convenience; Lucien was free to go wherever he wished. As she'd taken her wedding vows, Arabella had taken a silent vow all her own—she would not allow herself to fall in love with Lucien again. Last night had proven that there was a strong physical attraction, but that was all. Now she would be the perfect wife, pleasant and calm, always welcoming, but free to do as she wished, just like her husband.

The image of herself as a capable woman of the world stiffened her wavering resolve, and she managed a smile.

Lucien grinned in return, stepping forward to slip an arm about her waist and pull her to him. He touched the tip of her nose with his, resting his forehead to hers. "I may miss dinner, but I'll be back in time to tuck you into my bed."

His proximity sent shivers of awareness down her spine, yet still she managed to say lightly, "Come back whenever you wish. You are free to do whatever you want. I don't own you, Lucien. And you don't own me."

Frowning, he withdrew his hands from her waist. "Bella, don't—" He stared down at her face, a flicker of something in his green eyes. Then, with a heavy sigh, he turned away. "We will talk when I get back. There are things we should discuss."

Her heart skipped a beat. "What?"

He sent her a shuttered look, so fraught with unspoken meaning that her mouth went dry. "I don't want there to be any secrets between us, Bella. No falseness."

"Then tell me now."

He hesitated, then leaned over to place a kiss on her cheek, his breath shivering against her ear. "I don't have time. We will talk tonight and I will explain everything."

She watched him pull on his coat and walk out the front door. For a long time, she just stood there, fighting an urge to follow him.

"Where is Lucien?" Liza's voice woke Arabella from her reverie.

Arabella turned to Lucien's sister and tried to keep her smile from slipping completely off her face. Liza wore a muslin gown trimmed with aqua rosettes, the white skirt parting to reveal a pink satin slip. With her golden hair piled high on her head and a single ostrich feather dyed to match her slip, she looked regal.

"Lucien just left," Arabella said.

"Already?" Liza swung a baleful glare on Arabella. "What did you do to him?"

"Nothing. He received a letter and had to see to some business. He'll be back this evening."

"What business could he possibly have here in York-shire?"

Arabella stiffened. What indeed? She remembered the letter he'd held in his hand and how it had been crushed, as if he'd been none too pleased to receive it. With sudden clarity, she knew the letter had contained information about the jewels.

A plump dandy, with shirt points so high they grazed his cheeks, sauntered out of the morning room and caught sight of Arabella and Liza. "There you are! Been wondering where everyone went. Have all those plaguey guests left?"

Arabella gave a swift nod and refrained from pointing out that Edmund Valmont was a guest, as well.

"Thank heavens. Don't mean to sound unfriendly, but

it was deuced uncomfortable, talking to people I didn't even know—" He stopped, suddenly aware of the tension. "Oh, sorry. Did I interrupt anything? I'm bad about that, you know, though—"

"Edmund," Liza interrupted. "Miss Hadley and I were just getting acquainted."

"Were you, now? There you go, do the pretty to your new sister-in-law. Though you shouldn't call her Miss Hadley, you know. She's the Duchess of Wexford now."

A duchess without a duke, Arabella thought.

The door to the library opened and Robert wheeled out, a book in his hand. "Bella, where is Lucien? He promised to look at this for me."

"He is gone," Liza announced. "Your sister has already turned him away."

Robert regarded Liza with a flat stare. "Are you still holding to that idiotic story?"

Liza bristled, hot color in her cheeks. "It is not idiotic! Your sister tricked my brother into marrying her, and now she has forced him from her door."

Edmund chuckled. "Lud, Liza, what will you say next? You've got it all backwards, m'dear. Lucien is the one who—" He choked to a stop as he caught sight of Arabella's face. "I mean, I don't know for certain, but I would suppose—"

She took two steps toward him. "What do you mean?"

He backed away, his hands held palm out as if to ward her off. "Nothing! I was just thinking. Aloud. Do it all the time. Quite silly of me, but there it is." He edged closer to the door with every word.

Arabella crossed the space between them and poked a finger in the center of his straining waistcoat. *"Tell me."*

His eyes widened. "I can't—I don't—I haven't—"

"Now."

Edmund glanced about for help and met Liza's darkening stare and Robert's furious scowl. He sighed in defeat. "Oh, very well. I suppose you would have found out sooner or later, anyway. I mean, it isn't as if you can keep that sort of thing secret and—" He took a deep breath. "Lucien and Lady Melwin planned the whole thing."

Robert cursed. "Don't say another word, you fool!"

"No, explain yourself." Arabella frowned. "What 'whole thing'?"

"The wedding. He wanted to marry you, to do the honorable thing. But he said you refused him, so he finagled your aunt into helping him."

"Surely you cannot mean . . ."

Everything blurred to a halt. Aunt Jane and Lucien? Her mind froze, only one thought breaking free—she had to see Lucien. And when she did . . . She turned and dashed up the stairs to her room.

Robert whirled his chair around to face Edmund. "You fool!"

"I had no choice," Edmund said desperately. "Besides, it is all for the better. No sense in having a bunch of secrets lying around. Bound to stick their ugly heads up sooner or later, and then where would you be?"

Liza placed a hand to her forehead. "I don't understand. Why would Lucien do such a thing?"

Robert shot her a hard stare. "Why do you think?"

Her answer was interrupted by a clatter on the stairs as Arabella appeared, a shapeless gray coat tossed over her shoulders, worn boats peeking from beneath her gown.

"By Jove," Edmund exclaimed, his gaze wide. "What are you doing wearing that?"

"Bella," Robert called, but she didn't spare any of them a glance. She crossed the foyer, yanked open the front door, and slammed it behind her.

Cursing violently, Robert turned to Edmund. "Go after her, fool! Can't you see she's not in any state to be left alone?"

Edmund's eyes widened and he nervously fingered his shirt points. "But I scarcely know her. Maybe *you* should go and—"

Robert's fists slammed onto the arms of his chair. "Damn it! I can't! Now go and find her, and do not let her out of your sight until Lucien returns."

Edmund brightened. "There's an idea! Has the devil of a way with the women, Wexford does. Always did." He scurried to the door. "Never fear. I'll stick with your sister like a burr."

"Wonderful," muttered Robert, watching the door close yet again. He sat silently, his hands fisted about the arms of his chair, his knuckles white. After what seemed an eternity, he turned a baleful glare on Liza. "Well? Are you satisfied now?"

She colored hotly. "I made a perfectly logical error. Anyone who knows my brother would have done the same. He has always been set against marriage, and it is inconceivable he would wed in such a fashion unless forced to it."

"No one forced him."

"I still don't understand why he would stoop to such a stratagem."

"Because my sister would have him no other way, and he was determined to have her. He is in love with her— though I doubt he realizes it."

"I don't believe it."

"Don't you? Then explain why he watches her so closely, trying to catch every nuance of her expression. Why does he frown if she is frowning? Smile if she is smiling? Why is he doing everything he can to relieve her of the burdens of her life?"

"He must feel some sort of obligation—"

"Damn it, Elizabeth, listen to reason." He turned his chair and pushed it until he was within an arm's length of her. "You know your brother so well—have you ever known him to do anything that he did not want to do? Knowing the way he feels about marriage, do you think *anyone* could have forced him to the altar?"

Liza's stomach sank. How many times had she heard their aunt lament the fact that Lucien refused to listen to her? Lucien had done exactly what he wanted for years. Was it possible that he actually loved Arabella?

Liza had watched her brother struggle to hide the lingering scars left by his marriage to Sabrina. Lucien took everything to heart, including his many responsibilities. When his wife had died, he'd withdrawn inside himself, taking blame for Sabrina's wild, heedless behavior, wondering if he could have done something to stop what was, to everyone else, her inevitable end.

No amount of reasoning had ever been able to alleviate his pain. Then and there, Liza had been determined that her brother would not sacrifice himself again. But this time, perhaps things were different. Perhaps Lucien *was* in love with Arabella.

And now she'd ruined everything with her spiteful tongue. A great tear welled and slipped down Liza's cheek. All she'd ever wanted was to see Lucien happy. She pressed a hand to her mouth to stop her lips from quivering. She might as well return to her room and pack; Lucien would send her away when he returned, and this time she deserved it.

The tears fell faster and she searched for her handkerchief, finally finding the scrap of lace tucked in her sleeve. If her brother had committed such folly to win Arabella, then he was deeply, irrevocably in love. She only hoped she hadn't ruined everything for him.

As her tears thickened into a sob, a strong arm looped about her hips and she was unceremoniously hauled down into Robert's lap. He held her loosely clasped to his shoulder, looking down at her with a fierce sort of anger.

For an instant she sat frozen in his arms, her handkerchief fluttering to the ground. It was the first time any man had ever held her so.

"Clumsy, aren't you?" he said unsympathetically, pulling his own handkerchief from his pocket. "Must be your height. Has anyone told you that you are too tall?"

She wiped her face. "Not since I was a child, though I know my aunt thinks it will keep me from ever taking."

"Well, she is wrong. I like a tall woman." His face softened and his mouth curved in a twisted smile. "If I were standing, I'd say we are of a height."

She sniffed, trying hard to keep the tears from falling. "Are we?" she asked in a small voice.

He nodded, his gaze fastened on her trembling mouth. "I wouldn't even have to bend to kiss you."

Fascinated, Liza stared at him. Was he *flirting* with her? It was so hard to tell. There was some sort of pull between them; she'd felt it from the beginning. But surely he didn't find her attractive. She was huge, a giant almost. An awkward thing with a nose that belonged on a Roman statue. But lying here in his arms, his smile almost tender as he stared down at her, a stirring of something other than anger warmed her stomach. It was an amazing thing; in all of her eighteen years, no one had made her feel even the slightest bit pretty. Until now.

Robert smiled. "If you are quite through sobbing, I will tell you something."

"What?" she asked, blinking away her tears.

He leaned forward and whispered, "I think I know where the Captain's treasure is."

Liza had heard about the treasure; Aunt Emma was full of tales of all the places where it wasn't. "B-but your sister—"

"It is too late to worry about her. Only Lucien can undo whatever damage you and that ridiculous Edmund have done."

She nodded, a fresh wave of tears rising, her lip quivering. Robert's gaze locked on her mouth and for one horrifying instant, she thought he would kiss her.

But he didn't. Just as quickly as he'd scooped her up, he set her back on her feet. "Stop that."

"I can't help it," she wailed, mopping at her cheeks. "I've ruined everything."

"Nonsense." As her tears subsided into soft hiccups, he turned his chair toward the library. "Whenever you're done warbling, come and help me."

"Help you do what?" she asked, intrigued by his sudden air of mystery.

"Help me discover Rosemont's greatest secret." He sent her a strange smile over his shoulder, his gaze flickering across her hips and down her skirt. "Thank God you've got such long legs."

With that cryptic comment, he disappeared through the library door.

Awash in curiosity, Liza followed. She only hoped that she could be of more help to Robert than she'd been to his sister.

Arabella yanked open the gate and slammed it behind her.

"Miss Hadl—I mean, Your Grace," called Edmund.

Arabella walked faster.

The gate creaked behind her and the plump young man stumbled as he came abreast of her, his face damp with exertion. "I say, Miss—Your Grace—where, ah, perhaps I should—do you think—"

"Please do not bother yourself on my account. I would prefer to be alone."

"Alone? You mean by yourself? I don't think that's wise."

She jerked open the stable door and tromped in, immediately setting about saddling Sebastian.

Edmund stood watching her warily as if he would not have been the least surprised to see her sprout horns and fangs. "May I ask where you are going?"

"Away."

"Oh. And for how long?"

She leveled a long, hard look at him before gathering her skirts to one side and mounting the horse. Kicking her feet into the stirrups, she turned Sebastian to the open gate and walked him through.

Sputtering, Edmund scurried along beside her. "Miss Had—Your Grace! Lucien will want to know when to expect you home."

"Lucien can go to h—" Arabella swallowed the rest of the retort. She was wasting her breath; the person she really wanted to speak with was not here. No, her estimable husband was most likely sitting in a cozy tavern somewhere, ignoring his duties as a husband.

With a brief wave at Edmund, Arabella passed through the gate toward the main road and urged Sebastian into his version of a gallop, which was more of a lumpy trot. She rode down the road only a short distance before veering off across the moors. A chill wind tugged at the edges of her cloak and seeped through the thin dress, but Arabella didn't feel the cold. Warmed by the slow burn of anger, she trotted on.

It was infuriating to think of how she'd been played for a fool yet again. "All those good reasons for getting married—ha!" Arabella muttered.

Sebastian shied at a rabbit hole and Arabella steadied him, turning him onto a narrow path that cut across the moors toward Whitby. "What did that idiot think? That I would never discover his duplicity?"

She could still hear Edmund's voice explaining how Lucien had conspired with Aunt Jane. Once again, she had trusted Lucien and he had let her down. "Once a fool, always a fool," she muttered fiercely.

She'd search every tavern on the coast if she had to, but she would find her brainless husband and demand an accounting. By God, she would make sure this marriage of convenience was neither a marriage nor a convenience.

She wondered if Aunt Emma knew of Lucien's perfidy, then decided that of course she did. *I wonder who doesn't know about it besides me and Liza?*

Arabella scowled. First Lucien turned Aunt Jane and then her own brother against her. It was a good thing she'd found out what a scoundrel he was before her heart became engaged.

Though that wasn't strictly true. Despite her desire otherwise, she cared—far more than she should.

How dare he treat her so? To lie to her—and to marry her under such patently false pretensions! That was the most painful part of all. She had finally begun to hope about life with Lucien by her side. It hurt to watch that small, delicate blossom die, trampled beneath the arrogant boots of the one man she should have stayed far away from.

Sebastian dropped into a grinding walk as the path entered a small grove of trees. Arabella couldn't help but remember their night in the cottage—the whisper of skin over skin, of seeking lips and hot, drugging kisses. If she closed her eyes, she could see Lucien bent over her, his eyes dark with passion, his jaw tense with tightly controlled need.

She forced the images away, lifting her heated face to the cool air. Damn Lucien Devereaux. He had seduced her with passion and overwhelmed her with logical reasoning.

Sebastian jerked his head up and stumbled a little on the path. Arabella absently soothed him, a crease between her brows.

Why would Lucien have done such a thing? What could he have hoped to gain? Rosemont?

No, as much as she loved Rosemont, she knew it paled beside his other residences. So why had he gone to such elaborate lengths? What was the reason for his ruse? She frowned, absorbed in thought.

"What are ye doin' here, missus?"

Arabella turned to see Ned ambling up on a broken-backed nag. He was still dressed in his Sunday finest, a black wool coat that he'd worn to her wedding just this morning. His bony wrists stuck out from each sleeve a good two inches and made him look even lankier.

"I was on my way to meet His Grace. He is visiting someone in Whitby." She supposed she should call Lucien something less formal than "His Grace," but to do so would imply a closeness she was far from feeling.

"He's left the party already, has he?" Ned asked, surprise evident. "I jus' came from my sister's house and I

saw nary a soul on the road. Mayhap he went that way."
He gestured toward a narrow path that led off the main
road and into the woods. " 'Tis a shortcut of sorts, if ye
know where to turn."

Arabella nodded and nudged Sebastian down the path,
calling her thanks to Ned. Her mind was filled with uncertainty, her imagination rampant as she thought of Lucien's
machinations.

Lost in thought, she rode on. Sebastian rounded a wide
turn and pulled to a dead stop. Arabella blinked. There,
standing beside a narrow stand of brush stood Mr. Francot, his back to her. But it wasn't the sight of the solicitor
that surprised her. It was his companion. Standing beside
Mr. Francot, holding on to a small sack, stood Bolder.

Sebastian whickered a greeting to Mr. Francot's mare,
and the solicitor whirled around. Arabella captured a
glimpse of his pale face as Bolder yelled a violent curse
and ran for his horse.

"Get her!" yelled Francot, leaping on his mare.

Her heart pounding in her ears, Arabella whirled
Sebastian and urged him to a hard gallop. Though the old
horse was winded, he responded gallantly. Hooves thun-
dered behind her and Arabella leaned closer, whispering
words of encouragement. *Please, God, just this once, let
Sebastian fly.*

Chapter 27

Lucien checked his pocket watch for the fourth time. The minutes slowly ticked by and still there was no sign of Mumferd. *Bloody hell, where is that weasel?* Stifling a sigh, Lucien crossed to the inn window and lifted the edge of the curtain.

Hastings sat slumped on a bench in front of the stables, dressed in the shapeless coat of a common laborer. Hat pulled low, he braided a length of rope with the ease of long practice.

Other than glancing up whenever a horse arrived in the posting yard, he seemed immersed in his task. Impatient, Lucien dropped a coin beside his mug and went to join Hastings.

The valet remained seated, his hands never slowing as he patiently braided the rope. "This doesn't seem right."

"Yes, something has gone wrong. We'll wait five more minutes. I am anxious to return to Rosemont." *Anxious* didn't begin to describe it. Lucien couldn't stop thinking about the doubt that had clouded Arabella's eyes as he left.

He sighed and raked a hand through his hair, wondering if he dared to tell her the truth about the night in the cottage. Their relationship was still uncertain. Perhaps he should wait until . . . until what?

Hastings nodded toward the road. "There he comes now."

Lucien turned as a horse loped into view. Mumferd sat astride a large roan horse, his dark greasy coat flapping open to reveal a pistol strapped to his saddle.

Eyes narrowed, Lucien crossed the yard, a prickle of warning creeping between his shoulder blades. "Where have you been?"

"There was a bit of a turn-up." At Lucien's raised brows, Mumferd gave a placating shrug and placed his hand on his pistol in a meaningful gesture. "But all's well now. We've as much at stake as ye do."

Lucien regarded him narrowly, wondering what kind of a "turn-up" would make them willing to risk losing his participation in the auction. If there even was an auction. The thought tightened his throat.

"Mount up, guv'nor. I'm to take ye meself."

There was something forced about Mumferd's behavior. He moved jerkily, his eyes darting here and there.

Lucien turned and tossed a coin at Hastings. "Bring my mount, and be quick about it."

Hastings bit the coin before stuffing it into his pocket. Rising with insolent slowness, he shambled toward the stables.

Lucien shot a hard stare at Mumferd. "I hope this trip is not a waste of time."

Unease flickered in the man's murky eyes. "I don't

think ye'll be disappointed." His smile was as strained as his expression.

Tamping down his growing impatience, Lucien accepted Satan's reins from Hastings and swung into the saddle. With a swift glance at his valet, Lucien followed Mumferd.

Once on the road, the horses picked up a brisk canter, their hooves thudding heavily on the packed ground. They traveled for ten minutes in silence, Lucien's mind filled with foreboding.

Finally he pulled up alongside Mumferd and said, "Tell me about the sale. How many men will be bidding against me?"

Mumferd's gaze flickered. "Four. Maybe five."

Or maybe none. "I must admit, I am somewhat concerned why you were delayed."

"Oh, 'twas nofin'. Someone put their nose where it didn't belong. We put an end to her right enuff."

Lucien pulled Satan to a stop, ice clenching his heart.

"Why are ye stoppin'? We'll be late if we don't hurry along."

"You said *her.*"

Mumferd glanced nervously at a stand of woods just down the road. "Did I? Then ye didn't hear me right, guv'nor."

Lucien reached out and grabbed the bridle of Mumferd's horse. "*Who* did you put an end to? Tell me now."

Without warning, the man's hand jerked toward his pistol. Lucien knocked the gun away with a swipe of his hand. It went flying through the air as Lucien grabbed Mumferd by his muffler and lifted him from his horse, the informant's feet dangling, his hands clawing for release.

Mumferd's face turned red as he gasped for breath.

Lucien tightened his hold and pulled his face even with his own. "I will give you one chance to live."

Choking violently, Mumferd's teary eyes pleaded for release. Lucien threw him to the ground and quickly dismounted. The informant sprawled in the dirt, gasping for air, his hands pulling at his tight muffler.

Lucien yanked his gun free and cocked it, leveling it at Mumferd's head. *"Talk."*

Mumferd's gaze locked on the gun. He rasped out, "Nofin' happened to get ye into such a takin'! Someone stumbled on the boss as he was makin' a payment fer his shipment. B-but don't ye worry none. He's a soft spot fer women, he does."

"Bolder?" asked Lucien incredulously. Nothing he'd heard of the man had indicated a softness of any sort.

Mumferd's mouth tightened. "I'd not answer to the likes o' him fer a thousand quid! Bolder answers to me, he does, and a more shifty, no-account weaklin' I've never seen."

Then who was in charge of the smuggling operation? Lucien pulled the man back up to his feet and rested his gun barrel between Mumferd's eyes. "Where is Arabella?"

Mumferd took one look at Lucien's face and started sputtering, "She's in the cave. They were goin' to kill ye there, too. The boss, he got the idea that ye weren't on the up and up." He managed a shaky, pleading smile. "Please, guv'nor, you has to understand! I jus' follow orders. I don't make 'em."

Hooves thudded on the ground and Hastings appeared on the road, a braided rope looped in his hand.

Lucien lowered the pistol and Mumferd slumped with relief.

"Take him," Lucien growled as Hastings came abreast. "They have Arabella and I must reach her quickly."

The valet slipped from his horse. "I shall tie him up at once, Your Grace. Shall I give him to the local authorities?"

"Yes. Constable Robbins will be pleased to have a real smuggler resting in his cell. In the meantime, I will need this cretin's coat and hat."

Hastings nodded and gestured with his pistol. Complaining loudly, Mumferd complied.

"There, Your Grace." Hastings rolled the clothes into a ball and handed them to Lucien. "Be quick."

Nodding once, Lucien wheeled Satan and galloped away. He only prayed he would not be too late.

Arabella awoke slowly, pain flickering behind her eyes like steel pins. She moaned and lifted her head, aware that she sat bound to a pole, her legs curled to her side on a solid cold slab. Clenching her teeth, she opened her eyes to complete and utter darkness.

She immediately recognized the impenetrable black of an underground cavern. Waves slapped the stone slab and she could sense the tide surging against it. Perhaps she was in her own cave. She leaned against the ropes that held her and gasped in pain.

Her arms, bound tightly behind her, were completely numb. She tried to wiggle her fingers but could not. Whoever had tied her had wanted to be certain she would not escape. Forcing herself to ignore the agony, she twisted at the bonds, tears running down her cheeks.

Time crawled by, and she felt she must have been in the dark for hours before she heard the unmistakable sound of a boat. She almost sobbed in relief, straining her eyes against the darkness. *Please, God, let it be Lucien.*

Suddenly a lantern swung on the bow, the light blinding her. She squinted against it, her body trembling with cold and fear. A man climbed out of the boat as it reached the ledge, and with a swell of despair, Arabella recognized her captor.

Mr. Francot tied off the boat, then picked up the lantern and came forward. He bent his face to hers and brushed a strand of hair from her cheek with a surprisingly gentle touch. "Are you feeling better?"

"No," she managed to whisper through parched lips. "My head hurts."

He frowned and his fingers traced the bruise on her brow. "Bolder got a little carried away." The pale blue eyes met hers. "Never fear. I punished him for you."

Arabella shivered at the calmness of the statement and she felt an instant sympathy for Bolder.

"Are you cold?" Francot immediately shrugged out of his coat and draped it over her shoulders.

"Mr. Francot—"

"Please. Call me Steven. I have always wanted to hear you say my name."

She swallowed. "Steven." The name stuck in her throat like congealed porridge, but she managed a weak smile. "Why am I here?"

"Because you saw what you should not."

"All I saw was you talking to Bolder." She leaned as far forward as her bonds would allow. "Mr. Fran—Steven, I would never tell. I swear it!"

"Unfortunately, I cannot take that chance. How do you think I've been so successful? I am very cautious and I trust no one." He lifted a finger and ran it down her cheek. "Not even you."

"But I've been smuggling, too. It wouldn't make sense

for me to turn in someone who could identify me. And Bolder could do that."

"I know all about the smuggling at Rosemont. Who do you think supplied you with all that wonderful cognac your aunt loves?"

"You've . . . you've been helping?"

"As much as you would allow. Of course, I had to keep a close eye." He frowned. "People are apt to cheat an innocent female."

He set the lantern on a nearby barrel. Now that Arabella was no longer alone in the pitch-black cave, her spirit strengthened. She leveled a stare at Francot. "While I thank you for your seeming generosity, I did not need your interference."

"So Bolder told me, after that unfortunate incident when you relieved him of a very important cask." Francot's eyes glittered. "I was not happy to discover that you were involved so directly."

She clenched her jaw at his tight expression. "Why have you brought me here?"

"Ah, that is an excellent question. You, my dear, are about to witness an execution."

She could only stare at him, horrified.

"Don't look like that; I would never let someone harm you." He pulled a barrel beside her and sat facing her. "You look a mess. Let me remedy that." He carefully brushed dirt from her cheek and chin and tucked a loose strand of hair behind her ear. "There, that is much better."

It was all Arabella could do to sit still. "Thank you," she choked out, trying to focus on her surroundings, on anything that could help her escape. "If I am not to be executed, then who is?"

"It would be best if I—" He tilted his head to one side. "Ah, here he is now."

Francot stood as a dinghy passed through the mouth of the cave and began to cross the small lake. A man rowed steadily, his cap pulled low over his eyes, a greasy coat stretched across his shoulders. On the seat in front of him, Arabella could just make out a sack, filled with what appeared to be the outline of a man. Her whole body froze, her heart thundering in her ears.

Arabella recognized the fine black coat that showed beneath the sack. She turned wide eyes to Francot. "Lucien."

"I'm afraid so. He stole from me, you see. I cannot allow that to go unpunished or I would lose the respect of my men."

Fear congealed in her throat. "Your men?" she whispered. "Have you many?"

He smiled, a singularly sweet smile that terrified her worse than any threat. He leaned down and placed his hand on her knee, his heavy face only inches from hers. "After this next shipment, I will have money and power beyond your dreams, Arabella."

He tipped her face up until it was even with his, his eyes clouding, the lines about his eyes deepened by the shadows. "Had you waited, it would have been yours, too."

"I—I didn't know—"

"You will not reap the bounty of my wealth now." His hand tightened on her chin cruelly, his fingers bruising. "You have forsaken me and I cannot forgive that."

"You can't just kill him. He is a duke. Someone will look for him."

"Yes, he is a duke. And you care so much for that, don't you?" Francot sneered and he dropped his hand from her face. "Had I a title, you would have welcomed my suit. I thought I had put an end to that despicable duke's existence once. But he outmaneuvered me."

"Before . . ." Realization dawned and she gasped. "You set the fire in the shed!"

A grimace marred his features. "I had no idea you were in there as well, or I never would have blocked the door." He stooped until his eyes were level with hers. "I was in agony when I heard you scream. I never would have hurt you."

"You are hurting me now."

Francot's mouth twisted into a scowl. "But you are no longer Arabella Hadley, are you? You sold yourself for a title."

"I don't care anything for titles." *Only for Lucien*. The thought jerked her gaze back to the boat and she pulled at her bonds.

"Don't waste your time attempting to get free. You will only hurt yourself."

"What do you care?"

"Care? What do I *care*?" His voice rose, stiff with fury. "I even offered to buy that pile of rocks you love so much, and all for what?" The solicitor placed a hand under her chin and jerked her face back to his. "Why would I do that? To watch you marry another man?"

"No," she said, trying to channel her fury into cold, logical thought.

Francot's eyes burned in his pale face, his lips quivering. "Why did you do it? Why did you marry that cretin?"

Because I love him. The truth bloomed through her heart, warming her instantly. She would have married Lucien without the title, without the money. She loved him.

"You could have come to me," Francot said. "I would have saved you. But you didn't." He sighed and shook his head. "And now you will have the pleasure of watching your beloved duke die."

Arabella drew herself up, the cords cutting into her arms. "Don't, Steven. Please, leave him alone."

"Sorry, my dear. But I will see you a widow before the night is through. And then . . ." He leaned forward and rested his cold cheek against hers. "And then I will have you myself."

She jerked away, her distaste as bitter as bile.

He snarled and sank his hand in her hair, holding her face toward his own. "Don't ever turn away from me!"

Lucien gritted his teeth against the instinct to whip out his pistol and shoot the bloody bastard from where he sat in the boat, but Arabella was too close.

He rowed faster, hoping no one noticed that Mumferd's foul coat fit him much too tightly. When he reached the ledge, he looped the rope through the mooring, leapt out of the boat, and walked into the light from the lantern, keeping his head down and his face shadowed. But there was no disguising his height.

"What's this?" Francot's voice raised in surprise and he half rose from the barrel. Lucien broke into a run, his gun now drawn, but Francot yanked a knife from his boot and scrambled behind Arabella. With a vicious swipe, he slashed her bonds and yanked her to her feet. She gave a cry of pain as blood rushed into her arms. Cursing, Francot jerked her in front him, his blade to her throat.

"Drop the gun, Wexford. Or your wife will die before your eyes." Francot's eyes gleamed with malice.

Lucien tensed, his body aflame with the need to leap to Arabella's aid. But he dared not. Carefully, so as not to discharge the weapon, he placed his gun on the cavern floor.

"Lucien," Arabella gasped. A drop of blood welled at her throat and fell to her bodice.

Lucien clenched his hands. "Don't talk, Bella. Don't . . ." Emotion choked him. He would give everything he had to free her—his fortune, his lands, his very life.

He swung his gaze to Francot. "What do you want, you bastard?"

Francot smiled, his teeth yellow in the dull light. "The jewels. Now."

Lucien reached very slowly, very carefully into his pocket and pulled out the bag of jewels.

"Throw them over here."

Lucien tossed the bag so that it landed halfway between the two of them.

Francot's smirk disappeared. "You fool!" he snapped.

"If you want the jewels, come and get them," Lucien taunted.

The smuggler's eyes shifted between Lucien and the leather bag, then he shook his head. "No. You will slide it over here." He angled the knife, and another drop of blood dripped slowly down Arabella's neck. "Any more tricks, Wexford, and you won't be the only one to pay."

A cold rage filled Lucien. Whatever else happened here, Francot would not walk out alive. Lucien slowly approached the bag and pushed it with his foot. It moved several feet, but no more, still out of Francot's reach.

"Damn it! Move those over here!"

Only a few more feet . . . Lucien walked to the bag and placed his foot on it. With a sudden move, he kicked it past Francot. The bag hit the ground behind the smuggler, and a stream of glittering jewels broke free and slid across the wet rock toward the sea.

"No!" Francot cried. He instinctively took a step

toward the treasure, his blade dropping away from Arabella's neck.

With a cry, Arabella shoved Francot's arm and propelled him forward. He fell against a cask, but caught himself and turned, his knife blade clenched in his hand, an ugly snarl on his face.

Lucien dived for his gun, scrambling on the slick rock. His hands closed around the cold metal and he lifted the gun, took aim, and fired.

The blast caught Francot square in the chest. The knife flew from his hand as he staggered backward, hovering on the brink of the ledge. Hands clutched to his chest, he turned a white face toward Arabella, struggling for the breath to speak. "I—I . . ." A horrible gurgle rose from his throat, and he fell lifeless into the ocean.

Lucien caught Arabella in his arms and held her tightly. She sagged against him, her whole body trembling against his, but she was safe—safe in his arms.

Finally, when her trembling had eased, he pulled away and looked down at her. "Are you hurt?"

She offered a shaky smile. "Just my wrists."

He lifted one of her hands and ground his teeth at the sight of the scraped, bruised flesh. Cursing softly, he pulled his handkerchief from his pocket and ripped it in two, then bound each of her wrists with the clean, white linen. As he did so, his gaze fell on the red stain at her bodice. He tilted her chin up and examined her throat. Two thin lines met his gaze, the delicate skin scored just enough to bring blood. Lucien closed his eyes against the fear that chilled him. "I'm so sorry, Bella. I should have—"

Her fingers brushed his lips. He opened his eyes and found her bright gaze on him. "Lucien, there is nothing to be sorry for." A husky chuckle escaped her, though tears shone in her eyes. "You saved my life. What more could I ask?"

He gazed down at her, wondering at her strength. He loved her so much that just looking at her made his soul sing. He burned with the need to tell her, but now was not the time. Instead, he went to collect his heavy greatcoat from the boat.

She watched him, her eyes dark with emotion. "Lucien, what about the jewels?"

"When the tide lowers, they will send someone to dive for them."

" 'They'?"

He settled his coat about her shoulders. "The Home Office. I've been assisting them since the war began."

She glanced toward the black water where Francot had fallen. "I cannot believe he was behind the smuggling the whole time. I never thought he could . . ." She shivered and turned her face against Lucien's shoulder.

He held her there, sharing his warmth. He had so much he needed to say. But before he could tell her what was in his heart, he had to get her home and into some dry clothing.

He forced himself to loosen his hold and step away. "Your family will be wondering where you are. Come. If we wish to leave while it is still light, we will have to do so now."

When they reached the boat, Lucien looked at the cave opening and cursed. "The water is too high to use the dinghy. We will have to wait for the tide to go back out."

Sniffling, Arabella pulled free from his arms. "There is another way out." She pointed to the far wall where a narrow path led to a wide crack.

Lucien grinned. "With you, there is always another

way." He tugged the collar of his coat more securely under her chin and then collected the lantern.

Within minutes, they left the dark cave behind and were climbing the steep path to Rosemont.

Chapter 28

Liza stared up at the tree, whose huge branches swayed against the gray sky. The faintest hint of a lump formed in her throat. "Are you sure it is here?"

"Don't you listen to anything, brat?" Robert asked. "The painting led me to the book containing the family history—thus, the family tree. It took me a while, but"— he pointed to the great oak, his eyes silvered with excitement—"*this* is the family tree."

"I've never heard of a family having their own actual tree."

"And you know so many."

"I know all of the best families," she snapped, then grimaced to hear herself utter such an empty-headed platitude. What was it about Robert that brought all of her worst qualities to the fore? He was rude and insufferable, wallowing in enough self-pity to destroy an ordinary man, yet she found herself seeking him out.

Since their uneasy truce yesterday, when she'd made

such a spectacle of herself and almost ruined her brother's chance at happiness, Robert had allowed her to assist him with his search for the Captain's fabled fortune. Liza sighed, still not sure whether she was being punished or rewarded.

She glanced back at the house and remembered Lucien's face when he'd entered the house carrying Arabella. For the rest of her life, Liza would never forget his expression—fiercely tender, his eyes haunted. She'd known then that her brother was deeply in love with his wife. He wouldn't even let Aunt Jane and Aunt Emma tend to her, insisting that it was his right as her husband. He'd been so determined, no one had dared gainsay him.

But something was still bothering Lucien. Though Arabella had awoken this morning in a sunny mood, teasing Robert all through breakfast, Lucien remained quiet, his gaze never leaving her. Liza wondered what weighed on her brother's mind. Whatever it was, her brother was not one to let anything stand between him and what he wanted—and it was obvious that he wanted Arabella.

From both her brother's experience and the novels she'd read, Liza decided that men were much quicker to admit their feelings when faced with the imminent death of their chosen. She glanced at Robert and wondered how he would react if she were being held by a crazed smuggler.

Robert sighed impatiently. "Well, we've dug all around the—"

"We?"

A reluctant grin twitched the corner of his mouth, but he ignored her. "So the treasure must be *in* the tree. There is an opening halfway up."

She tilted her head back again and looked. Where the branches began to thin, there was a round hole in the trunk. She blinked. Just looking up into the swaying branches made her dizzy.

Robert tucked the papers into his coat. "I suppose we shall have to go and find Ned and get him to climb the dratted thing." He stared down at his legs with something akin to hatred. "I am no good to anyone."

Liza had to bite her lip against an overwhelming urge to soothe his creased brow with a kiss. *Heavens, what is wrong with me?*

But the rush of emotion gave her an idea, and she looked back up at the branches. Perhaps . . . She placed a slippered foot on the marble bench and stepped lightly up.

"What in the hell do you think you are doing?"

She wrapped her hands securely about a branch and pulled herself into the tree. "What does it look like?"

"For the love of— Get down from there."

But she was too far gone to stop now. For some reason, she had to help Robert succeed at something. She grasped a thick branch with both hands and pulled herself up, kicking impatiently at her skirts. "I'll have you know that I have climbed many, many trees."

Of course, that had been when she'd been a child, but he didn't need to know that. She was sure her skill would return as she progressed. Her foot slipped and for one fearful moment, she tottered. But her hands found purchase and she managed to regain her balance.

"Damn it, Liza!" he said, his voice hoarse. "Come down now!"

"But the fortune—"

"I don't give a bloody damn about the fortune!"

"Well, I do." She grasped a thick branch and tested it. It barely swayed, as she had expected. Perched on a sea cliff, the oak was subjected daily to hardy winds. A weak branch would have blown down long ago.

She carefully put her feet on the limb and reached for the one higher, stopping when her skirt snagged on a branch. "I should try to—"

An outburst of cursing met her words. Liza primly responded, "I'll toss an apple on your head if you don't stop saying such vulgar things."

"There are no apples in that tree. It is an oak and it is the dead of winter."

"Then I shall break off a limb," she replied hotly, gathering her skirts in one hand and wishing she'd thought to tie them up. Robert had to be the most ungrateful creature alive. Here she was, putting herself in the utmost jeopardy, and all he could do was curse at her.

"Liza . . . please . . . get down from there." Just the faintest note of supplication colored his words. "You will fall."

"And if I do?" She looked down at him, her heart suddenly lodged in her throat. "Don't pretend you would care."

There was a long silence and then he said, "Of course I wouldn't care, but Lucien might. And I damned well don't want to explain to him what a fool you were."

Her foot slipped off a branch and she made a mad grasp for a lower branch to regain her balance.

"For the love of—" Robert burst out. He had never felt so helpless in his life. His hands gripped about the handles of his chair, his palms wet. *"Get down from there now!"*

She ignored him, climbing with an assurance and competency that did nothing to ease his thundering heart.

"Stop glowering like that," she called. "If I fall, then you can catch me." She pulled herself onto a branch that creaked noisily in protest.

Robert pushed the chair closer to the tree, muttering

curses as he went. Didn't she know that he couldn't catch her? He was a cripple, for God's sake, unable to help himself, much less her. And if she died before his eyes . . . He bit his lip until he tasted blood.

She grabbed a bough above her head and hesitated one instant, her foot searching for purchase. To Robert's strained eyes, the branch looked much too thin to bear her weight. He wished with all his might that his legs were his own again. It should be him in the tree, not Liza.

"I'm almost there," she called down. The wind buffeted her voice and made it sound as if it came from over the ocean.

He could see her dress fluttering in the stiff breeze, the long pink skirts ruffling about the branches. Overhead, dark clouds swirled and the distant rumble of thunder seemed to portend disaster.

"Robert?"

"What?" he asked through clenched teeth. Was her foot wedged between two branches? Had she caught her dress on a branch and was unable to free herself?

"I've reached the hole. I'm about to put my hand in."

"Blast it, Liza! Forget the treasure and come down from there!"

"Don't be absurd. I didn't climb this stupid tree for nothing." The branches rustled around her.

"Well?" he finally said impatiently, wondering if he should fetch Lucien. Thunder rumbled again, closer this time and he looked uneasily at the quickly darkening sky.

"There is nothing in here but marbles," she said, disappointment evident. "A child's prank and nothing more."

"Then come down," he said, too relieved she hadn't fallen during her climb to even think about the treasure. "You had better hurry; it is going to rain."

"Very well. I just wish . . . Here, let me toss a few of them to you."

A scattering of small red balls came through the branches. Robert leaned over and picked one up. Made of red clay, it was inexpertly formed, too lumpy to be of use as a marble. He stared at it a minute before asking in an odd voice, "Liza, are there more?"

"A whole nest of them." She tossed several handfuls to the ground. They hit the walkway and bounced in different directions. "Perhaps we should—"

Thunder rolled overhead, and lightning crashed. Before Robert's horrified eyes, the tree exploded, the sound deafening. Pieces of bark and limbs flew through the air, the acrid smell of smoke clogging his mind.

Suddenly Robert was no longer on the cliff at Rosemont. He was at Waterloo, the rancid smell of death choking him, the metallic taste of fear filling his mouth. All around him, people were dying and he could do nothing to help them, nothing to stop the carnage. Nothing to keep the blood from soaking into the cold, hard ground.

Only this time, it was Liza.

Her scream rent the air. A haze covered his vision, as if a silk net had been stretched across time and slowed it to one endless heartbeat. As clearly as if he were beside her, he could see her tumble from the branches, her skirt tangling about her legs. She plunged headfirst, her arms flailing, her face frozen with terror.

Robert closed his eyes. Teeth clenched, he imagined himself reaching for her, catching her, holding her against him, safe and warm and so incredibly alive. No longer was he in his chair, but standing straight and tall, his arms extended, his hands grasping, closing about her.

For one long, breathless moment, he held her, his arms

tightly wrapped around her, his face buried against her bright hair.

Then, slowly, he raised his head and looked into her eyes.

"You . . . you moved," she said, her voice husky and trembling. "And I—" She gave a convulsive sob and buried her face in his neck.

Robert tightened his hold, afraid to breathe and waken from this dream. A dream in which she was safe and warm, alive in his arms. If he opened his eyes, he would know the truth; would see her crumpled form at his feet.

Her body quivered against his and he marveled at the faint smell of rose that lifted from the silken strands beneath his cheek. Terrified to waken, he simply stood, holding her.

After a long moment, Liza collected herself and gave a shaky laugh. She stepped out of the circle of his arms and looked down at his legs, her blue eyes shining. "Robert, it's a miracle."

It was at that second that he realized he was wide awake and he was *standing,* for Christ's sake. Slowly, afraid to move, he looked down at his legs, astonished to see his feet planted firmly on the ground.

Robert swallowed, intensely aware of every sensation—the feel of the solid earth beneath his boots, the sound of his harsh breathing, Liza's sweet scent lingering on his collar.

Joy exploded through his veins and he laughed as he caught Liza into a crushing embrace. The movement tilted his none-too-steady knees and sent them careening back to the bench, where he sat down so hard his laughter ended with a muffled grunt, Liza in his lap.

Red-faced, she scooted to his side. "I can't believe this!"

"Neither do I. But I owe it all to your pigheadedness." He chuckled and flexed his legs, one after the other.

Another rumble of thunder made him carefully stand. Though a tremor weakened his knees, he stayed erect. "We'd better get inside."

Liza swiped a hand across her eyes and stood. "Of course."

Robert looped an arm about her shoulders and said gruffly, "Just to keep my balance."

She nodded and did not move away, and he noticed that she was indeed the perfect height, the top of her head coming to his brow. They had taken no more than two steps when Robert stopped. His chair lay overturned amid swirling dead leaves and broken branches. Clay balls lay scattered along the path and throughout the brambles of the dead garden.

He removed his arm from Liza's shoulder and picked up the chair. With a surge of pure energy, he walked to the stone wall and heaved it into the air. It spun in the whitish glow of the approaching storm, the wheels spinning crazily. Then it dropped out of sight, leaving only the fading sound of crashing metal and wood as it bounced off the rocks and fell into the ocean.

Liza slipped an arm about his waist and pulled his weight against her. "Come into the house."

He nodded and turned with her. When his foot brushed by one of the clay balls, a faint gleam caught his eye. Brows drawn, he bent and picked it up. "Liza, help me gather the rest of these."

"But why—"

"Hurry. Before the storm arrives."

Liza frowned, but helped him collect all of the clay balls she could find. The wind increased with each passing minute and the thunder began to rumble closer and closer.

They found the last one and just made it into the house before the storm broke.

From the window of the morning room, Arabella watched as Robert and Liza ran inside. "Lucien!"

"I see him," Lucien said quietly. He came to stand behind her, his arms wrapping around her waist, his cheek against her hair, his own heart full.

Arabella turned her face against him and clutched his coat. Lucien soothed her hair. "Bella *mia,* don't cry."

"I'm not crying." She sniffed and pulled away to search desperately for her handkerchief.

He watched her dry her eyes. Seeing Robert walk had been her dearest wish, and he had been here, standing beside her, to witness it. As he would be with her from now on, sharing her joys and helping her through the painful times. *If she will have me.*

His breath caught in his chest as he looked at her. Luxurious strands of chestnut hair had pulled free from her ribbon and now curled about her face in a mussed tangle. Her eyes glowed a warm brown; her soft mouth trembled with emotion. Lucien rammed his hands into his pockets and forced himself to turn away from the delectable sight. They were alone, she was rested after her ordeal—now was the time.

He took a deep breath. "Bella, we need to ta—"

The door flew open and Aunt Emma rushed into the room, her gown obviously donned in haste. "Arabella! I don't know what—" She slid to a stop when she saw Lucien and stood uncertainly, wringing her hands, her eyes wide. "Oh! I didn't realize you would be in here. And I— Oh, dear!"

"Emma, Lucien is a member of our family now." Trust warmed Arabella's voice. Lucien's heart lowered. How could he tell her that trust was the last thing he deserved?

Reassured, Emma burst out, "Oh, Arabella, I think something horrible has happened. Jane—Sir Loughton—I should have told you about it, but Jane told me not to and so I didn't, though I knew I should, and I—" She stopped, dropped her face in her hands, and began sobbing loudly. "And n-now it's too l-late!"

Arabella paled. "The gaming debt."

Emma lifted her head, her blue eyes wet with tears. "How did you know about that?"

"I overheard you and Jane talking about it. And I . . ." Arabella stopped and glanced at Lucien, her cheeks flushing. But then she said in a resolute voice, "I have the money now."

So that was what the ten thousand pounds had been for. Lucien had suspected as much.

"If only Jane had known, then she wouldn't have—" Emma pressed her handkerchief to her mouth.

"When did she leave?" Arabella asked.

"Last night, after you fell asleep. She said it was just one night and that, all in all, it was a very fair offer." Emma fixed her wide blue gaze on Lucien. "Do they charge so much in London?"

Lucien managed to say with tolerable sincerity, "Actually, no."

"Well. That is something! At least she wasn't cheated."

Arabella made an exasperated noise. "Emma, there is no amount of money to compensate for a woman's virtue. Furthermore, I cannot believe Sir Loughton would make such a request. It is very improper."

Lucien could believe it; he'd seen the way the baron stared at Jane, as if he'd like to both strangle and kiss her at one and the same time. Since Lucien was very familiar with that feeling, he could only sympathize that circumstances had led the baron to such extreme actions. Before he could give voice to his opinions, there was a commotion in the foyer, and then Jane entered the room, looking slightly flushed, but unharmed.

Emma flew to her sister, flung her arms about her neck, and promptly burst into fresh tears.

"Heavens!" Jane exclaimed. "What is wrong with you?"

"With me? How are *you*? Are you . . . well? Did Sir Loughton—"

"There's really no need to discuss this here," Jane said hastily, glancing at Lucien and Arabella. "I'm perfectly fine."

Sir Loughton entered the room behind Jane. "And feisty as the devil, too."

With a deafening screech, Emma threw herself in front of Jane and glared at Sir Loughton. "*You bounder!* What do you want? Haven't you taken enough from her already?"

His eyes twinkled. "Not yet. I've one more coming to me."

Emma gasped. "I cannot believe this! Not content with stealing my sister's virtue once, you have the effrontery to demand it again! We'd rather pay you the money!"

Sir Loughton frowned. "Lord, no! I've too much coin as it is. In fact"—he glanced around the room, his mouth quirking into a grin when he caught sight of Lucien—"I've decided I need a spendthrift wife who will go through my fortune as fast as possible and spread it about the countryside."

Emma blinked. "A wife?"

The baron nodded, then turned to stare at Jane from

beneath his shaggy brows. "And I think I may have found one."

To Lucien's astonishment, something amazingly like a simper crossed Jane's thin face.

"You wish to marry *Jane*?" Emma said.

"Why not? Fine-looking woman, plenty of spice to her, and she don't bore me to tears, which is something I can't abide."

Jane sniffed. "That was hardly the way I would have announced it."

"It served, didn't it?" he demanded, his blue eyes sharp with amusement.

Emma clasped her hands together and smiled through her tears. "This is so romantic!"

"It is, isn't it?" Lucien said, coming forward to take Emma by the arm. He gently guided her to the door. "Perhaps you should all retire to the library to toast Jane's good news. I believe Hastings refilled the decanter with cognac just this morning."

Emma brightened. "Oh, the very thing! Come, Sir Loughton, Jane. I'll get some glasses. We have another wedding to plan!" Miraculously restored to spirits, she bounded from the room.

Sir Loughton caught Lucien's gaze and a moment of understanding passed between them. "Quite right, Wexford," the baron said. "We'll talk later." He reached for Jane's hand, but she turned to Arabella and gave her a swift hug. Lucien watched as Jane whispered something in Arabella's ear that caused her to chuckle and hug her aunt fiercely.

Sir Loughton coughed. "Come, m'dear. No more to be done here." He gently pulled his intended back to his side and they left.

Lucien crossed the room and closed the door. His aunt never cried. She never laughed, either, now that he considered it. He was beginning to see why Liza was so unhappy at Aunt Lavinia's.

From across the room, Arabella smiled at him, her gaze bright and unwavering. "You were saying something before they came in. What was it?"

Lucien raked a hand through his hair. "Bella, there are things we should talk about. I don't want there to be any secrets between us."

"No," she said slowly, some of the light fading from her gaze. "I suppose you are right. There are things we both should say."

There was a flurry of activity outside of the room, and Robert's and Liza's excited voices joined Emma's and Jane's. Lucien cursed as the door burst open once again, and Robert entered, pulling Liza behind him.

"Arabella! Look!" Robert held out his hand, an odd assortment of clay balls resting in his palms.

"Robert, your legs . . ." She couldn't seem to look away from the sight of her brother standing before her.

"Oh, Lord, you didn't know. I got excited and forgot—" He broke off when she pressed a hand to her mouth, then said gruffly, "Now don't go all missish on me. It was just a matter of time. You said it yourself, over and over."

"Only you didn't believe me."

He laughed. "Crow all you like." He selected one of the clay balls and handed it to Arabella, his voice quavering with excitement. "Look."

Arabella smiled uncertainly.

"Crack it open," Robert said.

She closed her hand over it and pressed. With a loud pop, the ball broke open, something sparkling among the broken bits of clay. *"Robert,"* she breathed. "The treasure!"

He laughed. "We're rich! I found it in the old oak tree in the garden."

"You?" Liza said, from where she'd been silently standing by the door. "What do you mean, *you* found it?"

"We, then," he said amiably, sending her a warm glance that made Lucien frown.

But he was instantly distracted when Arabella turned to him, her hand held out. "Is it of much value?"

He picked up the sapphire and held it toward the light. "The quality is astounding. How many are there?"

"I don't know," Liza said. "I didn't have time to see before the li—"

"We'll have to go back and check," Robert said, sending a quelling glance at Liza. "Only this time, I will do it myself."

Liza opened her mouth to protest, but Robert grabbed her hand and pulled her toward the door. He stopped there and tossed Arabella a grin. "Sorry to run, but Aunt Emma is waiting for us to join her in the library."

With that, he left, hauling a protesting Liza after him.

Arabella barely waited for the door to close before she crossed to it. She took a gilded chair from nearby and wedged it firmly under the knob. "There," she said with satisfaction. "That should keep them out."

Lucien's lips twitched.

Arabella walked to the settee and sat down. "Now come and tell me what it is you have to say."

Lucien took the chair opposite hers, wanting to see every expression on her face. He wondered desperately where he should start.

She cleared her throat. "I suppose you are going to tell me about when your father died."

"Yes." That seemed the best place to begin. "When I discovered the true state of affairs of my father's estate, Aunt Lavinia suggested I marry Sabrina."

Arabella nodded, her face shuttered, and Lucien continued quietly. "Bella, I told her no. Selfish man that I am, I preferred to have you with me in poverty than to live without you." A bitter smile twisted his lips. "But someone made me see the error of my ways."

Her brows dipped, but only for a second. When she met his gaze, a flicker of pain lit the brown depths to amber. "My father."

Lucien nodded. "My aunt had written him and told him the truth of our finances and that I was determined to wed you. He had not yet wasted your inheritance, and the idea of his daughter throwing herself away on a man who stood on the brink of ruin was untenable.

"Bella, I should have resisted, but he made me aware of the true horror of my future situation in such a way . . . Suffice it to say that by the time he left, I knew I could not subject you to the financial horror that awaited me."

And that, Arabella thought bitterly, was the ultimate irony. Rather than see his daughter with the man she loved, braving poverty together, her father had confined her to poverty in the country, alone and ruined. As the years passed and he lost more and more of their fortune, she wondered if he ever thought of the happiness he had robbed from her. "And so you married Sabrina."

"After I had given up hope of having you, I didn't care. Sabrina seemed like a logical choice. She was wealthy and willing to marry."

"Lucien, you don't need to tell me—"

"I want you to know. That way, nothing will ever come between us." Lucien shifted restlessly in his chair. "When

Sabrina and I were first wed, I had planned on using her fortune to repair my father's mismanagement. But after we married, I couldn't do it. The problem wasn't hers, it was mine. And though she was my wife, she was concerned only with her own amusement and not my dealings."

Arabella hoped Lucien didn't expect her to maintain such an attitude. She had every intention of being an active partner in his affairs. "That was very unnatural of her."

"There was very little that was natural about Sabrina," he said with a humorless smile. "Her moods were extreme, to say the least, and I was glad she took so little interest. I took what little capital I could raise and began to invest. It was a difficult venture and I put endless hours into it. Hours away from my house, away from Sabrina. I was gone so often, I didn't realize that her uneven spirits had progressed so badly that . . ." He stopped, his face shadowed with remembered pain.

"One day, I arrived home just in time to see her fly into a passion and attack one of the servants with her riding whip. If I hadn't been there, she would have killed the girl."

"Good God!"

"I immediately put everything aside and took Sabrina to the country, and placed her under the care of a physician. She hated it. She paced the floor and refused to eat. It was as if a wild animal had been caged. And she blamed me for her loss of freedom."

"Lucien, you were helping her."

"She didn't see it that way. After several weeks, she grew quieter, more docile. I thought she was better." He sighed and tilted his head back. "Eventually I was recalled to London to deal with some business matters. When I told Sabrina that I had to go, she asked me not to, begged me to stay with her. But I had been in the country for weeks, and my business . . ." He passed a hand over his eyes.

"You left?"

Lucien closed his eyes. "Not an hour after my departure, she slipped out of the house and rode a horse she knew was unfit. It bolted across a stream and threw her." He took a slow breath. "The fall broke her neck."

"Lucien, you cannot take responsibility for Sabrina's death. She was ill, her judgment impaired—"

"Which is why I should have stayed," he said harshly. "It is my fault that she died."

"Oh, pish-posh! What an idiotic thing to say. You cannot be responsible for anyone's actions other than your own." She looked at him thoughtfully. "Besides, how do you know staying would have made any difference? Chances are, she had already decided to leave and your being there wouldn't have changed a thing."

He shook his head. Arabella could tell he wanted desperately to believe the words, but couldn't.

"You know, Lucien, there comes a time when you have to let those who depend on you make their own decisions, and sometimes their own mistakes."

From outside the door came a burst of laughter, Robert's voice raised over them all. Arabella turned toward the sound. "It was the same with my brother. He was determined to join the war effort. He had a very idealized vision of battle and no concept of the true horror. I tried to tell him, but he wouldn't listen."

Lucien watched her closely. "So you let him go."

"He was eighteen at the time, a man fully grown. If I had forced him to remain here, he would have felt as if he were less than he should be. Less than a man. I couldn't take that from him."

Lucien's grip tightened on the chair arm. "There is more, Bella. About us. I haven't been fully honest with you."

She shook her head. "Lucien, don't. I al—"

"Please, let me say this quickly. When Constable Robbins came to arrest Wilson, I knew it was only a matter of time before he came for you, as well. I thought if I married you, I could keep you from such a fate. So I went to Aunt Jane and asked her to help me plan the night in the cottage. It was no accident, and I—"

In an instant, Arabella was kneeling by his chair, her fingers across his lips. "I already know, Lucien. Edmund told me."

Lucien caught her hand. "I shall have a few choice words for that jackanapes. He is a hapless fribble."

"Don't blame Edmund; he was very, *very* sorry. If it hadn't been for Liza, he would never have said a word."

"He is not as sorry as he will be." Lucien took her hand and placed it on his chest, where his heart beat steadily against her palm. "Bella, can you forgive me? I never should have left you all those years ago. It is my fault you had to endure such circumstances—"

"Pish-posh. Did you wager away my family's fortune? No. And neither did I. If this mess is anyone's fault, it is my father's. And I shall go to his grave this evening and have a word with him about it."

To Arabella's relief, Lucien's mouth twitched and some of the tension left his shoulders. "I still should have been honest."

"True. I suppose I shall have to punish you." And oh, how she would enjoy that, Arabella thought, looking at the strong lines of his face, the sensual curve of his mouth.

He raised a brow, his gaze suddenly hot. "And how might you do that, lady wife?"

She ignored the tingles that traced down her spine as his thumb traced lazy circles on the palm of her other hand. There was one more thing Lucien needed to admit to her. And it was the most important confession of all.

"Why did you marry me, Lucien? It wasn't just to protect me from Constable Robbins, was it?"

"No," he whispered, kissing her fingers and then pulling her into his lap. His arms enveloped her in a circle of heat. "I love you, Bella. I always have."

The words slipped into Arabella's heart and filled her with joy. He loved her. Nothing else mattered.

His kiss was as gentle as the drop of a snowflake, a cherished promise that quickly swelled into a blaze of passion. Without breaking the kiss, Lucien ran his hands over her shoulders and down her back to cup her bottom through the thin material of her gown. Arabella moaned against his mouth, her whole body instantly awash in desire.

Lucien finally broke the kiss, and stared down at her with a look of heated possession. "Perhaps we should retire to our chambers."

"But I've never been kissed in the morning room before. In fact, there are quite a few things I've never done in the morning room." She wiggled in his lap suggestively.

He growled. "You have a very interesting way of punishing a man, love."

She pulled away to hold his face between her hands. "Don't expect me to let you off lightly. You know I am a stubborn woman; what I start, I finish." She took a deep breath, then said, "I love you, too, Lucian—and showing you how much could take a long, long time."

He brushed a finger across her lips, his face alight with love. "Then we had better get started."

As she snuggled against him, a sudden thought made her chuckle.

Lucien drew away, a quizzical gleam in his eyes. "What are you laughing about?"

"Aunt Jane. Just before she left, she told me to call on her if I had any trouble getting you to come around."

His brows rose in an arrogant slash. "What was she going to do? Have her beau challenge me to a duel? I don't think Sir Loughton would oblige her."

"Oh, no. She said she'd teach me how to make her sheep tonic."

He blinked. "She didn't."

"Oh, she did. So be forewarned, Lucien." She placed her fingertips on his lower lip and traced it with a delicate touch. "The Hadley women always win."

His gaze darkened as he pulled her tightly to him. "As long as I'm the prize."

Chuckling, Arabella wound her arms around his neck and kissed him.